MW01107900

THE
THIRD
CORRIDOR

Angel Lynn

Futuristic Romance

New Concepts   Georgia

The Third Corridor is an original publication of NCP. This work has never before appeared in book form. This work is a novel. Any similarity to actual persons or events is purely coincidental.

New Concepts Publishing
5202 Humphreys Rd.
Lake Park, GA 31636

ISBN 1-58608-681-2
© copyright 2004 Angel Lynn
Cover art by Eliza Black, © copyright 2004

NCP books are available at special quantity discounts for bulk purchases for sales promotions, premiums, fund raising, or educational use. For details, write, email, or phone New Concepts Publishing, 5202Humphreys Rd., Lake Park, GA 31636, ncp@newconceptspublishing.com, Ph. 229-257-0367, Fax 229-219-1097.

First NCP Paperback Printing: 2004

Printed in the United States of America

Prelude

~ Play Possum ~
"...to pretend to be asleep,
dead, or unaware..."
--Webster's New World Dictionary, Third Edition

"What's happening?" Garret pulled the reciprocator from his head, dropping it to the floor as he rose quickly from the cot. The standby medical team immediately began their protocol examination, drawing fluids, checking for physical changes, and a barrage of questions to determine his mental status.

"What's your name? Where are you? How many fingers..."

Garret pushed them aside, and approached the habiliment, a large computer panel displaying rapidly changing numerical readouts. Just above a keyboard, a *Kineto-Neural Optic Emission*, or *KNOE* scanner, displayed a variegated, three-dimensional brain image surrounded by a near translucent skull.

Melissa turned her head to acknowledge Garret, allowing her eyes to momentarily leave the *KNOE*. "Your adrenaline levels were elevating and your heart rate was almost to a hundred and ninety. Your vitals were at critical levels. I had to reanimate you."

Garret bent over the console. He scanned the screen in front of him.

Melissa glanced upward again. "You're bleeding."

Garret touched his forehead and looked at the blood on his fingers. "What happened? Did I hit my head?"

"You tell me. That wound formed just before I disengaged the signal." Melissa was calm and professional, her eyes scrutinizing the monitor, and her fingers rapidly tapping at the keypad.

"How badly is she injured?"

"She has a mild concussion." Melissa pointed at the screen, which now presented a cross sectioned scan of a brain. A series of numbers was registering at the lateral sides of the *KNOE*.

Melissa traced her finger along the brain composite, stopping at the frontal lobe. "These readings are puzzling, though. Her serotonin levels are elevated and steady, but only briefly did they correlate with the same desynchronized beta waves you were projecting during rapid eye movements. However, I am now receiving high frequency beta waves from the frontal and parietal lobes."

"A neuropathy perhaps?"

"No, all neuronal transmissions are functioning normally, but she seems to be creating memories we typically find during alert wakefulness." Melissa stopped tapping the keyboard to look at Garret. "It's as though she's in an altered state of awareness, the same readouts the scientists recorded when conducting this experiment before."

She turned back to the screen touching it several times until a full body-scan appeared. She pointed to a deeply reddened area across the figure's left shoulder.

"What is that, a fracture?" Garret asked, touching an area on the screen.

"No, it's a physical wound," the staff physician interrupted. "Odd though, it is disappearing almost as rapidly as it appeared,"

He reached over Melissa's shoulder and tapped the screen to view the scan of the skull. "The concussion seems to be subsiding, also at a high rate of speed. Interesting." He rubbed an index finger across his lips. He then picked up his blunted stylus and began scrawling notes into his palm recorder. "She's stable. I see no reason not to continue."

"Should I try some cortex manipulations, Garret?" Melissa asked.

"No. I don't want to alter her natural thought formations. It may obscure the details of any data we collect." Garret fingered an intravenous line, now detached from its tubing, positioned over the inside of his forearm. Then he abruptly turned to Melissa. "Ah Melissa, it was invigorating. It was like being trapped in a vortex. We were accelerating, spiraling in a violent whorl. I thought my brain was going to implode. Then the ground came rushing through the blackness with such force..."

His expression grew smug. "Good thing you pulled me out or my body parts would've been splattered all over this room." He touched his forehead again and looked at the blood, mindful of the horrifying tragedy that took place, terminating the experiment twelve years prior to this. Garret managed to convince the *Committee on Research Expansion*, or the C.O.R.E., to resurrect the project, but he was warned to move forward with great caution.

"I only had enough time to initiate emergency shut down with your transmitter," Melissa informed him. She continued to work without looking up. "The disconnection between the two reciprocators must have nullified the event. When you became disengaged it caused an interruption in her brain patterns. A good thing too. Probably saved her life."

Garret leaned over the back of Melissa and pressed his lips to her ear. "You chose me. How touching," he whispered. "I believe you would have let her die. Nemesis does persuade you."

Melissa shrugged him off of her. She hated his frequent references to the Greek gods as though they controlled destiny. "I'm not jealous, Garret, and this is no joke. We need to re-examine this. If anything happens to either of you, the C.O.R.E will shut this study down for good."

Garret stood erect. "Coordinate my headset. I'm reconnecting with her."

"I can calibrate her readouts to your headset, but it may take you awhile to re-engage with her."

"Do it." Garret turned toward his cot, then stopped and looked over his shoulder. "Oh, and Melissa, don't abort under any circumstance. Not until the full eight hours has expired."

"But Garret..." Melissa ceased her calculations to object.

"That's an order Captain." He stifled her protest with his authoritative command.

Melissa snapped her teeth shut and jutted her chin forward. "Yes sir."

Chapter One

Hold tight Sera. The best is yet to come…

Sera was dizzy, and her vision was blurred. Her head was pounding, and she was sick to her stomach. She crawled to the top of a small, grassy hill to distance herself from the fire. Breathing heavily, she propped herself up on her forearms and knees. The top of her head touched the dirt and she looked beneath her body. She caught an upside down glimpse of smoke pouring out from the treetops in the forest behind her. Sera attempted to get to her feet, but couldn't gather enough stability to rise. Her throat and her chest screamed with rawness as she gasped for air. She feared that if she tried to breathe deeply she might vomit. On her left shoulder, her military insignia had been torn completely off of her waist length, khaki jacket. She had no tags on her, and it occurred to her that should she die, it might be difficult to identify her corpse--if she was ever found. The tear revealed a hefty abrasion on her shoulder, not fatal, but it was bleeding. The others had not been so lucky. Before her egress from the craft, she had regrettably viewed the mangled flesh that had once been her crew. It was a ghastly sight, one that Sera would put out of her mind quickly.

A sudden explosion interrupted her thoughts. Sera's body lurched forward. Flames savagely propelled upward, tearing a burning path through the tranquil sky. There would be nothing left but traces of ash. She felt a terrible pang in her chest. Her heart crushed with the agony of being stranded on an unknown planet. Yet, even in this moment of despair, Sera had the clarity of mind to realize her location on the hill placed her in plain view of any potential enemy, and that the smell of her blood might make her prey to some unforeseen creature. Her own safety was in question now.

Several yards ahead, and slightly to her right, there was a cluster of trees and bushes. Through it, Sera thought she could see a body of water. Forcing herself to her feet, she stumbled into the bushes. Once she was wrapped within the refuge of the thicket, she unzipped her jacket, removed it and collapsed to the ground. She used her crumpled jacket to rest her head, relatively sure that she was at least somewhat concealed from the possible dangers that lurked about. Sera looked toward the area she had just crawled away from. Smoke continued to billow forth in the distance. She watched despondently. Sera was alone. She needed to contemplate what her next course of action should be.

Sera lifted her head to survey the landscape, but because of her hazy vision she found it quite difficult. Squinting, she could see that the forest gave way to a horizon of far reaching, grassy lowlands, and she scanned the area, her attention suddenly drawn to a point in the distance. There was something moving across the land that looked much like a horse and rider. But her glimpse of it was a brief one, because the image vanished beneath the crest of the hill. With a steadfast gaze, she watched, and when it didn't reappear, she assumed it was a hallucination.

The sun was positioned just above the trees and Sera figured that it was late in the morning. She closed her eyes and forced them open again. It was imperative that she stay awake for her own protection.

Don't fall asleep, she warned herself silently, attempting to sit, but she was stiff with exhaustion. Her body wouldn't move and her mind relented the attempt to make it try. She inhaled deeply, noticing the slight aroma of eucalyptus and magnolia. The scent, along with the tepid, clean smelling air was soothing. Unconsciously, Sera closed her eyes.

Just for a minute…only for a minute.

Her thoughts drifted and her body felt like it was being tossed around on an ocean surf, rocking and spinning, coiling up, then down, her mind snapping back to reality for fleeting moments. She fell asleep, and the truth of what was happening to her became a distant reality.

Sera had no idea how long she'd slept. What she did know, when she started to wake, was that her throat was parched, her lips were cracked, and she was unbearably thirsty. Rolling to her back with a groan, Sera forced her eyes to open and found herself staring directly into the sun. The intense rays were piercing, painful almost, and she squeezed her lids. Her head was still throbbing, and her thoughts remained clouded, and although the ground continued to waver beneath her, Sera knew she had to get up. Pushing herself onto one elbow, and shielding her brow with her other, she took a look around. Bursts of light from staring into the sun were still hindering her vision, but through them, much closer than the first image, she again spied the blurred image of a horse and rider. Sera sat upright, grunting with the effort it took to do so. She rubbed her face, and then vigorously scratched her scalp. When she looked up again, the figure was gone.

This bump to my head must be tricking my eye sight.

Sera tried to clear her mind. What she remembered was tumbling out of control before her fall was abruptly terminated by her collision with the ground. She attempted to recall the objectives of her mission, but it was to no avail. Her head held only fleeting pictures of where she had come from. She did not know the name of her ship. She could not visualize the faces, or recall the names of any of her crew. Even the images of their ruined bodies seemed to be disappearing from her thoughts with unusual ease. Her mind felt like an empty void.

Oh my god. I've lost my memory.

Sera rubbed her forehead and then rose to her feet, stretching her back and limbs. Every muscle in her body tightened and pulled in the opposite direction. She was incredibly stiff and sore. She took a deep breath. Her nausea was subsiding, but her brain was still banging against her skull.

Sera smacked her lips, looking toward the water, hoping it wasn't noxious. When she bent to pick up her jacket, she heard a whinny, and froze in her bowed position, her sense of hearing perking to full alert. She heard it again. It was the unmistakable sound of a horse. Her eyes widened as she lifted her head only slightly without rising--four hooves. Her head tipped back and Sera looked up. There before her, a horse and its rider stood motionless.

Sera blinked.

Maybe it would disappear again.

It didn't. This was not a mirage. Sera straightened apprehensively, unsure if the nature of the encounter would be passive or aggressive. She quickly put on her jacket, the sudden motion causing her to sway in her upright stance. An intense feeling of blood rushing from her brain overcame her, but Sera fought to sustain her equilibrium. She needed to maintain control. It was imperative that she not alert the stranger that her physical condition might make her vulnerable to capture.

There was no movement between either of them for quite some time. It was as though one was attempting to ascertain the other's purpose. Sera observed that he was definitely male, or an unusually masculine woman. On his head he wore a black, cloth hood and a heavily meshed mask that hid his face. The bib of the hood draped his collar bones and was fastened in place by a leather gorget. The remainder of the hood protruded from beneath it. His gauntlet style gloves were thick and black. They, like the gorget, appeared to be made of leather, and were fastened with a single buckle. He wore a sea blue, hip length doublet, opened in front, and a tattered white shirt beneath. His colours were displayed on the left, upper front section of the overcoat. There was a darker blue crest of some sort, with a golden band angled across it. The band bore a lavender bloom that resembled a rose, and one of its pedals was pierced with an embroidered gold ring.

Sera slowly moved around him. His horse shuffled from side to side, and whinnied. There was a larger emblem, a coat of arms, centered on the back of the vestment, an oval frame entwined with ivy and a heraldic escutcheon centered on it. Three bands angled across it, one gold, one green and one red. Five blooms were positioned around its border. A lavender bloom, the same as the one on the front, was placed at the uppermost point. On the left point, the bloom was yellow, and a white one at the right point. Closer to the bottom tip, where the emblem bowed inward, there was a red bloom on the left, and an orange bloom on the right. Just below the bottom tip, there were three overlapping gold rings.

Around his waist, he wore a military belt. It was black and wide. An immense, double-edged sword and a smaller dagger, nestled in their sheaths, were hooked to the belt. His thickly woven trousers were ashen colored, and hugged powerful looking thighs. The trousers were tucked into heavy, calf length, black leather boots, buckled with three straps. More of the stranger's equipment was hooked to the saddle. A loop held a lance, broken and splintered nearly to its handle. There was a sack, a canteen, a bow and quiver with arrows. A badly dented breastplate and metal shield were both embellished with his crest. The ensemble looked antiquated. It had a medieval quality, and was definitely worn for battle.

His horse was a mighty brown charger, with a dense flank that was supported by sturdy, robust limbs. Its back was higher than the top of Sera's head. The bridle on the horse was trimmed in similar manner as the stranger's clothing. The headband was blue adorned with a lavender bloom patch. An actual gold ring pierced the embroidered flower. The cheek straps were gold colored with fringe gracing their length. Beneath the saddle, the body of the horse was draped from shoulder to tail in an elegant, but frazzled blanket, colored in a lozenge of blue and gold.

Sera carefully considered her options. Should she try to communication, or should she retreat? Did he want something from her? At first, Sera found his stillness baffling, until she noticed that the knight was wounded. A large tear in the right side of his jacket was saturated with blood.

The horse neighed, and pounded its hoof into the ground, bucked slightly then pounded its hoof again. It appeared distressed. Sera was about to speak when without anticipating it, the horseman suddenly began to sway, and he fell, hitting the ground with such force that Sera was sure he had broken his neck. The stranger lay immobile, flat on his back. For several moments, Sera stood still. She couldn't abandon him. Whether or not he was friend or foe, didn't matter. He clearly needed help. She approached him cautiously however, suspicious that his actions might be feigned, watching his chest expand and deflate. His breathing was rapid, but shallow, a clear indication he was in distress. Stooping, Sera started to remove the hood from his head, but his hand suddenly clasped her ankle, startling her. Sera shrieked and yanked away from him. She fell to her bottom and scuttered backwards, stopping when she was out of his reach.

"*ydor to...*" He held out his arm pointing toward his horse.

Sera understood his words but it was a language different from her own. She turned her attention to his horse and approached it.

Nice horsey. Now be still a moment. Sera stroked its mane cautiously, hoping it didn't bite. When the beast shifted its head to merely look at her, Sera reached up and pulled the canteen from a clip at the side of the saddle. She yanked the cap and the corked cap sealing it popped free. She shook it and then tipped it sideways. The canteen was empty.

Well, I hope that water is safe.

With the canteen in her hand she started for the bank. The charger followed along side her. *I'll just have to assume it is. Maybe it's why the knight came this way.*

When they reached the water's edge she found a rocky stream perhaps ten feet wide and about three or four feet in depth at its deepest part. The water was crystal clear.

It looks clean enough.

The horse dipped its head and started to drink, and Sera nodded, taking it as a sign that the water was safe, at least for the beast, probably for this land's inhabitants, and hopefully for her, as well. She filled the canteen, catching water streaming over one of the rocks, and returned to the knight.

He was pale and his lips were chalky, and he wasn't breathing.

Sera felt for a pulse.

There was none.

She dropped the canteen, and briefly began to panic. But then, without even realizing it, her reactions became automatic. She pulled off his hood, checked his mouth for obstruction and then sealed her mouth against his, pumping her breath into him. She then laboriously compressed his chest, counting...

One, two, three, four, five...and a breath...one, two, three...

Sera was quickly relieved when the stranger began to sputter, and then draw air into his lungs. The color slowly returned to his face.

"*Ydor...*" he repeated, after gulping a few breaths of air.

Sera hesitated, catching her breath. *He's probably dehydrated on top of everything else. He needs water.*

"*Ydor to,*" he continued to demand.

Sera pulled the cap from the canteen and lifted his head to give him a drink. He gagged, unable to swallow in his supine position. She tugged at his clothing and pulled him to a sit, but she couldn't hold him upright with one hand and put the flask to his lips with the other. He attempted to take it from her, but his arm fell to his side, and his body toppled backwards. Sera slipped the strap of the container over her shoulder and moved behind him. He was nearly limp, and it took all of her might to maneuver and lift his trunk. Finally, she was able to hook her arms under his, and drag him to a nearby boulder, and she reclined against it for support, bracing him in front of her. His head dropped back. His copper colored, shoulder length hair fell across Sera's shoulders. She brought the canteen to his mouth and he drank a modest amount of water. Sera remembered her own thirst and drank heartily. She was drenched from sweat and out of breath, but she held him tightly. His body was thick with brawn, and her arms barely reached completely around his broad chest. She felt his heart thumping furiously, as though challenging death. Sera too, could feel her own heart beating steadily against his back. She sat embracing him for a long period of time, using her bent legs and arms to hold him upright. He was silent and leaned heavily on Sera, crushing her chest. Blood from his wound soaked her sleeve and leg of her trousers. In her own weariness, Sera held no desire to move, but the muscles in her limbs began to burn so agonizingly, that she finally had to let go. Sera slipped out from behind him and managed to position him on the ground.

Several hours passed. The sun had begun to settle in the horizon opposite to where she first observed it. Earlier, while she had the benefit of daylight, Sera attended to the large gash in his torso. It was a long slash extending over his ribs from his midline, and ending at his right side. She saw no bone or internal structures, and no muscle appeared damaged, but she found herself picking pieces of what appeared to be the remains of chain mail from it. She thought that a small nick in a vein was the likely reason for its slow, but recurrent seepage, and Sera knew he could bleed to death if she couldn't get it to stop. She removed his upper garments, washed out the wound, and rolled his shirt to pad it. She used part of his doublet for bandages, by tearing the garment into strips, with two of the strips tied together and wrapped around him to hold the bundle of cloth in place. Apparently he had made a hasty exit from wherever it was he came, for the wound didn't look like it had received any treatment.

Now with that task finished, Sera had nothing much else to do. She glanced toward the area where her ship had crashed, and could no longer see any smoke. *The fire must have died quickly. I was expecting more explosions. I wonder why the fuel hadn't ignite?*

Sera attempted to replay the events leading up to her arrival on the planet, but could only muster fuzzy images through her still throbbing head. She sighed, wishing she could remember something--anything significant, as she watched the last ray of sunshine take cover below the horizon.

Sera remained awake well into the darkening hours, fighting against sleep, not only for fear of unwanted aggressors, but also to care for the injured knight. The moon was now full and high in the sky, glowing bright enough to give some light to the darkness.

The air had become dreadfully cold, and Sera shook with its chill. Earlier, the knight offered her a piece of flint rock from a small sash tied to his belt. Sera had a vague recollection of engaging in survival training and recognized the mineral. She gathered some dry branches and successfully built a fire, using the rock and buckle of her belt.

Realizing the knight needed the warmth as much as she did, Sera managed to drag him closer to the flames. For the moment, she wasn't afraid of him. He was of a little threat in his weakened state, even though he was awake and watching her, his eyes, nearly as dark as onyx--a stark contrast to his lighter hair and bronze coloring, followed her as she moved about. And despite his injuries, several times during the night he attempted to rise, but dropped quickly back to the ground.

Loss of blood could be very inhibiting.

It was late into the night when Sera eventually dozed off, no longer able to withstand the nagging need to sleep. When she opened her eyes again, the sky was beginning to glimmer with shades of red and orange, precipitating the release of an early morning sun. The magnificent colors outlined the massive clouds with shimmering borders, as though attempting to ignite them, but it had not yet warmed the air. The fire had settled to smoldering ash. Sera stretched and yawned. She had been sleeping sideways against the same large rock that she used earlier for support. It felt like a hard chunk of ice, and coldly slapped her body. She shivered and forced open her eyes. The pounding in her head continued. The clarity of her thoughts was improved somewhat, but not quite fully restored. How many suns had she seen rise? Was it one, or was it two? Then she remembered the knight, and cast her gaze toward him.

Something was not right with him. She moved quickly to his side.

His skin was cold and clammy. His lips were blue. His lids fluttered, and his eyes were rolled back in his head. His body shuddered uncontrollably, like a petit mal seizure, and it was more than apparent that his life was critically in danger. Sera ran to his charger and began searching for a blanket. A large woven sack, which hung around the pommel of the saddle, caught her attention. It was sealed shut with wax. Sera ripped it apart, thinking it might contain linen of some sort. The interior was also lined with a paraffin coating which enabled the putrid smell, now discharging from it to be preserved within, undetectable. Sera gagged with the sight of the bag's contents, and she turned away with abhorrence.

The bag contained a head--*a human head!*--sodden with blood.

Sera shrieked and tossed it away. For the brief moment that she observed it, Sera was able to identify a nose and mouth. Dried blood matted the hair on the decapitated body part to its scalp. Frozen with disbelief, she had forgotten that the horseman was in dire trouble. She then turned to him, and for an instant, thought of letting him die. Sera could not let him die, despite what she had just discovered. Her revulsion was oddly overridden by her fear of being left alone. His presence gave her purpose.

Turning to the horse again, Sera reached under its belly, unbuckled the girth, and struggled to throw off the saddle. She pulled the blanket from the charger's back, rushed to the knight, and threw it over him.

It had no affect.

Sera stretched out on top of him hoping in vain that this would provide him with warmth. It did not. She vigorously rubbed his arms and legs.

Nothing.

She had no choice. Sera unzipped her jacket and removed it. Then she removed her boots, socks and trousers. As uneasy as she felt about it, Sera removed her spandex camisole and underwear. Rationality convinced her that the warmest parts of her body would provide the stranger with the heat he so badly needed. Sera then proceeded to remove the rest of his clothes. She pulled his boots from his feet and trousers from his legs as she slipped beneath the blanket. She chided herself for neglecting to cover his unclothed chest during the night. Sera stretched out on top of him, exposing as much of her warm skin to his cold flesh as she could, her chest to his chest, her legs on his, her arms spread on top of his arms. Their intimate parts touched and Sera bit her lip.

He would be too incapacitated to notice, she hoped.

"Please, don't die." Her words were in his language. Sera could not fathom how she knew them but they were spoken effortlessly.

After what seemed like an endless time, his convulsions quieted to a tremor and she could feel his chest, which was against her breasts, ease from rapid respirations to more settled movements. His skin began to feel warm. With much relief, Sera remained on him for awhile to be sure that his body temperature was stable.

Naked…female…flesh.

His awareness funneled down to that one single fact, and he was immediately aroused. He hardened against her thigh.

Uh Oh.

Sera attempted to rise, but he clenched her wrists. Then using her arms as leverage, he raised her from his chest. He rolled and she was beneath him, her arms outstretched with his. He did not let go. It felt as though he would rip her shoulders from their sockets, and she cried in distress. His strength was mighty and with every ounce of her being she tried to escape, but she was pinned and powerless. Sera looked up at him. His eyes were glassy and bloodshot. He appeared disoriented and seemed to be looking through her, not at her.

"My blood with your blood," His voice hoarse but fervid. Again she understood the foreign language and this time the words caused her to shudder with a fear so great she could not scream.

"Let me go!" Sera begged. Her body, her life was at his mercy. His lips came crashing down against hers as he pressed his hips to her pelvis. *Cripes!* The man was huge. She squeezed her legs tightly together as he attempted to nudge her thighs apart. A losing battle.

Shit! Teeth down there would be so useful right now.

She bucked upward but realized her mistake immediately. He merely pressed his weight harder into her and she felt his member thicken even more.

Sera willed her body to relax. Fighting it would only increase the discomfort. But when his mouth moved lower to suckle her breast, she seized anew, and released an escalating and shrilling cry.

Sera squeezed her eyes shut. Penetration was imminent.

But then, all movement stopped. He went still.

Was it over?

Sera did a quick analysis of her body. *No*, he hadn't entered her. She opened her eyes. He was staring down at her, a stunned look on his face as he observed her terror stricken expression. His entire body shuddered as he fought for restraint. He blinked several times, then rolled away from her and onto his back, his chest rose up and down with great ardor. Sera wasted no time. She jumped to her feet and grabbed her clothes. She quickly put them on as she fled from him, running towards the stream, but her foot caught a rock. She tucked her chin to protect her face but was unable to bring her arms up in time. She stumbled into the trunk of a tree, slamming her forehead in the process.

"Ugh!" she bellowed. The collision was hard enough to cause her to rebound, and then fall forward again. Sera grabbed the trunk, and slid downward. The bark snagged the shirt she wore beneath her jacket. She scraped the skin on her face and chest as she slithered ungracefully to the ground. Sera continued to grasp the tree, dazed by the impact. She attempted to organize the chaos in her head, but the jolt that rocked her brain earlier, along with this new collision, only served to enhance her foggy thoughts. She was completely rattled and discomposed.

Sera twisted around and sat, leaning against the tree.

The stranger's charger had followed her and kept pushing at her with its snout.

"Leave me alone." Sera pushed the muzzle of the horse away from her, but it annoyingly kept nudging her.

"Get lost." She shoved the snaffle of the horse even harder. The horse snorted, spraying her with snot.

"That's just perfect," Sera grumbled while wiping the mucus from her face. "Thanks so much."

She rose from the ground and staggered to the stream. When she glanced back the charger was just behind her. She took off her jacket and leaned forward to splash her face.

Could this day get any worse?

Oh yea of little faith.

It could.

The horse bumped Sera's bottom causing her to fall face first into the water. Sera pulled her body upright, gagging from the water that invaded her mouth and nostrils. Her wet hair was plastered in strands about her face. Sera angrily dragged herself to the bank, turned to the animal, and stood nose to nose with it. The creature licked her face, covering her with slime again. Sera stood defiantly with her hands on her hips.

"Ya know horse." She poked a finger at him. "I am feeling quite hungry right now...horse."

She leaned in closer. "In fact, horse, I am hungry enough to eat, well... a horse!"

The horse stood its ground, undisturbed by Sera's threatening look.

Great, just great! She was being harassed by a horse now!

Sera dropped her head and almost smirked--*almost.* Her situation bordered on ridiculous. She could make an easy escape if she hopped up on the animal and took flight, but she had no idea where to go. Besides, the beast would probably return to its master and dump her at his feet with a mocking nicker and a snort. She stroked the horse's mane, wondering if it would allow her to ride it bare back. The animal was very large. If it bucked and threw her, she might have to add broken bones to her growing list of injuries.

Not a pleasant thought.

Sera touched the area above her right eyebrow to assess the damage. The abrasions covered the corner of her forehead and the area around her temple. She knew a bruise was likely beginning to form. She stretched and flexed her back. *Yep*, scrapes there too, those from trying to wiggle from beneath the savage when he was on top of her.

Sera was a mass of abraded flesh.

She gazed through the trees again. There was still no sign of him, so she decided to wash. Wearing only her undergarments, she dipped into the cool, rushing water, but did not dare linger within its cleansing embrace. She was frightened at the moment, but not hysterical.

A regimen of protocol tapped along her brain.

Observe, anticipate, communicate, negotiate.

She was comforted by the simple detail of knowledge, a strand of hope that tied her to a life she could not recall. Sera was a military educated officer, conditioned to handle hostile situations. It was likely the reason why she wasn't much offended by his attempt to rape her. She was exceedingly miffed at herself, however. It was a clear misjudgment on her part. True, he was incoherent, but she should have anticipated the chance for an attack. She was mostly disturbed that she had let down her guard in a moment of expedience to save his life. Blame that one on her present state of jumbled brain wave patterns.

I need to get a grip and think this thing through.

Sera emerged from the stream and sat in a small patch of sunlight peaking through the forest greenery. She combed her fingers through her hair.

Horse had deserted her. Likely, it returned to its savage master. Well, it was idealistic to think that she could get very far on foot. She pondered her unfavorable position, and concluded that she should remain with the horseman--if he hadn't already abandoned the campsite. She convinced herself of several rationales as to why this was her best course of action. First, he was presently incapacitated by his injuries and for the moment at least, would be of little threat, as long as she kept her distance. Okay, so the head in the bag was a serious consideration. She was however, in a strange and obviously archaic world, and his possession of the thing did not necessarily correlate to evil doings.

Did it?

Sera would file that one under *Review at a later date,* and her latter thought, that he might be a coroner, she would store under *Dumb rationales for having a head in a bag.* Next, she regarded her momentary lapse in sensible thinking. It also could have been a gross misunderstanding on his part as well. After all, he was disoriented and near death with a naked woman lying on top of him, one who had just finished rubbing him. He did gain his wits before he lost complete control. That behavior was promising. Third, any threat that this stranger posed might not even compare to the dangers in the land beyond. Finally, her most definitive reason was that she did not know the terrain and she was stranded. Escape was an option only once she assured herself that she wasn't going to end up in a bigger mess than the one she was in now. Sera stood and brushed herself off. What she needed to do was communicate with him, to negotiate a compromise about her situation, and convince him to help her. Sera rolled her head and shoulders in an attempt to throw off the humiliation, the pain and the isolation she was feeling. She returned to the camp refusing to be intimidated.

She decided that puffing out her chest in a demonstration of pride was not a good idea.

Sera found the stranger where she left him. He was sitting on the dirt leaning with one arm on a bent knee, and shaking his head as if he were attempting to regain his faculties. Her brave affront withered. She was suddenly very intimidated by his nearness, and his overpowering masculinity. He had a warrior's body, large and finely honed by practice of his skills. Sera allowed her eyes to briefly flick to his muscular chest and rippling abdominal muscles, covered only by the wound dressing. Just the right smathering of coppery male hair graced the front of him, converging just below his rib cage to a straight, darker line that descended and plunged below the waist of his pants.

Sexy.

It was the first word that popped into her head. Her heart fluttered.

Oh god!

Appalled by her unexpected reaction, she mentally threw down her misplaced libido and stomped it into the dirt. She would not permit the notion to wander any further, and was relieved that he had donned his trousers.

She did not want to look at *that* part of him.

Their gazes met and locked. Sera narrowed her eyes.

Dare come near me and I will cut off your…

Her warning expression was unmistakable, and he was perplexed momentarily, at the look she gave him, until awareness of what he had almost done to her struck him. He shut his eyes and wrenched his face as he gripped the realization of his actions. He had no recollection of the sensation of it, though the imagery of the occurrence was clear.

It was an unspeakable act.

He opened his eyes, and watched her side step toward the dagger still in the belt he wore earlier. Her wary gaze fixed with his. She removed the blade from the sheath and took a position several lengths away from him, where she sat with her arms wrapped around her bent knees, dagger in hand.

She deserved the comfort of possessing the blade.

He would allow her to keep it for now.

The sun by this time had risen far above the horizon, but the air around them was still cool. A slight breeze chilled Sera and she began to shiver. Noticing her discomfort, the knight picked up the blanket that was lying beside him and stumbled toward her, still weak from his trauma. Sera sprang to her feet, nearly losing balance herself. She held the dagger with two hands and pointed it at him. He stalled, no closer than several feet from her, and dropped the blanket.

He warily backed away, hands outspread, keenly aware that this woman who had shown him nothing but good will, could possibly and rightfully be the source of his demise. He had lived through too much to allow his downfall to be at the hands of a lovely stranger. For the moment it would be best to stay at a distance.

During the remainder of daylight, they sat facing, eyeing each other, a piteous pair of wounded foes, each ignorant to the other's purpose. Neither of them was well enough to move, but leery enough to forego rest. Finally, the knight rose unsteadily to his feet, staggered a bit, but found his composure almost immediately.

It was unsettling to Sera that he was regaining some of his strength, for as long as he remained physically weakened, her chances of protecting herself were greater. She worriedly watched as he made his way to the water. When he returned a short time later, he appeared slightly revitalized and clean and still wet from his bath. Sera's eyes followed the droplets of water that dripped from his wet hair, and streamed down his half naked torso, as he stood in front of her. His nearness made Sera nervous, so she fretfully pushed to a stand and once again raised the dagger. He extended his arm and offered her a drink from the decanter he was holding, but Sera refused it by shaking her head. The knight recapped his flask and tossed it toward her. It landed at her feet. He stood watching her for a moment, realizing her reluctance was likely due to her fear of him. Sera glanced at the container then returned her attention to him. Slowly she bent to pick it up. He nodded and smiled slightly. Then he turned his back toward her and went to his horse, offering her a fragment of trust that she would not try to stab him.

The charger had taken to some berries and was now refreshed with water and nourishment. It bobbed its head and neighed playfully as the stranger patted its snout, and brushed it gently. He then occupied himself with repositioning the saddle, as well as the bulk of his supplies and weapons cast upon the ground when the woman removed the saddle.

He noticed the sack was missing.

After a brief search he discovered it in some nearby shrubbery. He picked it up and examined it. The hook was unlatched and the seal was broken. He knew immediately that she bared witness to what was inside.

She could not possibly understand the meaning of this.

He returned to the charger and replaced the sack on the horse's pommel after wrapping it tightly with rope, a satisfactory attempt to avert the stench. He then turned toward her and wondered what she must think of him.

Sera was preparing to speak to him, carefully rehearsing her interpretation to ensure the words she used were correctly translated into his language. There was no room for error. But her plan had just taken a drastic turn for the worse. He was examining the woven bag that Sera tossed away after she viewed its contents. Now, he was looking at her, aware that she knew of his crime. From her sitting position, she watched him reach back, remove his bow from its clip, and an arrow from his quiver. When he placed the arrow in the bow and aimed it in her direction, the terror in Sera escalated. He could overthrow her with one shot of an arrow, and without ever actually touching her. Sera felt like the ultimate fool. Her life was about to end. He was going to kill her now. It had been a nice life she decided to presume. Sera said a little prayer and hoped he wasn't a cannibal too.

Perhaps, if she returned the dagger, he would show her mercy.

This seemed unlikely.

Be that as it may, it really did not matter at this point for he plainly held the upper hand. She could attempt to run, but the thought of an arrow in her back certainly was no more appealing than one through her chest. She knew that death would come more swiftly if the arrow pierced her heart rather than a lung, which might collapse, leaving her writhing in pain. Before she could react with any plan however, he rapidly drew back the bowstring and released it.

Sera screamed, covering her head with her hands.

The arrow whirred by her.

With disbelief she looked up, amazed that he missed her. He came toward her. She sprang to her feet and raised the dagger, ready to defend herself, but the warrior merely passed her by, his attention fixed elsewhere. Completely confused, Sera wheeled around to see where he had gone. The stranger was crouched over a small animal, dead from the arrow that pierced its neck. It looked like an oversized rodent with a pink tail and elongated nose. Its fur had a yellowish hue.

The knight plucked the arrow and picked up the animal, dangling it by its hind feet. He faced Sera. Her grip tightened on the dagger.

"I require my dagger if we are to eat." His voice was concise. His palm was open toward her, as if he expected that she would surrender the weapon. When she hesitated, he shook his head, and tossed the animal on top of the boulder to his right.

"Then you will clean the beast, and we will eat."

Sera's eyes swept from the creature to the dagger in her hand. The blade was her only source of defense, but it was true that the animal needed to be gutted. She was uncertain as to what she should do. He could have maimed her with the arrow as easily as he killed that animal. It was quite obvious he was capable of this, if that was what he wished to do. What use would the dagger be to her then? Moreover, Sera did not want to gut the creature, although she would if she was forced, but that was by no means, very appetizing.

Knowing that this went against all of her training and could possibly be her gravest act of insanity, she reluctantly turned the dagger, handle side toward him. She could see the headlines now. *"Military explorer goes numb in the brain after crashing her craft into the dirt."*

He moved closer to her. Sera's heart pounded and her hand began to shake as he reached for the blade. In one swift motion he grabbed her wrists, shackling her with his large hands. Sera pulled back furiously. Then she tried to kick him.

It was like kicking a rock.

Nonetheless, she continued her effort to free herself, but she could not match his size or his strength. Outmaneuvering him was impossible, and the blade was pointed in the wrong direction. Sera dropped to her knees and he too, dropped with her. The dagger slipped from her grasp.

"Pos sas lene," he whispered softly. She said nothing, but continued to struggle.

Finally realizing that her actions were futile, Sera went limp, sinking further to the ground, her head dropping. Her energy was depleted. Her resistance fled. Whatever his intentions, so be it. How half-witted of her to think she could trust him. This savage had no honest intentions. Sera was angry, deceived, and so terribly afraid of him.

"Your name?" he repeated, his tone still gentle. Sera looked up. What was her name? Yes, she knew at least her first name.

"Sera," she answered between panting breaths.

Was this all he wanted? Why would he use such a forceful manner to solicit such simple information?

All he needed to do was ask.

No, it was a tactic to disarm her. That was his aim when he grabbed her. He probably thought she was going to stab him.

Maybe she would have.

"Sera," he repeated. His voice was low and beckoning. A shiver coursed through Sera's spine. She shook the feeling away.

He released one of her arms to brush back a loose strand of her hair. Sera seized the opportunity and her hand flew to the dagger. With one turn of his foot, the sole of his boot flattened her hand, applying just enough pressure to immobilize it. He reached and grasped the handle of the blade, easing his boot enough for Sera to lift her palm from it. If she attempted to grab it now, one yank by him, and the sharp edge would slice her skin.

Sera stared at him. He caught sight of the purplish swelling on her forehead, and furled his brow attempting to recall the details of his transgression with her.

"You are injured." He sheathed the dagger and then gently ran his fingers along the bruised abrasions. "I did this?"

"No, but you were still the cause of it." Sera winced at his touch. Her eyes misted but she fought back the tears, releasing a single, stinging droplet that traced a path along her temple, anointing the scrapes on the side of her face. "When I ran from you."

Sera paused and took a deep breath, attempting to regain her composure. She did not want him to know how vulnerable she felt. She then defiantly stated, in her own language of course--no sense in provoking him, "You're a loathsome barbarian. I should have let you die. I'm going kill you when I get the chance."

"*Dialektos i Gaia.*" He released his other hand from her, held her at the shoulders, and stared at her steadfastly. "You speak the language of the Origins."

He pulled back from her slightly and studied her further, his eyes roaming her face. He inhaled sharply. "It is, as I had thought."

She had no idea what he meant, but at least she was free from his grasp. She did not move however. Sera was captivated by his closed lip smile that beamed with satisfaction. She desperately wanted to despise him for forcing her surrender, but the charming expression on his handsome, rugged face obscured the images of cruelty that she had been steadily gathering.

"Forgive me Sera. I meant you no harm." He moved his hands to cradle her head, intending on drawing her close, but then he noticed the discrepancy in the size of her pupils, one was larger than the other. He ran his fingers over the top of her head until he reached the lump in her scalp where she hit her head in the crash.

"The injury affects your alertness." He probed further. "Your skull is intact."

The pressure he applied to the swelled knot caused a surge of nausea and dizziness that consumed Sera. She swayed and then her body fell against him. It had been a valiant effort, but Sera could no longer maintain her stamina. He accepted her full weight on him.

"I need a nap." Sera reached for the ground.

He lowered her slowly. "Then have it. I will watch over you."

"Oh that's reassuring," Sera mumbled. She rolled to her side and closed her eyes.

So much for military strategy.

He sat next to her, and watch her, he did. Her skin looked soft and tanned, complimenting her hair, a brown so dark it was nearly black. The clip that held it in a twisted bundle at the nape of her neck had loosened, revealing wavy locks that stretched to just below her shoulder blades. It shimmered with a satiny luster where sunlight danced on it. Layers of it fell across her face and gently kissed her full, peachy lips.

Would those lips taste as sweet as they looked?

In time he would know this and more, now that he could relinquish his oath. He reclined to his side and propped his head with his hand. He continued to visually explore her. She was quite exquisite, physically fit. Her clothes were precise on her body, revealing gentle curves and round but not large breasts. He watched them move up and down steadily as she breathed. At the moment her jacket lay slightly opened. He was tempted to lift it for a quick peek. He had caught a glimpse of the tops of her breasts, the *rise* before, when she bent to pick up her overcoat. He would have feasted his eyes longer on them if his blasted eyes would have stayed in focus. He had also seen the thin piece of cloth she wore beneath, how her breasts rolled and the nipples pushed through the material when she stretched her arms to slip the coat on. It was nearly transparent, or should have been, the way it hugged those delicious looking mounds of hers. He cringed as a fleeting picture of what he tried to do to her passed through his mind. He had attempted to force his way with her, albeit he was hallucinating at the time. Still, his actions were not a circumstance favorable for a good beginning. He would have to earn her favor. Sera was the progeny of Gaia, the Ptino asteri of the Edict. She had been sent to him. It was fated that they be together.

Chapter Two

Sera awoke with a start. It was dark. He left her sleeping on the ground and had begun to prepare the meal. She moved to sit at the fire opposite him, devoid of thoughts, her face expressionless. The pain that hammered inside of her head continued to nag at her, although her thoughts were less disorganized.

The meat was tender, and tore easily from the bone. He ate ravenously. It had been many *rises*--days, since he had consumed such a fill as this. Only a few berries had touched his palate. His injury deprived him of the capacity to seek more sustenance, and the lack of water had weakened him further. It was because of Sera that he was able to enjoy this feast now. He was grateful to her and rued the actions, which guided her mistrust and ire of him. He would remedy that, find a way to show her that he was honorable.

"You must eat Sera, or you will be weak for our journey." He held out his hand and offered her a piece of the meat.

Sera turned her head away. She was annoyed, at him because of how effortlessly he gained control over her, and at herself for being in such a vulnerable situation. She should have made him her hostage when she had the chance. She should have tied him up. She should have taken his horse, used his supplies for survival, and waited patiently for rescue.

Should have, would have, could have. Blah, blah, blah. It didn't matter now. Sera felt fainthearted and defeated.

Accompany him on his journey? This, she should not do. If she left the area, her rescuers would not be able to find her. Surely they had been tracking her ship. Sera looked toward the sky, then back toward him. As she studied him, she became aware of a peculiar, unfounded need to be at his side.

"Your belligerence will not serve you well. Be incensed with me if you must, but survive for your own sake."

Sera twisted her mouth. It was watering. She was hungry. It made no sense to starve herself. She moved toward him and accepted the meat. She sat no more than a couple of feet away from him, momentarily forgetting her rancor, only to realize that her anger was suppressing her fright. Not a good thing. Predators can smell fear.

He could smell her fear, though she courageously sat near him. He supposed it was justified. Even sitting he towered over her by more than a head. She was not built like the female warriors he was accustomed to, large in frame and muscular like a male, and easy to charge without damaging. Sera was feminine and pleasing to the eye, but she was brave and fierce, a woman not to be underestimated. She would have to summon that ferocity within the next few *rises*, and he would do nothing to prevent it. He could only wish that her satiny smooth skin would not be marred too severely in the Challenge. He suspected it would be a brutal one. Scars would matter not to him. He would revere in them as a measure of both her outer and inner strength. The *Marks of Permanence* anywhere on her body would be cherished. He had no doubt she would survive. If she were truly disfigured however, it would likely intensify her anger and perhaps spur hatred toward him. Even with insignificant scarring she might still despise him. He did not think he could bear the loathing of such a beauty, from the woman who would be his wife.

"This is for you." The warrior carefully removed a small tin cup from the fire, setting it aside to cool. He had been simmering some kind of concoction. Sera wondered what was in the container, but did not have the ambition to ask. "It will ease the chiseling inside your skull."

Sera imparted a dubious look toward him, wary of his motives.

He was aware of her suspicion. "It will not tranquilize you Sera, only quell your discomfort."

The tin had cooled enough to be handled. Sera brought the cup close to her face and inhaled, detecting a slight, but familiar herbal aroma. Then she tasted the brew.

"Chamomile?" She looked up at him.

"We call it anthemis. There are other remedies mixed with it."

Sera sipped the tea, finding it quite soothing. His claim was correct, for within a short time the throbbing in her head diminished and she was thankful.

"The citizens who dwell in the Corridors of the Eighth Zone are allies to my zone." He poked at the fire with his dagger, clearing the ash and coaxing the flames to life. "The Corridors are safe refuge, but the Zone itself is large with areas that are unguarded. Many travelers pass through this Zone without detection. Our adversaries may lie in wait. We will sleep in cycle."

"I'll take the first watch then," Sera elected.

"If you wish." He sheathed his blade and reclined atop the dirt. "I have faith you will not slay me in my indefensible state."

Sera stiffened at his words. Had he understood her earlier threat that she was going to kill him?

"My rest is imperative if we are to reach my own Corridor, and you will not be secure out here alone. Wake me at half luna." He yawned, stretched his arms and placed one hand behind his head. The other hand gripped the hilt of his dagger. Sera watched him for several moments until his breath deepened into a peaceful rhythm. He was asleep. She looked at his dagger. His grasp on it tightened. He shifted his position and seemed to tense. She wondered if he slept with one eye opened. Disarming him would not be a simple task. Even if she did manage it, then what, kill him? He seemed barbaric at times, aggressive and foreboding, but he had done nothing that warranted her taking his life. Sera shook off the notion. She would not kill him, and she had already discarded her plan to run away.

Zone Eight. This meant nothing to Sera except to assume there were at least seven other Zones. She would later learn that there were in fact, ten Zones. Within the Zones there were Corridors or territories, whose residents claimed to be descendants of various *Origins.* Corridors were regulated by Chancellors of the higher *Origin* class, and each Chancellor was a member of the Magistrate Council, the ruling body of the Zone. All Corridors within the same Zone remained in good fellowship, but also held coalition with some of the other Zones. The Tenth Zone was an ally of the Eighth Zone, as well as, several others. The Fourth Zone however, was a bitter foe. This Zone was a monarchy. It had three kingdoms instead of Corridors, the First Kingdom being the most powerful. The other two were minor kingdoms under its rule.

Sera inhaled the evening air. It was fresh and amiable. The air was not nearly as chilled as it had been the previous nights. The fire gently crackled, and its warmth was satisfying. She grew drowsy, and fought to stay awake. Sera was bored stiff. With her memories in limbo, she had nothing much else to reminisce about, except *him*, and most of that was not pleasant. She rose to her feet to shake the sluggishness and walked to the edge of the bush. She looked out to the stars shimmering in crystalline rhythm across the abysmal sky. It was a clear night--*luna*. Her thoughts began to drift and bits of memory besieged her, a few recognizable faces but not much else. Did she have a family? Were they bereaved with her loss? If only she had a way to contact them, to let them know she was alive. For now, she was a displaced person in an alien world with nothing to do but bide her time.

When the moon reached its highest point in the sky--*half luna*--midnight, she knew it was time to rouse him. He rose readily and took his place at watch. Sera was appreciative that it was her turn to rest, but her sleep remained disturbed through most of the night. It was nearly *full luna* before her agitation settled.

"Sera." He shook her. The knight was crouched at her side. "Sera, you must awaken now."

Sera startled awake. It seemed as though only moments had passed since she had fallen asleep, but it was already quarter rise (dawn). Her mouth was sticky, and she smacked her lips. She thought that her breath must be horrid.

"Go away," Sera pushed him rather unobtrusively on the shoulder and turned over. The warrior grasped both of her shoulders from behind, picked her completely off of the ground and placed her on her feet. He swiveled her around to face him.

Now that got her attention.

"You must rise!" He shook her again, more vigorously this time. Sera's head bobbled a few times before she bolted it upright. She was irritated that he would wake her in such a rough manner, and was about to retaliate when he grabbed her chin with one hand and turned her head.

"Koitazo!"(Look!)

Sera could see two specks moving across the lowlands. "We must leave, now. There are intruders approaching!"

He was no coward. Under better circumstances, he would have boldly met his foe and slaughtered them. With his strength diminished however, there was a possibility he could be defeated. If he lost, they would take Sera. He would not put her in jeopardy.

He had extinguished the fire and camouflaged it. His charger was loaded and ready. He was dressed in the vestments that remained intact, his trousers, leather boots, and gloves. A small piece of his jerkin that was not used for his bandage was tied about his upper arm presenting a section of his crest. His weapon belt was secured at his hips. He was bare-chested, and Sera was momentarily dazed by how savagely handsome he looked.

He picked up her jacket and held it out to her. She stared at him stupidly, like a besotted maiden, until he became impatient and started to dress her. That snapped her from her trance. Sera snatched her jacket from him and immediately put it on. The warrior then mounted his charger and offered her his hand.

"Quickly Sera."

Sera hesitated, still apprehensive, but finally placed her hand in his and allowed him to pull her behind him. She shifted in the saddle barely large enough for two, realizing quickly how firmly she was pressed up against his back, his heat suffusing her clothing and warming her flesh.

Enticing heat…masculine heat.

Sera had little time to dwell on the awkwardness of it as he yanked the reins and the charger moved forward. They headed straight through the cluster of trees and toward the creek. The charger expertly maneuvered the rocks and gullies that presented along the path. They traveled along the water's shore until they reached a large, grassy clearing where the stream's edges expanded to a dashing river. A new forest was just ahead. They briefly stopped at the rim of the plain.

"What is your experience with a courser?"

Sera thought hard. She remembered something, a beach and riding along the sand, a dirt road along a field and jumping an old wooden gate. "I'm quite competent."

The warrior snapped the horse's bridle and it moved instantly, accelerating to a full gallop, gaining speed as it moved with swiftness across the field. In an instant protective response, Sera's arms flew around the warrior's waist and she held to him tightly. She feared that if it weren't for the high cantle at her back, and the pressure of his body against hers at her front, she would have been propelled from the saddle. This was unquestionably the fastest horse she had ever ridden, and it was exhilarating.

They reached the next copse safely. The warrior slowed the charger's gait to a trot and then to a steady walk as they moved through brush and into the wooded area. They followed the river bank traveling deeper into the forest, until it was well past full *rise* (midday). The knight seemed to have his bearings, guiding his charger purposefully. Sera removed her arms from around the stranger. She had not noticed earlier, but now her right arm felt wet. She looked at it and grimaced. From midway down her forearm, to the palm of her hand, she was stippled red. It canvassed the now dried, brownish tint of the blood which had painted her sleeve earlier. He was still bleeding. She wiped her hand on the leg of her trousers.

"It is a flesh wound, Sera. Not to bother."

"What's your horse name?" Sera asked, not wanting to think about the fact that the warrior was bleeding to death.

He grinned. She had no interest in knowing his name. It was well deserved. He had frightened her immensely, and she chose to keep distant, but he was no fool. He had no doubt that she wouldn't hesitate to rip the parts off of any threatening intruder.

He considered himself fortunate to still possess his appendages. All of them.

"Her name is Dex, and she is pleased to make your fellowship."

Sera smiled and patted the charger's hind quarter. She had developed a fondness for the creature, now finding humor in how the horse badgered her at the river. How awful of a man could its master be to own such a waggish creature?

They continued their journey in silence for what seemed like endless hours, until the rise began leaving them. It was nearly full *set* (dusk). Sera looked about. The forest was dwindling into tall underbrush, and the river branched into a smaller brook. They followed the capillary into a meadow dotted with a delightful sprinkling of turquoise flowers. The aroma was quite lovely, similar to the scent of lilacs. The warrior commanded Dex to stop. He surveyed the horizon and the dimming skies. "We will camp until quarter rise."

Sera dismounted from the horse and the warrior followed. The jolt with the ground caused him to grab the side where he had been wounded and he doubled over. Then he fell to his knees. Sera knelt and placed a hand on his back. She pushed his hair to one side, and felt his forehead. He was febrile.

"You need to rest." Sera placed her hands on his shoulders and urged him to sit. She unwrapped the bandages and grimaced. The wound was red and puffy and oozing, clearly infected. She rinsed the wound and attempted to cool him with water from the brook. Thick, dark blood seeped languidly, and Sera was forced to cut the sleeves from her jacket to create a new dressing. Using Dex's blanket would be her last resort. It was filthy. At least the insides of her sleeves were somewhat cleaner, and the thicker material would be more absorbent.

Throughout most of the luna, she attempted to arrest the bleeding by applying heavy pressure to the laceration, using her forearm. Rise seemed as though it would never break. Sera, deprived of sleep, was feeling thoroughly depleted of energy. Her head finally dropped to his chest, and she nodded off.

A tumult of flashing scenery and noises began obtruding into her thoughts, dashing lights, an explosion, fire, and the sound of her own voice echoing, Possum checklist complete. She was reading reports, and studying complex digital readouts. In her dream state, Sera reached, grasping for information, attempting to read the name tags of the people in the room, searching their faces for recognition.

The images were suddenly shattered as the warrior sat erect, throwing Sera sideways and jarring her from the smudged visions that invaded her dreams. The luna had passed and the quarter *rise* (dawn), was just beginning to crest the horizon.

"What is it? What's wrong?" Sera sat up and rubbed her face. He bid her to be quiet, pressing a finger to her lips. He tilted his head to listen. Sera attempted to listen too, and then she heard it. Horses were approaching. They both stood. Two riders appeared in the distance and were fast drawing near. The warrior yanked his sword from its scabbard. As the trespassers came closer, he was able to determine their colours. He was well seasoned in the garnishings of warriors from other Zones.

"The Fourth Zone. Stay alert."

Sera's heart began to thump without even knowing what the real danger could be.

He turned to her and firmly warned, "Do not speak your language ever, in the presence of others. They will surely strive to acquire you. Do you understand?"

Sera nodded.

The two intruders came to a stop three horse lengths away from them. The younger of the two wore a plain brown tunic and a crimson belt. He was a simple page. He bore no weapons except for a meager set of bow and arrows. The other wore the same styled, brown tunic, but the crimson star of the First Kingdom, was embroidered in the upper, left corner. A sword rested in his belt and he held a shield of the same colours and emblem.

"A mere squire." The warrior deemed this citizen posed little threat. The star lacked a piercing silver dagger, the badge awarded to the accomplished combatants of the Fourth Zone. Nonetheless, this apprentice of warfare halted before them and dismounted from his horse. He drew his weapon.

"I seek reprisal for the head of my master, King Zoren, descendant of Nyx, First Kingdom of the Fourth Zone," the squire declared, "and it is your head Jerad, son of Shegarth, descendant of Antheia, Third Corridor of the Tenth Zone, that shall give me deliverance!"

Sera looked at her warrior escort, Jerad.

The gap that separated them as strangers narrowed a fraction.

The squire sneered then snapped back his head, a common innuendo used among the Zones for intimidation and to show great detest. He raised his sword.

Jerad flashed a contemptuous grin. "Leave this place. You are a nuisance." He cocked his head and waved the squire off with the back of his hand, as if annoyed by his presence. "I see no herald declaring this Challenge."

"Do not ridicule me assassin," the squire refuted with a menacing voice.

"You servant, overstep your authority." Jerad's tone was cool and rigid. His arm was outstretched and he pointed a finger inches from the squire's nose. "You will regret your insubordination."

With this, the squire from the Fourth Zone drove his sword forward. Jerad parried and counter attacked with an oblique upper swing of his sword. The squire leapt back and attempted a cut of his own. Jerad anticipated the move and avoided it. He thrust his sword. The squire moved back and out of reach, but then lunged forward again and circled his sword to drive a blow. Jerad, extended his left hand and blocked the blade at the cross guard. Simultaneously, Jerad's sword made slanted contact with the squire's blade. With a great shove Jerad broke contact with the squire. Jerad then stumbled backward and became unbalanced. He slid to one knee. The squire lifted his blade to strike.

Sera gasped. She feared that Jerad, weak from fever and the loss of blood, was about to be defeated. With a quick exchange from her left to her right, the dorsum of Sera's foot came up between the squire's legs. "Wa!Ya!"

The squire's eyes widened as he released his sword. He grabbed his crotch and squeaked out a curse before falling backwards.

"Yo! Ten points!" Sera did a little jig clasping her hands above her and waving them.

Jerad surged, sword in hand, and jabbed it harshly into the dirt, taking with it, a chunk of the squire's ear. Blood began to ooze from the wound. Sera winced. The squire squealed with the pain, rose to his feet, and mounted his horse. He retreated, disappearing into the horizon. His page, who had completely avoided the conflict, followed closely behind him.

"He is spineless," Jerad stated complacently. "It would serve him right if I pierced his tail with my arrow, hence his citizens know of his foolishness."

He turned to Sera, and scowled. "You were not supposed to speak woman."

"I said it in your language."

"Wa Ya are not words in my language. I will be grateful if your intonation was not noticed."

"I have an accent? Not me." Sera threw her palms to heart and looked at him innocently.

Jerad rolled his eyes. "Let us hope that this brain damage you suffer is remedied with haste."

It was Sera's turn to scowl.

Jerad ignored her and instead took notice of the sword the squire abandoned in his recession. Jerad retrieved the item and examined it. The sword was a diamond cut, double-edged weapon with an arched steel cross guard. It glimmered in the light of the rise. The grip was ebony, exquisitely carved into a braided design. The pommel, like the blade, was a highly polished, steel orb. It contained a star shaped bezel holding a two karat ruby, the symbol and colour of the First Kingdom of the Fourth Zone. Jerad recognized the sword. It belonged to Zoren. His squire had either stolen or inherited it when Zoren was slain by Jerad. It was a fine sword, and masterfully forged. Jerad turned to Sera and presented it to her, hilt down, tip up.

"Your spoils, Lady Noble." He bowed to her. "I thank you for your assistance."

Sera was mulling over the integrated fighting skills she apparently had. She looked at him confoundedly, intrigued that he was arming her with a weapon. She accepted the sword.

"I'm a little surprised that you would give me a weapon."

"Why?"

"Am I not your captive?" It was meant as a mocking statement, for in reality, Jerad had shown her no sign that she was his prisoner. He treated her more like a traveling companion.

"Captive?" Jerad raised an eyebrow. "It would be quite contemptuous of me to entrap a descendant of Gaia, one whose status ranks higher than mine. I would surely be punished. My duty is to give you honor."

Sera rubbed her forehead. She did not understand. Her thoughts strayed to her own origins as her eyes wandered upward.

"Ah Sera, what is it you search for in the skies?"

"My people, they must be looking for me. I'm sure a rescue is on the way."

"Then let us hope that when they do, they will choose to point their feet to the ground instead of their heads."

Sera squinted at the odd comment. "You saw the crash?"

"Hmn." He splayed his hand through his hair. "I was being watchful of the shatter arrows being thrown by Nyx warriors. They are powerful and will split a man apart when they burst within the flesh. I had decided to arc along the edge of the grassland to avoid detection.

As I moved toward the safety of the forest, I spied an object, a person in the sky just ahead of where I rode. No higher than two of my lengths, the body appeared in the air from nowhere and tumbled to the ground."

He lifted her chin with two fingers. "I thought my eyes deceived me, but then I found you."

Sera blinked at him. She could see by his look that he believed the unbelievable tale. He had to be hallucinating.

"At first I thought you a spirit, but then I touched you and knew you were flesh," he paused, running his hands down her arms. "You are the Ptino asteri."

Sera quickly scanned her memory banks. Ptino asteri, bird star, starbird. He must have seen her ship when it entered the atmosphere. She didn't just merely fall out of it, drop through the sky and hit the ground. One thing was definite. He knew that she was not of this world, and amazingly he seemed to accept it as nothing extraordinary.

Sera's eyes browsed the skies, once more. "What is the name of this world?"

"Protogio."

"Pro-toe-j-e-o." Sera mouthed the pronunciation but without an interpretation of the words.

"Gaia and Protogio are linked. You must have learned of our connection through Argilos and Tomas, the two who came before you."

Sera shook her head. "I've lost my memory."

Jerad studied her with contemplation. One side of his mouth turned up in a half smile as awareness struck him. He moved his palm to her cheek. "Pure of mind."

Sera stepped back from his touch. "What do you mean?"

"It is a quote from the Edict of Oneroi." He reached out for her again. Sera took one more uneasy step backwards. He really shouldn't be touching her like that.

"Do you know my language?"

"I know some of the words. The two Gaians could not speak our tongue when they arrived. We spent much time learning to communicate with each other."

"Did you see my ship crash?" Sera looked at him expectantly.

"There was no ship, only you."

Jerad scanned the horizon, looking for any indication that other warriors from the Fourth Kingdom were present. Satisfied that they were relatively safe for now, he turned to Sera. "We must go now. I will walk for a bit. The brawl with the squire has enlivened me, but I fear it may pass before too long."

Sera decided that she too would walk and they both continued the trek on foot. Sera kept at least two horse lengths behind him. She was too deep in thought to keep his company. She was a bit disoriented, but there was no doubt that she had seen her dead crewmates and crawled from the wreckage. True, she hadn't actually seen the ship explode. She heard it, felt it, saw the flames, and she remembered being in it, well, sort of, although now, everything seemed to be one big blur. Jerad claimed that there was no ship. Maybe he just didn't see it. Perhaps she climbed a tree and what he saw, was her falling from it. There had to be a reasonable explanation. Sera strained to refine the intricacies of her voyage from her home planet to Protogio, but the memory she clung to, felt more like an illusion. It was fading from her reality like a long expired notion. Sera pondered that for a lengthy amount of time.

They walked for what seemed like hours. The length of the rise on Protogio seemed to correlate to what she was accustomed to. Sera noted the path of the sun through the sky, and its present position, directly overhead, told her that it was now full rise. At least she had retained her sense of time. It seemed trivial at the moment. She was exhausted and could not move any further. She stopped and sat on the ground. Dex stopped with her. Jerad kept moving for at least several paces. Then sensing isolation, he too stopped, turned around and noted that Dex remained with Sera. Jerad approached his charger and gave her the most inauspicious look, but stroked her gently.

"She is a loyal creature." Jerad rubbed the thick bristles on his chin. "I must question however, with whom she keeps her loyalty." He raised an accusing eyebrow at Sera and sat down beside her.

"Tell me how our worlds are linked," Sera was slowly growing frustrated by the black hole that was her life. She had been deposited on Protogio, without any inkling as to why she was there. Jerad seemed to know things about her that she herself could not recollect. Perhaps it would prod her into remembering.

"It is written in the *Protogio Principles: The Treatise of History, Doctrines and Rites*. It was centenaries, long ago…"

Jerad waved a hand through the air and began a summation of his world's history, including the tale of the *Origins*. Sera recognized some the names but her connection to them was impersonal. She thought he spoke of mythological gods but because Jerad referred to them as being tangible, she was not certain. When she questioned him about this, he repudiated the idea claiming that the ancients were ancestors, not gods. He told her of the link to Gaia and how the *Origins* ruled the peoples of both worlds for many centuries, but eventually they retreated from Gaia and came to live on to Protogio. A mighty magistrate intent on single rulership descended on Gaia. So great was his power that he gathered many followers. There were wars and crusades. No boundary was left uncrossed. The *Origins* were finally banished from the land.

"We always believed some of the Origins still dwelled on Gaia. When Argilos and Tomas arrived, we were sure of it. At first, it was presumed that they were the Gaians of the Edict, but the pieces did not quite fit. Now, with you Sera, my eyes could see no clearer."

Sera listened with interest. She would like to read more of the text from the *Protogio Principles*, and asked Jerad if it would be possible. He told her he possessed a copy of the book in his library and would show it to her.

"It is an enigma as to where the Origins first called home. Some say their beginnings were here, but out of boredom, they abandoned Protogio to find entertainment elsewhere. Others say they fled to us, falling from the stars," Jerad tilted his head and looked toward Sera with sideways glance. "Like you."

After pondering this, Sera commented, "Maybe they traveled back and forth."

"It is a possibility. Argilos and Tomas would often disappear, but then return to Protogio within several rises."

"How did they get here?"

Jerad turned to Sera and lifted his hand to her hair. He rolled a lock of it between his fingers, indulging in the silky feel of it. Sera's immediate impulse was to pull away, but she held herself steady.

"I was in the garden with my mother, and the Gaians appeared as you did, from nothingness." He leaned forward inhaling Sera's locks. "My mother was quite annoyed that they had crushed her favorite *betrus* shrub."

Jerad twisted a strand of Sera's hair and held it between his fingers and thumb. He moved his hand downward, allowing the strand to slide through his pinch. He tugged at it lightly before releasing it and smiled as the freed lock of hair sprung up into a perfect spiral.

"You have pretty hair."

Sera felt an unexpected flush rise to her cheeks. Not wanting to respond to his admiration, she pursued the previous subject. "Well, what did you do when the Gaians appeared?"

"I had never seen an Origin afore. I opened my arms and said 'welcome.'"

"I wonder how they did it, I mean travel between both worlds?"

Jerad straightened his back and pressed his palms onto his thighs. He tossed his head back. "Ah, that is a mystery. I do not know. As much as we asked, the Gaians refused to tell us. Their being here was doomed however. When the Fourth Zone learned of their presence, they sent warriors to our Zone."

"Were they captured?"

"*Ochi*--no. They returned to Gaia. It has been nearly twelve term cycles since they have been with us. Now that you have come into my keeping Sera, no one except those I can trust with my life, will know who you are."

"Who do you think I am, Jerad?"

"The Edict of Oneroi tells of the Ptino asteri who will unravel the mystery to use the Key to Orion's belt. As I have said, you are the one, Sera. It is plain to me. The Edict claims a bond will be forged with the Keeper of the Key, a joining so fierce that space and time cannot divide it. I am the Keeper of the Key, and you Starbird will be bonded to me. It is written."

Bonded? Sera furled her brow in confusion. "You're kidding, right?"

He blew out a gust of air. "I do not know how the Edict will be fulfilled. What I do understand is that I hold the Key to Orion's belt, and you possess the knowledge to use it."

Whatever it was she was not remembering, she was sure it wasn't that. The story was fascinating to say the least, but it surely did not refer to her. Jerad seemed to believe it however. It seemed pointless to argue with him about it for the time being.

Sera looked skyward again. "Isn't Orion's belt part of a star formation?"

"It is now, but Orion was an Origin of Gaia afore that."

"So what happens when I use this key on his belt? Do his pants fall down? Then what?"

Jerad tapped his finger to his lips as though he were in serious thought. "Perhaps you will have full view of his man parts."

Sera snorted. She should have been shocked at his comment but she wasn't. "Why, that would be sacrilegious wouldn't it?" she teased, delighted to have discovered he had a sense of humor.

"I supposed it would depend on what the Oneroi had in mind."

Jerad sighed, standing upright. He took Sera's hand and pulled her to a stand. "Come, you will ride now. We have only a short distance to go."

Sera withdrew her hand from his. He was beginning to touch her more freely, and she did not want to encourage him. Especially since she now knew that he expected to share some kind of bond with her. She would rectify that situation later, once she learned more about the *Protogio Principles* and his deeply rooted belief in this Edict.

Sera agreed to ride Dex. She didn't think she could walk much further. She was fatigued and very overwhelmed with the events of the last few *rises*. She lifted her foot to place it in Dex's stirrup. Jerad unconsciously and with no intention other than courtesy, moved behind her. He put his hands to her waist to give her assistance. His body was so close to touching hers that Sera could feel his heat. Jerad felt her body stiffen instantly and she cowered. He removed his hands from her and rested them atop of Dex, one arm on each side of Sera's body. He leaned closer. His warmth surged through her. She shuddered with the thought that even without fever Jerad's flesh would likely sizzle with sensual fire.

Jerad pressed his lips to Sera's ear. Sera's breath caught, part with apprehension and part with another feeling that she could not explain at the moment.

Desire maybe?

"Sera," he consoled softly. Again he seemed to chant her name, causing a tremor to erupt from deep within her. "If I so wished, there would have been favorable opportunities."

Truth be told, he wanted to touch her, to have her feel his touch. He looked at her hands, delicate but strong. He was hit with a jolt of arousal as he pictured those fingers caressing his body. Sera had laid hands on him, mostly to attend to his injuries. He liked the feel of that touch. When she rested her head on his chest in the savanna he longed to take her in his arms, but resisted. There would be plenty of time to hold her, to kiss the length of her, but only after he gained her loyalty, when she could give herself to him freely and without uncertainty. Jerad tore himself from his thoughts, stepped back from her and crossed his arms, his stance wide. His eyes roamed her backside, stopping briefly at her shapely bottom.

He drew a hardy gulp of air and held it, attempting to contain the longing building inside him. There was much to deal with first, her lack of trust in him being most significant.

He blew out an exasperated breath. "I think I will worship and adore you from afar for now."

Sera flustered at his words, unaware of his scrutinizing tour of her backside. Jerad stepped closer and his arm came around the front of her. He put a hand on her shoulder and turned her to face him. Sera tilted her head to look up at him. He was beautiful to look at, despite his ailing condition. It amazed her that someone as large and warrior-like as he seemed to be, could also be so amicable, chivalrous even.

"I warn you though it will only be from afar for a short time." His mouth curled devilishly to one side. "A very short time."

Chivalry indeed, the scoundrel! Sera bit her lip and averted her face to hide another blush. Her attention was drawn to the bandages covering his wound. They were damp but the bleeding had apparently subsided for the time being. When she tipped her head toward his face again, he turned away. The abrupt change in his mood was alerting. She stepped in front of him. Jerad was sweating profusely. His face was still pale and drawn. He remained hot with fever. He was not well. Worry replaced her tension. She wiped the sweat from his brow with the backs of her fingers, and hoped they would reach their destination soon. Being unfamiliar with the territory, Sera would be of little help in finding his Corridor should Jerad collapse. She knew that despite his obstinacy, if he did not reach his people soon, and receive medical help, his condition could become grave. Then she wondered what kind of medical aid it would be. It was pointedly obvious that care in this place could not compare to an advanced society.

He could still die.

Chapter Three

They had been traveling for at least three or four hours. It was *half set*--four o'clock in the afternoon. The tedium, combined with the scent of meadow flowers, which blanketed the savanna and the warmth of the beating sun was tranquilizing. Sera would have dozed, but she kept nudging herself awake over her concern for

Jerad. He walked the entire distance. Several times he had fallen to his knees, only to pick himself up and continue onward. Sera admired his stamina, and from her seat on Dex's back, she also admired the beguiling spectacle of muscle that flexed under the strain of his gait. She could not deny his physical allure, but there was another unsettling tugging that she could not describe. Even without the horse beneath her she had the unnerving sense that she would follow him into eternity.

Jerad smirked each time he turned his head forward. He caught her looking at his backside. It was gratifying to know she was attracted to him. He had waited too long to fully enjoy a woman's gaze, much too long to entertain the idea of a woman against his naked body. Such restraint he suffered in his quest, but no more. Sera would be that woman, for he never wanted another, until now. The thought of only Sera in his arms, in his bed, was quite appealing. How wise of the Oneroi to send a woman, to send *this* woman. Their union would be unbreakable and boundless.

Jerad slowed his pace until Dex and Sera were at his side. He hoisted himself to sit in the saddle behind Sera and reached around to take the reins. Sera impulsively sank against his chest. She marveled at how comfortable and natural it felt. An inaudible groan vibrated in Jerad's throat. Sera molded his embrace like a custom made glove. She fit his soul like she was born to be there. Sera proved her courage, fighting the squire from the First Kingdom instead of cowering, and her trust in him was beginning to emerge. She stayed by his side despite her misgivings of him. He was gaining her loyalty. In that moment Jerad knew. He would protect Sera at all costs, put her life before his, and give his very breath to save hers. There was a kindred spark flaring within him and it was glowing with intensity.

Could she feel it too?

They continued their junket through the plain. The terrain was beginning to ascend. At first, it was gradual, but then it became somewhat steep. Because it took much effort to climb, they dismounted from Dex to give the gracious mount ease. They finally reached the apex. It revealed only a gradual descent on the other side that tapered into another open field. Just beyond, perhaps twenty yards from them, Sera spied two steel masts protruding from the dirt. Each took ownership of a distinguishing flag bearing coats of arms. The posts were positioned at each articulation of a stone arch and its adjoining walls.

Jerad stopped and pointed toward the structures. "We are at the margin between the Eighth and Tenth Zones. We will be in safe territory soon."

Sera did not respond. Jerad turned to locate her. Sera was holding Zoren's sword, attempting to swing it, the weight of the weapon throwing her. She was frustrated with her inability to wield the blade and dug it straight into the ground. Jerad smirked and approached her from behind. He reached around each side of her and slid his hands down her arms. A slight tremor coursed through Sera. She gasped, but did not pull away from him. She dismissed the pleasurable sensation.

"It is a great piece of weaponry. Use two hands." He tugged her close to him, his chin at her temple, and pressed lightly against her. Sera sucked in her breath and gritted her teeth. She could feel his muscles flexing against her back. It felt rather...*nice*.

Jerad helped Sera lift and extend the sword. With both of his hands cupped over hers, he guided the blade in smooth long strokes, down to the right, circling and turning it left, then down again, their bodies swaying in rhythm with the gliding blade. "It is an intimate dance you play with the blade, Sera. You must anticipate your opponent's weakness and use the sword to bring him to submission."

I'll bet, she thought as she turned her head toward his chest and inhaled. He emanated an untamed and rugged essence that flooded her senses like frenzied pheromones.

Jerad released his hold on her, and drew his own sword. Sera nearly crumbled and fought to regain her composure. The abrupt separation and his physical lack of support made her realize that she had been unconsciously leaning against him. He stood opposite Sera, his feet widely spaced and knees slightly bent. One foot was slightly forward. His sword was extended at midline. Jerad lifted his chin and stood firmly. Every muscle in his chest, shoulders and arms rippled with intensity as he prepared for mock battle. He was the epitome of sinewy, warrior splendor, now towering in front of her. It was enough to make her drop her sword and dive for cover, under his body, naturally. Instead, she stood tall, all five feet, four inches of her.

"Sometimes a long stroke is needed." Jerad demonstrated the movement. A muscle in his jaw ticked with intimidation. "Sometimes only a quick thrust will do."

Sera stiffened with the sudden heat that coursed through her, pooling in places that were just unacceptable. She silently wondered if it were another kind of sword play he referred to. His affect on her was becoming increasingly alarming.

"Strike." His deep voice was commanding and defined.

"What?" Sera was jerked from her daze. "Oh..."

Sera imitated his position. She drew the heavy blade outward to the right and then forced it to the left. With a clang, it made perpendicular contact with Jerad's blade. The impact rattled her bones. Her teeth chattered. Sera dropped the weapon, and lost her footing. Unfortunately her back was to the slope of the hill and she toppled, somersaulting half its length. She stopped with a thud, her feet in the direction of the hilltop, her head to the bottom of it. Jerad was astride her instantly, dropping to his hands and knees.

"Always strive to unbalance your rival," he stated mockingly. His lips turned up in a smirk. Sera shook her head at him, but she could not resist returning a curt grin.

Jerad's chest thumped, as he gazed down at her. He swallowed hard. Her eyes twinkled when she smiled, and Sera indeed had the most stunning eyes, the color of sparkling, molten gold. They sang to him--a lulling melody as enchanting as a temptress' croon. Whenever he looked into those eyes it took every fibrous strand in his core to tear his gaze from her. Unable to resist the temptation any longer, Jerad angled his head and bent toward her. His lips surrounded her mouth, caressing her lips gently. He drew them between his own lips and sipped at the crease where her upper and lower lips met. Then he withdrew, summoning his well used self-restraint to retreat from the warm, tantalizing mouth that he had kissed a thousand times in his dreams.

"You breathe fire into my spirit, Sera of Gaia." His voice was low and sensual. "I do intend to have you, Starbird."

Sera felt panic rise within her. Although her initial feelings of animosity for him had softened, she still did not fully trust him. She did not trust what she felt when he was close, and she certainly did not want to ponder the kiss, that sweet, delicious, and much too short kiss. Right now she needed to put space between them, before she did something stupid like rap her legs around him, pull his face to hers and ravenously start tongue slapping him. No, Jerad was too much of a stranger with many mysteries surrounding him. Sera was a stranger to herself, the pieces of her past still lay unassembled, a lifetime of memories tucked in the pockets of her mind. She really needed to find something distasteful about this man who was beginning to make her hum with his every touch. So she pulled open her mental file cabinet drawer and yanked out the head.

He is a savage who severs heads. Disgusting.

There, that did it. She stiffened beneath him. Aware of the abrupt and negative change in her demeanor, he rose away from her and sat back on his haunches.

"Do not fear me Starbird. It was just a kiss I sought to steal from a rare beauty."

How noble, and damn didn't he reek of it.

In the days she had spent with him, he was ever the gentleman, bestowing nothing but respect on her, and she had not seen his fury. Even when he fought the squire from the Fourth Zone he demonstrated controlled expertise in his swordsmanship, maiming instead of killing. Sera sat upright and wrapped her arms around bent knees.

"Tell me about Zoren's head." The words heedlessly came to her lips. Sera pressed them together waiting for his reaction, hoping she wouldn't regret bringing up the subject.

Jerad closed his eyes tightly. He looked anguished. After a long silence, he finally managed to speak. "The head of Zoren was to avenge the atrocities he led against my house. The warriors of the Fourth Zone show no remorse in their brutal behaviors. They are barbarous when they advance. We are in constant watchfulness. Given the chance they would strip our lands of their resources, take us into slavery, rape our women..."

His voice trailed, recalling his own near violation of Sera, and he looked away from her in shame. "Ack, I am no better."

Sera tucked one foot under her and leaned closer, with full understanding of his dismay. "You did not make me your slave, Jerad." She splayed her hand and placed it gently on his chest. His heart beat steadily beneath it. "And you did not rape me."

Jerad regarded her from under half closed lids. He pursed his lips and ran his tongue along the inside of the crease. He could still taste her there. He wanted to taste more. Instead he placed the pad of his thumb under her chin and fanned two fingers along her mouth. Sera parted her lips slightly, allowing a tiny gust of air to escape, along with some of her misgivings toward him.

Jerad set his other hand over hers and lifted it from his chest. He turned her hand over and kissed her palm, silently thanking the Oneroi, once again, that the Ptino asteri was female, and that he was the one chosen to see her through the prophecy. The words of the Edict were most transparent.

She would be his.

They would--ochi, they must be bonded in the Vows of

Permanence. It will be, as it was written in the foretelling.

He stood. Turning his back to her, he wandered into the field, and looked out toward the horizon. Dex was strolling about in the grass, occasionally chomping a bit. Sera stood and went to his side. She placed a hand on his upper arm. His bicep twitched against her palm. He said nothing, but his breathing was heavy and labored and his fists were clenched. Without releasing his arm Sera moved to face him, giving him her full attention. The fury in his face was abominable and she released him, taken aback. Jerad stared over her head for endless seconds, but finally spoke, willing to lay open all that had driven him to the actions that eventually led to their meeting. He realized she needed to understand who he was as a man, before she would consent to fully be his woman.

"I went to tournament in the First Kingdom, not only to challenge Zoren, but to enact my revenge." He dropped his eyes to meet hers. "Zoren butchered my mother."

A pit formed in Sera's stomach. Her chest started squeezing tightly.

Jerad continued unrestrained. "He and four of his men came for the Gaians. My babe sister was only ten rises old. I thank the Origins that she was not with us on that rise. We all attempted to fight, but the Gaians suddenly vanished when Tomas received a mortal wound, a sword, through his chest. My mother and I were left alone to defend ourselves. We were defeated. My mother was raped by Zoren and another of his men, while three others held me immobile. Her throat was slit and her life was stolen. When they were through preying on her body, I was rendered unconscious by a blow to the back of my head. I awoke, face down in her blood, next to her bludgeoned, naked body."

Sera stood motionless, watching the dark, furious eyes erode to a troubled sorrow. She imagined the tortured, shameful guilt, coveted by a helpless boy restrained to witness the revolting discretion against the woman who gave him life.

"You were just a child."

"I was thirteen term cycles, Sera! Old enough to defend her!" He roared in reply, and then roughly grabbed her by the upper arms, his fingers dug into her flesh. "I will never forget her screams!"

Sera drew her fingers to her lips and sucked in a quivered breath. She understood his rage. She looked away, allowing herself a brief moment to digest what he had just told her. Sera's fingers curled. In the same situation she would have ripped Zoren's head from the neck that supported it. She would not have needed a sword.

"And this victory has given you satisfaction?"

He closed his eyes and snarled, "It did not bring me the relief that I had expected."

When he opened them again they were filled with a torment so deep that Sera felt as though she would fall into them and suffocate. But then his look softened. "It did however bring me to you my Starbird, and in that, I find much satisfaction."

Her heart wailed against her chest wall, and began to beat wildly with his words. Jerad wrapped an arm around her waist and drew her close. He arced over her, his weight nearly causing her to collapse. Jerad lowered his head toward her. His hot breath feathered the flesh of her mouth.

"Sera of Gaia," he gulped, "I am about to forfeit my faculties. The fever has taken its toll."

A shriek overhead caused them both to look skyward. A small hawk circled above. "Aryan's fledgling. We are close, but I fear my strength has reached its limits."

Jerad suddenly went weak, his knees crumbled. He threw a heavy arm around Sera's shoulder in a feeble attempt for support. She caved under the mass of his sinking body. They both dropped to their knees.

"Look beyond." He pointed out and across the field. "A gathering of trees, there. Just within its edge, a course will draw you riseward. Continue on this path until you reach the gulch. The trail will continue along its brim, and it will lead you around to a bridge and the First Corridor. If you get lost Dex should know the way. The watchmen at the reservoir will know my horse and will provide you with guidance. Tell them of my location. The Corridors are highly protected. You will find safe conduct there. It is setway, to the Third Corridor. Shegarth is a Chief Counselor and my father. Ask for him. At a steady cantor, you will make it there before full set. I am going down now Sera."

Sera wrapped her arms around him to prevent him from falling further.

"No!" she exclaimed, but she could not hold him and he dropped to the ground landing flat on his back.

"Get up!" Sera shook him forcibly. She slapped him hard in the face. He did not respond. She pounded his chest, but to no avail. Sera was frenzied, and she began to hyperventilate. He had a pulse. He was breathing, but he was absolutely dead weight. She would not leave without him.

Sera ran to Dex and yanked the canteen from its hook. She knelt by Jerad and poured the water on his face. He did not move.

She drew her hand back to slap him again but before it made contact, his left arm shot out and he blocked her. Jerad reached up, wrapped an arm around the back of her neck, and pulled her head toward his shoulder. "You wish to revive me by drowning and beating me?"

"It worked, didn't it?"

"Bring my consanguinity to me."

"No, we will leave together," Sera insisted, yanking him in an attempt to lift him off of the ground.

"You cannot carry me."

"Dex can. I will put you up there."

He chuckled weakly. "I might die on the way."

"You could die here. Such a fitting end for a knight to rot in a field with his eyes plucked out by fowl, and nothing to show for it but a decaying head. Besides we are almost there, right?"

Jerad gave consideration to her words, shaking his head, but it was her fit of might that encouraged him now. Sera straddled him, one foot to each side of his body. She squatted low, and dug in her heels as she grabbed his upper arms. With all of her energy she pulled back and forced him to sit. She held him there, grunted and heaved heavy breaths, daring him to fall over again. She suited him well, this mate of his. In the last few rises Sera of Gaia had already proven marked devotion for him, a warrior she still considered a stranger. He most assuredly would have died without the advent of their meeting. He would not spoil her perseverance now.

"Reserve my senselessness. You are a persistent woman." He closed his eyes. "I believe you were sent to me Starbird, to spite myself."

"Damn straight," she retorted.

He chuckled again and inhaled deeply, gathering energy from within. "Assist me to Dex. If I die on the way at least it will be while holding your delectable body."

Sera moved to his side and threw one of his arms around her shoulders. "Ready, set, go."

Sera summoned all of her power and pushed upward, bracing him against her. With a little help from Jerad--well, actually with a lot of help from Jerad--she succeeded in getting him to his feet and up on the charger. She retrieved the dropped swords and mounted the horse. Seating herself in front of Jerad, Sera took control of the bridle. Dex accepted her lead and they headed across the plain.

At the stone archway, they paused. Sera could clearly see the details of the heraldry now. Both were oval in shape, with a golden edge that was garnished with leafy vines. The background on the one to the left was pale. A deep yellow shield was centered on it, embellished with two jagged designs resembling lightening bolts, angled across it. One was black, one was silver. Three plume devices, one violet, one blue and one green, were positioned at the side and top points of the crest. Two golden rings that overlapped each other graced the point at the bottom.

"The coat of arms for the Eighth Zone," Jerad explained. "The First Corridor bears the black and the Second Corridor has the colour of Silver."

"And the feathers?"

"The device of high Nobility, the colours determining the Origins from which they descended."

Sera's attention was drawn to the other banner. This one was azure and had upon it three angled bars, one red, one green and one gold. Three roses at each point, yellow at the left point, white at the right, and at the top, the lavender bloom that also embellished Jerad's garments. Red and orange blooms edged each side further down, with the shield closing to a common point, where three golden rings overlapped at its bottom tip. It was the same crest that Jerad wore at the back of his doublet.

"The Tenth Zone. My region. There are three Corridors in this Zone. My kinsmen dwell in the Third Corridor. The highest standing Nobles in the Tenth Zone are descendants of Antheia, friend of the flowers, Chloris of flowers, trees and shrubs, Demeter who oversees growth. They blessed our land and gave us breath. The bloom was a gift that became our attribute. They also bestowed on us, the wisdom of cures from the foliage. We are healers first, guardians of our domain and warriors when needed."

Sera bid Dex to move and she headed riseward. "And the golden rings?"

"They are the badges of glory for courage and nobility, as are the daggers which puncture the stars of the warriors of the Fourth Zone. The rings are looped together to show our coalition among the Corridors. Only those who have mastered the battle skills wear the distinction of the gold ring."

Sera thought about the gold ring adorning both Dex and Jerad's garments. Jerad was of high standing.

Jerad slipped his arms around her waist, holding her tightly. He laid his head on her shoulder, trusting fully that Sera and Dex would guide them to their destination. "I will sleep now Sera. There will be much to come upon our arrival."

They continued on with Dex in a fixed trot, and reached the swelling of trees without haste. Sera did as Jerad instructed and followed the trail just inside the edge of the forest heading riseward, the trail carrying them in a persistent ascension. It was slow moving, but they were making progress. The hawk was swooping overhead, tracking the riders and squawking in its high pitched wail. He must have smelled blood.

The trees around them were majestic, burgeoning skyward and creating a canopy that girdled the trail. A laggard breeze gently created minute partitions between the branches above, allowing sprinkles of sunlight to prance around them. The branches themselves were long and limber, swaying like great wings and causing a wispy sound so sedating that even the most rambunctious of creatures would be lulled to calm. The air was damp and viscous, and an overwhelming scent of pine infused the air.

Sera yawned. She wondered how much further their traveling would carry them, and what she would meet with when they finally reached its end. Jerad said nothing else for the rest of their journey. He became inattentive, often swaying from side to side. With each unbalanced list, he jerked his head vertical, to right himself in the saddle.

The silence gave Sera pause enough to gather some remembrance of whence she came. She already knew that she was well educated and military trained by an advanced establishment. What disturbed her most however, was her lack of recall of the personal truths. She could see faces and recount flashes of experiences as a child and adult, fading in and out of her thoughts, either in slow motion, or streaming in fast forward, but details eluded her. She heard that amnesia victims often regain their memories when confronted with familiar items. It is why she could recall the frustration she experienced when studying the language that flowed effortlessly from her mouth now. It was a connection to ancient people of her world. She was quite fluently speaking Greek. In fact, she realized that he was speaking a selective form of Hellenistic Greek, ancient, but with some modern words intermixed. She had little difficulty understanding Jerad, but when Sera attempted to recall why she knew this language, it was too much effort to conjure even a simple memory. She also knew the Origins he spoke of were the Greek gods of mythology, and Gaia was the Earth she called home. All things Greek were flooding her thoughts, likely because it was being tossed at her regularly in the form of a six foot two Adonis by the name of Jerad, who happened to have his massive body wrapped around her at the moment.

Sera smiled. She liked the feel of him. She was starting to really like him.

Sera wondered about the possibility that there might be some mystical purpose for her being here. She would definitely study the Edict of Oneroi to learn more. Sera was certain that in her world reality was based on technology and the logic of science. Knowledge relied on research and not the predictions of prophecies. Although spiritual beliefs did still provide moral guidance, it did not direct their laws.

Separation of Church and State, Sera remembered.

She must have been sent here as a scientist.

"Well of course!" she shouted.

Jerad lifted his head from Sera's shoulder. "What is it?"

"I was assigned to this mission because of my expertise. I'm supposed to be here."

"I have already told you that." He nestled his bristly face against Sera's neck. It tickled and she giggled, but recomposed herself immediately.

"That means other travelers from my planet, Gaia as you call it, have been here. Otherwise, how would we know what language you speak?"

"I have also already told you that." He readjusted his head on Sera's shoulder while tightening his grasp around her waist.

Sera felt hopeful now. They would come for her. In the meantime it looked as though she would learn to adapt to this new world until her rescuers arrived. She assumed her mission was to explore and gather information. The happenings of the last rises had at least proven fascinating given the extraordinary similarities to a more brutal and unsophisticated age of old which she knew existed centuries before in her planet's history. Interesting to say the least, and linked somehow.

Sera looked to the skies.

But when would her rescuers come?

Chapter Four

They emerged from the thick foliage, and Sera was awestruck by the breathtaking view. They had come to the edge of a great crevasse, nearly two hundred feet across. Its walls dropped almost vertically from its threshold to a basin, about one hundred feet down. Then she noticed something peculiar. Along the opposite bank five solid stone columns, which appeared man-made, were embedded into the ravine wall. Every few minutes moderate volumes of water would gush from the spaces between. The structure appeared to be the makings of a drainage system. Sera's interest in the world she was about to enter piqued, for it was obviously not as primitive as she originally suspected.

Jerad instructed Sera to halt Dex. He moved in front of her and assumed control of the reins. His skin still scorched hot and the fever still had not passed, but Jerad sat upright, fully awake, adrenaline surging through him with anticipation of the events to come.

The trail led them to an area where the depth of the gorge began to shallow. The width too, narrowed to about fifty feet across. A wooden truss bridge gave them passage to the other side. The brushing of hooves against dirt shifted to a *clippity-clop* sound as horseshoes met wood. Sera attempted to squelch the nervousness that clung in her throat, pounded through her chest and plopped like stones in her stomach. She would soon meet Jerad's people, and she had no idea what to expect.

Two sentries stood at the far end of the bridge. On the upper left side of their vestments, they each wore a crest displaying the symbol and colours of the First Corridor. Neither device was embellished with a gold ring. They were unseasoned, but trained warriors. Sera stared curiously, noticing that one of the guards was a woman. In near unison they hailed Jerad with a raised fist, arm forward, and elbow bent to a right angle. Jerad slowed the charger's stride to acknowledge them and returned the same greeting. They responded by slapping their fists to the opposite shoulder and bowed their heads. Jerad nodded as he yanked the reins to steer Dex *setway*.

Sera marked his directions according to what she could best understand. The sun rises in the east--that would be *riseward,* and settles in the west--*setway*. He had also previously mentioned two other directions, *seatrail*--north. Likely there was an ocean or a large body of water in that direction, and *landtrail*--south. Zone

Four, where Zoren had reigned, was located toward *landtrail rise,* or in other words southeast. Sera mused at what it would have been like to come to this place without understanding the language. The outcome could have been much different. She might have killed Jerad. Worse yet, he might have killed her.

The marking of the First Corridor came into view rather quickly. A blue flag bearing an angled red bar garnished with a yellow rose and white rose stood perched atop a free-standing tower. The gold ring of honor pierced a petal on each bloom. The Tenth Zone's coat of arms, identical to the one Sera had seen on the banner at the arch, was artistically crafted into the column of the turret, with an inset of square, mosaic stones.

Sera looked up. There was someone on the parapet.

"Who approaches?" the watchman called out.

"Jerad of the Third Corridor, son of Shegarth, descendant of Antheia."

The guard moved along the platform and leaned through the crenel for a definitive look. He hailed Jerad with the same formal greeting used by the previous two guards. "Noble Jerad! It is due time you graced the First Corridor again. We wagered that you might not return."

The guard's gaze wandered to Sera.

Jerad's arm extended backwards. He wrapped it in a protective embrace around her back. "It is foolish to underestimate the power of allegiance. Advance your courier to my Corridor to announce my return."

The watchman returned his gaze to Jerad and nodded. He gave a shout to the area behind him, and then waved two red flags in purposeful movements to signal his message. Within moments a courser in full gallop sprang past, carrying the flag of the First Corridor. He held it high as he rode by, welcoming them.

Sera and Jerad pressed on, Dex at a slow, easy pace. The dirt road gave way to a tightly packed, cobblestone lane. The rhythmic sound of Dex's hooves returned as they moved along. By *three quarter set* they reached an arcade and the tower of the Second Corridor. They were received once again with a formal salutation from a guard in a turret, who informed them that they had been notified by the First Corridor and sent yet another courier ahead.

Full set was almost upon them. Jerad coaxed Dex to a fixed trot, determine to reach the Third Corridor before the *luna.*

Sera heard the sound of rumbling water. A high vertical waterfall came into view. It was preceded by the crashing rapids rushing toward the brink. A heavy mist drifted through the air, created by the plummeting torrents where it hit the rocks below. Sera turned her face toward the moist coolness of the spray, drawing in the damp, thick aroma of abundantly flowing water.

Here, a great system of channels constructed on high stone arches caught her attention. It was a facsimile of an ancient aqueduct construction that stretched from the waters and extended across the terrain. Sera recognized the structure. Her previous thoughts were confirmed. They had running water.

Jerad and Sera passed the final tower. Sera knew their journey was near to ending by the blue flag angled with the yellow bar and garnished with the lavender bloom. Jerad led Dex around the column, after being hailed by yet another guard, to a path which descended to a great stone fortress. The entire structure was mighty and so immovably reinforced, it must have taken years to build. The walls were over thirty feet high. It encompassed what seemed to be a vast amount of territory. The lateral wall extended far back, meeting a tapestry of craggy mountains that scaled the horizon. The forewall traversed *setway*, ending at a stout turret. A gatehouse was located midway along this wall. At the juncture of both walls and closer to them, there was yet another turret.

Three men appeared at the top of the first watchtower, two of them blasting a series of tones through cornets. The gatehouse doors swung open, and the arriving travelers passed through to the inner core of the stronghold. The couriers of the First and Second Corridors stood by. Villagers were excitedly gathering. With salutations and cheers, Jerad was welcomed home.

They entered onto a roadway, a stone path of flat, irregularly shaped, tan and gray pavers. It led to a tidy main square where the *agora*, or marketplace, was still bustling. There were non-collapsible, open air stalls intermixed with larger, more spatial infrastructures, some of wood, some of stone, but of humble design. It was the central hub of commerce, where citizens were busy buying, selling and trading a range of basic needs and luxuries. After spending days in the solitude of deserted terrain, the sights, smells and sounds penetrating the air stimulated Sera's senses anew.

There were baskets replete with scented flowers, and clothiers displaying fine cloth and finished garments. The aroma of apples and maple wafted through the air along with the smell of fresh baked bread and roasting meats. One section appeared dedicated to specialty shops where craftsmen were producing an amazing range of arts and crafts, including tapestries, paintings and sculptures, hand painted pottery and tablewares, and an array of exquisitely fashioned jewelry. The smell of heated metal drew Sera's attention to the blacksmiths pounding out horseshoes, as well as shields, swords and daggers being forged by master weaponeers.

There were weapons everywhere, highly visible, prominently displayed for purchase or sheathed in belts worn by citizens.

As they negotiated the path, all activity ceased. The citizens pushed toward the street to catch a glimpse of their returning Noble. It was clear that Jerad indeed held a position of leadership in his Corridor, evident by the number of fisted hands and bows of respect he received from the throng that gathered. There was no doubt that all rejoiced in Jerad's return.

Sera was keenly aware that she was an oddity to them. Curious stares repeatedly fell upon her, followed by much whispering. Her clothing was peculiar and surely like nothing they had seen before. It was dirty and torn, and she herself most certainly looked a wreck with her bruised and brush burned skin. If her hands had been bound, the onlookers would likely assume she was his prisoner. She was sure they were questioning her association with their Noble.

Sera's body lurched into an involuntary tremble. Jerad, aware of her discomfort, reached back, pried one of her hands from the cantle she was holding with a death grip, and pulled her arm around to his chest. He placed his arm over hers, fisted his palm over the back of her hand and placed it over his heart, holding it steady there. She was both amazed and touched at his willingness to display such public affection, even though it also served to increase the crowd's mutterings.

Sera scanned the crowd. The men were mostly clad in khaki or black trousers, tucked into various styled ankle or calf length boots. Some of the footwear had buckles and were fashioned with stiff looking leather. Others wore boots that laced and appeared to be made of a more pliable suede material. On top, the men donned plain tunic style vestments or white pleated gauze shirts with ballooning sleeves, many with drab colored doublets or hip-length vests over them. Some wore the vests alone, leaving their arms bare. To Sera's surprise, a good number of women dressed in trousers. Many also carried swords. Their fashions however, were somewhat more decorative--lace or beaded bodices with or without under blouses worn with pants or long skirts. Some wore plain chemise coverings with straight line or kerchief hems. Sera assumed that these people were the commoners of the Corridor. Her assumption was validated by their frequent parting to allow more colorfully clad, elaborately trimmed and crested Nobles to push their way to the front of the crowd.

The eclectic fashions worn by these people were a mix of contemporary dress with a more antiquated style and surprisingly more liberal than Sera had expected. None of the styles nearly resembled what Sera wore, however.

Sera noticed something else unusual. The streets were lined with lampposts, topped with lantern enclosures. A warm glow was emerging from them as the *rise* was beginning to settle. The light being emitted was not of flames, but from small cone shaped orbs, rounded at the top instead of pointed. They sat in the base of the lanterns, and appeared to be electrically powered.

"You have electricity here?" She peered around to look up at Jerad.

He gave her a confused expression.

"The lamps," Sera rephrased. "How are they powered?"

"Ah," Jerad responded with understanding. "They begin to glow as the air cools, usually when the sky grows dark."

When she looked at him inquisitively, he explained that the glimmer orbs, made by artisans skilled in glass blowing, contained the fluid from the bulb of the *crukis* flower. The flower, which grows along the mountainsides, survives by adapting its own temperature. During the *luna*, when the skies grow dark and the air becomes cooler, the liquid in the bulb thickens and turns opaque. It then emits a light that warms the flower. During the *rise*, the liquid thins and becomes clear, and the glow diminishes. There were two varieties of these plants, the white *crukis*, which cast a bright light and the blue *crukis,* which had a dimmer illumination.

"The fluid is like acid on the skin. It should never be touched except with a metal scoop." Jerad warned her. "Some have unfortunately found this out the wrong way."

"How long do they last?"

"A good orb will last about one rise cycle."--one month.

As they continued to pass through the main thoroughfare, Sera studied the orbs, watching the white lights brighten as the sky deepened. The noises of the busy marketplace were beginning to fade as they left the *agora* behind.

Sera relaxed against Jerad's back as she absorbed the beauty and peacefulness of the countryside. Various arteries extended from the primary road to taper into narrow paths. Some stretched far into the hillside where small, one story stone dwellings, were cradled within a mountainous backdrop. White or blue lights were glowing from the windows of many homes.

The tranquility surrounding them was interrupted by the sound of approaching horses. Several Nobles on horseback, both male and female appeared on the path. They strode up alongside Dex and slowed their pace.

One of the horsemen nearside to them spoke. "You bring victory to the Zone, Jerad?"

"Hmn," Jerad nodded. "Victory, the First Kingdom and much more, Corde."

Corde's gaze, as well as that of the others, fell to where Jerad held Sera's hand against him. Embarrassed, Sera attempted to pull her hand away, but Jerad tightened his fist around it to hold it in place.

"You display a blatant endearment to the woman. She is not a captive?"

"Not a captive."

"What of Sondra?" the women on Dex's farside questioned as she gave Sera a thorough looking over.

Jerad released an aggravated sound. "Thalia, you and the whole Corridor have known for many term cycles exactly what my intentions toward Sondra are."

He swung his head back in an irritated manner. "In fact, the whole blazon Zone knows of my intentions toward her!"

Thalia harrumphed in response but gave no other clue as to whether it mattered.

Jerad tossed a glance at a young girl riding just behind Thalia and motioned for her to come alongside Dex. She looked to be no more than twelve or thirteen term cycles. As she moved closer, Jerad reached a hand toward her. He stroked her hair and bent to kiss her forehead.

"You fair well, Phoebe?"

His brotherly affections toward her prompted Sera to take note of the honey colored hair and dark eyes that were nearly identical to Jerad's coloring, and just as strikingly stunning, in her female form. She was truly a beauty even in her youthful presence and showed every indication that she would blossom into a woman of tremendous loveliness.

"Ride ahead little sweet," Jerad instructed her. "Make ready for the Rite of the Cloak and the Vows of Permanence."

The girl glanced back at Sera, smiled shyly, and then nodded to her brother. Without a word she tugged at the reins and her horse galloped away from them. They disappeared down the *crukis* lit path.

Mekal, a Noble from the bloodline of Daedalus, First Corridor of the Eighth Zone, and a trusted friend of Jerad's, turned his horse to block the roadway. The charger reared and whinnied. Sera studied the crest at the upper left side of his tunic, a blue feather, pierced with a gold ring.

"You intend then, to create a ruckus, Jerad?"

"Is there any other way for this to be done?"

Mekal directed his horse to the farside of Dex. As they passed, his raised palm met Jerad's in a strong clasp that yielded to a knuckle to knuckle strike with fists--a cordial greeting between friends.

"She's a bit beaten already, would you say not?" Mekal flashed a cocky grin as his eyes drifted to Sera. "Are you responsible for that?"

Sera moved her free hand to the scrapes along her face. In her shabby condition she was not making a very grand impression.

Jerad grabbed the front of Mekal's shirt and bodily pulled him close. "What I am responsible for is none of your concern." Then he whispered in Mekal's ear, carefully lowering his voice to keep the others from hearing.

"I do not question the Edict of Oneroi. I bring the Ptino asteri."

Mekal pulled back. Once again his gaze fell to Sera. He leaned in closer, tilted his head and studied her quizzically. He furled his brow. His eyes, deep orbs of brown, roamed her person, and then grew distant as he searched his inner thoughts, seeking some buried truth. He fixated on her face again with a prolonged consideration.

Her eyes are golden.

Sera watched the knight examine her. He was a handsome man with wavy auburn hair and a moustache to match. His smile reached clear to his eyes. She liked him immediately, sensing a friendly demeanor. Something hitched in Sera's brain, a feeling of unconditional trust.

But why was he staring at her like that?

Sera sank against Jerad's back. She did not fear the warrior Mekal, but being the center of attention was very discomforting.

Mekal watched the woman shrink away from his scrutiny. He

had not meant to make her feel ill at ease. The warrior drew back and jerked his head to shake off his reverie. He returned his attention to Jerad.

Jerad regarded Mekal's inspection of Sera with suspicion, but disregarded his interest in her as simple curiosity.

"You are certain, Jerad?" Mekal questioned.

"As sure as the oath I vowed to keep at my mother's death."

Mekal laughed, a throaty deep bellow. He turned his horse about. "So you say the First Kingdom is now yours?"

"Mine whenever I wish to take it, prize of the challenge."

Mekal crooked an eyebrow. "And how did you manage that?"

Jerad waved his hand nonchalantly. "It was not too difficult, I wagered the spectrocorde."

Only Mekal and a few privileged others knew that Jerad, descendant of Antheia, was the Keeper of the Key. A secret he revealed to Zoren while they privately negotiated over the booty of their impending encounter. It was fortunate that the knowledge died with him.

"You are the most toplofty of brood, I swear." Mekal raised a fist. "I do stand with you, Noble Chancellor," he yelled as he sped off in the same direction that Phoebe had gone.

The others followed, leaving Jerad and Sera to travel the path alone.

The sky had grown dusky, giving a murky look to the horizon. Sera observed that the private dwellings were becoming increasingly larger as they moved on. Short, side roads, now opened into cul-de-sacs, containing gardens or fountains centered in the turn-about, where two and three story graystone manors stood. Most had pillared porches that extended the width of the buildings.

"These are the Noble Grandhouses. The clans of lesser Nobles and their bloodline reside within them."

Sera took in the sights with a childlike curiosity. Everywhere she looked, hints of familiarity struck her, but it was as though she was peering into a world of contradictory epochs where culture, fashion and architecture collided.

Then she saw it. They were nearing the most grandeur of structures in the Corridor--the castle. It was massive, with many levels, basking in the glow of hundreds of blue *crukis* windows set in the roofs of dormered balconies. She was awestruck by its shimmering, transcendental beauty.

The tallest structure was a cylindrical tower with a conical roof that jutted skyward from somewhere in the castle's recess. There were also several smaller, similar towers at the various corners of the castle walls, all reflecting a near topaz blue from the glint of their windows. At the top, a number of sentries paced along the parados. As Jerad approached, they stopped to hail their greetings to him.

Jerad turned to the path that led directly to the front of the castle. The most prominent feature in the facade was the grand entranceway. It was a fore building with an archivolt of roses in base relief that curved over glistening white, stone steps, longer at the bottom than top. The walls around it were constructed of the same ashlar stone except it cast a slightly grayish hue. It was a magnificent creation, reflecting its natural colors under the glow of white *crukis* lamps positioned on its columns.

"How many people live here?"

"Perhaps a thousand live in the Greathouse."

"One thousand?" The castle was as large as a small town.

"You live here, Jerad?"

"We live here, Sera." He raised her hand to his mouth and kissed her knuckles.

Sera opened her mouth to protest but snapped it shut. After all, she really had no place else to go. She might enjoy a bit of comfort during her stay here.

Jerad did not halt at the castle's entrance. He turned left and rounded the corner. The faint sound of a gong reached Sera's ears and increased in volume as they moved closer. She leaned to one side and saw a large number of people entering a tall, wooden, rectangular building. She and Jerad were heading in the same direction.

"It seems very peaceful here. Your people seem friendly."

"Do not be deceived by their civility. They can be as blood hungry and outraged as any berserk warrior, when it is fitting."

Sera gasped as Jerad reached around and pulled her into his lap in one sweeping motion, her feet dangling to one side of Dex. He paused and drew a deep breath.

He seemed worried.

Jerad lifted her chin and lowered his lips to hers. It was an affectionate and slowly rendered, closed mouth kiss. It spoke volumes of tenderness and caring.

A feeling of anxiety filled Sera. Something in the way he held her was frightening. When he raised his head to the skies, his words intensified her fears.

"By the utterance of the Oneroi, please do not let me have been mistaken."

Jerad was about to place Sera in danger, and it would be the only time he would ever refuse to safeguard her.

Chapter Five

Dex was in a full gallop. They made a stately entrance through the arena opening, to the cheers of at least fifty Nobles. Jerad brought Dex to a halt in the center of the floor. The Grandstage was a large open area, at least two hundred feet long and eighty feet wide with a thirty-foot ceiling. Tiers of bleachers surrounded the arena and were quickly being filled by citizens.

The crowd grew silent as Jerad lowered Sera to the ground first. When Jerad dismounted, he crumbled to his knees. Sera reached for him. He was still weak.

A page entered the floor, barely an adolescent, but much taller and stronger than Sera. He assisted Jerad to his feet.

"The pouch Sera, and my sword." Jerad spoke to her almost imposingly.

Sera did not hesitate. She removed the sack from the pommel. Then she withdrew Jerad's sword. She did not know why he wanted her to pull the blade from the sheath at his side, but she complied. The crowd stirred. Sera was shaking with a surmounting uneasiness. The spectators were growing in numbers, summoned by the gong outside. It continued to resonate its booming sound.

The citizens were beginning to push into any spaces they could fill, all Nobles, all crested and steadfastly watching them. Sera could not have anticipated such an exalted reception and she wished she could just crawl out the door and disappear into the sunset.

Jerad threw the apprentice from him and stood autonomously taking the pouch from Sera's hand. He nodded toward his sword. With both hands shaking, Sera extended it to him point up, hilt down, in the same manner that Jerad presented Zoren's sword to her. She heard murmurs from the onlookers and gathered that her actions, whatever they were, must be the reason for it.

The corners of Jerad's mouth turned upward slightly. She had done exactly what he hoped she would do, further convincing him that she truly was the chosen one of the Edict. Sera had no comprehension of her actions, but it was apparent to the spectators. She was permitted to handle a Noble's sword, a firm declaration that Jerad accepted her social position. Even more importantly, she had unwittingly held it out to him in a manner that symbolized equality. Once Jerad received the sword from her, he confirmed her status as being of Noble standing.

The governing body of the Tenth Zone was called the Magistrate Council. There were five levels within it. In ascending order they consisted of the Proletariat Council, Inceptive Chancellors, Noble Chancellors, Chief Chancellors and Chief Councilor Seat. The Proletariat Council was represented by three seats held by *hoi polloi*, common people, one from each Corridor. They were elected to their seats by consensus of the commonality vote. The next four levels, the Chancellor positions were reserved only for those of pure bloodline, direct descendants of the higher Origins Nobles. The Inceptive Chancellors were of minor ranking and like the Proletariat, gained their positions by vote of the Nobles in their respective Corridors. Noble Chancellors held a position of mid-standing, and Chief Chancellors occupied higher level positions. One of the Chief Chancellors also held the Chief Councilor Seat, the overman of the Magistrate Council. He was known as the Archon, or Chief Magistrate. It was his or her duty to settle disputes among the Magistrate members. The decision of the Chief Magistrate was final.

Typically two Nobles from each of the three Corridors would sit at each Chancellor level. There were no terms of service. Once voted to a seat, the position could only be relinquished through death, voluntary resignation or ousting because of a severe act of dishonor. Noble Chancellors, Chief Chancellors and the Chief Councilor Seats were only obtained through nomination by the Magistrate Council.

At the moment there were only four Magistrate members in-house, Shegarth, the Chief Magistrate, two Inceptive Chancellors, and a Proletariat representative of the common citizens.

Jerad stumbled closer and faced the Council members who were seated at the far end of the Grandstage. Despite his weakness he was clearly devoted to his purpose. He lowered to half kneel, sword blade resting across his bent knee. Shegarth rose to stand at the forefront of the Magistrate Council.

"Welcome home Noble Chancellor Jerad, honored warrior,

descendant of Antheia and," he smiled proudly, "my son."

Jerad bowed his head to the Archon. "It is with much sorrow that I reveal, Palos my arming squire, son of the Grandhouse Tim, First Corridor of the Tenth Zone, who accompanied me to the First Kingdom, was slaughtered at tournament."

A cry of agony arose from a section of benches, family and friends of Jerad's attendant.

Jerad continued, "Let it be known that he demonstrated great loyalty, courage and mastery of skill, contributing to my triumph in the final round. He has earned his gold ring."

"Present the badge of victory to his bloodline," Shegarth ordered.

A page appeared after a short pause. He carried a silver tray holding the badge, a crest with a white bloom centered on the red band. A solid gold ring pierced one of its pedals. He presented it to a young woman, the widow. She began to weep. An older woman sitting beside her, embraced her.

Jerad drove his sword into the ground with a mighty force. "It was not all for naught that his life was lost." He pulled the cords from around the pouch and turned it over. "I bring to you, the head of Zoren and my claim to the First Kingdom!"

The guillotined head rolled forward.

A clamor of cheers arose from the tiers. Feet rhythmically pounded. Sera grimaced. The air of approval at the obvious violence was unsettling, and the stench was horrendous. Sera started backing toward the exit in the building. She was among savages. This was much too clear. She really needed to get out of there.

"Be still!" Shegarth ordered the crowd, lowering his hands slowly, palms down.

"Noble Jerad, at the event of your mother's death, you swore an oath of abstinence until the time in which you could avenge the hideous acts committed against her. Although I realize you chose this course to feed your anger, the time has come to pass. On this very rise, let it be known that I declare you exonerated from your promise. You are free to present the device of your crest, to offer your cloak, at a time you deem appropriate."

Jerad stood, still facing Shegarth. "I will offer now to the one I honor." His voice was firm and determined.

The witnesses went silent. Sera had turned away and was almost to the opening leading outside when she slowed her pace, her curiosity overriding her want of flight. She was not sure if she understood correctly what the Chancellor said.

Did he say that Jerad was celibate?

Jerad crooked his finger toward a side entranceway. The young maiden, Phoebe came through it and approached Jerad. She was carrying a blue velvet pillow edged in gold fringe and bearing a long-stemmed, lavender blossom. Jerad removed the bloom from its resting place, holding it midway on the stem, between the thorns. He began circling the gallery, pointing the floret in the direction of the crowd. He located a female sitting in the benches and approached her. She extended her hand to accept the bloom, but Jerad shook his head, recanted, and placed it over the area of his heart. He bowed his head to her. Jerad drew his dagger, flipped it over, and placed it, grip first, into her palm. The crowd gasped. The woman scoffed at him.

"By my own volition, I bid to one who has shown great loyalty to see me home."

Jerad turned from the woman and faced Sera. Sera halted, her back still toward Jerad and the spectators. She had not seen what occurred between Jerad and the woman just moments before. Sera tensed, knowing that all eyes were on her, and that his comment was meant for her. Jerad approached. Sera could sense his presence behind her. With her escape plan now thwarted, Sera had but one choice. She turned to face him.

He offered her the bloom.

Sera paused.

What was happening?

She took several steps back and then hesitantly moved a few steps toward him. Jerad was offering her a token of gratitude. That was it. She really shouldn't decline it.

Should she?

It would humiliate him if she did, and she really did not want to dishonor the gesture, especially in front of his people. Besides, who knew what the consequences would be if she did indeed refuse to accept it. At the least, Jerad would be embarrassed and thus be angry with her. The worst, his people might become violent, and Jerad had cautioned her, just before they entered the Grandstage, that his people were not always congenial. Aggression was obviously not too much frowned upon in this place. Sera really had no desire to find out if it was true. She would accept his offering.

Sheepishly, Sera reached with her right hand, fingers widely spread. With much incertitude, she claimed the flower. At that moment a strange scintillation arced between them. Their bodies jerked at the same time. They held their breaths. Both Jerad and Sera stood motionless, gaping at each other, both still grasping the bloom, mesmerized by the enigmatic, ethereal haze that seemed to draw them together in a breathless melding of bodies, despite the three feet of space that separated them. When Jerad finally exhaled, Sera drew a breath so deep it felt as though she were capturing his basic essence. Sera felt nearly liquefied. She could swear that Jerad was drinking in her soul.

It was the snarl behind him that alerted Jerad. He released the stem, giving Sera full claim to it. He then raised his arm, motioning toward one side of the gallery, his eyes in a continuous fixation with Sera's. His expression was serious, but she could also detect his underlying uneasiness.

An arming squire approached, placed a dagger in Sera's left hand and draped a thick, long cloak over her arm. Jerad took the cloak, wrapped it around her left arm and once about her elbow. He drew a deep, anxious breath as he gazed into her confused eyes. He kissed her gently on the cheek.

With his lips pressed to her, he whispered, "Hold the collar with your hand. The cloak is not a strong thing, do not trust in it. Use it only for warding off the blade and to distract."

Then he warned, "She is scorned and will challenge you fully. The dagger requires the utmost in watching. Be steadfast, for she will show you no mercy. I trust you will not disappoint me."

Jerad cupped her face and whispered against her lips. "Once again, I beg for your forgiveness."

He moved away, leaving Sera staring at him in disbelief. Sera heard a furious growl. A woman with a dagger leapt from the benches and was heading toward her. Sera clenched her teeth and groaned. The legends of the Amazons came to mind, and they were all true. She found herself facing a gigantic warrior princess.

It was not a pretty picture.

She dropped the flower and transferred the dagger to her right hand. The woman lunged at her, and Sera was able to block the dagger hand of her opponent by grabbing her arm. She flipped the woman over her head, rolling backward on the ground to do so. They were both on their feet instantly, facing each other. Sera had a flicker of a moment to appraise the woman. She was clad in pants, and a sleeveless bodice embroidered with a yellow bloom and gold ring that pierced a petal. Facing this seasoned combatant was unnerving. Even worse, she wore a scabbard, a leather harness device held in place by a thick belt about her waist, and a strap which crossed her chest from her left hip to the opposing shoulder. It sheathed an immense sword. Sera leapt back in defense as the woman suddenly unbuckled the baldric and propelled it toward the chest of her arming squire, throwing him off balance slightly. The squire then draped a cloak over the woman's arm, and she wrapped it quickly. Sera was grateful that she would not have to face the sword, realizing her own inadequacy with the weapon. Not that she was any more proficient with the cloak and dagger, but at least this type of weaponry would allow her closer contact with her opponent, and the potential to disarm her with the martial maneuvers that she was more accustomed to.

"We the citizens in the Third Corridor of the Tenth Zone," cried a herald who had positioned himself on a high platform at the far end of the arena, "acknowledge that the warrior Sondra, descendant of Chloris, Second Corridor of Tenth Zone, accepts the Challenge for the Rite of the Cloak from…" He paused and looked at Sera, realizing he didn't know her name. He continued. "… this chosen woman, for the cloak of Jerad, descendant of Antheia, Third Corridor of the Tenth Zone."

The woman immediately began a succession of snaps with her cloak toward Sera's face, and rushed toward her. Sera, caught off guard, began stumbling backward to avoid the advances of the cloak, and to track the dagger being thrust at her. It thankfully did not make contact. Sera forthwith was out of control, and could do nothing but recoil from the aggressive charge. A cut, a thrust, another cut, and Sera finally managed to entangle the blade with her cloak, but the woman briskly withdrew it before it became trapped. This afforded Sera enough time to recoup, and she lurched at her adversary with several thrusts. The woman leapt back, beating off Sera's weapon with her cloak. She chortled at Sera's incompetence as she drew her knife horizontally and toward Sera's head. Sera reflexively crouched and surged, ramming her shoulder into the woman's stomach, knocking her to the ground.

She had a brief, irrevocable opportunity to jab her dagger into the woman's abdomen, but could not bring herself to do it. Sera's opponent reclaimed her stance unperturbed, and Sera could swear the woman mumbled the word fool under her breath. Leading with her right foot, the woman propelled an angled, upward thrust toward the bottom of Sera's rib cage.

A deadly strike if it had hit its target.

The barbarian meant to kill her!

Sera opposed the oncoming dagger with the folds of her cloak and attempted to drive her own blade toward the woman's side.

She missed.

The woman anticipated the tactic, leapt back and untwirled the cloak to its full length without releasing it. The cloak fell over Sera's head blinding her with the throw. Sera reflexively reached up and grabbed the garment.

It was a terrible mistake.

She exposed her midsection in the process.

Without warning, a biting strike to her abdomen caused her to seize and grab her side. Sera cried out, but with her position being most precarious, she had no presence to occupy herself with the pain. What she wanted to do was run, but was keen to her opponent's precipitance to make the kill. Sera caught sight of the impending blade. By mere intuition or perhaps it was by chance, she brought her cloaked arm toward the thrusting dagger, and somehow trapped it in several of the wrapped folds. The tip of it protruded toward her and barely missed slashing the skin of her cloaked arm. The woman jerked her cloak back and in one swift motion she once again had it wrapped around her arm.

Sera moved in and hooked her heel around the opponent's back leg. Simultaneously, she brought the flat of her dagger against the woman's cloaked forearm. The woman began pushing Sera's blade downward while jerking back on her other arm in an attempt to free her tangled blade from Sera's cloak. Sera resisted the pressure from the block, straining against the woman's superior strength.

She thought the blood vessels in her face would burst.

Sera angled her knife slightly. It cut through the opponent's cloak. A stain of blood seeped through the woman's skin, caused by the dint of the blade's edge. Sera pushed with all of her might against the arm of her attacker. She didn't know how she managed it, but Sera finally swept the woman's leg out from under her. The woman fell backward pulling Sera with her. As her back slammed against the ground, Sera's opponent thrust her trapped blade upward. It came dangerously close to Sera's chest. Sera arched her back, thus eluding yet another wound, as she fell to bent knees. Sera extended her arm and pinned her opponent's dagger hand with the flat of her palm. The knuckles of Sera's other hand felt crushed. She had fallen on them while still clinging to her blade.

She realized at once, that the point of her knife was inches from the woman's neck. Without hesitation she thrust it inward, and penetrated nearly a third of flesh until she felt resistance from the bone in her neck. Insensible to nothing but an innate need for survival, Sera, without thinking about what she was doing, ripped and twisted the blade forward, causing her opponent's head to rise slightly from the ground. The weight of the flesh against the blade gave added force to continue cutting until the women's neck was released from the dagger, and dropped back to the ground with a thud. Sera's hand swung inward, lacking further resistance. Sera raised the blade, ready to strike again, but her challenger was gurgling, and within seconds, the warrior Sondra was dead.

Sera dropped her dagger, appalled at what she had just done. She rose to her feet and backed away. Suddenly, she was overcome with pain. Sera pressed her hand to her side. Blood was flowing between the crevices of her fingers. Sera began to lose her senses, stumbling about until she doubled over and fell to the ground.

"The bloom," a voice whispered to her close to her ear.

"What?" There was clear agitation in Sera's voice.

"You must claim the bloom."

Sera did not recognize the voice but lifted up her head to see it was Phoebe who spoke to her. She attempted to locate the flower, having reason enough to conclude that for now, without full understanding of the consequences for disobedience, it was better to do as she was told. She didn't need anymore knives coming her way. It was then that she felt herself being lifted. Jerad knelt before her, and put her upright to her knees. She leaned heavily against his bent knee and supporting arm. The flower was in his hand. She looked at it, still thinking that it very much resembled an elegant rose in full bloom. Once again, Sera accepted it from him. She held the stem lightly, to avoid the prick of its large thorns.

There was stirring from the spectators, but whether it was friendly or hostile Sera could not determine. Her head and body began to sway and she started to fall backwards, but Jerad caught her in his arms. His look was intense despite its paleness from the physical disturbance to his own body. She began to drift again.

"Sera," he whispered to her, bringing her somewhat back to reality. Someone was tightly wrapping a bandage around her ribs.

She heard the sound of a cornet. The Chief Magistrate, Shegarth stood before them. "We will commence with the Rite of the Cloak on the fifth..."

Jerad interrupted. "No, we will do this now."

"That is highly irregular." Shegarth looked astonished. "She needs attention Jerad."

"I ask that the Magistrate Council does not question my motives. Grant me that this bonding will commence immediately."

"So be it then." Shegarth motioned toward an open doorway and the crowd parted.

An older woman approached, placed blue velvet cloaks, lined in gold satin around each of their shoulders, and fastened them about their necks with lavender, bloom clasps. The weight of the garment nearly caused Sera to fold to the ground.

"Let those present, hereby witness, the Vows of Permanence between Jerad, descendant of Antheia, Third Corridor of the Tenth Zone to..." Almost as an afterthought, Shegarth paused and looked back toward the Council for objection, then scanned the crowd.

Petri, younger brother of Sondra, stepped forward. He was leering at Jerad and opened his mouth to speak. Jerad narrowed his eyes and bared his teeth expressing a silent warning toward the adolescent to hold his tongue. Petri sneered, but said nothing. Shegarth tossed a glance between Jerad and the young Noble. Upon seeing that there would be no protest, he continued, "What is your name lady Noble?"

Sera threw her head back.

What the hell was going on?

Jerad spoke on her behalf, proclaiming loudly to the assemblage, "Her name is Sera!"

While still supporting Sera with his left arm, Jerad closed his right hand on the stem of the bloom she was holding. He raised it between them. Sera's hand dropped. Jerad motioned to Shegarth by jerking his head toward her fallen limb. The Chancellor lifted Sera's left hand and closed it around the stem of the bloom, just below and touching Jerad's hand. She felt the tips of the thorns pressing into her skin. It was uncomfortable. Sera struggled to maintain awareness and mulled over the idea that she was going to spend her entire time on Protogio with her head in a fog. She also wondered how much more damage her body would sustain before she was dead or rescued. At the moment not much else mattered. Everything around her was moving sluggishly, or was that just the way she felt?

Sera forced her attention to the rose that the two of them where holding. The realization of what Jerad was about to do came belatedly and she had no time to muster enough strength to protest. She was about to suffer another wound. Jerad closed his fist around hers, and then, he bore down on it. She felt the thorns pierce her skin.

What the...

Jerad gently opened her palm, and plucked her hand from the bite of the thorns. He turned the thorns toward his right palm and closed it around the stem. The Chief Magistrate fisted Sera's now lanced palm around Jerad's. Then he placed both of his hands around Sera's hand. He exerted pressure on it. Jerad offered only a slight tick in his cheek when the thorn's penetrated his own palm. The result was a mirror image of Sera's punctures.

The bloom was removed and placed on a sham. Blood seeped from where the thorns had broken through their skin. With the help of Shegarth, Sera's palm was pressed against Jerad's palm, the blood of their wounds mixing.

"Sera," Jerad called to her in a hushed voice, and she lifted her eyes to meet his gaze. He pulled her close and spoke softly against her lips.

"My loyalty for your trust, my strength for your honor, mind nurtures heart and flesh becomes one. Wherever you go I shall follow. Meaningless is one life without the other. My blood with your blood, Sera."

Sera was losing consciousness and her thoughts floated back to the woods recalling those last few words and how that utterance had terrorized her. Now Jerad spoke them to her affably.

"Speak the words, Sera," Jerad pressed the side of his face against Sera's cheek.

Sera shivered uncontrollably. She was cold. His cheek was warm and soothing against her face and she nuzzled against him.

What had he asked her to say?

Perplexed, she tilted her head back. "My blood with your blood, Jerad?"

It was a question, not a response, but it was all that Jerad needed. Shegarth furled his eyebrows at the incompleteness of the vow.

"It is enough to seal this," Jerad warned. "Be done with it!"

"Very well," Shegarth sighed. "By order of the Magistrate Council of the Tenth Zone, I seal this bonding of our Noble Jerad, descendant of Antheia, Third Corridor of the Tenth Zone to..." He paused, and then shrugged. "...to the Noble Sera."

Jerad lifted Sera into his arms. He swiftly carried her limp body toward one of the Grandstage exits, the flurry of sounds behind him becoming indiscernible and fading. Shegarth finished his declaration as Jerad disappeared with Sera through a postern.

"The ceremony of the Marks of Permanence will commence at three quarter set on the fifth rise from this determination," Shegarth called after them.

The crowd, were they cheering or jeering? Sera really did not want to know. She had gone numb and was no longer extant with her own body. Whether it was from shear terror or shock, she was paralyzed to intentional movement.

The world for Sera went silent.

Chapter Six

Sera became semiconscious as she was placed on a flat, cold surface. There were blurs of motion, people moving quickly around her. She watched through slotted eyes, catching a glimpse of shears, which the voice referred to as clips, passing hand to hand over her, and her top being cut away. Her head was tipped back and liquid drops were placed in her nostrils. She reflexively inhaled, noting a slight burning sensation in her nose and throat. White light radiated from a glowing dome on the ceiling above her. An unfamiliar female leaned over her then faded. Sera closed her eyes. She opened them again and two blurred, but familiar, male forms, speaking her language, began to take shape over her. She tried to reach for one of them, but her arm was like lead, and she could not lift it.

"She's rousing," a voice echoed.

"Holy shit! Look at these wounds."

Alarm bells resonated in her ears. People were rushing.

Bleep, bleep, bleep…

The ceiling above her, it was white, it was blue.

A recessed light in the ceiling, no, a dome light.

"What's happening to me?"

A crash… flames…

blood… my blood with your… I must be… I feel so woozy… I'm hurt…

I'm dying.

The tocsin warnings abruptly ceased. The two males evaporated, and the female re-appeared. The obscure voices of those in the room became more intelligible. On her left, a thick bandage was being pressed against her abdomen.

"The bleeding is heavy. A bit deeper and the blade would have pierced her liver." A male was speaking. She knew the voice.

It was not her language.

"You should let me do this, you are in no condition." It was a female voice. She did not recognize it.

"*Ochi*. I am responsible for her. I will need bergamot to relax these muscles."

Sera arched her back and moaned as a rush of pain struck her. She began to writhe as fingers delved into her wound. Through the lashes of her heavy laden lids she watched the *clips* pass over her once again, and then her pants were cut from her body. She tried to resist by reaching for her rent trousers, but someone had clasped her wrists and held them down.

"Lie still Sera. The belladonna drops should take affect soon."

Sera's body began to relax, intoxicated with the affects of the drug. The pain dulled. She slackened against the surface beneath her. Her eyes closed, and she drifted into blissful, muzzy waves.

"Twine... several," the male voice ordered, pausing between words as items were exchanged. "Clips, swab, stitch, clips..."

Sera was aware of the urgent commands, as she moved in and out of her stupor. Her eyes fluttered open to see the curved needle, with thread attached, moving quickly up and down, then scissors cutting and the same being repeated over and over again until her skin was sutured shut. A powder the male referred to as calendula, was brushed across her closed wound followed by a cold, sticky sealant. A linen cover was draped over her.

The woman moved to the man's side. Sera squinted to sharpen her vision. The woman was fair skinned. She had sandy wavelets of hair falling to the small of her back. It was pinned with a decorative clip behind one ear. She wore an ivory colored blouse with many closely spaced tiny, copper buttons down the front. There was blood on her clothing.

My blood?

Sera's attention wandered from the woman to the man. He sat facing away from her. He wore no shirt. Thick, defined muscles graced him from his broad shoulders down the length of his back and tapered to narrow hips. A single, thin scar crossed his right shoulder blade. The woman was attending to him.

"You look like *agelada* dung," the woman remarked.

He flinched as the cloth bandage was removed.

"The material is stuck to it. *Ack*, this is severe. You could have died from this." She shook her head. "It is infected."

She examined a couple of vials containing liquid, and prepared a medication. After drawing the liquid into a metal syringe, she pushed the needle into the male's shoulder and pressed the plunger. His shoulder twitched.

"Still yourself, it's just a bit of quassia for the fever and coriander for the infection." The woman finished injecting him then dropped the hypodermic into the slotted opening of a metal container.

The man placed a hand on the woman's arm. "How are you cousin?"

"I am well." She rummaged through her supplies, picked a couple of items and continued to attend to his wound. They conversed for awhile, about events and people, but the woman's attention soon strayed toward Sera.

"Who is she, Jerad?"

"I found her at the margin of the Eighth and Seventh Zones, near Eksaf 'anise."

"From your actions in the Grandstage, I guess you intend to keep her."

"It is fated, Ezra."

Ezra studied Jerad then tipped her head sideways as she considered Sera again. "Your consort is a near reciprocate of you, Jerad."

Jerad turned to Sera. "How so?"

"Her coloring, her hair is nearly the color of your eyes, her eyes nearly the color of your hair."

Ezra's eyes moved to the bandages on Sera's belly. "She will bear the same scar on her belly as you. Hers on the left mirrors yours on the right. It seems there is destiny to be revealed in all of this."

Jerad did not remark. He reached for Sera and stroked her cheek with his knuckles. He had not noticed how she emulated his image. A surge of affinity engulfed him. He and his Starbird were woven, two halves found wholeness, two hearts blended as one.

"You are an astute woman, Ezra, but I beg you to keep this observation of yours hushed for the time being."

The medication they had given Sera was making her groggy, but she fought to stay awake. She continued to watch as the woman wrapped a bandage around the man's trunk. She was suddenly aware of a stinging on her palm. Sera turned her hand over, held it close to her face, and attempted to focus on the three punctures and three small streams of blood, now smeared.

She couldn't remember how she had hurt her hand.

Jerad pulled her hand away and wrapped it in cloth.

His head dropped. "Aryan will not concede well with Sondra's death. Where is he Ezra? I must see him."

"He is expected home from the Second Corridor this luna. I saw Petri ride out on his charger, likely to hasten his return," Ezra paused. "Aryan finds great comfort with his falcons. He will likely go to them."

A line of worry crossed her face. "Please do not seek him out, Jerad. He must have this space of time to acknowledge what has happened."

Ezra once again turned her attention to Sera. "She looks very confused. I will stay here with her."

"*Ochi*. She will find greater comfort in my chamber."

"Jerad, she needs to remain in the infirmary."

"You have always been a prudent physician Ezra, but I will care for her in my residence. I have all the reserve I need there to ensure her recovery."

Jerad?

Sera's thoughts began to race. The events in the Grandstage flashed in rapid sequence. She came to full comprehension of what had happened.

A noisy crowd... The point of a knife slicing her... The resistance of a blade sinking into flesh... A flower... Thorns...

Jerad?

"Oh my god," Sera mumbled and made an effort to sit up. Jerad placed a hand on her chest to stop her. She resisted, grabbed his arm and pulled herself upright. She tried to speak but only managed to grunt at the dull burn and tugging in her side.

"What is it Sera?" Jerad grasped her shoulders to steady her.

Sera pulled at his right hand and held it with both of hers. She turned it over to look at his palm and found the puncture wounds smeared with blood. Her head fell back and she stared up at him with much bewilderment.

"Jerad, why?"

They were the only words that Sera could manage to impart from her quivering lips.

Jerad freed his hand from hers, placed a hand behind her head, and the other on her back. Sera relaxed into them, and he lowered her down.

"Sleep now Sera. We will talk later."

Chapter Seven

The room was dimly lit by the lamp on the stand next to the bed. The white glimmer orb had been covered with a thin cloth to subdue the lighting. It was *luna*. Sera was lying on her back and covered with a quilt. The thick mattress beneath her was part of a fluted four poster bed supporting a wrought iron canopy. It was curtained by deep green and burgundy draperies with an under layer of ivory sheers, which were knotted around the top of the posts, and hung down to the floor at the four corners. The top was open, and the ceiling above her was made of a glossy, slatted wood that looked like a dark maple. A large clothespress, with decorative carvings and golden accents stood against a wall. It had mirrored doors and was made of the same wood as the bed. It was definitely a masculine room. Jerad said he would take her to his dwelling. It was where she assumed she was now. She thought it might be a guest chamber, but Sera retracted the thought, knowing Jerad would put her nowhere except in his bed chamber, more precisely, in his bed. She wondered where he had slept. A turn of her head to the other side of the room gave her the answer. A plump pillow and casually thrown blanket were bunched together on a chaise in the corner, one dusty boot on each side, his clothing in a heap on the floor next to it.

Sera attempted to stretch. Her movement was shortened by a ripping pain. Each time she tried to move it would again tear through her. She tapped her fingers on the covers, and remained motionless, drawing shallow gulps of air, until the discomfort subsided.

She had been given a drug that blunted the pain. It caused her to float into a dreamlike state. She heard voices speaking in her language. She recognized faces and the ceiling of a familiar room. Then it was gone. The elixir must have been quite powerful for her to have such lucid visions, but it apparently had worn off. She wasn't feeling very dreamy at the moment. In fact, she was feeling downright irritable.

The wound was long, about six inches. She could feel its depth beneath the stitching. She recalled the bite of the knife as it sliced, and how the assault turned self-defense into murder. At least that is how Sera viewed it, as she pondered to no resolve, how she might have instead disarmed the woman.

What did I do to provoke her into attacking me?

It was her eyes that Sera would never forget--a dark jade and filled with rage. Her pupils dilated as her breath, her blood drained from her.

Sera stared into the eyes of a dying woman, one whose life she was responsible for taking.

My loyalty for your trust... flesh becomes one.

Sera ran her fingers through her hair as a lump squeezed control in her throat. She released a sob. The conversation between Jerad and the horsemen on the path now made sense. Mekal and Thalia more than hinted that there would be trouble, and Jerad sent his sister Phoebe to prepare for a ceremony. The woman who attacked her had been rejected by Jerad. That was what incited her fury toward Sera. The bloom was not a gift as Sera originally thought. When she accepted it from Jerad, she was also consenting to a betrothal. How could she have been so foolish to not realize it? She could have died, and most certainly would have, if Jerad had been unable to stitch her up. He saved her life. Yet, he was responsible for her present condition.

I trust you will not disappoint me.

Simple as that, *disappoint*. He knew what was going to happen. They all seemed to know, and she had been put on display for their entertainment.

I will be so disappointed if she cuts you to pieces, Sera.

Sera had every right to be angry with him, and she most certainly intended to be. He had become a real pain in her neck, thorn in her side, or hand, or something.

Sera let out an exasperated breath.

She didn't feel very angry--a little peeved, maybe.

How could she not be angry?

He certainly deserved her wrath.

She hurt all over.

His fault.

She'd been forced to kill someone.

His fault again.

She was wedded to him and through duplicitous means no less.

His fault! His fault! All his fault!

She had to get out of that bed. She needed answers, but when she attempted to sit, the muscles of her belly screamed in protest. Sera threw her left hand to the edge of the bed, pulled to her side, and groaned. Again, she panted short breaths until the throbbing diminished. It was then she noticed that her left palm, the one which bore the thorn piercings, was covered with a small, satin sash, embroidered with several lavender buds. It crisscrossed over the back of her hand and wrapped again around her wrist, where it was tied in place with a knot.

My blood with your blood.

Well, they were both certainly bloody enough.

Sera repeated those words to him only because she did not understand what Jerad wanted from her. She never meant to put a seal on a ritualistic decree.

This is outrageous, ridiculous and totally unacceptable!

Sera worked herself into a lather. She had an urge to unwrap the cloth and choke him with it. It was just the effect she needed. She pursed her lips and gritted her teeth. She clenched the blanket in fisted palms.

I'm going to ring his sinewy little... er big neck. How could he! How dare...

Sera stopped short of her last thought, frozen with the reality that swept over her.

Oh god.

She wasn't pissed.

She was flattered.

Damn him. Damn him and the edict he rode in on!

Sera guardedly pushed to a sit and cringed as she slid her feet to the floor. Her feet were bare, and sank into the plush carpet beneath them. It was an elegant floor covering, a deep beige color, with an ivy leaf pattern. If nothing else, Jerad certainly had refined tastes.

Sera moved across the chamber. The garment she wore was thin on her body, a white, long sleeved robe of crinkled cotton that laced up at the front. It gently molded her form from the shoulders to a drop *vee* waistline and swept lightly around her legs with long slits that revealed her thighs as she walked. She did not want to think about who had dressed her.

She passed through an arch opening about five feet across after pushing aside a long lambrequin. It was held in place by brass, floral sconces, and designed to cover the entire doorway. She was immediately bathed in the soft blue hue and penetrating warmth of a *crukis* skylight, encased in a ceiling that slanted toward an exterior wall. The outer room was spacious but sparsely furnished. In the center of the floor, there was a backless sofa with angled arm rests. A small table rested between one end of it and an oversized, cushioned chair. The floor was marble with a parquetry design, but was tepid to the touch, instead of cool.

A massive set of bookshelves that spanned the wall opposite from where she stood caught her attention. An impressive collection of literature crammed the shelves. Whatever answers she could not obtain from Jerad could surely be found within the pages of those books. Hopefully, she would be able to interpret them.

She leaned against a wall and observed the figure seated in a leather arm chair in front of an escritoire. She recaptured her anger.

Jerad was studying a clump of dried, purplish leaves, unaware of her presence in the room. He sniffed a handful. Then he picked up a quill and began to scrawl notes on a sheet of parchment. A white glimmer orb encased in metal caging, supported by a posted stand, provided him with the light to write.

"Plotting the demise of your next victim?" she paused for effect. "Or determining how you are going to fix them after you cut them up."

He looked toward her. His pensive expression softened. The sarcasm in Sera's voice should have been bitter to his ears, but instead, Jerad was relieved. Her voice was like honey and cinnamon, layered on a warm slice of bread, sweet, with a hint of spice. It set a blaze in his heart and lifted his spirits.

For two *rises* he was vigilant, silently begging the *Origins* for her recovery and beseeching them for mercy from her ire when she did awaken. Although, he would gladly face her hostility in lieu of the lifeless body he carried from the Grandstage. His gut retched. It was pointedly obvious that Sera did not have the skill to fight in that manner. He recalled the sound of tearing flesh and the smell of her blood saturating the air. Sondra nearly killed her. Death would have instantly fallen on Sera, if Sondra had not stumbled, as she lunged and swiped at Sera's belly. He watched helplessly as Sera's clothing stained red, and how her hand pressed against her flesh turned crimson. He damned the Oneroi, and fought to restrain himself from interceding, knowing that if he were to halt the Challenge he would be conceding to wed Sondra. Jerad would not lose Sera. He trusted the Edict and allowed it to continue.

In the *quarters* following the Challenge, Jerad sustained Sera's slumberous condition with his herbal concoctions, to spare her pain. Slowly, he eased the doses to bring her conscious awareness closer to the surface. It would hasten her recovery if she could move about, and get proper nourishment, but she was weak. Every time he lifted her to sit, she would slump helplessly in his arms. He coaxed water and thickened bullion down her throat when she was barely awake, applied poultice to her wound, and cleansed her perspiring skin, while she slept. Jerad spent restless, endless *quarters* tending to her needs, and pacing the floor when she had none. At times he placed his ear to her chest to listen to her heart, his face near hers to feel her breath, pressed his lips against her forehead to feel the warmth of her skin. All in an attempt to satisfy his need to be close to her--to affirm that she still lived.

He even brushed her hair.

Finally, he retreated to his journals, hoping that examining a few herbs would ease his tension, but it was a vacant attempt at distraction.

Jerad swiveled in the chair and leaned back. "Ah Sera, you are finally awake."

Sera studied him with quiet resolve. Jerad looked relaxed and content in his own element. The color had returned to his face and he was cleanly shaven. His copper hair hung neatly about his shoulders. He wore tan, suede trousers that were buttoned closed. They were tucked into well polished, black boots, and nicely hugged his thighs and hips. His shirt and vest were open at the front. The laceration under the right side of his ribs, still swollen, had been neatly sewn shut with a running stitch. Other than the dark circles under his eyes, he seemed none the worse for the wear.

He shifted in the chair and then pushed himself to a stand. His dark eyes wandered the length of her body. She was thinner and her face was drawn, but she was alive and would be well again.

As he approached, Sera felt the same allure that consumed her in the arena. It was as though she was bidding him toward her with a hushed urgency to have him near. It was unsettling.

He gently placed his hands on her waist, pressing her to his body. It caused a quickening in her belly that could only be described as yearning. The feel of him holding her was undeniably pleasant.

Not quite the perturbed reaction she was aiming for.

Her anger dissolved. She felt safe in his arms, wanting only to yield to the sincerity of his embrace. She was bemused by the contradiction of emotions that should have her seething at the man--most of her misery was his doing, but Jerad was unadulterated male, daunting and forbidding, yet kind hearted and caring. He stirred feelings in her that she could not readily identify or control.

Sera tipped her head back to look up at him as he bent to bring his cheek to hers. His breath was warm against the skin of her neck. She closed her eyes succumbing to the intimation that she was designed to be there.

"I have been beleaguered with worry for you."

He moved his arms to her back and pressed her harder against him. She tried to ignore it, but the ache in her side intensified. She recoiled with piercing pain as he squeezed her tighter. It was a sharp reminder of what she had done.

"I'm a murderer," she cried in a low aching voice as she grabbed her side.

Jerad grimaced and scooped her into his arms. She moaned with the sudden movement. He carried her to the bedroom, and placed her on the bed. Sera rolled into a fetal position, and whimpered.

Jerad crossed the room squatting in front of a low, ivory colored cabinet and opened the doors. It contained a number of glass vials and small, lidded crocks. He removed two items and went to Sera, placing the small vessels on a stand next to the bed. He sat on the edge of the bed and rolled Sera to her back. Tears escaped from the corners of her eyes. Jerad pulled the bed covering up to her hips, and began to untie her gown.

Sera reached for her body realizing that she was wearing nothing beneath the robe, but Jerad respected her modesty by keeping her breasts covered. She fingered the large bandage that covered her wound. Jerad took her hands and placed them at her sides. He removed the dressing, and glanced at her face. She was pallid and his concern returned. She should not have gotten out of bed. She needed more rest. One more *luna*. He would give her only a small dose of the sedative.

"What are you giving me, Jerad?" Her voice was scarcely above a whisper.

"The powder is saffron, for the pain and the bergamot drops will relax you."

"Herbs?"

Jerad pulled a cork from one vial and began to sprinkle the contents along Sera's wound. She felt instant numbness in the area.

"Tomas told us of your medicines. Our plants equal, some even surpass their effectiveness."

The next vial contained a liquid, which he drew into a small dropper.

"Inhale." Jerad placed the drops in her nostrils. Sera did as she was told, thankful that this land was not as archaic as she anticipated. Yet, there was nothing that could be done to save Sondra. Sera had unintentionally seen to that. Sera's bottom lip quivered and she began to cry. Jerad tenderly wiped her tears away with his thumbs.

"You bid to me a great honor in the Grandstage."

"I am a murderer," Sera sobbed with heavy heartedness.

"It is the way of things, Starbird."

Jerad moved onto the bed and pulled her into his arms. He covered them both with the quilt, and Sera drifted to sleep.

When she awoke again later, the first thing she noticed was the emptiness. She was no longer in Jerad's arms. Her blurred vision quickly cleared. The room was brightly lit with the *rise*. Sera sat up with little difficulty, other than the pulling of muscles, stiff from lack of exercise. There was some feeling of discomfort from her wound but it was tolerable. Jerad was asleep in the chaise at the corner of the room. One of his legs was stretched along the cushion. The other was bent with his foot resting on the floor. He was fully dressed. An open book was face down across his lap. Sera tilted her head to read the title scrawled on the cover, but she had difficulty deciphering the Greek letters from their upside down position. Her attention wandered to his right hand, which rested on his thigh. It was wrapped in a cloth identical to Sera's. She fingered the cloth on her own left hand.

"Conjugal clothes." Jerad had awakened and was watching her. He rose from the chair and sat next to her. He clasped her left hand into both of his. "Worn for five rises until the wounds are sufficiently healed, and the Marks of Permanence can be safely rendered."

Sera avoided asking him what that meant, leery that she would not like the answer, relenting to the idea that what she didn't know, couldn't annoy her.

On the far side of the room, an iridescent play of light caught her attention. An elegant crystal sculpture sat upon a table placed in the niche of a large bay shaped window. Sera stood, crossed the room, and moved closer to better examine the grouping of prisms. There were six connected pyramidal structures of various sizes. The design intrigued her. There was something familiar about it.

"*Poli omorfos, ne?*" Jerad followed to stand directly behind her.

"Yes, very beautiful."

"It is the spectrocorde, Starbird, the Key to Orion's belt."

"Oh, I see. So this is the infamous key. Isn't this what you wagered to gain the First Kingdom?"

"*Nai*--yes. It was a daring bargain, but if I had died, Shegarth would still have fought to protect it."

"Why would you risk losing the very item essential to the Edict you so believe in?"

"Vengeance can sometimes be a foolhardy thing, but it was the only thing Zoren would accept. Once I disclosed to him that I had the key, he nearly frothed at the mouth with the thought of gaining ownership of it. I waited until Zoren was ordained ruler of the First Kingdom with the intention of stripping the land from him. His death would be the ultimate prize."

He took hold of her wrists. "Let me show you, what I know of it."

Jerad passed one of her palms through the rays where the light of the *rise* arced through the beveled glass. It emitted a spectrum of brilliant colors and compelling musical sounds that caused Sera to gasp with a captivated delight. Then Jerad released her, and played a chord of notes, stroking the rays like the strings of a harp. A melancholy, yet hauntingly romantic melody trickled to her eardrums and floated into her brain until it was firmly entrenched in her mind.

Sera began to sway, her heart beat in cadence with her breathing as the euphoric aria captured and devoured her senses.

"Oh," she exhaled with a mesmerized whisper.

Jerad ceased playing. The sudden silence caused Sera to waver and she startled from her trance.

"I have the same response to it, Starbird," Jerad caught her against him. "My mother taught me the tune when I was very young. We played it quite often."

"Where did it come from?"

"I only know that it was created during the ritual of Eleusinian on Gaia."

Jerad told her it was written in the *Protogio Principles*. The esoteric event hosted by Demeter, was shrouded in mystery. Participants were forbidden to speak about it, but there was rumor that it involved moving from one world to the next. Most believed it was from life to death, but that was never proven. It was said that during one particular ritual, Artemis, who was in attendance, sought the means to protect her beloved Orion from imminent death by the scorpion. The Oneroi were also present. A pact was struck to ensure safe passage of the *Origins* when it was determined that their existence on Gaia was no longer beneficial. When the celebrations were over, the Edict of Oneroi had been proclaimed and Demeter was in possession of what became known as the Key to Orion's belt. With her permission, Demeter's handmaidens charmed it with the music and she declared the intentions of the Eleusinian complete. The details of the covenant were concealed.

"Most here think the sculpture is merely a unique piece of artwork. That it is, in reality, the Key to Orion's belt is known only to a sect of loyals, who have been ordained to protect it, even if the consequence is the spilling of their blood."

"But how did your family end up with it?"

"Demeter is an Origin of the Second Corridor in the Tenth Zone. She bequeathed the Key to the eldest offspring in her bloodline with the instruction that it should continue to be passed through each generation in this manner. My mother was the first born through the line, as am I."

"But you are a descendant of Antheia."

"*Nai*, Sera. Through my father. Offspring claim paternal bloodlines."

Jerad further explained that the sculpture, which was hundreds of centenaries old, came to be called the spectrocorde by one of his mother's ancestors. It was made to resemble the shape of the Mountains of Eksaf 'anise, located at the *setway* boundaries between the Fourth and the Seventh Zones, very close to where he found Sera. The *Origins* claimed these mountains as their place of transience. On Gaia it was referred to as Io's Curse of the Tombs. Many believe that the *Origins* passed from Gaia to Protogio by way of Eksaf, but how it was done was never determined.

"Could I have passed through that way?" Sera was beginning to believe that her visions of a spacecraft were just that, the workings of her imagination. In fact, the harder she tried to remember her landing on Protogio, the fainter the image of a ship crashing became, and a recollection of rushing toward the ground through open air was becoming stronger.

"I think it is highly likely you came here by way of Eksaf."

"But how?"

Jerad twisted Sera around to face him. "I could not say. It is meant to be revealed by the Ptino asteri. It is why I believe you were sent, Starbird. Through you, the mystery of the Key and its significance to Eksaf and the Edict will be revealed."

"What about the explosion? My ship..."

"Shatter arrows. They are a new-fashioned and markedly dangerous weapon, recently designed by our foes. I watched the warriors from the Fourth Zone shoot one into a bovine. Its flesh was shredded. There was also a large eruption of flames after an arrow was lodged in the side of a barrel that likely contained a blasting mixture. Their preoccupation with the weapon was probably the reason they did not notice you when you fell."

Sera looked over her shoulder and studied the sculpture, searching her brain for even a hint that she possessed knowledge of it, but there was none. She suddenly felt as though a heavy burden had been dropped on her shoulders. If she could not summon even an inkling of knowledge about anything Jerad told her concerning the Key to Orion's belt and the Edict of Oneroi, how was she suppose to know what to do with it? She did not like being relied on for a task as monumental as this seemed to be to Jerad's people.

"I think you put too much relevance on my connection to it," Sera stepped back from him, "and to you."

Jerad reached out and took her hands into his, looking down to where their conjugal clothes touched. "Perhaps, but I think the passing of time will be its revelation."

He released one of her hands and led her to the outer living quarters. The spicy scent of cinnamon filled the room. Sera located the source. On the table, between the couch and chair, a tea candle heated a potpourri bowl. Sera inhaled, savoring the scent.

"The scent of zeylanic pleases you?"

Sera's stomach gurgled. She smirked and lowered her head.

"Hungry?"

Sera nodded, and then jumped as Jerad lightly squeeze her ribcage. "Good. You have barely eaten for three *rises* and you are feeling a bit bony."

There was a knock at the door. Jerad bid the caller to enter. The door opened and a cart with covered platters was wheeled into the room. Jerad motioned the attendant toward the outside terrace. He took Sera's hand again and led her through the double doors to the garden.

Chapter Eight

The garden was a plush oasis of flora and greenery girdled by a rocky wall that ascended to about forty feet, high enough to allow privacy. Cascading water fell over one side of a ledge, pooling into a crystal clear, flagstone natatorium. There were hanging herbs and dwarf fruit trees, an unstinted variety of fragrant blossoms, and tall, wispy plants that tossed back and forth in the breeze. The blending of colors and scents, combined with the sound of the flowing water, created a tranquil and soothing atmosphere. The garden was a quiet, peaceful sanctuary.

Jerad led Sera to the privy, discreetly hidden behind a rock wall barrier and tall foliage. There were two basins. Both had water flowing through them, and were made of stone. The lower one served as a commode, the other was smaller and higher. It was used as a sink. There was a stack of folded towels and wiping cloths on a stone ledge just above the wash bowl. Jerad handed a couple of them to Sera. He showed her a dish of coriander paste, and produced a wooden toothbrush with stiff bristles, for her use, after breakfast. Sera accepted the amenities from him, glad that she wouldn't have to forgo proper hygiene. Then it dawned on her. How had she been relieving herself while she was bedridden?

Sera looked down at the latrine and her mouth dropped open. Jerad took note of her wide-eyed, mortified expression. With understanding of what she was thinking, he gently placed a hand to her shoulder.

"I am a physician, Sera. I have cared for many who have needed assistance with this."

"Lucky me," she groaned inwardly. "Spare me the details."

"Do you need help?"

"No!" she yelled quite loudly.

"Then I will leave you to your privacy," He grinned at her adorably embarrassed face.

Sera emerged from the privy a short time later, sporting a look of chagrin. She found Jerad in a corner of the garden, sitting on a curved bench, in front of a small, rod-iron table. She sat next to him. He placed a dish of food in front of her. Sera stared at the breakfast on her plate. There was an array of finger foods that looked appetizing enough, but despite her hunger, she could not eat. Jerad, however, was devouring the food in front of him. He had eaten very little these past *rises* and was quite famished.

He stopped abruptly. "You are not eating. Are you ill?"

"It's a barbaric custom."

Jerad stared down at his plate, confused. "It is only food."

Sera rolled her eyes. "No you *dufus*, that whole thing with the cloak."

"It is an accepted way. Just two rise cycles afore, Thordo challenged Fresdel for his betrothed, Camdariel's hand. Fresdel won the Rite of the Cloak, although it was not without consequence. He suffered many wounds in the Challenge... and what's a *dufus*?"

Sera ignored his question. "And Thordo died?"

"No, but he was so impaired that he relinquished the Challenge, unable to continue, less he endanger his life. Camdariel was disappointed but not devastated. She would have accepted either for a husband."

That word again, disappointed, as if maiming and killing were no big deal. These people were too casual about such a thing. Sera felt a pit form in her stomach as she mentally relived the terror of being attacked, forced to defend her life, and the blood bath that followed when she sliced Sondra's throat. She gulped.

"So I did not have to kill her?"

"The point of your blade was at her throat. Had a halt been called, you would have been deemed the victor."

Sera narrowed her eyes as a rush of anger consumed her. "You mean to tell me that all I had to do was yell the word halt?"

She was furious with Jerad for withholding such important information from her. "Why didn't you tell me this!" Sera wanted to hit him. "How could you do that to me... to Sondra!"

"You would prefer to have been slain?"

"What are you talking about?" she snapped.

"Had I told you that you could halt the Challenge, once you had Sondra under your blade, you would have done exactly that."

"So?" Sera's voice cracked with indignation.

"Sondra would have denied the victory and killed you."

"That wouldn't have happened, if I would have refused to continue to fight her."

"Ah Sera, but it would have. Sondra, as well she knew, was at the mercy of your blade. She should have called a halt. In her pomposity, she did not. Sondra would not have stopped until one of you was dead. She had a streak of malevolence in her soul."

"Why did you force me to challenge her? Why didn't you call for a halt?"

"It was the only way to break my betrothal to her and bond with you, as the Oneroi intended, as I desired."

Sera flew out of her seat and stood rigid. "Your betrothal to her was your problem, not mine!"

Sera disregarded his comment about the Edict, not wanting to deal with that issue at the moment.

"You challenged when you accepted the bloom. I did not force you."

Sera plopped back down in her chair grabbing her side and wincing. She dropped her head and pulled at her hair. "I shouldn't have done that."

"Then why did you?"

Sera shot her head up and glowered, "I... I thought it was just a gift."

Jerad shrugged. "It would not have mattered. I offered you my crest and it angered Sondra. She would have tried to kill you whether you had accepted it or not. You had no choice."

"So what would have happened if Sondra had killed me?"

"Then I would have regretfully been mistaken about my assumption that you were the Ptino asteri."

Sera looked at him with distaste. Jerad and Sondra were promised, probably since childhood. He had taken an oath of celibacy and would not marry her until he avenged his mother's death. Sondra had patiently and faithfully waited for him, loved him from a distance.

"How could you be so cruel?" She scowled and turned away from him.

Jerad placed a hand under her chin to turn her head. She jerked away and refused to look at him. He was ugly to her right now.

"Look at me Sera."

When she continued to refuse, Jerad grabbed both of her shoulders and forced her face to him. Sera gave him the most appalled expression she could muster.

"We were childhood friends, Aryan, Mekal, Sondra and I, all from Noble clans. It was only fitting to our parents that Sondra and I become consorts. I never cared for her in that way. She was, as a sister. Long I asked her to break the betrothal, but she would not. I warned her that I would somehow force a Challenge. I did not... I never wanted to take her for a wife. I thus told her many times. She would not listen."

"She loved you though, didn't she?"

He shook his head. "Sondra had a cold heart. She loved only

status and power."

"But isn't a promise, a promise?"

"It was not a promise I chose to give. If she had agreed to my wishes, the betrothal would have been dissolved without repercussion. She was being stubborn. Sondra had a conqueror's mind. She could not vanquish me and that was a stab to her pride."

"She waited for you."

Jerad burst into a deep roar, throwing his head back.

"Sondra waited for nothing. She bedded half of the male warriors in the Zone. In fact Mekal, Sondra, and I were in the Great Hall one *luna* enjoying the spirits. Sondra solicited the company of one of the male guests. She nearly tupped him at our table, the brazen woman. She gave her charms freely and assumed she could still have me in the end. She made me look like the fool."

"Isn't that prohibited?"

Jerad snorted. "She was a free woman with the right to do as she pleased. You see my Starbird, she proved that her loyalty toward me was less than honorable. All knew what she was about. Sondra had no shame."

"I believe where I come from, women who do those things are called whores."

"Here too. To openly display loose virtues is severely frowned upon. It is wiser for both men and woman to be discreet with their private affairs, less we become daft like the fools in the Seventh Zone."

He paused a moment then grimaced. "Aside from this Sera, you saw her. She was nearly as big as I am. She was bigger than many of the males who dwell here." He spread his arms and elevated his voice an octave, for emphasis.

Sera pursed her lips together to suppress a smile. There was no humor to be found in the death she caused, but Jerad was right. The woman was a gargantuan.

Jerad leaned in toward Sera, propped a forearm on his thigh, and lowered his voice. "Her breasts were like rocks, not smooth and soft like yours." His eyes darted to Sera's breasts. Sera's eyes went wide at his bluntness.

Then he shuddered. "She would have pulverized my delicate manhood."

Sera scrunched up her face and pressed a fisted hand to her lips, but she couldn't contain herself.

"Ha!" Sera laughed and slapped the back of her hand across his chest. "Your delicate manhood. Give me a break."

She shook her head, still chuckling. It figured. Every time she was almost successful at not liking him, he did or said something that made her feel lighthearted toward him. Once again her anger toward him slipped away.

Jerad picked at his food, biting into a piece of flatbread, and washing it down with the herbal berry tea in his cup. Sera's stomach growled. She was suddenly hungry, and the food was now looking more tempting. She picked up a soft yellow cube of fruit and bit into it. It was delicious, somewhat bittersweet. While enjoying her breakfast, Sera mulled over their conversation. She imagined Sondra, an oversized, but handsome warrior woman, throwing one of her studs over her shoulder and running off to toss him in her bed. Sera lowered her head and wondered how she ever managed to defeat the woman. Then she felt a twinge of sympathy for Jerad. Sondra had humiliated him. Sera peered at him through the corner of her eyes.

"Are you really a vir... " Sera stumbled over her words. It was an embarrassing question, but she was curious about the reference made to his oath. "I mean, you have never been with... oh never mind." Sera turned a healthy shade of red.

Jerad placed a hand behind Sera's head, drawing her face to within inches of his. He slowly shook his head from side to side. "Never, but soon with you, wife."

Sera almost choked. When he closed in for a kiss, she turned her head away and Jerad pulled back. Undeterred, Jerad grazed her cheek with his knuckles. He ran the back of his splayed fingers along her throat and over the top of one breast. Sera didn't move. She didn't jerk back. She didn't even flinch.

Oh sure Sera, nice message you are sending here. Turn away from a kiss but let him play with your boobies.

She clasped her hands together and firmly pressed them on the tabletop, resisting the sudden desire to jump in his lap and rub up against him. The idea of so much untouched masculine flesh was tempting, and he apparently was hers to take.

Aw geez!

Sera dropped her forehead to her fisted hands. How could she think such a thing after all he'd put her through?

Jerad narrowed his eyes, noting that her nipples were peaking beneath her attire. A smile curved his lips. He was pleased with the cover garment the seamstress brought her to wear. The thin material betrayed her body.

He brushed his palm against her exposed thigh. Sera stiffened. She picked up her cup and swallowed arduously, trying to ignore the lusty sensations holding her hostage. Jerad pressed his lips against her ear, sending a thrilling shiver along the back of her neck.

Well that certainly didn't help.

Sera released a small, strangled cough and cleared her throat. Then she held her breath and counted to ten, remembering that counting to ten was supposed to be good for something.

Jerad reached for a piece of flatbread. He scooped a small amount of a dark orange topping from a bowl and dabbed it on top.

"Here."

Sera reached for it but he stopped her hand and brought the bread to her mouth instead.

"Open your mouth."

"And say ah?" Sera jested, but as soon as the word ah left her lips, he popped the bread into her mouth. She closed her mouth with a small chortle. It tasted like peaches. It was good.

Jerad watched the even line of her jaw work as she chewed and the sensual motion of her throat as she swallowed. When her tongue dabbed at the corner of her mouth to retrieve a stray drop of jam, his groin, which had been perpetually tight since the moment he first laid eyes on her, swelled torturously fuller against the seam of his trousers. His hand came up to reach behind her head, and he bent toward her. This time she did not turn away. Sera's belly tensed as she anticipated a kiss, but Jerad dragged his tongue across the crease of her mouth, withdrew, and savored the flavor of jam and her lips with his own tongue. Sera gasped at his intimate boldness. He smirked at the shocked look on Sera's face.

"What?" he mocked. "Did you think I was going to kiss you?"

She was fun to tease.

Sera's mouth fell open. She couldn't tell him that it was exactly what she thought, but before she could snap it shut he drew her mouth to his, and tasted her from the inside out.

The man was a virgin rake!

She should have pulled back, but her tongue reacted like a hungry vulture and she plunged the depths of his mouth instead. He responded by devouring her, exploring her with his own tongue until she sighed into his mouth and her body melted into his. Jerad relished the feel of her against him as she surrendered to his seductive siege.

He ran a hand along her side and slipped it into the opening of her gown, smoothing his hand over her breast and gently kneading the supple mound. Her nipple hardened under his palm as his lips moved to kiss and suckle her neck, her shoulder, and then trail back to her mouth. His craving for her became so intense he had to fight the impulse to rip open her robe and take her right there on the bench.

"Ahem!"

Sera and Jerad froze. Their eyes flew open, their lips still locked. A woman was standing on the terrace looking quite abashed at interrupting their private interlude. Phoebe stood next to her giggling.

Jerad withdrew his hand and slowly released Sera's bottom lip from his teeth. He rose from the bench, thankful he was wearing a longer tunic to hide the obvious bulge in his crotch, especially with his babe sister standing there. He had forgotten that the seamstress was due to arrive. Jerad gave Sera an affectionate kiss at her temple, took his leave and headed to the infirmary.

Chapter Nine

The poor woman apologized at least a thousand times for her rude intrusion in the garden. Sera nonverbally thanked her at least a thousand times for her rude intrusion in the garden. Phoebe just sat on the chaise smiling at Sera, not caring who intruded on whom.

Mesari the seamstress visited, at Jerad's request, to measure Sera for a wardrobe. It was actually a thoughtful deed, considering Sera had nothing but her birthday suit to wear. It was also somewhat surprising that her rogue of a husband didn't just keep her naked and waiting in his chamber. She had a feeling she would be constantly dodging his pursuing hands, not that she was putting much effort into the dodging.

In Jerad's absence, Sera had taken the opportunity to bathe, thankful he had given her the opportunity to do so, out of his sight. She had just finished donning the single gown that Mesari brought for her to wear until her clothes could be sewn, and was smoothing the wrinkles from the full length, silky garment, when she heard the rustle of the lambrequin door curtain. She looked up to see Jerad standing in the entranceway of the bed chamber.

Jerad returned from the infirmary. His mind was not on his duties. It was the first time he was away from Sera's side. Being separated from her left him feeling vacuous. He could not concentrate. The taste of her, the feel of her heated body against him unrelentingly suffused his senses.

There had been work to do. He tended to a child's bothersome cough, removed a large splinter from a finger, and applied ointment to the stiff joints of an elderly woman. The most pressing matter, that required his attention, was to extract a bantam knife from the foot of a citizen from the village. The commoner and his cohorts had taken up the sport of kotopoulo, a game of tossing a blade, half a finger long, at an opponent's feet. The object was to get as close as possible without causing injury. Jerad dislodged the blade successfully. He stitched the wound, applied pain killers and antiseptic before he bound it. He sent the young man hobbling away with a warning to hone his reflexes if he wished to avoid becoming a cripple in the future. He could almost predict another dagger in the foot would present to the clinic before the end of the rise.

Jerad always found much satisfaction in his work, but this rise he was filled with discontentment.

Ezra noted his solemn visage, watched his frequent sighs.

With a shake of her head and a roll of her eyes, Ezra finally insisted that he return to his Sera, avowing that she would rather work alone than withstand another moment of his gloomy facade. She assured him that he would be sent for if she required his assistance. Jerad readily and gratefully agreed. He finished some minor tasks with haste, and left Ezra to handle the activities in the clinic.

"That was quick." Sera pulled her calf length boots onto her feet and looked up at Jerad. She could tell by the admiring expression on his face that he liked what he was seeing.

Mesari was bending to pick up the cover garment that Sera had worn for three rises, intending on delivering it to the laundry. The look on the Noble Chancellor's face told her to make herself scarce. With a word to Phoebe, that it was time to leave, Mesari rushed toward the door, paused briefly, crossed her right fist to the opposite shoulder and bowed. She promised Sera that she would have several items of clothing ready for her, on the next rising. She also promised to knock.

Phoebe started to follow, but when she reached her brother, she stopped. "May I go with you to the Grandstage this rise, brother?"

Jerad gave her a loving smile. "Of course little sweet. Wait for us in the outer chamber."

Phoebe threw her arms around her brother's chest and hugged him tightly. Jerad kissed the top of her head. Sera was warmed by the fondness they shared. A stitch of remembrance, an affinity crept upon her and took hold. A face formed in her thoughts. She too had a sibling, a brother.

Phoebe released her hold on Jerad and bound out of the bed chamber, a happy and carefree glide in her steps.

"She is special to you." Sera watched the child disappear through the curtains. A slight ache rose in her chest.

"I would guard her with my life."

"Phoebe and Mesari seem close, as well."

"Mesari mothered her when our own died, though she was only twelve term cycles herself. They are together often. They are good friends."

Jerad turned his attention to Sera. He noted her forlorn expression. "What is it Starbird?"

"I'm homesick. I want to go home."

Jerad moved toward Sera and embraced her. Sera laid her head against his chest and accepted his comforting.

"You are home, Sera."

Home, she thought. What if he was right? Was this where fate had meant to put her, or was she in this place by mere circumstance? Sera tilted her head to look into Jerad's eyes. She was suddenly overcome with the sense that she was glimpsing a reflection of her own soul. There was an unspoken harmony that mixed between them. It shook her to her core. No, there was nothing random about their meeting. Jerad had said it, and she could feel it resonating within her. Their paths were woven, boundless.

He was half of her flesh.

Her longing for Gaia drained from her.

Jerad moved back from her and held her hands. Then he imparted a scrutinizing, heated look along her length that left her feeling as if her clothes were dripping right off of her. Sera smiled. She was becoming accustomed to his desire for her. She was starting to almost welcome it…enjoy it…almost. Sera released a hardy breath. Sera wanted Jerad. This she could admit to herself. It was as if she had always known him. Yet, there was something, a barrier that still fed her wariness, an apprehension that had little to do with the fact that they had only met a few rises ago.

She could not quite put her finger on it.

"What do you have on under there?"

"Under Where?" Sera snorted at her unintentional pun.

Jerad moved closer, his mouth curved into an impish grin.

Sera skimmed her hand along the sword belt at his waist and then along the hilt of the sword. She looked up, smirked, and flicked a single finger under his chin.

"Wouldn't you like to know," Sera teased, as she turned to swagger away.

Jerad caught her about the waist with one arm and pulled her back against his chest. "Perhaps a pair of knee breeches?" His voice vibrated enticingly against her ear.

He referred to the tight fitting half trousers that the women wore under their skirts, which served to preserve their decency, should they engage in a fight, or a great wind caught their hems. Unfortunately, Mesari did not realize that Sera had no such undergarment and failed to bring one.

"No." Sera had no idea why she was indulging him.

"Then what?" He playfully stroked her ribs with his fingers, tickling her.

"Stop it!" she laughed.

"Tell me or I will torture you."

Sera continued to struggle from his grasp, laughing, twisting her body. He held her captive with one arm, and was relentlessly tormenting her with the other hand.

"Nothing!"

Now why did she just admit to that?

Jerad stopped abruptly, and a sensual flicker appeared in his eyes. He groaned, turned her, grasped her about the hips and pulled her against him.

"I liked that scanty, lacy loin you wore under your own trousers. Perhaps Mesari could fashion one or two or ten pairs for you."

Sera bit her lip at the reminder that Jerad had removed her clothing in the clinic. She went still, her abashment apparent, but she had little time to dwell on it. Jerad reached in front of her and began gathering up her skirt.

"For now I will see what is under here."

Sera grabbed the hem of the gown to stay it, feigning indignation. Jerad's attempts weren't forceful. His actions were merely mischievous. He could have easily stripped the gown from her body if that were his intent. Then he ceased, releasing the garment with a chuckle . He curved his palms around the back of her head, and nuzzled his cheek to her forehead.

"I tease you Sera." He kissed her brow and whispered in a husky voice, "I already know what is under there."

Sera skewed her face. He *did* know. Jerad had seen her naked more than she cared to think about. She *did* think about it however, and an unexpected heat slunk along her flesh. For a brief moment, she had a tantalizing thought of his hands roaming her unclad body.

Jerad released her and scanned her body once more. His dark eyes smoldered. The garment hugged her like a second skin. It draped smoothly over her shoulders and clung to her breasts. Her nipples nudged through the material and he was certain he could see a hint of areola. His gaze moved lower to the curves of her waist and hips, then further to the juncture between her shapely thighs where a slight, triangular swell was visible through the material. There was no other way to describe it.

She looked--*provocative*.

Jerad harrumphed and moved to the clothespress. He opened it and withdrew a long, white satin cloak. He arranged the garment around her shoulders and drew it closed at the front. Satisfied that it sufficiently covered her, he fastened it at the collar with a lavender bloom clasp.

"We leave the dwelling today. I would suggest, *strongly* suggest, my Starbird, that you retain the modesty of the cloak, less I find myself set to lay waste to any man in the Corridor who sets a lustful eye upon you."

Jerad took her wrist and led her from the bedchamber. Phoebe was patiently waiting outside. Jerad pulled out a drawer in the desk and reached behind the back of it. He retrieved a ring of metal keys--skeleton keys, Sera recognized. They left the dwelling, and entered a hallway. It was a short passageway that ended with a solid wall on one side and a large, wooden door on the opposite end. There were several doors along the walls to either side.

"These apartments are all part of our residence."

He inserted a key in a lock and opened the first door, located directly across from the living chamber. Inside and to one side of the room, an accouterment of weapons, armor and tools, were hung on walls or neatly placed on racks. On the other side of the room, bundles of both practical looking and luxurious fabrics were neatly stacked on shelves. Jerad approached a blue, velvet roll and fingered it.

"If you wish for an item to be sewn by the seamstress you may choose any of these materials. Her payment is usually a bit of extra cloth to use as she pleases."

He then moved to a large coffer and opened it with another key. It was filled with a variety of colored gems in various sizes, along with gold, silver, and reddish metal nuggets.

Jerad scooped up a handful. "These can be used in the *agora* for purchases. Some merchants will also barter for ready-made goods. You will learn what is valuable to each merchant, and use your judgment to trade for the goods you want to obtain."

He pulled a small, leather sack from a pocket on the inside of Sera's cloak and dropped in the pieces. He drew on the string laced around the opening to close it, and replaced it to the cape's pocket.

"What is here is yours, Sera."

"How did you get all of this stuff?"

"There are mines throughout the mountainside. Our laborers excavate the raw materials, and they are paid either in raw materials, food, or wares. I earn my keep as defender of the Tenth Zone and with my position as Noble Chancellor on the Magistrate Council. Sometimes I receive goods for my healing skills. Some items I earn through contest."

Sera's attention was drawn to the sword she recognized as Zoren's, but then she noticed something else. On the weapons rack a familiar blade was tucked into a baldric. She recognized that hilt. It was Sondra's blade.

"Why is this here?"

"I laid claim to it for you."

"I don't want it."

"You have earned the right to wear it, Sera. It is acceptable."

Jerad lifted the blade and held it out to her. Sera turned her head away. Remembering her lack of sword skill, Jerad recanted. Her refusal was probably for the best. She might cut off her own arm. He would have to teach her how to use the blade first. Jerad returned the weapon to the rack.

Jerad led them from the room after closing and locking the chest. He then locked the door.

"This room is kept locked, mostly to dissuade temptation, although I doubt anyone would be foolish enough to try and breach it. The living chambers of all Nobles in the castle are well guarded, though its inhabitants are highly trustworthy.

Jerad slipped into the living chamber to return the key ring to the drawer. He reappeared, holding two keys. He locked the door to their private chamber, and then clipped the keys to his belt.

"The remainder of the rooms I keep unlocked."

He opened another door further down the hall. Cool, damp air rose from the depths of what looked like the entrance to a cellar. Jerad uncovered the *glimmer orbs* anchored to the stone walls, as they descended a flight of stairs. It led underground to a small pantry, where a modest amount of edibles, some fresh, some cured, and a stock of hard beverages and wines were stored.

"This is our personal stock. It is checked daily by the *kitcheners* to ensure the food is fresh. What needs to be consumed immediately is taken to the main kitchen to be used or sent to the commoners to be given away."

There were three rooms remaining, two comfortably furnished guest bedchambers, and a large, empty room with a large balcony that overlooked the castle's courtyard.

"If you find a use for this space Sera, you are welcome to it."

Sera's immediate thought was to make it a sanctuary to hide from her consort's overactive libido, but *ochi*, he would likely find her there.

She would probably let him.

They passed through the door at the far end. Jerad slipped a key into the keyhole. With a couple of clacking sounds the deadbolt slid into place.

"I only lock the main entranceway when I am away from our apartments."

They descended a stairwell, which rounded to a lower level and terminated into what appeared to be a larger, central spine. It was wide enough for the three of them to walk side by side and still allow ample room for others to pass. They were hailed by the watchman, who was posted there, and Jerad handed him the keys. The guard clipped them next to others on a ring attached to his belt, and the three of them continued on their way.

The walkway was lit by a row of blue *crukis* windows, separated by mullions that lined the wall on one side. Being that it was early in the *rise*, the windows were presently clear. A large mural ran the expanse of the opposite wall.

The painting depicted the birth of Protogio and progressed through various stages of its history. It included life size exhibits of daily life in the Corridor, craftsmen at work, warriors at swordplay and citizens engaging in festivities. It ended with a great winged creature swooping down on a battleground, which was being fought under a darkened sky of falling, luminous stars.

It took a moment for Sera to realize that she was looking at a rendition of the Edict of Oneroi. She dug in her heels to slow their pace. Jerad noticed her interest in the artwork, and stopped to oblige her.

Phoebe took Sera's hand and looked at her with an approving smile.

"My sister is intrigued by you."

Sera patted Phoebe's hand, feeling a bit uneasy at the girl's enamored expression. "I am no one special Phoebe."

"Oh, but you are." Phoebe pointed to the eyes of the Ptino asteri painted on the wall and then cast her gaze to Sera's eyes.

"The color of your eyes is unique, Sera. Not another has been seen with such." Jerad offered an explanation. "The artist was likely spiritually inspired when he painted it."

"Its a coincidence, Jerad," Sera gawked at the face of the creature, entranced by its golden eyes, set deep into a human-like face, cleverly painted so that its gender could not be defined. Its head was graced with black, feathery looking hair that draped over the creature's shoulders. The silvery body was that of a bird, with two broad, fully extended wings. On its back sat four omnipotent deities, who appeared to be giving powerful command to the flying beast beneath them.

"The sons of Hypnos, Sera. They are collectively known as the Oneroi."

"Is that bird supposed to be me?" She creased her brow at the hybrid. "How ludicrous."

A rumble swelled in Sera's gut as a laugh burst from her lips. "Oh that's priceless. It's just the way I want to be immortalized!"

Jerad examined the mural, and then turned to her, perplexed.

"Four men riding me?" Sera quipped. She chortled, and then bellowed an uncontained guffaw. She wiped at tears that welled in her eyes.

Jerad glowered at her. He shook his head, unsettled by her ridicule of the Edict. She did not understand the significance of the divination. Protogio's survival, its future, depended on her knowledge of the Key to Orion's belt. Without it, his world would be destroyed. Jerad swallowed his rising indignation, allowing that her amnesia caused her ignorance, and proceeded to tug her down the passageway. To his annoyance her laughter resonated throughout the hallway.

"I am glad you find our doctrine so amusing," he groused, as they moved down another hall and through an arcade. It opened to the outside courtyard. Two guards hailed them as they passed through, as did a number of citizens who lingered about the outside area.

"Jerad, that can't possibly be me. I am just a person." Sera stated emphatically.

Jerad glanced at his sister. Phoebe looked affronted by Sera's behavior. "You are offending my sister."

She was offending him as well.

Sera noted Phoebe's distress and stifled her mirth. "Oh, Phoebe, I don't mean to upset you. I am sorry,"

Sera pulled Phoebe into a hug. "But you need to understand that it is just too unbelievable to think of myself as some kind of divine, saving grace. I barely know who I am, not alone what I left behind."

It was Phoebe who halted this time. She frowned.

"Brother, if she cannot accept her moira, who will save us when the Nyx warriors come?"

"Have faith, little sweet. All will come to pass as predicted." Jerad attempted to console her. He was not sure he believed his own words.

He sighed with exasperation.

Jerad hoped that the mural would have triggered some awareness within Sera. Nothing else had worked so far. The spectrocorde, although its euphonic spectrum affected her, as he knew it would, was of no help. Giving her fragments of Protogio history and bits from the Edict had not worked either, nor did telling her the story of the Gaians who came before her. She needed to read the Edict of Oneroi in its entirety. He withheld showing it to her at first, concerned that she might suffer anxiety if too much returned to her at once. He meant only to encourage her memories and gently guide her into acceptance of her fate. It was his obligation as Keeper of the Key, so he suspected, since the Ptino asteri had been delivered unto him. It was what he was sure the Oneroi would expect of him, and nothing less. He would have to think on this.

"Come my ladies. All will be well." Jerad motioned them on with a sweep of his hand, but he continued to share Phoebe's uneasiness.

Chapter Ten

It was a spectacular showing of flexing muscle and clashing swords. There were at least twenty Nobles in the Grandstage arena proudly demonstrating their warrior skills. Phoebe explained that on every third *rise*, the squires and sometimes the pages, warriors in training, practiced quintain and running at the rings. Both feats were performed on horseback. In quintain the participants used lances to charge at a target attached to an arm. The arm extended from a pole and was designed to swivel around and slap the horseman if the lance was ill placed, often knocking the rider from the horse. Running at the rings was also accomplished with lance and horse. Wooden rings, with a center opening, two to four finger widths, were suspended. The object was to collect as many rings as possible with the tip of the lance. Both sports were relatively safe and served to enhance the visual acuity, accuracy and discipline of the younger warriors, before learning to joust against another horseman.

More able warriors often milled about, tittering at the clumsiness of the less experienced Nobles, taking bets at who might be successful and who would be downed first. Some participated to offer training. More often than not, and to the agitation of the Master Trainers, the apprentices would be crowded from the Grandstage floor. The arena would then erupt into full-blown jousts with the seasoned, gold ringed knights' intent on flaunting their prowess. During the joust exhibitions, metal or leather armor would be worn and the lances were weakened to splinter easily. The lances were also rebated or blunted. Even still, it was not unusual for injuries to occur. At these times Jerad and Ezra were kept very busy in the clinic, unless of course Jerad himself had sustained an injury, and he spent a *rise* or two recuperating, only to be continually chastised by Ezra for his foolishness. Fortunately it did not happen often, as Jerad was quite skilled with the joust.

On this *rise* sword practice would prevail over all events. The Masters would see to that. The ability to wield a sword was highly valued by Nobles and Commoners alike. It was their primary means of defense against their enemies. All citizens in the Zone were encouraged to learn the skill, although only Nobles were granted the privilege of showmanship within the walls of the Grandstage. Commoners held their demonstrations in the hills and open fields. Sometimes the Nobles joined them.

The swords were rebated to diminish the possibility of fatal injury, but as with the lance, a few hard blows could cause severe bruises or broken bones. The intent however, was not to harm, but to disarm.

At one end of the floor, youngsters, who had not yet reached their maturity, were also involved in the swordplay and dagger maneuvers. Some were eagerly snapping cloaks and swiping at their opponents with wooden daggers. Others were trying their hands at the sword. Phoebe was one of them. Her male opponent matched her height, but he was more muscled. He still possessed an adolescent physique however, not quite as brawny as his adult counterparts. Phoebe disarmed him of his sword a number of times. She had remarkable skill even at her young age, but took her own share of defeats. At the moment, she was sitting on her bottom, having been bested by her contender. He held out his hand and pulled her to her feet, then laughed and embraced her in a solid hug. It was then that Sera took notice of the pleasantries that passed from one Noble to the other. Despite their aggressive natures, the citizens seemed to be an affectionate horde. She observed a female warrior smack the bottom of a male as he entered the arena. Another male leaving the floor threw his arm around the shoulder of his male opponent and leaned on him, as they conversed with each other. Amid their bantering and swordplay, they touched each other, *a lot*, but all in the show of camaraderie. They truly seemed to care for each other.

Through the corner of her eye, Sera caught sight of a sword propelling through the air. She turned to see Jerad standing over his female striver with the dulled tip of his sword planted firmly at her throat. The woman laughed and cried for a halt. Jerad moved the blade aside, offered his hand and pulled her to her feet. The woman lightly slapped his cheek with an open palm before exiting from the playing field. Jerad thwacked her butt. Sera's spine stiffened at the gesticulation, and she was surprised by the twitch of jealousy that suddenly enveloped her.

The fondness these citizens displayed toward each other was going to take some getting used to.

She attempted to shake the unfounded feeling and turned her attention to one of the Master Trainers.

Herus was one of four trainers present. She was a tall, older woman, at least fifty *term cycles* in age. She exhumed pride and confidence with her skill. Sera watched her with both enthusiasm and appreciation, as she faced younger, stronger males and females. She moved with unrestrained gracefulness. Her silver braid flittered about her head. Her sword slashed through the air with such ease and precision that Sera guessed the women must have spent much of her life engaged in combat. The gold-ringed feather badge on her vest verified that it was true. With little effort her challengers' swords were flying. She brought the best of the best to their knees. She snorted as she stood over a Noble who she had thrown to his back. Warrior after warrior faced her, and she defeated them all. When she grew tired of toying with them, she moved to her juvenile apprentices. With the youngsters however, Herus' demeanor changed. She instructed them with firm but motherly guidance.

Herus was a respected woman. Her advice and experience was well received by all.

"She's amazing, is she not?" A woman sat on the bench beside Sera.

"Remarkable," Sera replied without averting her attention from the activity in the arena.

"She's a grandmother, you know."

Sera turned her head toward the woman. She recognized her. "You are Ezra."

"*Nai* Sera. I am surprised you know me considering your condition that rise."

Ezra reached for one of Sera's hands and held it between her own. She looked up to examine Sera's face.

"Your color is good. Are you still in pain?" She smiled gently at Sera.

"Not much. Jerad said he will remove the stitches on the next rise."

Ezra's attention was drawn to the Grandstage floor. Sera followed her gaze to where Jerad was facing his next rival. The swordsman, who engaged Jerad, was large and well muscled. His tawny mane was thick and full. It framed a face that looked harsh and fervid. A picture of a ferocious lion formed in Sera's mind. An uneasy feeling washed over her. There was something frighteningly familiar about him, but she was sure that she had not seen him before.

With swords raised, their match began. They quickly began crossing ground. Others in the arena scurried from the floor to give the fighters liberty. Sera watched the combatants with mounting anxiety. There was a belligerent edge to the competition that appeared to be more of a confrontation than just a friendly sport.

Sera turned her head toward Ezra and watched the woman's expression turn grim.

"They have been the best of confidantes since childhood," Ezra remarked, as she tracked the movements of Jerad and the other swordsman. There was a twinge of worry in Ezra's voice.

Sera allowed her gaze to return to the arena. The warrior rushed at Jerad, putting him on the defense. He began a relentless attack with his sword. Jerad blocked and retreated, but only briefly. Jerad gained the offensive and advanced toward his opponent. The fray grew to such a contentious pace that Sera was near fretting. It looked as if Jerad's contender meant to do him harm. Because Ezra appeared as equally distressed as she did, Sera assumed that the encounter was more than a typical game of practice. She was thankful that the blades were dulled. The thought of Jerad being hurt was upsetting. At first, she attributed her feelings to her sense of humanity, but realized her concern for the other warrior was less than compassionate. She wanted to see Jerad's opponent lose.

Silently she cheered Jerad on. He was her warrior, her consort, her *friend*.

How had she grown to care so deeply for him in such a short time?

And why was no one stopping this clearly, reckless match?

Sera looked about the arena. All eyes were centered on the pair, but not one citizen seemed willing to interfere. Even Herus, who watched the two warriors with a disapproving expression, did not move to suspend the battle. It was allowed to continue until both men were sweating and out of breath. Amazingly, all attempted strikes were blocked by both combatants with neither succumbing to any harmful blows. Jerad finally called for a halt, despite the fact there was no victor.

The Grand Masters moved in and then waited to see if their intercession was required. The match had quickly escalated dangerously close to becoming a full-fledged Honor challenge, and this they could not allow. Not without the Magistrate's consent. The warrior dropped his sword first, and Jerad responded in like. There appeared to be a collective sigh of relief that flowed among the observers in the Grandstage. Herus approached the warrior and whispered something to him. He stormed to the side of the arena floor, but not before scoffing savagely at Jerad. Herus shook her head at Jerad, and Sera noted the muscles in Jerad's jaw tense. Something was definitely wrong. She had a sense of impending doom, and knew with profound awareness that it was her marriage to Jerad that caused the discord.

The other Nobles in the Grandstage returned to the floor, and as if nothing unusual had just occurred, all activity returned to normal. Sera however, could not as easily put the incident to rest.

"You know the one who fought with Jerad?"

"Ah, but *nai*. He is my consort, the Noble Chancellor Aryan, of the Second Corridor."

Sera looked toward the arena. Aryan was glaring in their direction. His baneful expression bore into Sera with such intensity it caused her to shudder. Sera looked away. She did not have the courage to stare him down, nor did she wish to compete with him, should he become further antagonized. He could strike her down with one blow. She decided to ignore him.

Ezra released her crushing grip on Sera's hand. She had been holding it tightly while suffering her own anxiety over the match between Jerad and Aryan. Sera looked down as Ezra withdrew her grasp. She noticed that Ezra's left hand was tattooed in a delicate vine of yellow rosebuds and leaves that began on her palm and wrapped around her wrist. It ended at the back of her hand. The design was elegant, aesthetically pleasing to the eye. The colors were brilliant and the shading was creatively embellished to give it a three-dimensional illusion. Sera was tempted to ask her about it, but now, did not seem like the appropriate time.

"His scowl is for me as much as it is for you," Ezra shot a defiant, but flirtatious smile in her husband's direction.

Aryan leered back, fixating his glare on the two women as he buckled his baldric into place. Then he slowly and deliberately withdrew his broadsword and began to diligently polish it. Ezra was not intimidated by his attempt at provocation.

Sera however, was very daunted by the looming warrior. She stole a skewed glance in his direction and then briskly averted her gaze. "Why is he so angry?"

"He does not like my conversing with you."

"What have I done wrong?" Sera bit her lip, not sure she was ready to hear the answer, but it was too late. The answer came.

"Ah Sera, you have done nothing wrong, but you should know, it was his sister you killed. They were *gemini*."--twins.

Sera grimaced. Her muscles tensed. That explained why he looked so familiar. Aryan shared many of Sondra's features. The woman she killed was the sister to a close friend of Jerad's. Aryan must deeply hate her for what she had done. At the moment, Sera could not have felt more like an outsider, an intruder. What did the rest of the Corridor think of her?

"May I ask you a question, Ezra?"

"If you wish."

"Why are you so accepting of me?"

Ezra looked at her with a confused expression. "What do you mean by this question?"

"Why is everyone around here, except for Aryan of course, acting like my killing Sondra is no bid deal."

Sera watched Ezra as she mouthed the words *big deal.*

"Your words are strange Sera, but I think I understand what it is you ask. I will try to explain."

Ezra paused momentarily and hissed in her husband's direction. Aryan's eyes narrowed and the fierce looking man snarled back at his petite wife. Under different circumstances, Sera would have viewed Ezra's lack of intimidation with more amusement, but at the moment she was relieved to see Aryan turn and stomp away.

"Sondra was not so highly respected here," Ezra continued, ignoring her consort's annoyance with her. "Aryan's family grieves, but others, they do not. No one here expected less than a battle for Jerad's crest. It was no secret that when, or if he married, it would be to another. What is much a surprise to all, is that it is you who stands breathing instead of Sondra. You have earned much respect for your courage."

Like I had much of a choice, Sera thought.

"I could have called a halt had I known about it." Sera whispered with a culpable breath.

"Had you done so, the outcome would have been less than favorable for you. Sondra had an unnatural obsession with Jerad. Your death would have been her pleasure. She too could have called a halt, but Sondra was presumptuous, and I suspect she repudiated the notion that you had bested her. It is merely the way of things sometimes."

Jerad had said much the same, yet it didn't alleviate Sera's anxiety. After witnessing what was supposed to be merely sport between Jerad and Aryan it was apparent that the matter had not been put to rest.

Ezra nudged Sera with her elbow, shaking her from her thoughts. "Beware Sera."

"What?"

Herus was standing before them, motioning for Sera to enter the arena.

"Your presence has been noticed."

Ezra placed a hand on Sera's upper arm and leaned toward her, careful to hide her words from Herus. "Do not refuse that one. She does not fare well as an enemy.

Then she chuckled. "I will take my leave now before I find myself tripping on my own feet in the middle of the Grandstage."

Ezra looked toward the door. Aryan was waiting for her. His mood appeared unaltered. "Besides, my consort is pounding his chest and growling at me."

She dashed for the door and disappeared with her husband.

Herus approached, grabbed Sera's wrist and yanked her from the bench. Sera opened her mouth to protest, but instead found herself at the mercy of a *big, bad mama* called, Herus.

"Come girl, don't be shy. We have much work to do if we are to make a fighter out of you," Herus bellowed in a robust voice.

"But... no... wait." Sera attempted to pull back, but Herus had a firm grip on her, and was literally dragging her to the middle of the floor.

"It was by the grace of the Origins, Noble Sera, that Sondra did not split you in two."

Herus made no recourse for Sera to respond, and before Sera could say *boo hoo,* or *help,* a blunted sword was shoved in her hand. Herus took a stance in front of Sera and raised her blade. Sera lowered her sword to her side. Herus scowled at Sera's defiance, but Sera made a quick recovery, moving toward the great warrior woman. With her modesty in tow, she softly whispered close to Herus' ear, "I am not wearing any underwear."

Herus jerked her head back and she gave Sera a once-over. Then with instant understanding she roared with a boisterous laugh, drawing the curious attention of those nearby. Sera blushed profusely. Herus slapped her on the back, sending her body flying forward at least several feet, but at least the woman had the decency to make no further comments on Sera's state of incomplete dress.

"Off with ya!" Herus motioned to the onlookers, shooing them away. They immediately obeyed, returning their attentions to their own activities.

Sera was *off the hook.*

Relieved, Sera turned to leave the arena, but Herus caught her arm.

"Not so fast girl!"

Crap.

* * * *

Sera's hips were flexed to a ninety-degree angle. Her knees were flexed to a ninety-degree angle. She was chair sitting against the wall, except there was no chair beneath her. She had been in this position for at least a *quarter segment*, but it felt like a full *rise*. In two hands she held a sword that probably weighed five pounds, but felt like fifty. Every now and then Herus would strike Sera's blade with her own, from the right or from the left, or from overhead, daring Sera to fall over or drop the sword. Sera gritted her teeth, her perspiration drenching her. The muscles in her thighs ached, the muscles in her butt ached, the muscles in her arms ached, but Herus was relentless. Each time Sera began to slide downward, Herus hoisted her back up. Who would have thought that inactivity could be so exerting.

Jerad, still engaged in his sword sport at the opposite side of the arena, occasionally glanced her way, a jocular grin on his lips. Sera responded with a pointed, *I'll get you for this*, glare, in his direction.

"Discipline girl! Pay attention. You will have time enough later to attend to your consort!" Herus clanked her blade against Sera's once more. "Let your mind be master over your fatigue and victory will be yours!"

"If you are done torturing my wife, Herus, it is time we took our leave." Jerad approached, and stood just behind the woman.

Herus frowned, more disappointed than disapproving. "Very well. You are finished for now, Noble Sera.

Sera blew out the breath trapped in her lungs and slid to her bottom. She could have licked Jerad's boots at that point, dirt and all, she was so grateful he had finally come to rescue her. Herus grabbed Sera's arm and with a quick jerk, pulled Sera to her feet. Jerad moved in and caught Sera as her knees began to buckle. Herus stood by, laughing.

"She is lovely. A strong woman. It is a good choice you have made laddy." Herus slapped Jerad's shoulder approvingly. Jerad rolled his eyes. Herus consistently referred to any man, even those only slightly younger than she, as *laddy*. He did not mind. Despite her gruff demeanor and her oft condescending way, he was fond of the woman.

Jerad took Sera's hand. "Come my *tharros*, we are expected to sup with the Magistrate Council this luna."

He called her his *heart*. Sera's own heart skipped a beat with his term of endearment. His affection warmed her immensely.

Jerad turned to Herus. "A pleasant rise to you, Herus."

"*Nai*, of course, and to you, laddy boy!"

With Sera's hand still in his own, he moved to leave the Grandstage.

"Thank you for your help," Sera politely remarked to Herus. What she really wanted to do was get out of there as fast as she could and never again be caught in Herus' presence. Unfortunately her quivering, lower limbs would only allow her a clumsy, limping escape.

Chapter Eleven

Jerad pushed the door open, and he entered the dwelling. Sera followed, closing the door behind them. He began unhooking and releasing his accouterment, dropping it to the floor. Without looking back he proceeded through the doubled doors leading to the garden, stripping his clothing until he was completely unclad. He crossed the stone terrace, and slipped into the tarn.

Sera removed her cloak and boots and sat at the pond's edge. She pulled her skirt up to a modest height and dipped her aching limbs into the soothing waters. Jerad's back was toward her, allowing her to discreetly and shamelessly peruse his naked backside. A subtle tingle crept through her, then surged, pooling at her feminine muscles. They clenched in aroused delight. He was a much tempting sight to behold. Jerad abounded in masculine flesh. He had broad shoulders that tapered to a taut derriere and powerful, exquisitely sculpted thighs.

And she was married to it...

Ahem... Him.

She blew a slow, appreciative puff of air and wet her lips. She continued to admire the attractive view, until Jerad sank below the surface, and out of her sight.

Oh nai.

She definitely wanted him.

Jerad broke the surface of the water just below the cascade and Sera watched him shower. He was seemingly oblivious to her presence. Sera bent toward the water, swirling and scooping it with her hand. When she looked up again, Jerad was lazily prowling toward her, his dark, passion filled eyes locking and capturing hers.

Look away Sera, she pleaded with herself, but *her self* just did not listen.

Sera's breath quickened at the imminent view, and the likely onslaught to follow. He began to ascend, the water becoming shallow around him. His skin was wet and glistening.

Oh Lordy me!

It wasn't like she hadn't seen him naked before, but that was different. He was in the grips of death then.

Jerad paused, thigh deep in the water. Sera finally managed to snap her lids shut, but only briefly. They flew open like they were spring loaded and she was eye level with a part of him that showed every indication of being fully, *really fully*, alive.

Now how the hell was she going to handle that?

Sera's heart started pounding wildly. She felt a tremble begin in the tips of her fingers and toes that vibrated through her until it gathered in a strangle hold inside her throat. She swallowed a hard lump. A ripple sparked low in her belly, causing a radiating heat to imbue her flesh. Sera thought to jump into the pool to extinguish the flame that was slowly searing her with heightening arousal, but that would only bring her closer to the source of the fire.

She wanted him to touch her, but not now. It was too soon.

Run, she told her feet, but they were immobile beneath her. Sera looked down at her betraying appendages, somewhat baffled that her mind would so forcefully fight what her body most assuredly wanted.

Move damn it!

Her feet disobeyed.

Awe cripes! She looked up.

Jerad stood still, hands on hips, naked, and oh so proudly erect-- in more ways than just one, flashing a handsomely broad and devilish smile.

Then he--*Oh gawd*, he flexed *it*, and it bobbled, up and down, up and down. He waggled his eyebrows at her.

Sera threw her hands to her face and dropped hear head, but despite herself, she burst into laughter. She was embarrassed and amused. Jerad was over her in an instant. It was then that Sera discovered that her hand had a mind of its own as well, because the little traitor fit itself nicely around his hardness and stroked it like it was a beloved pet. Jerad groaned with her unexpected touch, his breath growing heavy with desire.

Sera's entire body went into mutiny. Her knees bloomed open in wanton longing and her nipples budded as Jerad pressed himself against her, forcing her back to the ground. He fit his hips snuggly between her thighs.

"So, what's up, doc?" she asked nervously.

Now where did that come from, and why was she thinking about a carrot?

"Need you ask?" He inhaled sharply, and stroked his erection against her.

Nope, not a carrot.

Zucchini maybe.

"I am hopeless to deny the hunger for you, that thrives within me, wife."

And outside too, she thought, feeling his member hardened even further.

Being fully clothed and draped by a wet, nude, hard body was undeniably erotic.

Jerad's mouth descended on hers, his tongue seeking entrance. Sera willingly parted her lips, responding by thrusting her tongue to taste him. His mouth was so tight on hers that she could scarcely breathe, or perhaps it was just that she had forgotten how to breathe.

Nai, she was breathless in the throes of his delicious trespass, an aching urgency building inside her.

The rational side of her brain, the one that should have been screaming, "Stop before its too late!" had given furlough to her sensibilities, and seized her apprehension along the way. Sera's qualm wilted to Jerad's seductive foray.

Oh hell! She was his wife. She was obligated to perform her wifely duties, right?

Wifely duties.

Yah, uh huh.

There was another name for what she was feeling at the moment, all of it pleasant, and well beyond her spousal obligations.

Sera closed her eyes and tried to inhale, catching his breath as it entered the chamber of her mouth. His hands moved to the neckline of her dress and he slipped the material off of her shoulders, exposing the tops of her breasts. He kissed the swollen flesh there. One hand cupped the bottom of her breast through the material and Sera arched up to greet it, as his thumb played across her hardened nipple. He splayed the fingers of his other hand through her hair and grasped her locks to tilt her head back. Then he suckled at her throat. Sera's hands roamed his body, seeking, caressing him along his muscular back to his firm buttocks, as she slowly rocked her pelvis against him. Jerad responded in like manner.

Jerad shifted to one side and gathered her skirt to caress the bare skin of her thigh. He ran his palm down the outside then up along the inside, relishing in the feel of her satiny flesh until he reached her juncture. He stroked his thumb along the crevice hidden beneath her curls, barely brushing her hardened nub. Sera bucked and moaned at the incredible sensation, ready to combust at any moment. He groaned at the heated moisture he discovered there.

A loud screech caused Sera to open her eyes. A falcon was circling the sky, high overhead. Sera's eyes wandered to the top of the escarpment above the garden. There was a male form on the ridge above. Sera could not make out his features. The light of the *rise* behind him cast him into shadow, but nonetheless, there he stood, motionless, watching.

Sera stiffened. Jerad felt her grow rigid beneath him and drew back to query her sudden change. He followed her distracted gaze toward the ledge, and then released a frustrated grumble.

For the love of the Origins! Was there some amoral plot to keep him from mating with his wife?

Jerad rose to his feet and donned his trousers. He approached the embankment and began climbing upward, using the thick, ivy branches growing from the wall, for support. Sera rearranged her clothing to cover herself and watched as Jerad reached the onlooker. Both men disappeared beyond the ledge.

"Aryan my confidante." Jerad greeted the warrior with a halting tenor.

Jerad raised a palm to receive an informal greeting, summoning every thread of self-restraint to keep from strangling the warrior for the interruption.

Aryan did not respond. Jerad lowered his hand.

"You are always welcomed at my door, but perhaps it is the door you should use when you call."

Aryan stepped closer to Jerad and sniffed hard. He snarled, curling his lip with distaste. "I can smell her on you."

Aryan gave a visible snap of his head to show his disdain.

Jerad clenched his fists. He knew what the warrior was about. He meant to antagonize Jerad, and indeed his crude comment left Jerad feeling indignant.

"I suggest you keep thoughts of my consort out of your head,"

Jerad responded caustically. His palm landed on Aryan's groin with a forceful clench, "and from here."

Aryan was immediately enraged. He drew back a fist and connected it to the side of Jerad's jaw. The blow was hard enough to unsteady Jerad, but not enough to cause him to fall. A trickle of blood emerged from the corner of his mouth. Jerad wiped it with the back of his tightened fist. Aryan stood grounded, with a look of disgust. Then he darted a pointed finger at Jerad.

"She is dead because of you."

Jerad grabbed Aryan by the shoulders facing him squarely.

"She is dead by her own doing. She could have refused the Challenge. She could have called a halt."

"And disgrace her honor? You knew she would never have done that."

"You know, as do I, that it was her pride she defended, not her honor."

"You have committed a betrayal against my house, Jerad."

"And what of you? What is your rendering of this?"

"It matters naught what I think. My mother is grievous and infuriated. As the oldest scion it is expected that I will bring charge."

"And what of your sire? Is it not his place to bring implication to the Magistrate Council?"

"My father dithers with his loyalties."

A wise decision, Jerad thought. Aryan's father Angus, now retired, once held the Chief Council seat. He and Shegarth were still close confidantes. Jerad expected that Angus was in despair over the loss of Sondra, but he was a just man. Angus would have investigated the circumstances regarding the Challenge for the Cloak, and found the outcome did not breach the boundaries of their laws. Creating discord on this issue, which could divide the opinions of the Magistrate Council, would be an irresponsible thing for Angus to do.

Jerad considered briefly, that he should reveal Sera's true identity to Aryan. He, just as Mekal, had taken an oath of guardianship of the Key. Aryan, much like his father, was an honorable man. It would then be Aryan's obligation to protect the Ptino asteri, to protect Sera, and disloyal to the Edict to find antipathy against her.

Jerad immediately squelched the thought. Aryan, as it was with many of his kinsmen, had grown apathetic toward the Edict, believing it to be a disputable myth--a child's tale. Some had even come to question that the *Origins* ever existed and that Gaia too, was the workings of an ancestor's imagination. Aryan might balk at the idea of Sera being the Ptino asteri. It was better that Aryan thought that Jerad merely wanted Sera as wife, less he mention Jerad's notion to others.

Ochi.

If it became known that Sera was the Starbird of the Edict, the Fourth Zone would in like hear of it. As had happened with Argilos and Tomas, they would surely descend on the Tenth Zone with a vengeance, seeking to claim both Sera and the Key to Orion's belt. He decided that the fewer who knew, the safer Sera would be. It was of utmost importance that he did not risk the passing of the prophecy and the future of Protogio. He must guard Sera's relevance to the Edict with his life.

Jerad looked at his friend. Not once could he recall Aryan ever looking at him with such contempt. It was disturbing, but also understandable.

"It is *my* honor you should defend my friend. Sondra was not fitting to take for a wife. Always, you have known what I intended when it came time to offer my crest. Do you deny it?"

Aryan's flinch did not go unnoticed by Jerad, but as soon as it appeared, it was gone. Aryan's countenance hardened. His arms came up between Jerad's, and with an outward thrust, he forcefully disengaged Jerad's grasp on him. Aryan hooted twice, calling his falcon. The bird came to perch on his gauntlet.

Jerad cocked his head back. If Aryan was of mind to be his foe, so be it.

"You are trespassing on my property Aryan," Jerad stated firmly, showing little emotion, other than the slight twitch to one side of his mouth. He deeply regretted the loss of Aryan's friendship. Since childhood, they had been as brothers-- inseparable. He could only hope that some *rise*, Aryan would come to understand and mayhap absolve him.

Aryan backed away. His glare fixated on Jerad. His expression warned of retribution as he disappeared around the corner of the castle.

Jerad returned to Sera.

Sera was sitting on a divan near the bookshelves. A book was open on her lap. She had found the journal of Argilos and flipped it open to the first page. There was a time of entry and information on the Gaians' first *rise* on Protogio.

It read:

First Hour 0900: We are amazed at the vivid colors and realistic images that our linking has created. Thomas verifies that his visions coincide with mine. It is indeed fascinating. There are people here and they call this world Protogio. We are enthralled with our ability to interact with such imagery, but they are irrelevant to our work. We will try to ignore them, but their interest in us might make that an impossible task.

Linking?

There was something bothersome about the word.

Sera did not read further. Her thoughts were suddenly distracted by Jerad's story of the Gaian's who had visited Protogio before her arrival. Jerad claimed that the Gaians often appeared and disappeared like magical spirits. This puzzled her. It was irrational to think such a thing. Perhaps they were merely being elusive with their arrivals and departures, not wishing to disclose the location of their ship. Such a sophisticated vessel might incite fear in a culture as primitive as this one. Or it could be that they needed to keep it safe from confiscation by the Protogions. Sera could readily envision the people here dissecting the craft to inspect its workings, thus leaving her fellow travelers stranded. Another, but more unlikely thought, occurred to her. Was it possible that there was an advanced technology on her world that she had yet to recall, one capable of transporting a person from place to place without use of a vehicle? It would explain Jerad's claim that she too had appeared from thin air. Sera turned her head upward, looking through the *crukis* skylight window. Was there a ship out there awaiting her call?

The explosion.

Sera's heart sank. The one face she remembered from the crash, was the same face she recalled while watching Jerad hug Phoebe.

Her brother.

Was he dead? Had she transported from the spacecraft before it exploded?

Sera slammed the book shut and dropped her head with a despondent sigh.

Why can't I remember?

She was pulled from her thoughts when Jerad returned to the chamber. He sat facing her, spreading one leg to each side of the bench. Sera looked up at him, and they silently stared at each other for several moments.

A crushing sense of guilt was consuming Jerad.

Damn you Sondra. Why did you have to be so stubborn? I did not expect your blood on my hands. I never wanted you to die!

He had caused such tremendous sorrow within Aryan's clan. How much more havoc would he reap for the sake of the Edict? How many more of his kinsman would question his loyalty before this over?

Jerad reached out to skim a thumb along Sera's cheek. It was soft and warm under his touch.

So lovely.

And those eyes--eyes that looked like they devoured the sun.

Did others feel the same when they looked at her, or did this strange allure he possessed for her belong solely to him? Aryan's comment about Sera's scent, and the thought of Aryan observing Jerad's lovemaking with her deeply irked him. The idea of Aryan- -*of other men*, obsessing over Sera, left him seething. Despite the Edict an overwhelming need to care for Sera engulfed him.

Sera is my wife.

Jerad felt reckless where Sera was concerned. All of his actions, since finding her, had been committed impulsively, irrationally, when he had never done so before. At swordplay or table gambling, even in the hunt for wild beasts driving them into traps, or over cliffs to the waiting arrows of his hunters, always he acted with tactic in mind.

Until now.

With Sera, he had no plan, knew not where this plight was leading, except that it must be allowed to go forward.

A knot wound tighter than a bow string squeezed inside of his chest. He dismissed the sensation as mere anxiety over the immense responsibility bestowed on him as Keeper of the Key and his obligation to his people.

Nai. There was an extrinsic command that was driving his actions.

And his infatuation with Sera.

He had married her by order of the Edict, he rationalized. The Oneroi were to blame for this peculiar devotion he felt for her. They were guiding his and Sera's fate and feelings. There could be no other explanation.

"Who was that?" Sera finally broke the silence.

"Aryan, Noble Chancellor of the Second Corridor."

"He is your friend, isn't he?"

"That is a thing that is in question at the moment."

Sera lifted a finger and traced it along his furled brow. He was strikingly handsome, but the fidelity she felt for him went well beyond simple physical attraction. There was an odd pressure in her heart when she looked at--when she thought about him, and she could not escape the nagging command that impelled her toward him like an overpowering magnetic force.

"He frightens me, Jerad. Even Ezra seemed unsettled by his aggression in the Grandstage earlier this rise."

"I would agree. There was much anger in his sword."

His expression softened.

"Do not fret overmuch my Starbird." He leaned forward and gently kissed her lips. "His growl is oft worse than his chomp."

Sera pursed her lips and drew her eyebrows together. She did not believe him.

Seeing he had done little to alleviate her concern, and not knowing what else to say, he did what any sensible male would do.

He changed the subject.

"What is this you are reading?" He turned the book to get a better look at it. "Ah *Nai*, the Gaian's journal. It was left behind. I learned some of their language, but not the letter symbols. I have been unable to discern the written words. Do you understand it?"

Sera nodded.

"Read it to me."

Sera inadvertently opened the journal to the last entry and read the passage.

Final Hour 1500: We have completed the final phase of our journey and have much to report, but the circumstances in our research have taken on more complexities than we had anticipated. Although our research has only carried us through a single day, our time on Protogio has extended over several weeks time. We suspect there is more authenticity to this venture than anyone would allow us to believe, but I feel it is something we must explore further. In regard to the people here, I have endeared them to me. I cannot deny that I will truly miss them. For now, the Chief Councilor Angus has informed us that the soldiers from the Fourth Zone are marching toward us. We will likely, not be present, to witness the final outcome. I bid you farewell my precious Protogio, and I leave you with these last words:

In the quiet of the night when cool, gentle whispers of breezes

caress my face with a glimmer of starlight,
I am lured by majestic visions, which draw me
deeper into the depths of this mysterious porthole,
 revealing brilliant horizons beyond,
too far to reach, yet dear to my heart,
I will never forget you, my castle in the air."

Sera stared at the words, studied them, memorized them. She laced her fingers together and pressed her clenched hands to her lips.

1500...military hours--three o'clock p.m.

Phase.

A single…day?

A string of disjointed pictures and voices played through Sera's memories. She could see her own hand penning words,

POSSUM, Phase I: 0800.

And hear her own voice saying, *Yes sir…got it…*

Jerad watched as Sera's expression turned from awareness to confusion. "You are remembering Sera?"

"I thought… there was something. I don't know." Sera shook her head. "It was nothing I understand."

She looked downcast. Jerad could not even imagine what it would be like to be tumbled into a foreign place with his mind a stranger to itself. His heart was suddenly heavy with compassion for Sera. How disturbing this dilemma must be for her.

He had done little to comfort her, yet she followed him blindly, trustingly.

"If ever you return to Gaia, you must seek Argilos out." His comment forced him to consider the possibility of Sera leaving him. Jerad cringed. He did not welcome the sinking feeling that thought gave him, and the likeliness that it would occur.

I am her husband.

The reality of that fact hit him harder than a falling boulder to the head. In that moment he realized that he was more than *just* her husband. He would die a thousand deaths if he ever had to let her go.

Chapter Twelve

Jerad and Sera were summoned from the dwelling, by courier. Their supper would be taken in Shegarth's private meeting chamber, a stately room just inside the Great Hall. Following the meal, the Magistrate would hold assembly to discuss Zone issues among other matters.

Jerad pulled out a chair next to Phoebe and motioned for Sera to sit. He took a seat in the chair on Sera's other side, the first chair next to the head of the table. Sera looked from one end of the impressive table to the other. It was a massive, oval shaped piece, made of ebony, large enough to accommodate at least forty people. Small daggers for cutting food and bowls of water with cloth napkins used for cleansing hands, were set about the table.

Sera ran her fingers along the tabletop, leaving a trail of smudges on the highly polished, black wood surface. She surreptitiously glanced around to see if anyone had taken notice of her minor indiscretion, and wiped the evidence clean using the edge of her conjugal cloth. A low chuckle resounded in her ear and she turned her head in time to see Jerad's amused grin.

"I used to splotch this table with my sticky little fingers when I was a child." His eyes twinkled as he fondly recalled the memory. A puckish smirk crossed his face. "Too much temptation for a boy who reveled in mud frolicking."

Jerad flattened his palm against the surface. When he lifted it, he left behind a perfectly shaped handprint.

"A small token for the chamber maid I tormented with my leavings. She is an old woman now, but I am sure she will be endearingly ruffled by my little gift."

"You are quite the mischief maker husband." Sera smiled. She wished she had known him as the impish boy he apparently used to be.

Jerad appraised her with genuine warmth. It was the first time she referred to him as *husband*, and he liked the sound of it on her lips--lips he now bent toward to brush with his own.

Smacksmacksmack.

Phoebe's lips were puckered and she was making kissing sounds in his direction.

She looked like a fish.

Jerad reached around Sera's shoulder and lightly smacked the top of Phoebe's head in response to her teasing. "Button it up sapling."

Phoebe stuck her tongue out at him.

Sera quietly laughed.

"Tsk, tsk my begats, must I send you to your chambers without supper?" Shegarth, who had just entered the chamber, did not miss the sibling exchange. There was immense affection in his countenance as he gazed upon his children. Shegarth placed a kiss on Phoebe's cheek and moved behind Sera. He set a large, friendly hand atop of her shoulder and offered an accepting nod as he passed by. Sera nodded timidly in return. She remembered his presence in the Grandstage the *luna* of her arrival. Now, with less commotion surrounding her, she saw the evidence of paternity in his character. His features, his stature, the way he walked, were so obviously akin to Jerad, save the salt and pepper hair.

"Father." Jerad stood and inclined his head toward his sire. The two men embraced briefly.

Shegarth took his seat at the end of the table, nodding and greeting the arriving guests. The table would be full this *luna*. Along with the members of the Council, kindred and close friends were present. In two *rises* Jerad and Sera would receive their Marks of Permanence. By invitation, these guests had come to witness the event.

"Welcome everyone." The Archon stood and raised his goblet.

He turned to where Jerad and Sera were sitting. "And welcome to my daughter of the Mark, consort of my son, Jerad."

He tapped the base of his cup twice on the table in a congratulatory toast, and took a sip. The rest of the guests did the same. Sera shifted slightly at being the center of attention once again, but she accepted the acknowledgement graciously with a slight bow of her head.

A memory surfaced. Sera turned to Jerad, and smiled brightly. "Let me show you how it is done where I come from."

She raised her goblet and Jerad followed her lead. There was the tiny chime of crystal touching crystal as she tapped the rim of her glass to his. Sera entwined her arm around Jerad's bent arm, and brought the cup to her lips. She took a sip. Jerad peered at her over the rim of his own cup as he drank, enjoying the intimacy of the Gaian practice.

"I think I much like your way better," Jerad set his goblet onto the table, and then he frowned. "Though I am not sure I wish for you to share this gesture with others."

...men.

"*Ochi,* Jerad. Only with you." Sera smiled. There was a sultry flicker in her eyes.

She slowly licked her lips. Her expression hinted sensual

promise. Jerad hooked a finger under her chin and traced her bottom lip with his thumb. Sera tentatively drew the tip of it into her mouth and then coyly lowered her lashes, somewhat surprised by her own playful behavior. Jerad beamed a dazzling, white smile, taking thorough pleasure in her unrestrained dalliance, meant solely for him.

His eyes darted around the table. The guests were quietly engaged in their own discussions and paid them no heed. He growled from low in his throat, wishing they were alone.

The platters arrived with a variety of steaming foods and cold dishes. They were arranged along the length of the table, and the guests began to serve themselves, passing the plates when they had taken their fill.

Sera nibbled at her food, much of it unidentifiable by shape and color, but tasty to the palate nonetheless. She attempted to listen to the casual conversations, but her thoughts kept drifting to the Argilos' journal. The looming prickle of finality that the entries seemed to imply unsettled her. She was pulled from her thoughts by a sudden barrage of questions directed her way.

"Sera, what Zone do you call home?"

"I... uh," her mouth dropped open, but what could she say?

"What bloodline Origin do you claim?"

"How came you into the company of the Noble Jerad?"

Sera's head bounced from face to face.

"Hush!" Jerad intervened. "As you all well know, my wife has had a trying few rises."

"Is she ill?" the woman across from her remarked as she stared at Sera's bewildered expression.

"Of sorts, Rhondia." Jerad placed a reassuring arm around Sera's shoulder. "A blow to her head has left her vacant of her memories."

"What a terrible thing!" Rhondia replied. The other guests murmured their agreement.

Great. Now she was being pitied.

Sera could not have felt more pathetic, but much to her relief the subject was quickly forgotten as the guests began to converse on new topics.

The supper was nearly finished and the dishware was being cleared. Guests began rising from their chairs bidding their thanks to Shegarth. The room emptied until all that remained were the Magistrate members, Sera and Phoebe.

Sera turned to Phoebe. "Where did everyone go?"

"To find their amusements." Phoebe looked pensive for a moment, then she grew cheerful. "I will show you my chamber."

Phoebe looked to Jerad and he nodded his approval. He took Sera's hand and gently patted it. "The Magistrate Council has orders of business to attend to. I am sure you will find it tedious. I will find you when we have finished.

An attendant entered the room and placed a small stack of papers in front of Shegarth. The Chief Magistrate shuffled through the documents and began passing them to other Council members.

Phoebe yanked Sera from her chair, pulled her across the room and out of the room. Sera spared Jerad a quick glance before Phoebe closed the arched, wooden double doors. Phoebe took Sera's hand and began to run with her. Sera dug in her heels. She did not want to run through the halls like a frolicking youth.

She was much too old for that!

Disappointed, Phoebe slowed her pace.

She led Sera through a maze of hallways until Sera knew she was hopelessly lost. Phoebe finally halted near a guard who stood in front of a single doorway. The guard raised a fist, slapped it to the opposite shoulder and bowed his head. He then removed a key from his belt and slipped it into the door's keyhole. With a click he pushed the door open for them.

Sera peered into the cavity, but all she could see was the beginnings of a twisted staircase that disappeared around a curved wall.

Phoebe clasped Sera's hand once again and they began to ascend. After what seemed like endless upward spiraling, it finally dawned on Sera that they were climbing to the top of a tower. She questioned Phoebe and indeed it was the tallest tower in the castle- -the very same one that caught Sera's eye outside of the castle.

Sera was a bit winded when they finally reached the door at the top. Phoebe in all her youthfulness was barely out of breath. Phoebe opened the door and pulled Sera inside.

My goodness! Sera's eyes widened.

* * * *

The Inceptive Chancellor Rhondia, a Noble of the First Corridor, waited until the doors were closed before speaking. "The Noble Chancellor Aryan will not present himself this luna?"

"He has given his pardon for this assembly." Shegarth answered impassively. He made no further comment, but knew it was futile to hope there would be no issue with the Challenge that occurred for the Rite of the Cloak.

"There is rumor that Aryan will seek requital for Sondra's death." This statement came from the Inceptive Chancellor Jason, who was seated at the opposite end of the table.

"It is more than rumor Chancellor. I spoke with him last luna," Chief Chancellor Fremi, a female of the Second Corridor, chimed in. "His clan pressures him."

"I heard as much Fremi." Jason agreed. "My consort is friend to Ezra, and they spoke earlier this rise. But I am told that Aryan struggles with his anger, his loyalty to our Noble Jerad, and loyalty to his kinfolk."

Shegarth watched through the corner of his eye as Jerad's disposition visibly stiffened. "What penalty do they seek?"

"His clan seeks Sera's servitude in their house for her remaining term cycles."

Jerad clenched his fists. *Never.*

"They would own her like a slave?" Shegarth straightened and raised an eyebrow.

"Ah Archon, slave is such a harsh word." Rhondia responded to his look of surprise. "After all we do not adhere to bondage as do some Zones. *Ochi*, she should be allowed to move about freely, perhaps even continue to dwell in the house of Jerad, but she would be indentured to Aryan's clan house."

"I do not find the request much severe considering they have lost one of their own." Fremi added.

"Would you agree to those terms, Jerad?" Shegarth looked at his son. All heads turned to Jerad and the Council silently awaited his response.

"*Ochi*. I will not allow her to become a common thrall." Jerad did not attempt to hide the irritation in his voice.

Shegarth was not surprised by his son's reaction. Jerad was never one to compromise his convictions and his devotion to Sera was acutely obvious. As Chief Magistrate however, it was Shegarth's obligation to oversee Council deliberations and his duty to remain unbiased, despite the fact that it was his son who was the focus of this charge. Additionally, it was preferable to settle disputes civilly rather than through the Challenge, and in this particular case, a Challenge that would most certainly bring no contentment to all involved. Sondra was dead, and nothing could amend that circumstance.

"The Magistrate could urge them to consider a lesser punishment, Jerad, one that is shall I say, of a less lengthy in term." Shegarth stood as he presented his appeal. "Would the

Magistrate consent to a compromise in punishment if the clan approves?"

There were several nods of agreement. It was a reasonable proposal.

"You misunderstand Council members," Jason interrupted. "Servitude is only their first request. They wish the marriage bond be severed as well."

Jerad jerked from his chair nearly toppling it. "By what reason!"

"They claim a tainted bloodline."

"What is it of their concern as to the bloodline from which she was sired?"

Shegarth held up a hand and commanded them to hush. He ordered his attendants to leave the chamber, and then turned to the six Proletariat representatives of the common citizens. He bowed his head.

"I beg for your pardon and mean no condescension to the people of our Zone. We will deal with the municipal grievances momentarily. For now I must ask you take your leave while we discuss this delicate matter further."

The Proletariat commoners conceded to his request and Shegarth escorted them to the door. He thanked them and apologized for the disruption, then soundly closed the door when they were gone from the chamber. He was relieved they gave no protest. It was essential that the forthcoming discussion be handled with the utmost discretion.

Shegarth returned to his place at the table and took his seat. He exhaled harshly as he rubbed the back of his neck, attempting to ease the knot that was forming there. He lifted his head and fixated on Jerad's face.

"As Keeper of the Key, son..." He cleared his throat and rectified, "...Noble Chancellor, it is your duty as well as ours to ensure the pure bloodlines not be corrupted, less the Key fall into unsavory hands."

"She is at the least of a Noble house with an allegiance Zone, is she not?" Rhondia looked toward Jerad and awaited his answer.

Jerad did not respond, and he would not lie, though he was sorely tempted.

"We realize that a bond between you and the female has transpired, but we must question if your enchantment with her has misted your logic."

Jerad bit back the anger that the accusation caused. Losing his temper would resolve nothing. He drew a deep breath and reined control over his precarious emotions. "I assure the Council that my judgment in regard to Sera is perfectly coherent."

"Your allusive behavior causes suspicion, Noble. If you make her Origin clear to us," Jason urged. "We might deny the demand to annul the bond."

Jerad slashed his hand through the air as he infused the Council with a look of indignation. "Her status was proclaimed with the handling of my sword."

Shegarth placed a firm hand on Jerad's forearm. In want to settle this without bloodshed, he beseeched his son. "Sera's identity could change this entire circumstance."

Shegarth knew the truth. He and Jerad had spoken in length about it. There was no doubt in his mind that Sera was exactly who Jerad claimed her to be. Though he disagreed, Shegarth fully understood Jerad's refusal to enlighten the Magistrate Council. Their carelessness with the two Gaians had ended tragically, and Jerad would not risk Sera's life.

Jerad glared at his sire, concern betrayed in his unblinking eyes. He subtly shook his head from side to side. Shegarth tipped his head in return, confirming that he would respect Jerad's silence.

Jerad turned to address the assembly. "Sera's status exceeds that of every Noble in this chamber and in that I ask you to take heed. Her loyalty lies where it should and not with that of our enemies."

The Noble Chancellor Larz, who had remained quiet during the discourse, leaned forward to speak. "Council, we talk of punishment and of descent, but we have yet to determine if a crime has indeed been committed."

"An unjustifiable death has occurred by a fatal blow, purposefully delivered," Fremi said.

"*Nai.*" Jason rose from his chair and with his palms raised upward, he gazed around the table. "Such is forbidden in a simple Challenge for the Rite of the Cloak. It is as such according to our laws. Can one here deny this?"

Silence washed over the chamber. Jerad gritted his teeth and muttered an oath. Even he could not refute their laws.

"Then we do concur that punishment must be rendered."

"The fault lies with Sondra!" Jerad roared before another word could be spoken. "She should have called for a halt!"

"Someone most certainly should have called for a halt," Larz added with a near sarcastic tone. He leaned back in his chair and crossed his arms.

Murmurs erupted from the Nobles around the table, and the

volume of their voices quickly increased as they began to argue among themselves.

"Order!" Shegarth bellowed.

All conversation ceased.

"I agree a halt should have been called, but I plead with the Magistrate to consider the circumstances. Had Sera called a halt, she would have relinquished Jerad's cloak. If Jerad had called a halt, he would have relinquished his claim to Sera. Additionally, we have questioned the numerous witnesses present in the Grandhouse that luna, and they all agree that Sondra had obvious intent to kill Sera. Had I foreseen the outcome of the Challenge, I would have called a halt myself and left the decision of victory to the Council."

"My honorable Nobles, in defense of the Archon's words, I was present in the Grandstage and the deed had been done before any of us had the clarity of mind to call a halt," Rhondia defended, petitioning the Council for leniency.

"Regardless," Fremi looked at Rhondia to dispute her claim. "Sera should have withdrawn her blade. She should have cried a victory."

"It was clearly and act of censurable misconduct," Jason agreed.

Shegarth drew his brows together. "Sondra would have retaliated so say the witnesses. Sera's only recourse would have been to turn and run. There is no honor in that."

Larz gave pensive consideration to the Council's discussion before adding his own thoughts. "*Nai*, that is true Archon, but in doing so it would have given enough space in time to call a halt."

"Sera could not have possibly known that." Jerad argued. "She is not of our Zone."

"Ignorance of our laws is no excuse, Jerad. It should have been explained to her."

Jason moved away from his place at the table and walked its length until he was alongside Shegarth's chair. He nodded to the Chief Councilor, before turning to face the Magistrate Council. "Failure to adhere to the Zone's dictates resulting in an unlawful death shall be declared as the crime. Are all agreed?"

A mutual response of *Nai* was voiced by all members, with the exception of Shegarth, Rhondia and Jerad.

Rhondia pursed her lips as her eyes darted between Jerad and Shegarth. Her expression was apologetic. Her shoulders slumped and she uttered her *Nai* as well.

Jerad turned helplessly to his sire. "Father…"

"My hand will be forced with this my son. Will you accept any compromise, Chancellor?" Shegarth's tone was sympathetic and he shared his son's distress. The Council appeared settled on their decision.

Jerad's chest heaved. The tempo of his breathing quickened as a burgeoning outrage assailed him.

Restraint be damned!

He would kill for Sera if forced to.

Jerad unleashed his anger. "Sera stays with me as she is. The bond will not be severed!" He slammed his fist against the table top.

"Aryan's clan has the right of it to issue a Challenge, Noble Chancellor."

"Then the Challenge will be accepted." Jerad lowered himself to his chair. Anger radiated from his tense expression, as he responded to Jason's warning.

The matter was closed for now.

Chapter Thirteen

Phoebe was a slob. There was no other word that came to Sera's mind. Every bit of floor space in the enormous, circular bedchamber was covered, leaving little of the carpet visible to the eye. Clothing was scattered, hanging from Phoebe's canopy bed or crumpled in piles. Books, weapons, and debris that looked suspiciously like the remnants of food, were carelessly tossed about.

"Do you not have a chamber maid, little one?"

Phoebe merely shrugged, telling Sera that the elderly maid was too frail to climb the lengthy stretch of stairs each *rise* and came only once every few *rises* to do the cleaning.

"Surely Mesari must scold you for this?"

"Mesari is not my keeper," Phoebe responded defiantly.

Feeling she had no authority to further scold the girl, Sera relented and followed Phoebe to the balcony overlooking the Zone.

The landscape was speckled with white and blue *crukis* lights hinting at life below. There was no moon this *luna*, Sera noticed. The darkened skies served as a vast milieu for the twinkling stars above.

Orion's constellation was among them, shining high over their heads and winking brighter than any other stars in the sky. Phoebe described its pattern to Sera pointing one by one to each star and naming them all, but it was the belt of Orion that intrigued Sera the most. She stared at the three stars for a long time watching as the constellation traversed counterclockwise in its journey through the lunar sky. Sera knew immediately that she had seen it before, but somehow it looked different. She didn't know why.

What do you want from me?

She frowned when no answer came.

Who am I to these people? Why am I here?

Her brain responded with an ominous silence.

"Are you listening Sera?"

"What? Oh, I'm sorry Phoebe I was just..." Truthfully, Sera had only been half listening to Phoebe's girlish chatter, nodding occasionally and adding a few *uh huhs* for good measure.

"Never mind." Phoebe brushed of her annoyance, took Sera's hand and pulled her back inside. "I will sculpt your hair."

Sera was in no mood to have her hair fussed with, but feeling a bit guilty over having ignored Phoebe, she reluctantly consented. After shoving aside a heap of items from her bed Phoebe directed Sera to sit. She began brushing and tugging at the strands of Sera's hair all the while prattling to Sera about her friends and favorite things to do. Sera was sure the girl would never come up for air.

"Done!" Phoebe finally announced. She gave Sera a hand mirror and pulled her over to a larger one standing in the corner. Sera surveyed Phoebe's work and was astonished to discover that the girl had talent. Sera's hair was pulled tight on the sides with only a few wisps left free in the front for bangs. In the back Phoebe had woven the strands into an intricate overlapping pattern and then secured the loose ends with six, golden beads.

"I will do your hair for the Marks of Permanence."

Sera was about to ask about that when she spotted a very sad looking excuse for a doll sitting on Phoebe's bed. Sera crossed the room and picked it up.

"Where did you get this?" Sera stared at the misshapen toy in her hands. The eyes were two misaligned buttons and the smiling yarn mouth was sewn askew. The hair flared around the oversized head making the doll look as though it had received a terrible fright. The arms were evenly sewn, but one leg was longer than the other, and the dress was a patchwork of mismatched materials. It was thread bare and evidently well loved. It gave new meaning to the word rag doll.

Sera thought that it had to be one of Mesari's early attempts at sewing. She could only hope that Mesari's skill had improved given that the seamstress was in the process of creating a wardrobe for her.

"Jerad made it for me when I was only two term cycles." Phoebe spoke through a wide yawn as she crawled onto to the bed.

Jerad made this?

With his own two hands?

What a caring thing to do, Sera thought.

And how contradictory--ferocious warrior, tender nurturer.

How sweet of him. How appealing… and handsome too… and a good kisser.

A girl could swoon.

Sera hugged the doll to her bosom. It was a gift from the heart, created out of love for his sister. Sera recanted her original thought. The doll was the most beautiful thing she had ever seen. A twang plucked in the center of her chest. Sera gulped with the sudden gush of emotion assailing her. Her heart was singing Jerad's name. It amazed her how only a few *rises* ago her life had been thrown into a turmoil of uncertainty, but now just the thought of him soothed her, eased her bereavement of a misplaced past. At that moment Sera wanted to be with her husband.

Phoebe snuffled and turned over. She had fallen asleep while Sera was admiring the doll. Sera was grateful for the opportunity to slip away. She tucked the doll next to Phoebe and quietly left the tower bedchamber.

Sera snaked her way down the spiral of stairs hoping the guard was still posted at the bottom door.

What a boring job standing watch over a door must be, Sera judged as she pushed the door open.

Or not… she reconsidered, startled to find a woman pressed between the guard and the wall. She cleared her throat.

"I beg your pardon Lady Noble." The guard backed away from the woman and bowed toward Sera. "I thought you had retired with the Noble Phoebe for the luna."

"Never mind." Sera slashed her hand through the air. "Would you be so kind as to direct me to Shegarth's apartments?"

The watchman readily obliged her. Sera repeated the information twice and thanked him. She started down the passage, but then stopped and turned around. Her eyes swung between the guard and the woman.

"As you were, warrior." She gave him a sly smile.

Having the courtesy to look abashed, he lowered his lids and repressed a grin.

Sera snorted and walked away. She whistled a tune, and a clamor of words filled her head as she remembered her favorite love song. She traipsed through the halls and after a few wrong turns and further directions from late *luna* strollers, Sera finally found the familiar double doors to Shegarth's hall. Sera eased the door open and peered in. The Magistrate Council was still deep in discussion. Sera discreetly retreated without being observed. She found a bench and sat down to wait for Jerad.

Jerad remained with Shegarth after the Magistrate Council dispersed. They discussed the charges and how they might effectively guard Sera should the Challenge be lost. Both agreed that if Aryan's clan were to win charge of her, then the Magistrate would be told that Sera was the Ptino asteri. Though Aryan might be reluctant to believe it, the information might give him pause enough to prevent Sera from being harmed. Aryan had been ordained as one of the Guardians of the Key. Despite his anger, he would be forced by the Magistrate to honor that vow. Jerad was not satisfied with this decision, but dead men offer little protection, and if he were to die…

Blasted. He could not think on it.

It was nearly *full luna* when an exhausted Jerad finally left his father. He intended to retrieve Sera from Phoebe's chamber and take her to bed, but found her curled up on a large cushioned bench in an alcove just a few paces down the hall. She slept on her side with her back to him, her arms folded comfortably across her belly. Jerad sat behind her and placed a palm on her thigh. She stirred slightly but did not awaken. His attention was drawn to the weave in her hair.

Another victim for my sister to ply her craft on. His lips turned up into a half smile as he admired his sister's work.

He fondled the mesh with a delicate stroke, aching to thread his fingers through it, undo it, spread the dark, wavy mane around Sera's head as he kissed her beautiful face.

Should he wake her?

Ack. He could not disturb her. They had found little peace since coming home and she looked like a seraph in her tranquil slumber, unaware--innocent. Her chest rose and fell with such contentment that Jerad's own breathing caught the rhythm and eased some of his woes.

Jerad splayed his fingers through his own hair and sighed, weary from this *luna's* events. He contemplated all that had been argued at the assembly, holding no blame against the Council for their conclusion. It was justifiable. An untenable death had occurred in what should have been a simple Challenge for the Cloak.

Hades blood. He could skewer himself for the wretched blameworthiness he felt about the whole thing.

It was for the best that he informed the Council he would accept a Challenge even prior to it being declared. The Magistrate was being naive if they expected to negotiate terms of punishment with Aryan's clan. Jerad knew Aryan's kin well, having spent much time in their company. He was keenly aware that their anger would supplant any penalty offered, other than corporeal punishment. They would seek blood for retribution and nothing less.

What a burden the Origins had bestowed on him.

Why?

Why had he been chosen for such an arduous task? Why had another not been favored?

Sera, that was why.

She belonged to him even before he met her, and no one...*no one* would take her from him. The thought of another having her rattled his sanity, boiled his blood, tore at his heart.

His body jolted against the invasive and unwanted vulnerable feelings.

Duty, he convinced himself, *and Honor.*

Jerad unclasped his cloak and nestled himself against Sera's back, covering them both with his mantle. His attraction to her was merely physical, the intention of the Oneroi to keep him at her side, to ensure he would protect her--so the Edict could be fulfilled.

Nai. That was a good explanation for it.

Chapter Fourteen

Sera slowly opened her eyes. She did not remember falling asleep. It seemed like very early in the *rise*, but she felt revitalized for the first time since entering this alien world. She took a deep breath and attempted to stretch. Several things occurred to Sera as she fully awakened. She was pinned to a rock hard wall--*a breathing wall*, by a bracket of muscled steel. A large masculine arm was wrapped around her and a hand was slipped into the top of her dress, covetously cupping...*her breast?*

That had better be Jerad behind me, she mused, but knowing it could only be him.

Sera snuggled against him then stiffened, suddenly disturbed that he would take such intimate liberties while she was in a state of unawareness, but more so with her own feelings that she liked it. That was quickly replaced with distress that a passerby might have seen them there. She was relieved to discover they were covered by a cloak. All thoughts dissipated when she realized that she had to *pee--badly*. But she couldn't move.

Sera poked Jerad with her elbow. His grip around her tightened.

Damn. Just wake him up Sera.

Jerad snored.

She took pity on him. He was tired. It must have been a long *luna* for him, and god only knew they hadn't had much rest. Sera wriggled out from under his arm and carefully climbed off of the bench. She paused briefly to admire her husband's gloriously formed body, and then strode off down the hall.

When she reached the end of the passage she looked left and then right.

Hmn. Which way should she go?

She had come from the left last *luna*. Sera shrugged and turned right. She soon found herself standing in a large open vestibule, an exhibition hall she believed, if the numerous sculptures, tapestries and paintings were any indication.

"Don't move," a voice echoed from across the room. Sera stilled, but she wasn't afraid. She recognized that voice. It was a kind voice, a trustworthy voice.

A head peered out from behind a large canvas set on an easel. Sera smiled.

"Why do you wish that I not move Noble Mekal?"

"Ah Sera, you know me."

"From the path in the village." She nodded.

He looked pleased.

"You have not answered my question Noble."

He moved around the canvas, crossed the room and came to stand in front of her. When she saw him on the path, he wore the colours of the Eighth Zone, a blue feather pierced with a gold ring, anchored on a black, jagged bar. His attire on this *rise* was much more casual, a loose flowing, black, pullover shirt hung over tan, suede trousers. His attire was smudged with paint. Sera peered up at him and studied his face. It was a face that made her feel quite comfortable--and his eyes. She knew those eyes. Sera drew her brows together.

But from where?

The thought was interrupted when Mekal brought his hand to her chin and he turned her head from side to side.

"*Nai*, a fine subject to grace my canvas. You will let me paint you, gracious lady?"

He stepped back from her and bowed.

"I would be delighted Noble Mekal, but I have a more urgent need at the moment." She leaned in and whispered, "I need to find the...uh...facilities."

Mekal tipped his head in questioning regard. "And what facility would you like me to direct you to?"

"Ya know, the bathroom?"

"You wish to take a bath?" He tipped his head to the opposite side.

"No, not the little girl's room."

"I don't believe we have a gathering place for our female youthlings."

"No damn it! The toilet! I have to pee!"

Exasperated, Sera dropped her head and scanned the floor. This was embarrassing. Why didn't he understand her?

What the hell did Jerad call it?

Actually he hadn't called it anything. He just showed her.

Mercy, was she going to have to explain it to Mekal?

"So many words for one little room."

Sera looked up to find Mekal was smirking at her. Her eyes widened. "You're teasing me?"

He smiled broadly and pointed to a door at the back of the gallery.

"Very funny. Ha ha." Sera brushed by Mekal, tossing him a sneering look. She didn't think it was possible but his smile expanded even further, and his shoulders shook with his brief, convulsive laugh. When he could no longer see her face, Sera's feigned expression relaxed. Her frowning mouth was replaced with a grin. Though she could not say why, she felt an unqualified allegiance with Mekal. It was poles apart from the feelings that Jerad stirred in her. Jerad made her heart dance, awakened her passions. With Mekal she did not feel such a physical yearning. With him, she felt a friendly, collected ease.

Sera finished taking care of her needs and emerged from the privy chewing on a fresh mint leaf she had picked from a bowl near the wash basin. At least she hoped it was a mint leaf. It tasted like mint anyway. She shrugged and headed toward Mekal, glancing at a small canvas she was passing. At first she thought it was a painting of a bird, but did a double take and stopped when she realized it wasn't a bird at all. It was an image of a man with wings--artificial wings.

A kite, she thought. *No, no, a hang glider.*

Mekal came to stand beside her. "Daedalus, of whom I am a descendant, was an Origin with great ingenuity. He fabricated the wings and gave the Eighth Zone the gift of flight. We refined its design. The glide flyer is one of my Corridor's greatest achievements."

"You fly?" Sera was astounded that they had such knowledge.

"All in the Eighth Zone take wing. It offers expedience to effectively survey the territory. Our Sky Sentries also do battle from the air."

Sera leaned against a pillar and crossed her arms. "Well, I'm impressed."

It would have been convenient if one of them had flown overhead when she and Jerad were traveling the plains.

Mekal set one of his hands on top of her folded forearms. "I could teach you to fly, Sera."

He watched her face brighten, but it was not for him or his suggestion. Her attention was drawn beyond him.

"Or not."

Mekal turned his head to the voice to see Jerad crossing the gallery. He released Sera's arm as Jerad stepped between them. If Mekal had not known Jerad for most of his life, he would have taken pause with the ferocious expression Jerad directed his way. Instead, Mekal returned Jerad's avaricious glare with an expression of unspoken humor. The jealousy on Jerad's face was so vivid that Mekal could have pressed a canvas to it and made an impression. Jerad had always been the impassive sort. Seldom did he show emotion over much of anything, least of all a woman. It was touching to see his friend in such a tattered condition, and quite amusing.

Mekal casually strolled to his pallet of paints, and dabbed a brush into a tray of pale green. He swept it along the canvas.

"Do not question my integrity, Noble," Mekal spoke from behind the easel. With certainty, Jerad should not have a care where he and Sera were concerned. Mekal did not even consider *those* kinds of thoughts toward her. He liked her well enough, and her body was beguilingly touchable. Yet, he lacked what should have been a purely male reaction to her.

Mekal wrinkled his brow.

How odd. It was rare for him to be unaffected by a beautiful female. If there was anyone who loved women, married or not, it was Mekal, but with Sera it was unthinkable, forbidden somehow.

Jerad grunted. He would trust Mekal with a sword at his back, yet seeing him touch Sera left him feeling antagonized. He had never felt such a quirky sensation afore.

What was wrong with him?

"You do not wear jealousy well my friend." Mekal continued to paint without looking up from his canvas.

"I am not jealous," Jerad emphasized his words, a bit too zealously.

"You're jealous?" Sera looked at Jerad with both surprise and skepticism. "Of him?"

She pointed a finger in Mekal's direction. *Could Jerad actually have feelings for her that went beyond his damn fidelity to his Edict?*

Mekal turned his head away to hide his chafed pride. Sera was not attracted to him either. He sighed. *Dikaios, dikaios--Fair is fair.*

Jerad opened his mouth to vocally deny Sera's question when a child suddenly came running into the gallery.

"Noble! Noble!" The boy rushed toward them, his chest heaving for the breath that his long sprint through the castle denied him.

"What is it child?" Mekal inquired.

"Ezra…in the infirmary." The boy bent in half and pressed his palms to his knees. He panted heavily before speaking again. "Dagur was kicked by his horse. His face is crushed."

"Blood Hades! I have told that old man to take caution around those wild destriers of his!"

Jerad grabbed Sera's wrist and he ran with her from the hall. He pulled Sera through the hallways at such a hard pace that she had to hike her skirt to keep from losing her footing. They rushed through the castle, down one hall and then the next until they finally burst through the infirmary doors. Sera's lungs burned as she gulped for air. She watched as Jerad flew toward the plinth where the injured man was sprawled, and writhing in pain. Ezra was trying to force a long metal tube between his teeth.

Sera's stomach flipped when she realized the extent of the man's injuries. His nose was pushed to one side, his cheek bone was indented and his jaw was clearly out of place. Blood seeped from his mouth and nose as he gurgled for breath.

Jerad grabbed the tube from Ezra and made his own attempt to push it into the man's mouth. He tried to reset the man's jaw but its shattered pieces shifted abnormally at Jerad's handling. With a cracking sound Jerad repositioned the man's nose. The man continued to retch in his need for air.

"*Blasted* Ezra! We have to enter his throat!"

Ezra rose immediately and gathered supplies. Sera moved to a far wall and leaned helplessly against it while she watched Ezra and Jerad work. There was nothing she could do. She looked up at the blue ceiling, and the large white *crukis* dome light affixed to it, and shuddered with the memory of almost dying in this room.

Sera returned her gaze to the table. Jerad's masterful hands swept along the old man's neck as he counted the ridges beneath his skin. She winced when he plunged a thin blade into the injured citizen's throat. There was much blood at first, then hardly any at all, and Dagus had stopped jerking and moaning his pain, thanks to the remarkable properties of the herbs they used.

Ezra slipped a curved, metal cannula through the opening they created.

"Breath curse it," Jerad murmured through gritted teeth as he inserted a small plunger into the tubes inner core. He withdrew fluid to clear the opening.

Everyone in the room tensed.

Almost immediately Dagus tugged a breath through the newly formed airway. His chest began to move up and down rhythmically.

Simultaneously, Ezra, Jerad and Sera blew out the air in their own lungs with relief.

Jerad walked to a large basin of flowing water in the corner of the room. He threw off his bloody shirt and began scrubbing the blood from his hands. He dipped his head and drenched his hair and face.

"Noble, noble! Is he dead?" A young woman burst through the door and threw her body at Jerad's feet. She hugged his calves. Jerad bent and grasped one of her elbows, assisting her to stand.

"He is alive, Helen. We can only wait." Jerad nodded to where Dagus was resting. Helen followed his gaze.

"You saved him." She turned back to Jerad, grabbed his head and pulled it downward. She planted a kiss on each of his cheeks before moving to Dagus' side. Helen cautiously touched Dagus' chest and surveyed him from head to toe. She bent and lightly pressed her lips to his forehead. Ezra placed a sympathetic hand on Helen's back. Helen lifted one Dagus' hands to her cheek.

"Oh father, you old fool. I thought I lost you," Helen sobbed.

Sera watched Helen briefly before looking at Jerad. He was staring at his palms. His fingers were clawed and his hands trembled. Sera placed a hand on his shoulder. Jerad balled his hands into fists and then dropped them to his sides. He moved to a cot, slumped down heavily, and lowered his head.

Sera sat beside him and began wiping his forehead with a drying cloth.

"What you did was incredible."

Jerad looked toward the plinth where Ezra was immobilizing Dagus' jaw using a large metal band that circled him from under his chin to the top of his head.

Helen was gone. She had left the clinic without saying a word.

"It may have not been enough."

"But he will live?"

Jerad drew his brows together and pursed his lips. Concern was etched on his face.

"His condition is grave. I know not what damage there is inside." He closed his eyes. "If only Tomas had remained long enough to teach us the rest, to show us what to do to help the crushed bones mend."

"Tomas?"

Jerad nodded. "The ability to apply the throat tube was a gift from Tomas. He too was a physician and a scientist. He taught us some of the surgeries."

"Everyone here speaks often about gifts, from the Origins, from the Gaians. Why is that?"

"Most of our knowledge was not gained by our own means, Sera. What wisdom we do possess was given to us by the Origins and then some by the Gaians who followed." Jerad rubbed his forehead then raked his fingers through his damp hair. "We would not have survived otherwise. When the Origins abandoned us, our progress stopped. Even our numbers do not change. For every one that dies, only one is born. Argilos and Tomas brought hope to Protogio. We thought that our stale existence would finally come to an end. We are trapped in oblivion, disregarded and forgotten.

The Edict promises a continuing future for Protogio."

"I still don't know what it is I can do." Sera frowned. She would be lucky if she could remember how to tie a knot. "I should read the Edict, maybe that will help."

Jerad propped a booted foot on top of the cot and pushed himself against the wall. He extended his hand toward Sera. She shifted to his side and he wrapped a strong arm around her shoulder.

"I think now could be no worse or better than later. I will get the book for you when we return home."

"Yes, I think its time. I think I am ready now to read it," Sera nuzzled into the crook of Jerad's shoulder and Jerad tipped his head to rest his cheek against the top of her head. They both closed their eyes.

A slight tugging on Jerad's hair caused him to stir. Both he and Sera opened their eyes to discover an adorable child, who looked to be no more than three term cycles, had climbed on top of the cot. She sat on her haunches staring at them with the wide-eyed face of innocence. Jerad reached out and stroked the tiny girl's mop of yellow curls before lifting her into his lap.

Helen stood in front of them with three more small children in tow. She held out a squawking creature between her two hands. Sera blinked at it with astonishment. It looked like a disfigured chicken. The fowl had eight claws at the end of each foot, a squared, red beak that opened horizontally, instead of up and down, and the sound it made seemed more like a throaty rasp than a cackle.

"I am deeply grateful, Noble Chancellor. Please accept one of my best fowls." Helen held the bird out to him. Its wings sprang to life. It croaked and flapped wildly, scattering feathers about the room.

"*Ochi*, woman. Keep your *kotopoulo* to serve your clan. When the harvest is brimming and you have plenty, I will be honored to sit at your table and enjoy one of those fully cooked meals you are famed for."

Helen smiled and nodded.

The little girl perched on Jerad's thigh tugged his hair once again. "My grandpapa will be alright, Noble Jerad?"

"Your papa is a strong warrior, little one, but *ochi,* I cannot promise he will live."

Tears began to fall from her eyes. Jerad cradled her in his arms and hugged her to his chest. Sera's heart twisted at the sight, and she swallowed a lump in her throat. The girl looked so strikingly tiny and frail against Jerad's massive form, but the delicate way in which he held her was touching.

"Ah, little one, no matter what happens he will always be with you in here and here." Jerad pointed to her heart and her head. "He loves you and you love him. That can never be taken away."

Jerad leaned down and kissed the tip of her nose. He set her on her feet and patted her bottom. "Off with you now. Your mother needs you."

He watched her toddle over to her mother and siblings. Helen was blessed to have birthed four sweet babes. Though large families did still exist, most females of his generation had only one sireling, and some had none, not by their choosing. He and Ezra had been studying herbs to try to correct the problem.

Helen tucked her *kotopoulo* under one arm. She hailed and bowed. The four children did the same before following their mother out the door.

"That was kind of you," Sera's admiration for him was growing by leaps and bounds.

"Helen is overwhelmed with four children to feed, none older than six term cycles. Her husband mined the hills and was killed in a collapse. Her father is her only remaining kin. I could not accept payment from her just now, but I also did not want to insult her either. She earns her keep by serving meals in the agora. She can compensate me later."

Ezra appeared with a clean, linen shirt for Jerad.

"Much thanks, Ezra. Go home. You look tired." He yanked the garment over his head.

"*Nai*, but I will be back to relieve you later. Dagus will need watching through the luna. I will retrieve our apprentice to help."

Chapter Fifteen

Sera's pace was slow and deliberate. She was lost in thought, wondering how her disarrayed emotions had suddenly untangled themselves. Her heart found a peaceful acceptance, and a touch of something much deeper, with every glance she tossed Jerad's way.

Jerad remained in the infirmary attending to Dagus. He and Sera had eaten a light meal there. Their conversation during the meal remained casual, with Jerad telling Sera stories about the adventures he shared with Mekal and Aryan when they were young. He subtly brushed over any tales of Sondra. Sera listened with interest, thoroughly enjoying his company. She openly regretted that she could not offer more about her life to him as well.

"I do not need to know the details of your life to be enamored by your beauty and spirit, Sera. You are a remarkable woman," he told her, his words warmly wrapping around her.

She was delighted and soothed by his praise.

Sera stopped briefly to trace her fingers along the crease of her lips. They still tingled from the caressing touch of his mouth against hers, a gentle but passionate kiss they shared before she left him. She did not object when he sent her off alone. Her solitary walk through the castle was a much welcomed reprieve to consider what was happening to her feelings.

So many of Jerad's inherent qualities had been exposed to her over the last several *quarters*--Phoebe's doll, his courtesy towards Helen, the way he held the little girl preciously in his arms, his determination and concern with saving Dagus, and being clearly upset about not being able to do more--She had seen the slight, misty blear in his eyes, though he did well to hide it.

Jerad was kind, considerate, and attentive to all those around him, and especially to her--most especially to her.

And his touches--oh heavens!

His touches were like Elysium come to life.

All of it set the compassionate man he truly was apart from the fierce knight who frightened her at first. It seemed like eons had passed since that time.

Damn if that plunking in the center of her chest didn't start playing her again.

Sera was besieged with a growing awareness that she was falling fast, and she knew without uncertainty that Jerad would be there to catch her. If Sera had any residual doubts about Jerad they had dissolved on this *rise*.

Sera grinned.

It really was not all too dreadful.

Mesari and Phoebe were waiting at the door outside of the apartments when Sera arrived. They were accompanied by two attendants who held a stack of bundles containing the neatly folded clothes that Mesari promised to deliver.

The entourage followed Sera into the residence, and Mesari

directed the attendants to deposit the packages on the bed before dismissing them. Mesari and Phoebe stayed to help Sera smooth and hang the finely made garments. There was an assortment to choose from, altered to a near perfect fit on Sera's body.

"Oh my, what is this?" Sera held up a red leather bodice with two dags in the front, and a pair of black leather trousers. It had three buckle enclosures and a dipping waistline. The material was supple to the touch. The design seemed quite daring.

"If I wear this my stomach will show."

"You have such a nice figure, it will look wonderful on you."

"This is allowed?"

"It is a much accepted style," Mesari assured, "and a good material for sword sport."

Okay, so skin is in.

Sera could deal with that. Perhaps she should get her belly button pierced and shock them all.

"This is gorgeous."

Sera donned a sleeveless, full length, emerald gown. The bodice top was an embroidered satin with a cross-corded back and cinched waistline. From the waist, the gown was silk and slit down the front, revealing the black lace underskirt beneath. On her feet, she wore cross-gartered, black suede boots that ended midway up her calf.

"These clothes were already sewn. I only needed to alter them. Your gown for the Marks of Permanence will be finished and delivered at the morrow's quarter rise." Mesari remarked casually as she continued to hang Sera's clothes.

Seeing an opportunity, Sera finally asked what the Marks of Permanence entailed.

Mesari looked surprised by Sera's ignorance, but Phoebe quickly interrupted to explain Sera's memory loss.

"How awful." Mesari grabbed Sera and threw her arms around her.

"Actually," Sera admitted, "I am starting to get used to it."

"Well, then." Mesari took Sera's hand and they both sat down on the chaise. "Betrothals are arranged by parents while their children were young. This is done to ensure the continuation of the pure blood lines, and to retain one's Noble ranking. Once the betrothed reach the appropriate age, usually nineteen term cycles, they take the vows in a ceremony called the Rite of the Cloak. At this time, the groom presented his crest to his bride. The couple would then be draped in the colours of the male's clan. Vows of

Permanence or the words of promise are then pledged. The blood marks are rendered and blood is exchanged. In the Tenth Zone it is with piercing by thorns from the flower crest. In the Eighth Zone, a slash is made across the palms of the betrothed by a tiny, honed blade attached to the end of the plume. In the Fourth Zone it is done with a dagger. Once the blood between the pair is mixed, they are considered mated."

"Is it was permissible for the betrothal to be broken by the promised couple?"

"As long as both agree. The unwanted betrothal would then be annulled peacefully. If one does not agree and there is another suitor, then a Challenge for the Rite of the Cloak could be issued. A Challenge can only be made by a suitor of an acceptable bloodline, and when there is assurance that the crest would be accepted if he or she won. "Otherwise," Mesari shrugged, "There would be no point in challenging."

Challenges for the Rite of the Cloak did not require consent by the Council. There was only one reason to engage in such a Challenge. The reward to the victor was obvious. It did however require at least three non-clan witnesses to arbitrate any disputes about who had won the Challenge.

Sera already knew much of this, but it was the explanation of the Marks of Permanence that had her sitting motionless with wide-eyed astonishment and her mouth agape. These marks were to be inked into her flesh during a final celebration several *rises* after the vows were exchanged. Jerad alluded to this but Sera had not questioned him further.

Sera dragged her fingers through her hair and then opened her palm to study the conjugal cloth. She touched the area under her ribs where the blade had sliced her. She thought about the mixing of blood and marks so permanent they could never be erased. Sera looked at her left ring finger. It was not like wearing a ring. Yes, she remembered. This was what was done on Gaia. The married couple wore rings once they completed their vows--rings so displaceable that they could be removed at will.

The Marks of Permanence were just what they claimed to be.
Permanent.

They could not be hidden or denied. They were there for all to see, permanent markings to swear devotion to one's consort, sacred and binding. In just two *rises* she was expected to receive those marks, indelible engravings, never to be removed.

Then another thought struck her. "What if one dies and the other wants to re-marry?"

"A small knotted vine with the new consort's colours is added to the first."

"So a person could end up with markings all over them by the time they themselves die?"

Mesari laughed. "Just how many consorts do you assume one will lose and gain in a lifetime, Sera?"

"The way you guys like to hack each other up, probably a lot."

"*Ochi*, Sera, one does not lose a consort often, except maybe in old age, but when it does happen, it is acceptable for the widowed man or woman to take a lover if marriage is not desired of course!"

"These rituals of yours are incredible." Sera mumbled.

"It is the way of things, Sera."

"So I keep hearing." Sera frowned.

Despite her hesitancy about taking the Marks of Permanence, Sera was amazed to realize that she wasn't opposed to it either. She had seen the elegant design on Ezra's hand. It was quite lovely.

What a fierce and wondrous way to declare one's love! she thought, stunned by the sudden quickening in her heart. And Jerad would share this with her? Is that what he felt towards her, or was he doing this because of the Edict?

What if she was to be rescued? Would she return home bearing those marks? Could she even will herself to leave Protogio?

Would she want to?

"My brother loves you," Phoebe abruptly blurted, as though she had been reading Sera's mind. Sera and Mesari turned to stare at her.

Sera's eyebrows lifted. "What makes you say that Phoebe? He has only known me for a few rises?"

"He looks like a mush cake when he is around you," Phoebe giggled. She plopped down next to Sera and began working a small plait into one side of Sera's hair.

"Well of course he loves you, Sera," Mesari responded to Sera's look of doubt. "There are many women in the Zone who wished to be joined with Jerad, but he never showed interest in presenting his crest."

"*Nai*," Phoebe nodded. "Merati was even willing to challenge Sondra."

Sera's ears perked up. "Who?"

"She greatly desired my brother. Whenever she visited our

Corridor, she would always follow him about doing that woman thing with her eyes."

Phoebe's awkward demonstration of batting eyelashes made Sera laugh.

"Her feelings for Jerad were quite zealous, and she had the skill to match Sondra," Mesari added.

"She was beautiful too!" Phoebe exclaimed. "And also very nice. Not like Sondra who always pinched my ears."

"So why didn't she challenge Sondra?"

Should she even care?

Yes she cared.

"Jerad told her not to. He told her he would not offer her his crest."

"Hmph," Sera sighed. She had a lot to think about.

Phoebe held up a mirror so Sera could examine her hair. Sera nodded her approval, and then looked over her new wardrobe. There were two more pairs of trousers, a couple of blouses and vests, knee breeches, and another dress and skirt.

"Where are my jammies?"

"Your what?" Mesari questioned, unfamiliar with the term.

"Ya know, nightshirts, stuff to sleep in?"

Mesari chuckled. "I don't believe the Noble requested any."

Argh! The man was utterly incorrigible! Sera threw up her hands and marched from the bedchamber. Would she ever have any control of her own life in this place?

Her forward progress was briskly arrested. She slammed into Jerad's hard chest with a resounding *oomph* that was expelled from her lungs. He grabbed her shoulders to steady her and then held her at arms length.

"Are you alright, Sera?"

"Fine," she grumbled. "Just fine."

"You look beautiful wife."

"Thank you." She lowered her lashes and blushed prettily.

Good god!

Was she really that daft that a simple compliment from him could make her weak in the knees?

Apparently.

Sera looked up to meet his gaze. Gracious if that man didn't take her breath away!

Oh well, sleeping naked with him might have its advantages. She chose to ignore the perilous fluttering in her heart.

Chapter Sixteen

The Great hall was brimming with Nobles when Jerad and Sera arrived. They entered to the sounds of merry conversations and laughter. The aroma of roasting food wafted through the air as serving attendants scurried about, keeping the cups of the guests well filled.

Sera looked around curiously.

Long aisles on each side of the hall were separated from the large main area by thick, stone columns that ran both lengths of the enormous room. The columns jutted upward to meet the high ceiling, and were joined to their adjacent pillars by intricately molded arches. Below each arch, spindled railings enclosed a second floor. There were citizens along the upper level, many standing against the balustrades to watch the activity below. A large banner was suspended from a vaulted ceiling. It displayed the Tenth Zone's coat of arms. Three smaller banners hung beside it, baring the blazonry of the allegiance Zones. The majestic room served as a refectory, as well as, a place for entertainment. It was warmly lit, cheerful and welcoming, despite its expansive size.

Jerad scanned the room as they moved through the crowd. Sera couldn't help but notice that he seemed a bit edgy, but did not get the chance to question him about it amidst the constant greetings they received. Sera watched as yet another Noble approached Jerad. Their raised palms met in a strong clasp followed by a fisted knuckle to knuckle strike. To Sera, the Noble respectfully nodded.

The supper gong clanged, indicating that the meal was about to be served. Jerad and Sera took their seats at the table on the dais, a place occupied by the highest ranking Nobles in the hall. Presently, it was the Magistrate Council and their consorts.

"I see that Aryan remains absent," Jason remarked.

All eyes drifted to the two empty chairs reserved for Aryan and Ezra. Sera took notice of the cogitative glances exchanged between the Council members, but did not understand. Sera gave Jerad a perplexing look, hoping he would explain what was happening.

He did not.

Sera should have been irritated by that, but something deep within her entrails warned her that she would prefer not to know.

She also surmised that it was likely she would find out soon enough.

"Perhaps it is a favorable circumstance?" Fremi offered.

Jerad cast a glance toward his sire. Shegarth stroked his beard as he returned a doubtful visage.

"I think it is not likely," Jerad stated dryly.

With a resigned sigh, Shegarth motioned toward the next table. As it was the custom for every chair on the dais to be filled, he requested Mekal and Herus to step up. They readily obliged, of course. Sitting at the prominent table was an honor not to be refused.

Mekal kissed Sera lightly on the cheek as he took the vacant seat next to her, surprised by how spontaneously forthright it seemed. The gesture was an accolade of sorts, he supposed. He was fond of her and nothing more.

Sera looked at Jerad and shrugged.

Jerad eyed Mekal with circumspect. His unconscious self was telling him that Mekal was safe refuge for Sera, but his conscious self had weighty objection with Mekal touching her.

It was irrational thinking.

He trusted Mekal.

Jerad willed the negative feeling away.

When the guests in the Great Hall had eaten their fill, and the plates were cleared, they coalesced into small gatherings. A company of musicians began playing an upbeat tune. Some of the Nobles danced. Others tapped their feet as they chatted with their acquaintances. Many indulged in drink and game playing.

Mekal followed Jerad and Sera to the gaming tables, now set up along one side of the hall. They sat down to play a game called *merrills*. The game boards contained three concentrically placed squares connected at the mid points of their sides. Peg holes were evenly spaced around each square. The object of the game was to get three pegs in a line. This was called a *mill*. Once a mill was formed, one of the opponent's pieces could be removed from the board. Each time a player lost a peg he could choose to quit and take his losses, or he could add a gemstone to the ante and continue. The game was won once a player reduced an opponent's remaining pieces to two.

Jerad explained the rules to Sera and she challenged Mekal. She found her skill without haste, winning two of every three matches against him. Mekal finally threw up his hands after losing a handful of gems to her and turned the board over to Jerad, who smiled wickedly at Sera. He was a master at this pastime. His arrogance was quickly stifled. Sera defeated Jerad with little effort, drawing an appreciative chuckle from his lips.

"You are ruthless, wife."

"Yes, yes I am," Sera replied smugly as she scooped her winnings over to her side of the table.

"It seems you have met your match, Jerad." Ezra joined them, softly tittering at the double meaning behind her statement.

A rhymester approached the table. He was adorned in clashing colors--a block styled tunic of red and purple, and stockings striped in orange and blue. He looked quite comical. Sera nearly laughed at his motley appearance. Ezra did laugh.

The rhymester threw a fist to his shoulder and bowed so low, Sera thought he might fall over. He then bolted upright and stretched an open palm towards Mekal, cleared his throat and began to speak.

"The artist!" he announced. "Unwavering hands that hold the tool to dance the paint in final song."

He turned to Sera and tipped his head.

"Beauty preserved in endless time."

"Kudos!" Mekal reached into his cloak, withdrew a stone and flipped it to the man.

The bard bowed his thanks.

Sera assessed her collection of gems, pointed to a green one and looked up at Jerad. He shook his head. She pointed to a blue one and he nodded, letting her know it was a worthy reward for his short verse. Sera dropped the recompense into the man's palm. He looked at the gem and blinked. He dropped to a bent knee and kissed her hand before dancing merrily to the next table.

"How much did I just give him, Jerad?"

"Enough to keep him happy for seven rises."

"Enough to keep his woman happy for seven rises," Ezra corrected. She rolled her eyes. Such generosity was in Jerad's nature.

He was a good man.

It made what she was about to tell him that much more difficult.

She inhaled deeply, and her voice grew somber. "Aryan follows behind me, Jerad. He means to declare his claim this luna."

Jerad closed his eyes and nodded. "I expected as much."

"What's going on Jerad?" Sera asked.

Jerad held Sera's hands. "I wanted to spare you the worry, but…"

He was interrupted by the increase in mutterings and the crowd parting around them.

Aryan was stalking toward them, his boots treading against the floor with intense and hostile purpose. His expression roared with an unheard growl so fierce that Sera shuddered.

Oh, this does not look good.

He stopped an arm's length away from them. His eyes bore through Sera and then moved to do the same to Jerad.

Ezra grabbed Sera's forearm and motioned her to back away from the two men. Mekal came up behind Ezra and Sera, put a hand on each of their shoulders, and pulled them both even farther back. Many others were also moving away.

Aryan snapped his head back and curled an upper lip. Herus stepped forward along with other warriors, ready to pull the two men apart. They would not allow the Challenge to erupt in the Great Hall where others might be hurt.

"You must have dug her up from the muck in the Seventh Zone," Aryan snarled at Jerad.

Jerad went rigid with anger and his hand flew like lightening to Aryan's throat. "Consider this fair warning. Do not insult my wife."

This was the second time Sera had heard a deprecating reference about the Seventh Zone.

"Ezra, tell me about the Seventh Zone."

"*Ochi*, Sera. I do not think that you wish for me to expand on Aryan's insult."

"I do," Sera pressed. "How am I supposed to defend myself with ignorance?"

"I suppose it is only fair Sera, if you wish to know.

The citizens of the Seventh Zone are descendants of Himeros and Dionysis. They are hedonistic, incestuous and prone to overindulge in intoxication. The men are vile and aggressive, and the women lewd and shameless. Many are laden with scabs and diseases from a multiple of encounters with unclean men. Their offspring, many sired by couples who share the same bloodline, are often deformed or daft. That is, if they even survive the birth."

Well, Sera bristled, *that was quite a hefty insult.*

She was deeply offended and blushed with embarrassment.

Jerad stepped closer to Aryan. "Let it go, Aryan."

Aryan shoved him.

The murmurs in the crowd grew louder as the Nobles in the hall began to debate the issue amongst themselves.

"Your deceit brings misery to my family."

"That was never my intent, Aryan."

"You degrade your own bloodline by mixing it with a Seventh Zone whore."

Aryan was pointing directly at Sera, but his eyes remained fixed on Jerad. "I know where you found her and frankly, my Noble, I am disgusted and flabbergasted!"

Jerad felt the burning rush to his head as his fury escalated. He clenched his fists. At that moment he wanted to kill Aryan for his slander.

"My clan will not condone this revolting act of disparage. By justifiable cause sanctioned by the Magistrate Council of the Corridors in the Tenth Zone…"

Aryan swiftly drew his sword and jammed his blade into the wooden floor. It landed solidly between Jerad's feet. Jerad stood unflinching. Having sported the sword against Aryan on many occasions, he knew the warrior's precision with the blade was impeccable. He also knew that this would not be the time or the place that Aryan would choose to splay him open.

"Death Challenge!" Aryan spit venomously.

The hall fell silent.

A Death Challenge.

The glass Ezra was holding slipped from her hand, hit the floor and shattered. She truly did not believe that her husband would go this far.

Jerad had thought it, and now it had been declared. He was not in the least astounded that it had come to this.

"Aryan! Jerad! Is this necessary? Will an Honor Challenge not suffice?" Shegarth bellowed.

"Indeed Nobles. We can forbid this type of Challenge," Jason asserted.

Aryan turned a hostile leer to the Council members. "Do you tell me that my sister's life is worth naught?"

"State your terms, Aryan!" Shegarth snapped at him.

"If I am victor, it will be his blood in exchange for my sister's blood." Aryan looked pointedly at Jerad, "and this hypocrisy of a union will be forever severed! If I lose, Sera will give servitude in my house."

The members of the Council nodded. It was both appropriate and acceptable. Shegarth had no recourse to disagree. He was outnumbered.

His heart grew sick with worry. He knew Aryan and he knew

his son. It would be a brutal battle, as both warriors were fearless and unrelenting, and they were equally matched. Neither would yield to the other's sword. There could truly be no winner in all of this.

"Do you accept Noble Jerad?" Shegarth's voice actually cracked with the agony he was feeling.

"I accept."

What other choice did he have? The Council had given their consent.

Ezra moved forward, but was stopped when Mekal grabbed her upper arm. "Do not interfere Ezra. This matter must be settled. It is better for a man to face his anger than live a life in agony and merely pretend he is happy. This way is often the remedy."

"I am the one who killed Sondra." Sera wrenched her hands, feeling suddenly faint. "Why does he challenge Jerad instead of me?"

A strangled noise that was half chuckle, half cry emerged from Ezra's throat. "He could not have Sera. Look at you, and look at him."

Sera glanced down at her body, then to Aryan. It would be pure insanity to think she could fight a man that size even if he was blindfolded and had both his hands and feet tied.

"I can fight," Sera defended herself.

"Not like a warrior, Sera, and most definitely not with a sword."

"Can't the Magistrate Council stop this?"

Mekal gave Sera a sympathetic look. "It is they who approved it. The Challenges are a civilized way of diffusing anger, of settling disputes."

Civilized?

If Sera hadn't been so upset, she would have laughed in Mekal's face.

"But one of them will die!"

"It is possible."

"No," she whispered.

"It is the way of things, Sera."

"I am so sick and tired of hearing that."

A fight arose behind them, and it was then that Mekal realized that many arguments and riotous aggressions were erupting in the Great Hall. He had to remove Sera, else he may have to guard the Ptino Asteri in the midst of a chaotic melee.

That could prove difficult.

Mekal grabbed Sera's wrist, ushered her through the columns

and into one of the side aisles. At the same time he signaled his page. The boy was immediately at his side.

"Cry the herald, boy. A Death Challenge has been issued."

Mekal then dragged Sera down the aisle and hustled her away from the Great Hall.

Jerad turned to catch a glimpse of Sera leaving with Mekal.

"*Nai*, I see how faithful your whore is," Aryan taunted. "She has already chosen your successor."

Jerad growled and punched Aryan in the nose. Aryan moved to retaliate. They were both subdued without haste.

Chapter Seventeen

By these teachings we unveil the prophecy which will come to pass. Heed our warning, a great evil will descend upon you whose course will be to eradicate the power of justice with a wave of great devastation, the likes of which you cannot comprehend nor have ever witnessed afore.

Be not caught unaware, for a baneful warrior through the line of Nyx will seek to annihilate your people and claim that which is not his to hold. A messenger will be sent from Gaia carried through the belt of Orion and arising from the Mountains of Eksaf 'anise. Know these signs that the Edict is upon you. There will be two in number, separated by past and present but linked, and whose presence among you will both stir chaos and destroy it. One will be called the Ptino asteri who in truth will be of spirit, but flesh to the touch. The Ptino asteri will be pure of mind, will have dominion over creatures, and will forge a bond with the Keeper of the Key. This bond will be a joining so inherently seamless it will cross the boundaries of the heavens. Not a citizen, assemblage, beast, or natural substance will have the power to put it asunder.

There within this melding, the mysteries of the key will be revealed as the bonded are torn apart by flesh but not of spirit. The Ptino asteri will deliver unto you the prior one. They will face and exterminate thine enemy. Look riseward and your eyes shall be opened. This edict will have come to pass. Doubt no more the prophecies of the Origins.

Sera studied the Edict of the Oneroi. A shivering chill blew threw her spine.

Pure of mind.

Her memory loss. It's what Jerad had told her.

Sera rubbed her thighs and arms. She was definitely flesh to the touch, but what did the Edict mean by *who in truth will be of spirit*? Jerad thought she was a spirit when he first saw her.

She didn't feel like a spirit.

...the one prior--Argilos or Tomas?

She was bonded to the Keeper of the Key--Jerad. His self-fulfilling prophecy maybe?

What if it wasn't?

...within this melding, the mysteries of the key will be revealed as the bonded are torn apart...

Sera closed her eyes and began to tremble.

The Death Challenge.

Was Jerad about to die?

"Go to hell, Orion." Sera waited for the lightening bolt to strike her down.

She had to protect him. She could not allow Jerad to face death for her. The thought of losing him was pure anguish. He gave life to the very blood that coursed through her.

She had to stop this insane Challenge.

But how?

* * * *

Jerad entered the dwelling and sank into the chair in front of his escritoire. He propped his elbows on the surface and dropped his forehead to his hands. His mood was thick with uneasiness at the impending Challenge, and with agitation that Mekal escorted Sera home--that she left without him.

Sera stood at the garden doors and stared at the splashing waterfall, as if it would wash away her woes. She was tormented by the possibility that Jerad might be taken from her, that his life might be ripped away.

If Aryan wanted the marriage dissolved, so be it. Jerad would have no reason to fight if she refused to be Jerad's wife.

"It was not proper that you left my side, woman."

Sera took a deep breath. What she was about to do was appalling. She bit back her guilt reminding herself that she was saving his life. "It seems that you have failed to tell me much about what is proper in this god forsaken place!"

"Why are you annoyed with me, woman?"

I'm afraid for you, Jerad.

"Because," Sera stiffened.

"Ah, that does make it clearer to me." He stood and crossed the room until he reached her. Sera turned to face him.

"I am likely to return to Gaia. What if I am already married? What if I have children? Have you thought of that?" She lifted her chin a notch and crossed her arms.

"Are you? Do you?" It was something Jerad had not even considered.

Sera lowered her eyes. What was she feeling...*innocence?*

In clipped pictures, two faces came to mind. She recalled the pain of a disastrous relationship, did not remember passion, only contempt. The second and more recent left her feeling empty. While thinking of either of those faces, nothing in her stirred. She raised her eyes to Jerad, *and oh*, how everything in her stirred. Sera steeled herself against the emotion.

"No, I don't believe I am married." She just could not deceive him about something like that.

"Perhaps you have many lovers." He crooked a worried eyebrow. The idea of it disturbed him deeply. "The unruly promiscuity of some Origins is legendary."

Sera frowned. Her body railed against the very idea of libidinous indiscretions. The thought of engaging in such actions felt immensely--*foreign.*

"Well that would be a big myth," Sera mumbled under her breath. "At least concerning me."

Jerad ran his thumb across her lips. He actually smiled.

"I am glad of this Sera. As for the question of children, that can be easily examined."

"Oh, no." She pulled back from him. "There will be no examining and no more touching!" She shook her head vehemently.

He narrowed his eyes and firmly grasped her chin with one hand, tipping her head to search her eyes.

She averted her gaze and groaned. Her heart began to ache.

"Tell me what is wrong, Sera."

"I want to go home," she lied. "On the next rise I will leave for Eksaf 'anise and wait for my search party."

"The Challenge is next rise."

"There will be no Challenge if I refuse to be your wife."

"What is this you are saying?"

She moved away from him and began to pace the room. "You put me on display for the amusement of your people, made me a pawn to annul your betrothal, knowing full well there would be no other challenger." She stopped and glared at him. "You used me!"

Jerad moved closer to her and folded her hands between his palms. "I did not mean to take unfair advantage of you, Starbird."

"I will not take your Marks, Jerad!" The perilous words choked free of her throat. She pulled out of his grasp and stepped back.

Jerad's eyes flew wide. He stared at her. Sera's eyes met his stark gaze.

Her heart sank.

The expression on his face--a twinge of anger mixed with hurt and confusion--it was dreadful. She tried to walk away again, but Jerad stalked after her. He grabbed her shoulders and turned her around.

"You *will* take my Marks."

"Is that an order, sir!" Sera became incensed at his demand.

Good.

This might be easier if her own anger could be provoked.

"You would dishonor me in this manner?" Jerad was stupefied. He shook his head. "Why Sera? Why do you refuse?"

Sera tightened her lips and jutted out her chin defiantly.

Because it would kill me if you died.

"Because I don't have to if I don't want to!" She yelled and stomped her foot.

Why did that come out sounding so childish?

His anger emanated and he paced toward her, backing her against the wall. "That is worse than a betrayal!"

Sera sucked in a breath. She had never witnessed his anger before. It was frightening, and it was all her fault.

What if he hit her? Ochi, he would never hit her.

"You will take my Marks, if I have to tie you to a column and sew your lips shut to keep you from protesting!"

Sera began to quake. His bass voice was cavernous and rattling to her bones. "My strength for your honor! I could be dead on the next rise and you spurn my Mark?"

A twinge of shame rushed through her gut. She resisted her mind's plea to throw herself into his arms, to confess that she was baiting him, to admit her distress, her devotion. She hated what she was doing to him, what she was doing to *them*. Sera turned her head away.

"I won't do it."

His expression hardened. "I will put you out of the castle to fend for yourself, strip your status, declare that you are used. Anyone who wished, Noble or otherwise could claim you and have his way with you."

He lied.

"Oh, another detail I see you forgot to tell me about!" Sera glared at him. "The only thing those Marks are good for is to hide these ugly scars!"

She lied--again.

To her, the Marks of Permanence were beautiful.

Sera tamped down the thought and cast him a defiant look. She stomped to the couch and sat down. "I am going to sleep now."

"You will not sleep on that. Now get into our bed." Jerad pointed toward the bedchamber, confused by her behavior.

"No, I choose to sleep here," Sera stated firmly.

"Perhaps you would prefer Mekal in your bed, woman?"

"What?" She looked at him with utter dismay.

Mekal? Should she drag him into this and let Jerad think--no, she couldn't do it. Not unless she had to.

She hoped she wouldn't have to.

"Jealous?" Her mouth spewed the word before her brain could stop it.

Jerad gritted his teeth. His body went rigid.

He turned from her and went to a sideboard. He removed a decanter, popped it open and gulped until it was emptied. With a sideways toss, he threw it across the room. He spanned the room with three contentious steps.

Jerad stilled before her, breathing arduously. He smoothed his hands beneath the collar of her bodice and caressed the back of her neck. Then he yanked her toward him.

"Do you want me, Sera?" His voice was low and eerily calm. There was little inflection in its tone.

She did, but she could not acknowledge it. She tried to free herself, but he swept an arm around her waist and crushed her against him.

"I will not die without knowing the feel of my woman's flesh." He turned her toward the couch, threw her down, and flattened her with his body. "I will have you now."

Sera screamed and tried to escape from beneath him as he fumbled with the lacing of his trousers. "No, Jerad. Stop!"

She managed to free her hands. Jerad closed his eyes just as Sera pressed her thumbs into his lids. He howled and pulled back. With one swift roll Sera was on the floor. She scrambled to her feet and ran toward the door. The blindness was only temporary, and Jerad, regained his sight quickly. He lunged at her and pinned her to the wall. He spun her around.

"Am I so repulsive to you that you will not share my bed with me, wife?" Anger, doubt and hurt, mixed with the effects of the liquor coursed through his blood. It was obscuring his judgment.

Was he mistaken about the Edict?

Was he mistaken about Sera?

"Have I been a fool? Has Aryan unclouded my eyes?"

Sera furled her brow. "I don't understand."

"Are you nothing more than a Seventh Zone whore?"

Sera did not respond. If it would keep him safe, she would let him think as he wished.

"Mayhap an emissary for the Fourth Zone?"

Sera remained silent.

Jerad pressed his palms against the wall, enclosing Sera between his outstretched arms. He tilted his head sideways, his face just a hairsbreadth from Sera's.

"Who sent you, Sera!" His words were hostile and grew deafening to her ears, but as quickly as his voice escalated however, it became subdued and daunting. "Whose bed will you share if I am downed by slaughter?"

"No one's!" she cried.

Oh god! Don't break now. Sera inhaled, held the air inside of her lungs briefly, and then released a quivering breath. She had to convince him their relationship was over. Sera pursed her lips and drew on the last bit of her reserve.

"Then why do you refuse me?"

"I am not your wife, and I never will be." Her gaze dropped to the floor. She dared not look him in the eyes for fear he would see the deceit in her words. "I don't want you."

"I--I don't even like you very much," she whispered.

Jerad stared at her incredulously for several heartbeats. Without warning he drew back his fist and slammed it into the wall behind her. It hit with such tremendous force the wall splintered.

Sera's mouth dropped open, but she could not speak. She could neither inhale nor exhale. It was as though she was bound at the neck.

Jerad laughed mockingly--not at her, at himself for being such a fool.

Sera gulped.

She had driven him over the edge.

Sera could bear no more. She was on the verge of tears. She pushed his arm aside and ran from the residence, through the castle passageways and out into the Corridor.

Sera made her way to the *agora*, slowing her momentum as she reached the main commerce area. She mingled among the citizens hoping she could avoid drawing attention. She sighed with relief. The market was bustling with activity, and no one seemed to notice her presence among them.

Now what? Where could she go? Eksaf 'anise was the only logical choice. She would have to obtain a horse and provisions. She would also have to hire a guide because she did not know the way.

Sera had no gemstones. She fled from Jerad without taking her cloak, desperate to escape him before she caved in to her emotions. She could not go back to retrieve it.

Damn it. She hadn't been thinking very clearly when she left.

The sound of a lute diverted her attention. A young minstrel, poised upon the stump of a tree, was strumming a lovely melody. Sera moved closer to him, attracted by the wistful composition. The musician nodded his head to Sera and began playing a livelier tune. His voice chirped a song.

"She came from a place far beyond to grace our humble land. She healed his soul and brought him home, and won our Noble's hand."

It only took a few seconds for Sera to realize that he was singing about her. When he finished, there was applauding behind her. Sera turned around. Every onlooker crossed a fisted arm and bowed to her. Sera grimaced.

So much for being incognito.

An elderly woman, cloaked and hooded approached Sera and knelt by her side. She placed an exquisitely delicate flower in Sera's hand.

"A precious Iris for you, my Noble, an offering from my garden. It will bless you with fortune and hasten your melancholy."

Sera graciously accepted the flower and sniffed it.

Was her sadness that obvious?

"It's lovely. Thank you."

The woman grabbed Sera's other hand, and looked up at her hopefully. "A blessing from my Chancellor's lady?"

Sera observed the feeble woman and frowned. What could she possible say to appease her?

"Uh," Sera hesitated, "health and wealth?"

"Thank you my lady of the Greathouse, thank you, thank you." The woman kissed Sera's hand repeatedly, and then gave her a toothy smile before backing away.

The sky suddenly grew dark and all heads turned upward. Though it was only just nearing *full set*, ominous gray clouds converged, shrouding what was left of the light from the *rise*. Thunder crackled and lightening burst. The assemblage in the marketplace scattered. Doors slammed and shutters snapped shut. Within moments the *agora* was deserted and Sera stood alone.

"How prophetic." Sera grumbled and rushed toward the nearest shelter she could find, a gazebo in the middle of a flowering garden. She lapsed to the wooden floor. Rain began gushing from the heavens. Sera cried out and wept in concord with the abysmal skies.

Chapter Eighteen

Jerad sat on the floor propped against the wall. His legs were outstretched to their full length and his head drooped heavily to his chest. His arms were limp at his sides. He grasped a half-empty decanter. Some of its contents puddled on the floor next to him.

There was a pounding on the door.

Or was it inside his skull?

Jerad lifted his head and stared at the door. He grimaced. His head rolled forward and fell once again to his chest. The pounding sounded again. He threw back his head, banging it on the wall behind him.

"*Ack!* Enter!" He snapped.

The door creaked opened and Mekal stepped in. He paused, and then scoffed at the heap of Nobleman, slumped on the floor.

"Disgraceful." Mekal shook his head from side to side. "What a sight this will make on the walls of my gallery."

"Mekal." Jerad closed one eye. "Stop moving, both of you."

"Come then, up we go." Mekal crouched to help Jerad to his feet, but before the two of them were fully upright, the drunken knight fell forward and landed on top of Mekal.

"Kiss me or get off, my drunken *filos*."

Jerad rolled to his back. Mekal pulled him to his feet and threw one of Jerad's arms around his shoulder. Jerad's knees started to crumple, but he caught himself and stiffened. He broke free from Mekal. Swaying, he bent and picked up his carafe. Mekal snatched it before it reached Jerad's lips.

Mekal took a hearty drink from it and set it down.

Jerad's body teetered, but Mekal caught him. He dragged Jerad to the garden pool, and dropped both of them to their knees. Mekal shoved Jerad's head into the water, and then pulled him out by the hair.

"Mekal," Jerad choked.

"*Nai*, a good rise to you too."

He submerged Jerad's head again.

Jerad's hand came back to grab at Mekal, but before it made contact Mekal jerked Jerad back, this time setting him on his rump. In a surrendering gesture, Jerad held up his hands. He rose clumsily and stumbled back to his bottle of drink, attempting another round.

Mekal came up from behind him and yanked it away. "Let us walk. Shall we?"

He braced Jerad's sagging form against him and they circled the room several times, until Jerad's weighty bulk began to exhaust Mekal. He released the drunken warrior. Jerad staggered backwards, tumbled over the sofa and onto the floor.

He grumbled an oath.

Mekal moved to the other side of the couch, and helped Jerad up. Jerad gripped Mekal's shoulders, swaying as he attempted to focus on his friend's face.

"Are you here to abuse me?"

"Of course."

"Aryan is a great warrior." Jerad's vision reeled and he closed his eyes. He drew a deep, exasperated breath and sank into the oversized chair. "I fear my annihilation draws near."

Mekal settled onto the sofa and propped his foot on the opposite knee. "He is no greater a swordsman than you, Jerad."

"*Nai*, it is true, but I am drunk."

"As is Aryan. I just came from his dwelling."

Jerad lifted his bloodshot eyes to Mekal. "How so?"

"He wishes not to challenge you."

"Then why does he?"

"You know the answer as well as I, Noble. His clan seeks it and he is fiercely loyal to his clan. They refuse to believe in Sondra's disreputable behavior."

"Sondra is dead. It cannot be undone."

"And most believe it could not have ended any other way, *filos*."

"I do know this, as I believe Aryan does, but he will still make a good show of the Challenge."

"Hmn," Mekal replied rubbing his chin. "Of that I have no doubt."

He studied Jerad briefly. He had never seen Jerad quite so agitated. "Tell me Noble, it is unlike you to take to so much drink. What else troubles you?"

"Did I react with haste, Mekal? Should I have wedded Sondra?"

"*Ack! Ochi!* Sondra was a Gorgon!" Mekal released a strangled sound from his throat. "She would have stripped you of your flesh and fed it to you for supper."

Jerad tangled his fingers through his hair and dropped his head to the back of the chair. "I took to drink last luna because I thought I had made a grave error thinking Sera was the Ptino asteri"

"And now?"

"She is the one. I have no doubt. Too much of the Edict is passing." A slight smile crested Jerad's mouth as he recalled first meeting Sera.

"When we were near the riseward boundary of the Eighth Zone, a *Chuger* appeared from behind a boulder, ready to be feasted on."

Mekal raised an eyebrow. The animal that Jerad described dwelled nowhere near that area. They were typically found at least twelve *rises* further toward *Landtrail*.

"And I swear on the souls of the Origins Mekal, the foolish animal looked as though it was about to stroll right up to her. It served us well for a decent meal where few creatures are known to wander. She has dominion over beasts, just as the Edict proclaims. Even my horse favors her more than me."

Jerad frowned. "Sera left me, Mekal. She refuses to take my Marks."

"And this disturbs you?"

"It does not greatly disturb me." Even as he denied it, his chest squeezed with a heavy aching.

"What does irk me is that it was I who was chosen to be bonded with her, as dictated by the Origins. It is blasted curse!"

"A curse you say?"

"Her blood surges through my veins. It consumes me. I felt it the moment she appeared in the air."

"In the air?" Mekal asked curiously.

"*Nai*. It is true. Those barbarians from the Fourth Zone were testing their shatter arrows and were too distracted to see her. She appeared suddenly and plunged to the ground."

"And what did you do?"

"I fell off my horse."

Mekal snorted. It was well too obvious his friend was besotted with more than his spirits. It was no hex. It was a matter of the heart.

"*Agapao.*"

Jerad raised his head. "Love?"

Mekal smirked. "You love her."

Jerad narrowed his eyes. His confidante looked much too amused. He would like to thwack that sappy grin clear from his face.

"She will not leave my head! The Oneroi has bewitched me with lust for her to ensure their decree is fulfilled. It is simply that!"

"If it is as you say, then there is naught a reason for the Challenge."

Jerad raise an inquisitive eyebrow. "By what reason?"

"Accept the terms of the charges. Dissolve the marriage and relinquish Sera to servitude in Aryan's clan. If she truly is the Ptino asteri, the Edict will come to pass regardless."

"Give up Sera?"

It was unthinkable.

Jerad sneered at Mekal. "So that you may have her?"

"What is this you assume? I have no design for her."

"She is charmed by you."

"*Bah*!" Mekal slashed a hand through the air.

"She did not deny it when I asked."

Mekal watched Jerad thoughtfully, wondering why Sera reacted as such. Mekal had no answer. He and Sera were friends, nothing more.

"Regardless, I am powerless when she is not with me. I am incapable of giving her up."

"Yet you say it does not bother you that she refuses your Marks," Mekal replied, leaning lazily against the arm of the couch.

"Unquenched desire. *Nai*, that is it. I have not been able to join with her. It is maddening."

Mekal burst into laughter. "You have not consummated your marriage?"

Jerad was seriously going to clout his dear confidante--just as soon as the floor stopped moving.

"After all of our conversations about seducing a woman and you have been unable to bed your own wife?" Mekal pressed his lips together, desperately resisting the unbearable urge to badger Jerad about this amusing disclosure.

"It was not for lack of trying!" Jerad barked. He then lowered his voice. It was quite humiliating. "The doing is not the same as the telling."

Jerad's expression turned gloomy. "I am lower than a slimy *flub* at the bottom of a swamp, Mekal."

"Why do you say such a thing?"

"I nearly took her in the forest against her will. If it were not for her blood curdling scream, I surely would have. Then I tried to do the same thing to her on the last luna."

"I am sure she appreciated that."

Jerad grunted. "She hates me, and I do not blame her."

"Nonsense. I see the way she looks at you, *filos*. She loves you." Mekal cleared his throat. "I would however, suggest a gentler approach with her."

"Such as, my almighty and wise mentor?" Jerad asked acerbically.

Mekal snickered at his sarcasm. "What do you do when your horse throws you? Walk away?"

"*Ochi*, I stroke the creature gently before attempting to mount it again." Jerad paused to consider the humor in his statement. "But Sera is not a horse."

He angled his eyes upward in thought. "Although she does have nice teeth."

Mekal laughed, leaned forward and slapped Jerad on his back. He stood, offered his hand and yanked Jerad to his feet. "Come my friend, you have a bigger bird to spear at the moment."

Jerad rose, returned a slap to the side of Mekal's shoulder, and nearly fell over. "You have been loyal my confidante, all these term cycles. Yet, it was always Aryan I gave first regard to."

"There is no shame in being second to your right. It has ever been an honor to be called your friend, Jerad."

Mekal turned to leave.

"Mekal."

Mekal paused and looked over his shoulder.

"I will see you at the Grandstage, my friend."

"You shall." He confirmed with a nod.

Mekal closed the door behind him and leaned against it. *What a muddle his confidante had gotten himself into. Now, where could Sera be?*

Chapter Nineteen

Sera tried to sleep with little success. The damp, wooden boards beneath her held little comfort for her aching body, and the short, narrow benches could only suffice as a place to rest her head. They were much too small to recline on. Her arm was numb from laying her head on it. She was cold and thirsty and miserable.

A slight tugging on Sera's finger roused her, and she lifted her head. A tiny shrew was nibbling on the tip of her fingernail. She raised her other hand, and with a single finger, gently stroked the tiny body of the creature. She expected it to flee, but to her surprise, it did not. Instead, it climbed onto the back of her hand, stood on its hind legs, front paws dangling, black eyes staring, and twitched its pink, little nose. Sera picked up the shrew and cupped it between her palms, glad at least for some minute company.

Sera looked at the brightening sky, and shivered with the chill of the *rise*. The marketplace was stirring to life. She did not hear the horse drawing near but heard the clacking of boots striking the gazebo floor as someone approached from behind her. Before she could turn around, a cloak was draped around her and two large hands framed her shoulders.

Sera turned to look.

Mekal was thoroughly aggravated with Sera when he set out to find her, and meant to tell her so. She set his friend's heart to tatters with her behavior, rejecting him when he was willing to die for her--and insinuating that there might be illicit affection between her and Mekal himself?--well, that was simply detestable.

Mekal had every intention of laying his ridicule upon her, but reeled in his irritation when he saw her face. The sorrow he glimpsed there was heartrending. She was pale. Her eyes were red and swollen. She looked so thoroughly defeated--so *sad*.

"You have been crying." He felt sympathy for her instead.

"What are you doing here, Mekal?"

Mekal released her and stood. He strolled to a bench and sat down, propping his elbows on the railing behind him.

"I was worried about you." He realized then, that he truly was.

"Yes, of course. You are a guardian. It is your duty."

"*Nai*, I am a guardian, but perhaps it is also something else."

"Something else?"

"I could be missing my sister."

"What has that to do with me?"

"When Jerad brought you to the Corridor, my memories of her returned. Close to your age she would be now, a mere twenty term cycles."

"I am much older than that."

Mekal shrugged. "If you say."

"Where is your sister?"

"My mother had gone feebleminded after my sister's birth, spewing nonsense about the Origins appearing to her and telling her that Ekaterina must be sacrificed."

"How frightening."

"I was but seven term cycles and did not fully comprehend, but it was clear that my mother was not in her right mind. Despite our close watch on her she still managed to slip away with Kati. Ten rises we searched for them and when we finally found my mother, she was alone. Ekaterina was gone."

"What happened to her?"

"My mother claimed that all would be well. She had done as the Origins of her visions had instructed. She left my sister in the Mountains of Eksaf 'anise. We never found her. Kati was but six rise cycles then. There is no possibility that such a young babe could have survived.

When I first saw you, there was a familiar presence about you, your posturing, the way you looked. I thought perhaps--*Ochi.* I was mistaken. Ekaterina's eyes were a very deep brown."

"Like yours?"

"Like mine."

Mekal stood and treaded across the wooden floor. He folded his arms and leaned his shoulder against one of the gazebo's wooden posts.

"Your place is at your consort's side, Sera. Jerad is distraught by your denial of him and will not have full wits when he battles Aryan this rise."

"He still fights?" She asked disbelievingly, standing abruptly. "B--but I told him I would not be his wife! Why is he still challenging?"

"*Ah*, now I can put purpose to your reasoning, foolish as it may be." Her intent was to stop the Challenge. It made perfect sense to him now. "Of course he still fights, woman. Your honor has been besmirched."

"Shit, Mekal! Take me to him now!"

Sera slipped the shrew into the pocket of the cloak, not giving a thought as to why she was keeping it.

Mekal mounted his charger without hesitation. He hoisted Sera to sit behind him in the saddle.

"Hurry!" She ordered Mekal.

Sera read about the Challenges in the *Protogio Principles* and could even understand why they might be necessary. Understanding however, did not mean that she was willing to accept.

There were three types of Challenges considered legal by the Zone dictates. The first, was the Challenge for the Rite of the Cloak. The second, an Honor Challenge could be issued for lesser crimes such as thievery or slander. Severe injuries might occur during an Honor Challenge, but death blows were not allowed. The rivals fought until one of them called a halt, or in the case of obstinacy, until the Magistrate Council called a halt and decided on a victor themselves. The Death Challenge could only be issued when a horrendous crime had been committed. Murder, rape and torture were among these crimes. With a Death Challenge, only the rivals could call a halt, and whoever called the halt would forfeit the Challenge. If it so happened that one of them fell unconscious or lay mortally wounded before dying, the other contender could call for a victory or slay the rival if he wished to do so. Such was the nature of the Death Challenge.

Guilt for crimes was decided by the Magistrate Council. It was based on the evidence presented and with witness testimony. Once guilt was determined, the victim of the crime could offer for approval, what they deemed to be an appropriate punishment. Though most disputes or accusations were settled to the agreement of the victim and without a Challenge being issued, occasionally the victim or the victim's clan would be so outraged by the violation that only a public, physical pummeling would satisfy them. A Challenge might then be requested. Challenges were a catharsis of sorts, and served to alleviate anger and dispel further violence or retaliation by those involved. Both the Honor Challenge and Death Challenge required approval by the Magistrate Council, and the rules guiding them were very strict. First and foremost, rivals of the Challenge must possess evenly matched skills. If this was not possible, the Magistrate could deny the Challenge. Second, at least three non-biased witnesses from Magistrate Council had to be present. Third, the criminal could refuse the Challenge, but in doing so would have to accept the harshest of punishments agreed upon by the victim and the Council. The same would occur if the offender accepted a Challenge and lost. However, if the offender accepted and won the Challenge a less severe punishment would be rendered. No further retribution was allowed by the victim, and the matter would be considered settled.

Sera knew she could not call a halt to the Challenge. She could only hope that she wasn't too late to beg Jerad not to go forth with it. She could plead for mercy from the Magistrate Council, or perhaps Aryan's clan would take pity on her. She would publicly swallow her dignity if she had to, and if all else failed, she would throw herself between Aryan and Jerad. She would do anything to save her husband--*anything*.

"Will we get there in time?" Sera was immensely worried.

"It depends on how many contenders are present to demonstrate their skills."

Challenges gave opportunity for the apprentices and squires to earn respect and recognition among their peers and superiors. Jousts, blade competitions, and quintain were the sports of choice. The tournaments typically began in the early *rise* with the least experienced competing first.

The event often drew an excess of spectators, and this Challenge was no different. When rumor spread that the two Noble Chancellors were to battle, many outside the Zone, intent on traveling elsewhere turned their horses about and made haste for the Third Corridor to watch or participate in the events. Indeed, the Grandstage was overflowing with citizens clambering for space to witness the Death Challenge between Jerad and Aryan, a rare event in the least, and one not to be missed.

The merchants from the Zone were delighted. Many arrived during the *luna* to seize the opportunity to sell their wares and fill their pockets. Sera was appalled at the festive atmosphere and cheerful demeanor of the citizens. Wagers were being made, and from the looks of the gems being used, the stakes were high. Long wooden tables and makeshift booths were assembled along the main path. There was music and dancing, and the bartering and buying of goods. Colorful streamers were hung about, and citizens were proudly displaying the crests of their Zones. The marketplace was brimming with activity and was so overcrowded that Mekal abandoned his attempts to maneuver his charger and hired a stable master to care for his horse. He and Sera were forced to walk the rest of the way. The crowd had begun to swarm, attempting to get closer to the Grandstage area. Weaving through the nearly impenetrable throng was proving to be an arduous task. Not that the *hoi polloi* would be allowed inside. Only Nobles were permitted entrance to the arena. The commoners were left to rely on the mouth to mouth relay to describe what was happening in the Grandstage.

Sera's heart beat quickened to a panicky rate when she heard the shouts arising. Jerad and Aryan had entered the floor.

"Oh, Mekal!" Sera wailed above the noise of the crowd. "We have to get there!"

"*Nai!*" Mekal yelled back. He gripped her arm and jostled forward. "Aside! Aside now for the Noble Sera!"

The crowd slowly parted.

Delilah was perched on Aryan's thick leather gauntlet when he entered the floor. The falcon was hooded, but the raptorial bird was unusually agitated this *rise*.

The spectators clamored and stomped their feet at first glimpse of the warrior. The noise grew even louder when Jerad entered on the other side. Jerad scanned the gallery, locating Ezra, Mesari and Phoebe, but Sera was nowhere to be seen. He was downcast by her absence, proof that she did not care.

He turned his attention to his rival, watching as Aryan placed Delilah on a wooden block near the side of the Grandstage. In like with Jerad, Aryan had forgone wearing the metal armor often donned during hazardous Challenges, choosing the leather coverings instead. The softer material allowed more freedom of movement, but also made the combatants more susceptible to injury from a strike.

A long lavender scarf was tied about Aryan's upper sword arm, the scarf Jerad's parents forced him to present to Sondra at his maiden tournament, and along with it, his betrothal to her. He was just ten *term cycles* old then. Jerad winced with guilty conscience at the memory, remembering how awkward and juvenile he felt at the time. To him, it was just a game he played. Never could he surmise that it would come to this.

Aryan circled the Grandstage.

Delilah flapped her long wings and frantically rubbed the straps of her hood against her perch.

Jerad assumed a defensive stance, arm crossed over the front of his body, gripping and releasing the hilt of his sword. He would not draw first blade. If Aryan still intended on fighting him, he would have to make the first move.

Aryan bit his lower lip, exposed his teeth and gnarled. He drew his sword and rushed forward. Jerad met him with the clashing of their blades.

The straps of Delilah's hood broke loose and it fell to the ground. Bated, her preying eyes locked on the flailing scarf tied around Aryan's arm.

Fluttering--wings--prey.

Delilah flapped her mighty wings and swooped, latching onto Aryan's arm and pecking at the lavender scarf. Jerad froze. Aryan flinched, startled at his well-trained falcon's attack. He recovered instantly and called off, attempting to flush the bird from its game. The knot on the scarf came loose. Delilah snatched her quarry, clamping it in her beak. She circled high and then dove toward...

Sera.

Sera stood in utter fear as the falcon descended. She raised her hand to protect her face as Delilah came to rest quietly on her uplifted arm.

Thank goodness Mekal's cloak was draped over her. Even so, she could feel the bite of its talons. Delilah opened her mouth. The scarf fell to drape around Sera's arm. The spectators gasped and then silence echoed through the arena. Jerad and Aryan abandoned their conflict and watched.

"Shoo bird," Sera cautiously muttered, not quite knowing what else to do.

Get this thing off of me!

She stared into its eyes--eyes that were remarkably the same color as her own.

Bird eyes--I have bird eyes--ugh!

The tiny shrew made its appearance, sniffing its way from the cloak pocket. Delilah uttered a snarling growl. The falcon stooped, plucked the shrew and swooped vertically upward. She made a tight circle and ascended, before flying out through the open transom in the Grandstage ceiling.

Mekal snorted at the bizarre occurrence.

The spectators stared at Sera with revered awe.

"Dominion over beasts," a voice in the crowd croaked out. The conjecture rippled throughout the crowd.

"The Ptino asteri," another voice resounded.

Damn! Sera turned away.

Mekal grabbed her shoulders and turned her back. "It is too late, Sera. They know. Face your citizens."

The crowd was disturbingly quiet. A Noble dropped to his knees as one fist flew to his opposite shoulder. He bowed his head. One by one the witnesses followed the Noble's gesture until they were all dropping to their knees en masse.

Oh god! Sera gurgled. *Get me out of here!*

Aryan threw down his sword and spread his arms open with his palms toward Jerad, making himself vulnerable to the thrust of Jerad's sword. "I call a halt. I unsay all charges."

Jerad stared at Aryan as his declaration took hold.

"This is finished." Jerad dropped his sword. With a clang it landed athwart along Aryan's sword. "I accept the halt."

"*Ochi!* You will finish this Aryan!" A woman in the bleachers narrowed her eyes at him and snarled.

"Mother! Sondra's arrogance was her downfall. You know as well as I that Sera had no choice but to defend herself."

With his arms still outspread Aryan faced the Magistrate Council, and in a voice loud enough for all to hear, he bellowed, "I loved my sister as I do my clan, but Sondra would have indeed killed Sera. The Death Challenge against my Noble friend was unjustly granted. Further I relinquish any claims to injustice and request that the Noble Chancellor Jerad and his consort be exonerated."

Shegarth stood and faced the Magistrate Council. "Is all agreed?"

The member's of the Council solidly responded with *Nai*.

Aryan's mother could not contain her fury. She shrieked and leapt from the benches. With dagger in hand, she lunged at Jerad. Aryan blocked her way and easily subdued her. He carried her from the Grandstage as she kicked and screamed. A string of curses spewed from her mouth. Aryan would return her to the Second Corridor where the rest of his clan would retain her until her anger subsided and she would listen to reason. There would be no further retaliation. His mother knew this, and he knew his mother well. She would eventually accept the truth, her anger would turn to grief for the loss of her daughter, and she would, in due time, heal from this unfortunate ordeal.

Sera watched as Jerad stalked toward her. Unlike the crowd, Jerad was not affected by the spectacle that had just taken place. His eyes were narrowed and he looked angry.

"*Pfft!* Now you decide to come to me! I risk my life for you woman and you have not even the deference to be at my side?"

Sera opened her mouth but he pivoted away from her and stormed off. She ran after him, and Mekal followed them.

"Jerad!" Sera caught him at the top of the hillside just outside of the Grandstage. He turned to face her.

"If I had been splayed open in front of these witnesses, would you have cried?"

Again Sera opened her mouth, but nothing came out.

"I think not!" Jerad's eyes shifted and he snarled at Mekal. "I see whose company you prefer."

Sera was distraught and confused. She wanted to reclaim her past, yet didn't care if her memories ever returned. She wanted her people to rescue her, yet she wanted to stay with Jerad. She wanted to wrap her arms around him and embrace him. She wanted to run. What she did was nothing, except stare numbly as Jerad walked away.

Sera turned to look at Mekal and groaned as she noticed a large crowd of citizens gathering at the bottom of the hill. They were staid by a number of sentries who stood in line in front of them. A cheer went up as Sera scanned the crowd, a mix of Nobles and the *hoi polloi*, and every one of them fell to their knees in praise of her.

Sera rubbed her forehead wearily. "Word travels fast in these parts."

Mesari approached, followed by Phoebe.

"Come Sera! Come! We have much to do!" Mesari reached for Sera's arm. A sentry stepped between them. Mekal waved him away.

"W-what?" Sera was feeling quite dazed with all that was happening.

"The Marks of Permanence! It is already past quarter set. We have less than four quarters to ready you for the ceremony."

Sera's head bolted upright.

Jerad was angry with her. Would he still take the Marks? Would he forgive her for hurting him if she took the Marks? Could she still go through with it? Yes, she confirmed solidly. She would and wanted to with all of her heart.

Chapter Twenty

Jerad was stupefied and skeptical when Mekal advised him that the women were preparing Sera for the ceremony.

He was elated.

He would *not* be elated!

Then he saw her. Sera was stunning. She wore his colours, a lavender gown of luxurious velvet, in two pieces so that her belly showed.

Jerad inhaled sharply.

The things his tongue could do to that navel of hers.

He exhaled a slow lingering breath.

The waist of the skirt was braided in the blue azure of his Zone. It hugged her hips then gently flared to sweep the floor, longer in the back than in the front. The material outlined her thighs...

He closed his eyes, imagining her luscious thighs wrapped around him.

The short-cropped bodice had long, campanulate sleeves and was tied together in a knot between the hollow of her breasts, giving him a tantalizing view of their rounded shape, as the material molded perfectly around them.

Jerad sighed a quiet groan, working that knot free, in his mind's eye--with his teeth.

Sera came to stand beside him. Her hair was beautifully woven with lavender buds, obviously the handiwork of Phoebe. A hint of patchouli teased his nostrils, a soothing aroma that was alluringly sensual, obviously Ezra's doing, as she knew how much he enjoyed the scent.

She looked like a tempting enchantress from a faraway land, and he adored her.

He stiffened as she met him with beckoning eyes.

Lust, nothing more, he tenaciously reminded himself.

The material felt sumptuous against Sera's skin. The top barely covered her chest and was cut short enough to reveal the scar from Sondra's blade. She did not care. Sera felt sensuous and feminine. She knew the appreciative eyes of the guests followed her as she moved through the hall, but there was only one man who captured her interest.

Jerad was exceedingly handsome in his wedding regalia. He wore an azure, velveteen hip-length, doublet. It was studded in silver and had rolled epaulet pads twined in lavender cording that emphasized his broad shoulders. A black leather belt sheathed his sword and rested neatly on his lean, masculine hips. His tight, black leather trousers and sleek, thigh high boots sent a delightful tremble through her.

Was he still angry?

Sera saw the flicker of passion when his gaze fell upon her, and with it came the hope that he still wanted her, but then his countenance abruptly changed.

They stood before Shegarth, who would lead the ceremony. Shegarth's eyes darted between Jerad and Sera. By the looks of his son, one would think he had been throttled and dragged to the chantry to be sacrificed, and Sera looked like she had lost her dearest friend.

Shegarth shook his head.

What senseless misfortune comes from hearts in denial.

Well, at least they had both come forth. He feared that one would show without the other, making for a most embarrassing situation.

He turned his attention to the guests and spoke loudly. "Once again I implore, will there be any protest to the Vows between the Noble Jerad and the Noble Sera?"

There was no objection heard from the Nobles in the hall.

"Very good." He clapped his hands together. "Then let's proceed, shall we?"

Shegarth held out his hand. Sera knew what to do. Mesari acquainted Sera with the aspects of the Marks of Permanence. It was the reason Phoebe presently stood to Sera's right. Sera thought it more than appropriate to choose Jerad's sister as her paranymph. Jerad stood to Sera's left, and Mekal was on Jerad's other side. Sera assumed that Mekal was chosen to be Jerad's groomsman. Sera was also told that Mekal was the artisan who would ply the Marks of Permanence.

Sera placed her left hand in Shegarth's palm. Shegarth untied the conjugal cloth and removed it. He draped it over his wrist. He then extended his palm toward Jerad.

Jerad's eyes riveted downward and he hesitated. Sera held her breath and waited for what seemed like an eternity, and released it slowly when Jerad finally responded.

Shegarth took the ends of the conjugal cloths and in symbolic gesture tied them together. He held them up for the witnesses to see.

"Join hands, children."

Jerad did not move.

Shegarth shot an irritated look toward his son. He picked up Jerad's hand and slapped it into Sera's. Jerad's fingers reflexively closed around Sera's hand. He shifted slightly as the warmth from her flesh and a sense of comfort surged through him. Their thorn marks touched, flesh to flesh, for the first time since receiving them. Jerad resisted the temptation to cast his gaze toward Sera. He desperately wanted to see her face, but felt it better to remain detached. He would not allow her to scathe his honor again.

"Jerad and Sera, do you swear to the Council and all here that witness, to accept the Marks of Permanence of your own accord?"

Jerad nodded reluctantly.

Sera shifted beside him and held up her free hand. "Wait."

Jerad squeezed the hand he was holding, applying a steady, increasing pressure, threatening to break her bones if she humiliated him now.

"You're hurting me," She mumbled.

He loosened his grip and glowered at her.

What was she up to?

Sera turned to completely face Jerad.

She untwined her fingers from Jerad's hand and pressed her palm against his. She took a deep breath. Her golden eyes lifted to meet his dark, brooding stare. "My loyalty for your trust, my strength for your honor…"

Jerad's heart beat erratically when Sera began to speak.

"…Mind nurtures heart and flesh becomes one…"

His anger began to melt away.

"…Wherever you go I shall follow. Meaningless is one life without the other. My blood with your blood, Jerad."

Her words deeply enraptured him, and she was here to take his Marks.

To cover her ugly scars.

Those words bit hard, supplanting the vows she now spoke. He responded by turning away.

Sera bit her lip. A stinging in her nose and a tightness in her chest seeped through her. He was shunning her. It was a painful reality check.

Don't cry! Don't cry! Don't cry!

She swallowed it away.

At least Shegarth seemed pleased with her. He smiled at Sera amiably as he motioned for them to sit down. "Well done, Sera."

To Jerad, he flashed a frosty, sidelong glare.

Jerad strode to a bench. Sera followed. He poured wine from a flask and offered it to Sera. As if of their own determination, his eyes flickered to her face. He watched her take a sip.

She had such a lovely mouth.

He took a hard gulp from his goblet, reining the urgent stirring that crept through his loins.

The Marks mean nothing to her.

Mekal sat on a small stool in front of them. Phoebe sat to the side. Mekal rummaged through his dray of art reserve and prepared to administer his craft. He had already formed a picture of the workmanship that he would permanently enchase upon their skin. A steady hand would be required to manage the intricate design he intended for the Marks of Permanence. With Jerad being a Noble Chancellor, and Sera being of Gaian Origins, it would only be fitting that the consort markings be an aesthetically perfect piece of artwork demanding of the Nobles' status. He would commit these marks with great pride.

Mekal began with the Challenge scar under Sera's rib, etching woven green vines, tiny leaves, and lavender buds along its length. He did the same to their palms tracing the thorn piercings to create tiny lavender sprouts twined together with vines that wrapped not once, but twice around their forearms. He was diligent in his workmanship, lifting his incisor and precisely placing the tip to ply the indelible mark, stopping only to re-ink it.

Nobles approached to offer their congratulations, but none lingered overlong. The tension between Jerad and Sera was a palpable thing. Mekal concentrated on his work, dismissing all expectations for reasonable conversation with them.

Sera gritted her teeth and flinched each time the point made contact. It burned.

"Why is it we can't have anything to numb the pain?" She referred the question to Jerad, but he gave her no answer. He merely stared straight ahead.

Mekal twisted his mouth at Jerad's indifference and offered Sera the answer. "The Marks of Permanence should not be taken lightly, Sera. They are considered a sacred endowment. To endure the pain of receiving them is to avow one's abiding love and devotion."

Was that what Jerad felt for her? Sera looked at Jerad. He continued to ignore her.

No, he didn't love her. Sera's chest constricted with that definitive. He was only doing this because of the Edict. She sat in silence, wondering why she had consented to do this.

When the Marks of Permanence were completed, Mekal dusted the imprints with a drying powder and lightly brushed them off. He examined his work, pleased with the outcome. He stood to gather his things, motioned to Phoebe to follow him and they left to join the rest of the guests.

Perhaps some solitary time together would allow Jerad and Sera to resolve their differences.

Sera shifted restlessly beside Jerad, not knowing what to expect, waiting for what seemed like an eternity, for Jerad to respond. At last he turned to her, momentarily assaying the legend beneath her rib, and his crest upon her palm, so reflecting of his own, an intimate sharing of promise between them. He was rapt by how strikingly magnificent Sera looked bearing the Marks of Permanence--*his Marks*. The infatuation nearly disarmed him. He lifted his hand to touch those Marks, but stopped midair, remembering what he intended to say to her.

"I have been overly presumptuous and inconsiderate, Sera." He let his hand drop to his side. "You are my wife, but I will respect your wishes. I will not touch you again."

Jerad stood, spun on his heels and quit the hall.

"But I want you to." Sera whispered.

He did not hear her.

Within moments he was being marched back to the Great Hall, a humbled expression on his face. Shegarth caught him storming from his own marriage celebration and peevishly ordered him back inside, following Jerad to the table on the dais. Shegarth motioned for Sera to join them and she took a seat next to Jerad. He did not look at her. Attendants appeared with platters and the meal was served.

Sera found the mood less than pleasant.

This was suppose to be her wedding feast for goodness sakes, but it seemed more like a funeral!

Jerad refused to speak to her. He refused to even look at her. Shegarth kept rubbing his temple. Mekal attended to his food, and Aryan--for the love of the holy keepers, whoever they were, conversed with Jerad as if nothing foul had occurred between them. Yet even Aryan sat gloomily slumped in his chair.

Sera tried to speak to Jerad again. He blinked and turned his head away. Sera glared at him. She huffed and pursed her lips.

Words could hurt, but his silence was breaking her heart.

To hell with it! She'd had enough. He was acting like a total--a total--

"Jackass!" Sera snapped as she stood and stomped away. Phoebe's lower lip rolled into a pout and she glowered at Jerad. She stood abruptly and followed Sera.

Aryan leaned in toward Jerad. "What is a jackass?"

"I do not know, but I think that it is not a good thing." Jerad grumbled, as he watched Sera move down the rows of tables.

"Hmph," Aryan replied as he scanned the hall to locate his wife. Ezra sat at the table farthest from the dais, the tables reserved for the Nobles of the least status. "Is it anything like a crackbrain?"

Mekal looked up from his plate and lifted an eyebrow.

"It was Ezra's choice of praise when I declared the Challenge. She has been in a foul mood ever since." Aryan frowned.

"It is why she sits there." He tipped his head in Ezra's direction. "Her intent is to publicly scorn me."

The muscle in Jerad's jaw ticked as he watched Sera sit next to Ezra. He clutched his mug in his hand, lifted it to his lips and took a large swallow. He could already hear the gossip mongers' fabrications as to why his wife left her place next to him. What he should do is tramp right down there, carry her back to his table and tie her to her seat!

"What irritates you, *filos*?" Mekal leaned in toward Jerad. His tone was discreet.

"Look where she sits, at the lowest ranking table in the hall."

"What of it?"

"Her place during the meal is with me, yet you see how she refuses me."

"And you have welcomed her with open arms?"

"She wishes to humiliate me as Sondra did," Jerad scowled.

Mekal scratched his chin. "Hmph, now I see what motivates you Chancellor, yet I remind you that Sera is not Sondra."

A serving maid approached. She bent over Jerad in a dramatic manner as she set the next course on the table. Her buxom breasts were clearly visible and dangled flagrantly close to his face.

Both Aryan and Mekal snorted.

"Eunice, I swear you have a nose for trouble." Jerad blinked at her cleavage, rolled his eyes and turned his head aside.

Eunice rose slowly and looked down from the platform to where Sera sat.

Troubles in the bedchamber, and so soon.

How fortunate for her. She would enjoy a swiving with the Noble Chancellor.

"Why Noble Jerad, I am only doing my job."

"And what job might that be sweet?" Mekal asked as he stroked her bottom.

Eunice cast a lingering glance toward Mekal. He was handsome and virile.

She would like that one too.

She swaggered back to the kitchens.

"Are you still angry with Sera?" Mekal returned to his conversation with Jerad.

"*Ochi*, it has passed."

"Then why do you punish her so?"

"As I said, I will not tolerate my wife shaming me."

"And she has behaved so disgracefully, has she not?"

"Meaning?"

Mekal dramatically threw his hands up.

"After all, she was dropped on her head, killed another, married off to a stranger, and told she was expected to save our world. Who is to blame? It is no wonder she hasn't jumped from the nearest balcony, but she takes your Marks and gives you vows instead. How dare she rebel because you eschew her every attempt to get your attention! Shame on her!" Mekal bantered. "She must be daft as the rise is long."

Jerad narrowed his eyes at his confidante's sarcasm. "She takes my Marks and gives me vows out of preservation instinct. It means naught to her."

"*Ah*, but *Nai*. Unrequited passion is indeed a sting to a man's pride," Mekal mocked. He rubbed the pad of his thumb against his index fingers a hairsbreadth from Jerad's nose.

"What are you doing?"

"I am playing a tiny little lute for your tiny little pity spree."

Jerad sneered at him.

Eunice returned and leaned over Jerad to refill his cup, giving him another eye full of her hefty bosoms.

Sera felt like the googily green-eyed monster. If the little slattern bent over her husband one more time to show him her breasts, she was going to kick the *shi*...

She did it again! Bitch!

Sera threw down her napkin and snapped to a stand.

I'm going to pound her into the dirt!

Every one of her nerves was screaming with raw fury. She stopped suddenly when Mekal whispered something to the servant, who then hurried from the room. Sera sat back down.

Mekal had spied the daggers of rage on Sera's face as a reaction to Eunice's coquetries.

It was not good thing.

A nasty turn was about to erupt and it was his obligation to spare his Noble friends from further humiliation. Mekal grabbed

Eunice's arm and pulled her downward. He whispered enticingly in her ear before discreetly nipping at the lobe. She giggled. Mekal told her to meet him outside the kitchen in one *quarter segment*. She smiled at him amorously before removing herself from the hall. With hungry eyes and a skewed grin, Mekal watched her strut away. Eunice was a voluptuous little strumpet with a licentious appetite. She would do nicely for him this *luna*.

Mekal glanced toward Sera, relieved to see that she was no longer advancing. With the situation diffused, he returned his attention to Jerad.

"You hide behind your arrogance and your pride, Chancellor."

"What do you badger me about now, Noble?" Jerad leaned back in the chair and crossed his arms.

"Only a brave man has the strength to seize a gift which might make him vulnerable."

"Are you calling me a coward?"

"If the boot fits…" Mekal let his remark trail as he took a bite of his food.

Jerad chortled.

Afraid of what?

Making love to Sera, of loving her?

Did he love her?

He could not answer his own question. Jerad slumped in his chair, wallowing in his misery.

Misery wants company, but Mekal was in no mood to oblige. He bid his leave-taking and left the hall, heading in the same direction that Eunice had gone.

The life of a guardian was a hazardous undertaking, but someone had to do it.

Jerad's scowl clashed with Sera's crestfallen expression. He felt a pang of guilt. If she kept looking at him like that he was going to finish the deed she attempted the luna afore and poke out his own eyeballs. Jerad slammed his mug on table.

Hades' fetid breath.

He did not even care about the Edict any more. He wanted only Sera, to hold her in his arms, protect her, cherish her, love…

Feeling ambushed by such intense feelings, Jerad lifted a shield to his heart, rejecting the barrage of emotions assailing him. He flew to his feet with such haste, his chair toppled to the floor. Jerad left the hall without giving Sera a second glance.

He had to think.

Sera watched him leave. Her bottom lip quivered. Ezra gave her a sympathetic pat on the hand. Phoebe huffed. But Sera's mood suddenly and drastically changed. She became riled, consumed by a fierce possessiveness and a rampant, potent determination.

Damn it all anyway!

She might never gain his love, but she was most certainly going to claim his body.

It was time to put an end to this ridiculous game.

* * * *

A crooked smile crossed the face of the swordsman facing Jerad. "I do think a more importunate Challenge is about to come to pass, Chancellor."

Over Jerad's shoulder, he watched the Noble Sera approach. Her rapid gait was stiff. Her angry eyes were steadfast on Jerad. Before Jerad could turn to see what his opponent was referring to, he felt the point of a blade in his back.

Sera was behind him, arm outstretched, massive double edge sword in hand.

Blasted!

Why had she chosen Zoren's sword? It was so heavy her extended arm was beginning to ache. Sondra's lighter, single-edged blade would have been a better choice for Sera's size but *those* wounds were still too fresh. Sera decided that it was better that the sword was kept out of sight for awhile.

"Draw your weapon, barbarian."

Jerad's jaw ticked and he gritted his teeth, astounded by Sera's audacity.

How dare she.

The others in the Grandstage laughed. The challenger in front of Jerad sheathed his sword, rubbed his bristled chin and backed away.

"This should be quite amusing, Chancellor." His smirk only served to irritate Jerad further.

Without turning, Jerad placed his hand to the hilt of his sheathed sword. "Dear wife, I fear I will humble you here today."

Sera forced a puff of air through her pursed lips as if to say, *yah right.*

Such mettle did his wife possess. Jerad turned slowly to face her. His breath hitched in his throat. *By the Origins she was beautiful when she was angry!*

Sera was fire and fury, emphasized by the bright red vest and pitch black pants she now wore.

And Zoren's sword? Who did she think she was fooling? She

could barely lift the blade, yet her determination was clearly evident by the fierce look on her lovely face.

He couldn't wait to get his hands on her.

"State your charge."

"Spousal neglect."

"And what penalty do you seek?"

"Your bed. With you in it." Sera boldly jerked her head back, heedless of who might hear her. He was her husband and she was taking him down.

Jerad actually blushed at her bold request, but regained his wits quickly. "I should warn you wife, the last time a consort challenged her husband for such plunder, she found herself in a state of undress for seven full rises."

"Oh yah?" Sera looked at him defiantly. "So tell me Noble husband, who actually won that challenge?"

Jerad choked back a laugh. Battle lust or bed lust, it did not matter. She was his wife and one way or another, he was taking her down.

With a lightning blitz, Jerad swung his arms. His clasped fists crashed down on Sera's wrist rattling her with such pain that she dropped the sword. Sera yelped and grabbed the throbbing appendage. She felt like a fledgling novice, but she was a stubborn one, and determined not to surrender. It was better that she no longer had the blade. It's not like she knew how to use it anyway.

Sera crouched with her feet widely spread and knees bent. Her arms were stretched out, her hands clawed. Strands of her dark hair loosened from its weaving and were tousled about her head. Sera blew a wayward tendril away from her face.

Jerad chuckled. She looked like a wild animal ready to pounce, needing to be tamed.

Before he could ponder the thought any further, Sera hurtled toward him bringing a foot to his chest. Jerad was caught completely off guard. The blow knocked him off balance and he landed on his rump. Laughter from the onlookers filled the room. Sera too had been thrown backward by the force, but they were both immediately on their feet and she was charging again, throwing her shoulder with all of her might into his abdomen. He stiffened. Sera bounced, landing on her backside again. Much to her dismay Jerad flew forward and grabbed her arms. He twisted around, tossed Sera onto her back, pinned her arms over her head and crushed her with his body. All in one sweeping motion.

Again more sniggers could be heard.

"You are defeated." His face was merely inches from hers.

Sera thought briefly that she might bite his nose, but instead tried to buck him off. She stilled when she felt a thickening bulge press against her thigh.

"Settle yourself, woman," Jerad whispered. "I do not wish an audience for this grand but intimate greeting." He bent his face close to hers, his eyes twinkling with mirth. She was at his mercy.

"Let me up, you're hurting me. I...I can't breath."

His insolent grin was *pissing* her off.

"You are talking, therefore you are breathing."

He did not move.

"I'm going to faint." She rolled her eyes back into her head as if fainting.

He chuckled.

"I'm going to scream!"

"So scream. Who here will help you?"

"Let–me–up," she snarled through clenched teeth, emphasizing each word.

"No."

No?

He pressed his weight harder against her. "Address me as master and say *please*."

Sera looked at him, and *oh* if looks could kill. "No way! Get off of me!"

"I think not."

His calmness was infuriating. "Get off of me, you big oaf!"

He pressed his full weight down on her, smirking.

Damn! He was enjoying this!

Sera relented as she struggled to suck air into her lungs.

"Okay. Okay," She croaked. "Uncle."

Jerad shook his head. "*Ochi*, I said call me master, *kopella*."

Wench? Was there a Greek word for wench?

Evidently.

Well, that did it!

She bit his nose--hard.

Jerad let out a painful howl and he began rising off of her, but Sera rose with him refusing to release her teeth.

With a great show of force, and drawing on every warrior skill afforded to him through relentless training, Jerad, mighty warrior, descendant of Antheia, Third Corridor of the Tenth Zone...

...grabbed her breasts and squeezed--in full view of their entire audience.

Kollef, one of the men in the room could no longer contain himself. He dropped to the floor, rolling with laughter.

What a pitiful pair they made with Sera's mouth clamped to Jerad's nose and Jerad bent inelegantly over her, his hands clamped to her bosoms.

Sera gasped and her mouth fell open. She jumped away from Jerad, crossing her arms over her chest protectively. He rubbed his nose. Their eyes collided in a blazing lock.

Stubborn beautiful madwoman!

Gorgeous warrior jerk!

Sera turned on her heels and stormed away spitting, "Damn Greek speaking, medieval barbarian!"

"Does she talk to herself often?" Kollef grinned, recovering from his fit of hysteria.

"Only when her mouth is not otherwise occupied," Jerad replied, more amused at Sera now, than angry.

The snickers from the onlookers served to further inflame Sera's temper.

"I heard that!" She sputtered without looking back. "Go boff yourself!"

Jerad was utterly shocked. Never would he have expected such a vulgar suggestion from his wife's mouth. He tracked Sera's movement but watched only momentarily.

With a quick stride Jerad was instantly behind her. Sera shrieked as he wrapped both arms tightly around her, pinning her arms to her side. He easily lifted her feet from the ground.

Sera squirmed and flailed her legs in a futile attempt to break free. She jabbered threats toward him as she struggled.

"Ah, I think you shall not leave me so quickly my foul-mouthed captive."

"She puts up a mighty fight, Jerad," Corde sniggered. "I bet she is quite the spirit in the bed chamber."

Jerad flashed a searing look. "Stifle that crude tongue of yours, Corde! She is still my wife, and you will respect her as such."

Sera blushed. To add to her humiliation Jerad shifted her to one arm while still restraining her. He effortlessly bent down and picked up Zoren's sword, stood and tucked it under his belt.

"I believe that this now belongs to me."

He set her down.

"As does this." His eyes poured over her body with carnal intent.

Jerad grabbed the front of her vest and pulled her out of the arena.

When they were away from the earshot of the others, he abruptly turned, throwing her a fierce look. "Barbarian? I will show you what kind of barbarian I am, *siren*."

Sera's lip contorted, her eyes narrowed, and she sneered at him. Jerad shook his head and dragged her to the stable just outside the Grandstage.

"Why did you bring me here?"

He said nothing, but did release her briefly.

She watched as he retrieved a rope from one of the stalls. Her eyes widened and she turned to run. He grabbed her around the waist and hauled her back. She landed flat against his chest. A *woosh* of air escaped her lungs. Jerad grabbed her hair, wrapped it around his hand and tugged on it. He turned her around and tipped her face upward. His lips curled aloft. He seized her mouth in a deepened kiss, ravenously probing with his tongue. Sera's efforts to resist were futile. At first she furiously tried to pull away, but her body, as it seemed always in want to do with him, betrayed her mind. She returned his kiss, sinking into him. With his mouth still clasped to hers, he took both of her hands and wrapped the rope around her forearms until he reached her elbows.

Her arms were hog tied before she realized what was happening.

He released her lips. Sera looked down at the ropes and then back to Jerad. "What do you think you are doing?"

"What I should have done a long time ago. Claiming what is mine."

Jerad held the free end of the rope and pulled her toward the castle, leading her like a slave. They passed Ezra on the way.

"Good luna to you, Jerad and Sera." She greeted them casually, as if a warrior dragging his bride by a rope were an ordinary occurrence.

"And to you, Ezra," they both responded simultaneously.

Ezra continued on her way without looking back.

Chapter Twenty-one

Some honeymoon this turned out to be.

Kinky bastard.

Jerad's hands grazed lazily over the lush material of her vest and trousers--just before he cut them from her body. She stood there naked before him, in their bedchamber, with her back against the bedpost. He had tied her hands to the canopy rail above the bed, the rope now replaced by the shears of the bed curtain. She did not resist him, but instead watched with anticipation as a thick haze of yearning swept over her.

Jerad responded with a deep, appreciative look before settling into the chaise. He sat fully clothed, lounging with one foot up and the other on the floor. He sipped wine from a crystal chalice.

His eyes roamed her body, ravaged her mentally, scorched her erotically.

Sera noticed three distinct movements on Jerad's face. His eyebrow twitched, his nostrils flared, and a devious grin crept across his lips.

Jerad gritted his teeth. She was glorious. Her skin sparkled like the early *rise* against a misty sky.

Why had he cut her clothes off her?

It only served to bring his blood to a roiling simmer. Never had his lust escalated to such heights afore. He could not help it. Once he laid claim to her in the Grandstage, he felt a raw, primal need surge through him. When he led her to the bedchamber and tied her to the bedpost, he became absurdly predatory, like a great falcon swooping down on its prey.

Like the Ptino asteri in the mural, he mused, except it was *he* who had captured her.

Now he sat like a daft fool, trying with every shred of his will to beckon his inner restraint. He dare not touch her, lest he explode in his trousers.

That would not do.

Jerad tensed against the blistering desire taunting him, resisting the building urge to shed his clothing, plunge deep inside her and thrust with all his might until he found his release.

Ochi.

He needed to love her gently, with his lips and his hands, caress her skin, her soft, silky skin--that now flushed with a passionate glow, begging him to plunge deep inside her and thrust with all his might until...

Ack, and blasted!

Jerad expelled a harsh breath.

He knew the female form, knew it well in fact. Being a physician afforded him such knowledge. With his patients, it was a sterile situation, his interest being clinical at best. As a warrior he laid hands or body against women in the midst of competition or battle, with only an ever so slight titillation that dissipated quickly in the throes of the contest.

Purely platonic events.

Ochi. He had never physically engaged a woman, though there had been plenty willing to enlighten him to the art of lovemaking. It had been difficult to resist, the restraint excruciating at times. With Sera, it would be markedly different. She was his mate, his wife. They were bonded. It was his right, and his privilege. He could touch her, with his fingers, with his mouth, and with his body--learn to heed to the simple and complex nuances that revealed a woman's passion--Sera's passion, and how to elicit responses to give gratification to her needs.

And he was now free to unbridle his needs as a man.

At the moment, a very aroused man.

The expectation was nearly killing him. He craved Sera beyond all rationality.

He needed to get himself under control.

"Untie me Jerad," Sera pleaded.

She could have wiggled free. The bonds Jerad tied around her wrists were not very tight, but he did not know that, and she was enjoying his dominance over her.

He shook his head slowly and deliberately from side to side. He knew she could wiggle free, but as long as she was willing to play this game, he was more than willing to accommodate her.

Fine, Sera thought. *I'll play the game.*

If it was seduction he wanted, it was seduction he was going to get.

Sera inhaled slowly and stretched her back, causing her breasts to jut and roll with the motion. She met his gaze with an enticing come-hither look and brazenly licked her lips. Jerad released a choked groan and tossed his head back. He laughed softly, then returned a whetted gaze in Sera's direction. She was assailed by a pulsating ache in her most private, feminine place. It threatened to undo her. She responded with a shrewd smile.

He stood and picked up a blue, bell-shaped piece of fruit from a bowl to his right, and approached her with smoldering eyes.

"I find food to be a very sensual thing, don't you Sera?" He suckled the fruit, and then bit into the soft flesh.

Without touching her, he leaned his face toward her and pushed the fruit from his mouth to between her lips.

He certainly did like to play with his food.

Sera clamped her lips around it and crushed it before leisurely working it around in her mouth and swallowing it. A stream of sticky, blue juice dripped from the corner of her mouth, trailed down her chin and along her neckline before it curved inward to rest between her breasts.

Jerad inhaled sharply, and leaned forward to lave the little juice path from her chin. Sera's head fell back and she moaned. He suckled around the edge of her jaw, tasting both her sweetness and that of the fruit, following the trail from her neck and collarbone to the mound of her breast and the crevice in between. Her nipples peaked with his delicious laving as he gently took one between his lips, flicked it with his tongue, drew it into his mouth and released it. Not once did he touch her with his hands. Sera's breathing deepened. She wanted, no, *needed* more. When his teeth grazed her other nipple, Sera thought she would jump out of her skin.

Jerad released a low, seductive chuckle and backed away from her. He returned to sit on the chaise and leaned back, folding his arms across his broad chest. He casually rested a booted foot to his opposite thigh.

He should have fled the room.

He was perilously close to rupturing.

Sera was still trembling from his touch. She blew out a nervous breath, suddenly feeling vulnerable and exposed. He was playing her like a fiddle.

"I thought you were supposed to be a virgin!" she snapped.

Jerad leaned forward placing his chin atop clasped hands. His elbows rested on his slightly parted knees. There was a wicked gleam in his eyes.

"I will have you know Starbird, though I have not physically indulged in my own pleasure with another, I am far from innocent. I have spent many long term cycles and cold, lonesome lunas considering what I would like to do to my woman."

Sera's body shuddered as she contemplated his unsatiated imagination gone wild. She gulped.

Sera was in deep, deep trouble.

"Okay then doc, let's play."

"Do you challenge me again?" He crooked a slanted, cocky smile that caused Sera to chuckle.

She bit her lip. This was serious business. "Take off your clothes and let's find out."

He laughed, and moved toward her, stopping a hand's width from touching her.

Oh *Nai!*

Even without fever he did radiate a blazing heat all his own.

Jerad leaned in, pressing his clothed body against her nakedness. He placed one hand over her bound hands and the other on the back of her thigh. He nuzzled his face into her hair.

"Your scent drives me to madness."

If Sera had thought that being clothed next to a naked man was sensual, this was positively volatile. She was on fire.

Jerad stepped back from her, and removed his shirt, yanking it over his head. He reached and threaded his hands through her silky hair, pulling the rest of her weave apart and draping the strands around her shoulders. The flower buds holding the weave came loose and bounced to the floor.

He bent toward her and touched his mouth to hers, plying her lips until they molded to his and he was able to slip in his tongue. He explored and plunged, withdrew and plunged again, groaning with pleasure at the mere kiss. Sera returned the same, savoring the taste of him, the feel of his soft tongue as she caressed the inside of his mouth. He drew both of her lips between his and then nipped at the bottom one before tearing away from her.

She sighed and then tensed with uneasiness as Jerad sat on the floor in front her. He wedged his knees between her legs, forcing them apart, admiring the view as he did so. Sera flushed. His warm breath wisped against her intimately. A shiver ran up her spine.

"Jerad don't...untie me."

"I have no plans to untie you just yet." He twisted her words.

"No, that's not what I..."

She gasped, unable to finish her words. His fingers came up to her curls and he parted her folds. He brushed his thumb against her. Sera arched and threw her head back, quivering at his touch. He examined her, experimented, kneaded her buttocks and inner thighs. He trailed his fingers along her inner flesh and fondled the small swelling there. It stiffened and throbbed. He rotated it between his finger and thumb, and while he manipulated her, he brought his other hand to her sheath and stroked a finger inside, then two. He smiled at the building moisture and the scent of musky female arousal. Jerad shifted against his own urgent need, but did not relent. He continued his finger thrusting and massages, until he fully understood her need. A rush came over Sera, followed by an intensified shutter as Jerad leaned forward and his moist tongue tasted and suckled her.

Sera screamed and she reached her first peak.

Oh my freakin' stars! Where did the man learn to do that!

It was a rhetorical question.

Sera was tight, *very tight*, and he was pleased to discover that she indeed was not a well used woman. Jerad thrummed restlessly. He could wait no longer. He stood and turned to retrieve his dagger from the table. He faced her, and began unlacing his trousers, further aroused by the sight of her passion-glazed eyes and flushed skin.

"I think wife, you have been duly punished."

Between heavy breaths Sera lowered her head looking at him from under her lashes. Her voice trembled in a whisper. "No husband, I think not nearly enough."

Jerad growled deep in his throat, a prowler's cry before the pounce. He slid his trousers down his firmly muscled legs only to realize he had not removed his boots. He briefly looked at his trapped pants then up again at Sera.

Oops.

Sera suppressed a smile.

Jerad shrugged and waddled toward her, manpart leading the way--like a moisture seeking divining rod.

She laughed at his ungraceful charm. With one slash Jerad cut the shears binding her. Sera brought her hands around his shoulders and leaned against him. Jerad dropped the dagger, slid his hands around to her back to caress her bottom. He pressed her closer, possessed with a torrid, innate longing to plunge inside her.

He backed her onto the bed, kicking off his boots and trousers, before coming down on top of her.

Every muscle in his body began to ripple as Sera's body lay beneath his. He seized her lips for a deep, shattering kiss and smoothed his hands along her sides until he had both of her breasts cupped. He brought his face between them, kissed the inside of one soft mound, then the other. Sera splayed her fingers through his hair and nuzzled her cheek against the top of his head. He moved up again to take her mouth. Jerad eased a thigh between her legs. Sera's breath quickened as his member grew thicker and he stroked it against her.

Jerad groaned.

It was sweet agony.

He grasped her buttocks and pressed harder. He needed to ravage her--now.

Jerad moved over her, inflamed by the beauty beneath him--his woman.

He poised the tip of his erection at her cleft.

"Sera."

There it was again. He exhaled her name with a feathery breath, a sensual moan of aching desire, like the utterance of a mating call. She could refuse him nothing when he said her name like that.

"Take me, Jerad."

There were no simpler words than that.

Jerad closed his eyes, wanting to relish in the sensation. He entered her and began a slow lingering slide inward. Sera released a soft cry at his fullness, drifted, savored, tipped her pelvis upward and begged for more.

He stopped.

Stopped?

Why did he stop?

Maybe she really did have teeth down there.

Jerad clenched his teeth, taking a mighty hold of his restraint, his mind in a stagger over what was just revealed to him. He expected that Sera had known a lover or two.

Not this.

Pure of mind, the Oneroi had authored, but pure of body, as well?

This was unforeseen. He would have accepted her regardless, but in the depth of this new knowledge, his feelings for her heightened.

His first--*her* first. His--only his.

Before, now, always.

Forever *mine*.

"What's wrong?" She stared up him. He looked awestruck. "What did I do?"

He kissed her worried brow and chuckled softly against her forehead. "It is not in what you *have* done Sera, but in what you have *not* done."

"I don't understand."

"Sera, *suzugos*,"--beloved, he crooned in a bated whisper. "If I had gone any further I would have hurt you."

He rewarded her confused look with an adoring smile. "You are untouched."

Her countenance was one of total astonishment. "I..."

A virgin?

Who Knew?

She didn't.

"W-What?"

Sera searched deep within the crevices of her mind, but came up empty. Not one face was perched upon her libido.

Save Jerad.

It made sense to her now, the barrier in her head, the resistance she could not explain, her subliminal conscious protecting her body from unguarded desire.

"But, I'm too old to be…"

He withdrew from her and Sera mewed a protest at the loss of him. He pulled her from the bed and stood her in front of the clothespress mirror.

"What do you see, Sera?"

Sera meekly lowered her eyes unable to look at her naked form. Jerad's arm came up around her to cup her chin. He turned her face to the mirror.

"Do not be ashamed wife. Look at yourself. Look at us."

Slowly, Sera lifted her lashes to meet their reflections.

"What do you see? What do you feel?"

"Um, two naked people?" She blushed.

…and hot male flesh prodding my backside.

"I see my wife, a beautiful and intelligent *young* woman. I see myself with my woman, two souls brought together by fate and good fortune."

"You don't see the Starbird of the Edict?"

"Whatever the future holds, Sera, so be it. What I see, what I want only to see, is you."

Jerad turned Sera to face him. He drew her close and kissed her.

"Come woman let us make this a proper marriage," he murmured against her lips.

Jerad scooped her into his arms and gently lowered her onto the bed, stretching out beside her. He showered her lips, her breasts, her belly with tender kisses. He returned to cover her mouth with his own as he eased his body over hers, nudging his hips between her thighs. This time he kept his eyes open, wanting to watch the face of this woman, taking her lover--taking him for the very first time.

He did not want to cause her pain, but knew it could not be avoided. He slid inside of her and edged deeper, locking his gaze with hers. He felt the resistance, pushed and broke through.

Sera gasped as he filled her and tears sprang to her eyes. At first there was pressure, then immense, shearing pain--a thorn tearing flesh--and then...*bliss.*

They were one.

A seamless bond.

Jerad went still, basking in her liquid heat, allowing her to relax and accommodate him. To Sera, the sensation was mind bending and overwhelming--his searing flesh against hers, her body pressed beneath him, and feeling the length of him embedded deep inside. Jerad held her face in his hands and kissed her tenderly. He felt her relax and he began to move, slow and lingering strokes at first, then quick short thrusts, then long, penetrating strokes. Sera rocked gently, moved faster, ground against him. She met him stroke for stroke, opening and accepting him as he pressed harder, pushed deeper. She moaned at the delirious waves seeping through her flesh as she climbed higher and higher, bursting through a riptide of ecstasy so intense she thought she might blow apart.

She cried out.

Jerad thickened and pulsated in response to her heightened pleasure.

"Sera."

The sound of his voice caught in her ears like an entrancing melody.

"By the Origins, Sera!" Jerad rasped out between ragged panting as she clenched around him. He slammed harder...once...twice...three times. A guttural sound escaped his throat and he sent the essence of his manhood spilling into her chamber.

Satiated, he collapsed on top of her as she went boneless beneath him. Neither of them moved for quite some time.

"You are the finest woman, Sera." He pulled her into his arms.

She did not respond. Totally exhausted, she had fallen asleep.

Chapter Twenty-two

Jerad was tossing *kupas* at Sera and she was catching them with her mouth. They were enjoying a time of leisure and privacy in a secluded nook within the forest. The hidden garden was located just outside of the Corridor's walls and a short walk from its main path. The solitude was a welcomed reprieve. Ever since word spread that the Ptino asteri walked amongst the citizens, Jerad and

Sera had found little peace. Hordes of people, unable to suppress their awe, persistently followed the couple about, gawking or begging for blessings. The Guardians of the Key were summoned to safeguard them, but Jerad and Sera had grown weary of their constant presence as well. On this *rise* they managed to elude the elite sentries along with the scrutiny of the citizens, and secret themselves away.

"I use to do this with popcorn," Sera parted her lips to capture another piece of the small ocher colored fruit. The *kupas* were sweet and juicy, and grew on vines in bunches. They reminded her of the grapes she ate back home, except the skin protection was much more fragile. It split easily, and the juice inside was a viscous fluid instead of a squashy solid.

Home.

Sera crinkled her toes into the soft, grassy rug beneath her bare feet.

This was her home now.

Parts of her memory had been returning over the last two *rise cycles*, snippets of the life she led before. Nothing significant. Just short little recollections brought on by her present experiences. It did not matter. Sera was happy and content. Not once did she ask to go back to the Mountains of Eksaf 'anise. She did not want to leave. If a rescue party were to ever locate her, Sera would tell them as much. She would stay on Protogio.

Jerad sat cross-legged about ten feet away from her, thoroughly enjoying the relaxing moment. *Rise* after *rise* the Edict had loomed heavily in his mind. He knew by its prediction that Sera would be taken from him. When, where and how, were the only questions. But for now, if only briefly, he was able to put that away. His mind and his heart were at ease. He would cherish Sera for the time they had left.

"What is popcorn?" Jerad tossed another *kupa* her way. Sera caught the fruit and clamped down on it. The skin snapped and the thick liquid flowed onto her tongue.

"It's dried corn." Sera swallowed the fruit, trying to determine a way to explain. She had yet to see anything that resembled corn on Protogio. "It's a little kernel from a vegetable cob that pops open into a fluffy tasty treat when you heat it."

"Might be good," Jerad dashed off another *kupa* in her direction. Sera snatched it out of the air, tossed it skyward and caught it with her teeth.

"You are talented wife."

"Yep, real talented." She snorted.

"This could be a useful skill, Sera."

"Oh yah, right! About as useful as a campfire in a tree house!"

Jerad tilted his head, considering her words. When her humor finally touched his wit, he whooped with laughter, and pitched a *kupa* toward her taking direct aim at her shoulder.

"Hey!" Sera protested and snatched it with a backhanded catch.

He flashed a sly smile as he launched another, this time taking aim at her forehead. Her hand shot up and she repelled it. Jerad's eyes widened with amusement at her swift reaction. He started flinging *kupas*, one after another, in rapid succession.

With the eye of an eagle and unfailing reflexes, Sera either deflected them or caught them with her hand. Of those Sera did catch, she hurled back at Jerad. The delicate skins burst on impact, leaving splotches of *kupa* juice dripping through his hair and down his torso.

Realizing his disadvantage, Jerad finally halted his attack. An amorous gleam appeared in his eyes. "Ah, but *nai*, my wife does have many useful talents, and she will show one to me now by licking this off!"

Sera laughed, jumped to her feet and started to run.

Jerad's long stride and quick step brought him to her instantly. He lunged at her and tumbled her to the ground. Sera squealed and twisted around to face him. He stole an affectionate kiss, before tickling her mercilessly. Sera screeched and chuckled as she struggled to get free, but then Jerad covered her mouth with his hand.

"Shh." He pressed the finger of his other hand to his lips and gazed beyond her.

"What?" She mumbled from beneath his palm.

"Stay down,"

"Why?" Sera lifted his hand from her mouth.

"Shh! Look. A *kinkashou*, Sera. She is about to give birth."

Jerad pointed and Sera turned to her belly. Her attention was steered to a small fury creature, sitting upright on its hind legs and staring at them. Its little snout sniffed the air.

The two foot long creature had thick, calico fur of browns and greens. Its face and claws were shaped like a ferret's but much larger. The long tail, resembling a monkey's tail, extended back and helped the creature balance on its haunches. Sera noted the six mammary glands, pinkish and swollen, protruding from a rounded, very parturient belly.

The animal went down on all fours, toddled amazingly close to Sera and sat up again. It wriggled its nose and eyed her with tawny, oval orbs. Sera sat back on her haunches and stared back.

"You have command of creatures, Sera," Jerad whispered in her ear. "I think she will allow you to touch her."

Sera hesitantly reached a hand toward the creature. It did not move. She put a palm to the *kinkashou's* belly and marveled at the feel of the pups rolling around inside.

"How adorable!" Sera exclaimed.

The expectant mother whimpered, gave one last sniff to the air and scampered into the bushes.

"Come we will see it." Jerad motioned to Sera and they crept noiselessly on hands and knees toward the creature's hideaway.

Sera pulled the branches aside. They watched cheek to cheek as the miraculous event unfolded. The *kinkashou,* now on her side, continued to whimper and pant with laboring breaths. It paid no heed to her observers, as the moment of bringing forth life engaged her. One by one five pups, eyes sealed shut, emerged. With tiny puling cries, they searched and prodded for the sustenance that only their mother could provide. The new mother lapped them clean, guiding each one of them to a teat. Their hungry complaints settled to suckling sounds.

Jerad smiled warmly, watching Sera's joyful expression as she admired the new creations.

He pulled back from the grove that contained the tiny nest of newborns. He sighed as his notice fell to Sera's petite but sturdy frame, feminine and graceful, yet strong. She had delectably rounded hips--woman's hips--*child-bearing hips.*

Something stirred deep inside him.

He leaned in, and inhaled her fragrance. It was a hot *rise* and he could smell her sweat. It was rousingly affable to him. Jerad was intensely and uncontrollably excited by this woman who was his mate. She was the most magnificent woman he had ever known, and he desired her with sudden demand.

Jerad moved toward her and caught her unaware. Grabbing her at the waist from behind, he jerked her from the bush and turned her so she was supine beneath him. His mouth claimed her neck and his hand moved immediately to her breast. Sera gasped and came to full comprehension of what he was doing. She reacted the way any good warrior's wife should.

Sera flipped him over her side and sniggered, as he landed flat on his back.

A bass, seductive tone reached Sera's ears as Jerad chuckled. He sat up and smiled vibrantly. Sera expected a swift assault, but Jerad reached for her, pulled her into his arms and cradled her in his lap. Tenderly, he splayed his hands across her belly in a gesture that could only mean one thing.

Sneak attack, no fair!

Sera's heart liquefied and she sank into his embrace.

And then...

Jerad moved in for the kill.

"I love you Starbird." He gazed at her adoringly.

Slam dunk!

Was that her heart bouncing off her diaphragm?

It must have been. How else to better explain the rebounding lump that soared upward to catch in her throat, only to crash back to her chest with a resounding thump.

Jerad pulled her close and nuzzled against her cheek as he held her. He did not wait for her to respond to his words.

He kissed her hungrily, savagely--like a man seeking his last breath.

Sera was his, only his, and he would love her thoroughly.

Jerad pressed his tongue into her mouth, as his fingers worked the buckles on her trousers. He pulled her blouse free and skimmed his palm across her ribcage until he reached her breast. He caressed her gently. Sera's body hummed to life.

I love you.

He said the words and she would cherish them as she questioned her own swelling heart. Jerad was her past, her present and her future. Her life, her memories began and would end with him. Only Jerad held any meaning for her now.

Sera looked up at him, but instead of returning a warm, fuzzy expression, a devious glimmer graced her face.

She stayed his hands.

"It is my understanding husband that you have a fetish for knots."

Jerad crooked an eyebrow. He had told her what he wished to do to the knot on her wedding garb.

Sera lifted her mouth and kissed him briefly before pushing him onto his back. She straddled him, and bent to nibble his ear, moved lower to kiss his chest. She took a masculine nipple with her teeth and nipped it gently. Jerad's deep voice rumbled at the immense pleasure Sera was giving him.

She moved lower, and lower still, until she reached the cross-lacing of his trousers and began pulling the cording through the grommets with her teeth.

His straining manhood eagerly popped free.

He gurgled as she took him into her mouth. A somatic tremor marched torridly through his body.

"Ah for the love of Himerus woman! Such a gift you give to me!" His ragged voice praised her, his quaking loins thanked her, but then he could bear no more.

Jerad grasped her body and urged her upward. As he dragged her along his own body, he pushed off her trousers. Then he sat up, threw her trousers over his shoulders and clasped her behind the knees to draw her legs around his waist. His hands slid along her back until he had her bottom cupped in his palms. He lifted her and began teasing her with just the tip of his erection, lowering her and lifting her again. Sera writhed atop of him seeking fuller penetration. Jerad withheld, savoring her growing desire. When he could no longer control his intensifying need, he sank her fully onto him, with one downward push on her hips.

They both groaned in cadence.

He lifted her, withdrawing part way and plunging again, over and over until the erotic wave crashed over, sending them both into an explosive climax and leaving them clinging and crushed against each other, joined in breathless heap. He flexed inside of her, savoring the afterglow of energy well spent as her feverish spasms continued to engulf him.

Loving Sera felt natural.

Sera drew a deep, satiated breath as she nestled in his arms. Jerad had an innate sexual prowess, and he had unleashed it on her. He was her protector, her soul mate, her companion. Gaia be damned, and all the memories that eluded her. Jerad was all hers, flesh and soul.

In that instant, Sera knew that she loved him too.

Chapter Twenty-three

The Ptino asteri will forge a bond with the Keeper of the Key…
…none will have the power to put it asunder…

Sera and Jerad left their haven hand in hand, regretting that their brief, but enjoyable interlude had to come to an end. The rise was growing long and they told no one of their plans. It was more than likely the Guardians were frantically searching for them, concerned that malevolence had befallen them.

They encountered Ezra on the path back to the Corridor. She was mounted on her horse and was trotting toward them. She smiled widely upon seeing Jerad and Sera, and halted her mount to greet them.

"There the two of you are! The Corridor is in a ruckus over your disappearance, but I suspected you had sneaked away."

"Have you come to find us Ezra?" Sera asked.

"Ochi. I am going to gather some reisha. Our stock is low."

Jerad frowned at her. "Those mushrooms grow in the setway forest Ezra. It is nearly a three-quarter segment ride from here. You cannot go there without escort. The glide flyers have caught sight of a band of Nyx warriors lurking along the margin."

"I will be fine." She patted her sword.

"Your blade will be of no use against a number of seasoned warriors Ezra."

Sera looked at Jerad. "Go with her. I will get Dex from the stable and meet you there."

"I need no escort, Jerad. You can not leave Sera unprotected."

She had no sooner made her assertion when a Guardian came galloping on his horse. He tugged the reins and his horse reared on its hind legs as it halted. Dust from the path kicked up around him. He dismounted and greeted Jerad with a nod and fisted salute. He did the same to Sera, but with her, he dropped to one knee, indicating her higher status.

Sera winced, still uncomfortable with her pedestal ranking.

"Guardian, accompany the Noble Ezra to the forest. She is in need of medicinals and should not go alone," Jerad instructed the warrior.

"Ochi Chancellor. I cannot. The Archon has half the sentries searching for the two of you. Our orders are to return at once should we learn anything."

Jerad twisted his mouth. He would not force the warrior to countermand his task. He did not want to leave Sera, but knew she would be safe with the Guardian. He finally agreed.

"Very well then. Return my wife to the Corridor and inform the Archon that we are safe."

Sera rose to her toes and lightly kissed Jerad's lips. "I will be along soon, likely with a horde of guardians following behind me."

Jerad slid his hands around her waist and pulled her close. "See that you are wife. I grow restless when we are apart for too long."

Truer words were never spoken for as soon as Ezra and Jerad were out of sight, Sera felt an uncomfortable tightness in her chest. It was as though a piece of her heart followed him.

Sera turned toward the Guardian and he assisted her onto the horse.

The service entrance located at the Corridor's *setway* wall was no more than a quarter segment away. It wouldn't take long to have a horse saddled, and she would be back with Jerad in a heartbeat.

They passed the aviary on their way to the stables. The horse tramping around in the grass, Aryan's horse, Sera recognized, told her that the Noble was likely inside. On a whim, Sera ordered the Guardian to stop. She dropped from the horse and instructed the Guardian to stay outside. Sera stood at the entrance to the sanctuary and peered in. Aryan was on the far side of the bird confine, standing with his back to her. He seemed oblivious to her presence. .

Sera fingered the leather baldric she was wearing before sliding her hand to the hilt that was protruding from the attached scabbard. It was Sondra's blade. Sera wore the sword only because Aryan's clan complained that her refusal to don it was the same as proclaiming that Sondra's life was not worth acknowledging. It was an insult to the clan.

Go figure.

Additionally, to have the Ptino asteri displaying their kinswoman's possession was deemed a great honor, testimony to Sondra's hand in fulfilling the Edict of Oneroi. It was the least Sera could offer them, but she did so with tremendous qualm. It hung heavily around her, a constant reminder of what she had done.

Sera mentally recited the words she wanted to say, but in the end decided to let her feelings speak of their own accord. She stepped inside. The falcon perched on Aryan's gauntlet, spread her powerful wings. Her head snapped to and fro before fixing her eyes onto Sera

"Aryan."

He stiffened at the sound of Sera's voice. He did not turn around. The mighty bird continued to watch her.

Sera pulled the sword from her belt, held it out on two palms and stared at it.

"I feel no triumph in possession of this."

Her voice was intensely serious, but her face was saddened. "The thought of how I acquired it only brings me misery."

Aryan still did not move. Sera sheathed the blade and moved closer to Aryan.

"Though, I suppose it is what I deserve," she sighed. "I cannot bring her back and if I could change what I did, I surely would." Sera's shoulders slumped and at the same time Aryan turned to look at her.

Sera looked up. Aryan's expression was devoid of any emotion. "I am so sorry, Aryan. I will carry the weight of it until I take my last breath."

There was nothing more she could possibly say.

Aryan watched her silently. Sera turned to leave.

"Sera."

Sera stopped at the door. Aryan set the falcon on its block and walked up behind her.

"I must beg your forgiveness for my vulgarity in the Great Hall. I am quite ashamed at my behavior. Had I known you were a virgin…"

Sera felt a crimson heat flush through her cheeks. She spun around. "How do you know about that?"

"Your chamber maid has a very large mouth."

"How many people know?" she asked, dreading the answer.

"I think it is common knowledge. The woman is quite the gossip monger."

"Sheesh!" Sera dropped her face to her hands. Mortification struck solidly. "Why didn't she just parade the sheets through the agora?"

"Ack, woman, if we still did that half the linens would likely be white." Aryan's mood almost seemed to lighten as her embarrassment heightened. He grasped her under the chin and tilted her face upward. His stoic expression softened.

"I…" Aryan was interrupted by a commotion outside. He released Sera and went to investigate. Three of his warriors were approaching with haste, shouting as they halted their mounts. One quickly jumped from his charger. The second handed down the warrior she carried and he was laid upon the ground. He appeared to be badly wounded, a dagger wound through the belly it seemed. Aryan recognized him as the sentry posted at the *setway* tower.

"What goes on here?" Aryan demanded.

The injured warrior lifted his hand to grasp at Aryan's tunic, heaving for breaths and shuddering with pain.

"Easy Charon." Aryan attempted to calm him. "I need to understand what has happened."

Charon swallowed a gulp of air. "The Noble Jerad and the woman came to the gate on a single horse. Betur was just behind them, also on horseback."

Aryan was acquainted with Betur, a cocky young apprentice with high spirits. His family dwelled in the First Corridor. "Nai, I know him…Go on."

"When they came through on the other side I saw only the single horse carrying the Chancellor and the woman. I was suddenly hit from behind. The blow did not bring me down. I drew my dagger but before I could strike, a blade pierced my belly. I was only half aware, but I saw Betur signaling toward the forest."

The female among the trio, Teri, stepped forward. "Apparently Betur was alerting the Nyx warriors. Charon managed to signal us after Betur had gone. We investigated the forest beyond the setway bridge. We found the bodies of the sentries who were posted there. They must have been alerted to the trouble and gone to help." The warrior paused and pressed her lips into a thin line.

Aryan stood and faced her. "What else, Teri?" He eyed her sullenly, sensing he would not like what she was about to say.

"We also found Ezra's dead horse."

"Ezra was the woman with Jerad?" Aryan jerked around to affirm what he did not want to hear. Sera stood in the aviary doorway. Her hands covered her mouth. Her eyes were wide with fear. She returned a horrified nod.

Aryan's controlled demeanor turned furious and he began to bellow orders.

"Teri, take Charon to the infirmary, then have the sentries find Betur for questioning. We may have other turncoats among us!"

He motioned to the second warrior. "Go to the Archon and inform him the Nyx warriors have taken Jerad and my wife! Have him send warriors to the landtrail forest. It is likely they will not cross through the Eighth Zone. There are too many glide flyers about. I suspect they will make their way through covered trails. We may be able to block them before they leave the Zone!"

He grabbed Sera's wrist and boosted her onto his horse. He mounted in front of her and they galloped toward the stables.

"Corde is exercising some of the warriors in the hillside, tell him to return with the men to the Corridor and make provisions at once!" he roared at the Guardian who followed them.

The Guardian looked at Sera and then back to Aryan.

Realizing his reluctance to leave his charge, Aryan snapped. "I too am a Guardian, warrior, and well above you in status. Do as you are told!"

The Guardian left immediately.

They entered the stables and Aryan ordered the stable girl to start saddling the coursers. He turned to Sera. "I should have sent you with one of the warriors. I will return you to the safety of the castle before I leave for the Fourth Zone."

A terrible sense of doom spread through Sera's chest. A ringing started deep inside her ears and altered to an annoying buzz. She swallowed a hard lump of air as an overpowering feeling of time ticking away consumed her, along with a strange sense of being summoned.

She moved toward the stable girl who was scurrying to complete her orders.

"This charger first," Sera directed, pointing at Dex. The girl looked at Aryan, who was busy on the other side of the stable, then back to Sera.

"I outrank him child," Sera stated firmly. The girl stared at Sera, knowing that she dare not disobey the Ptino asteri. She saddled the horse.

Sera led Dex outside without notice from Aryan. She mounted the horse and spurred into an immediate gallop. Sera reached the setway gate before Aryan realized what she was doing.

"Blasted! Never mind the horses, girl. Get word to Shegarth to gather as many warriors as possible without risking the security of the Zone. They are to leave at once. Tell him I am in chase of the Ptino asteri who is heading to the Fourth Zone. Can you handle that?"

The girl nodded and briskly left the stables on horseback.

Aryan mounted his horse, thankful he had brought a canteen, his bow and arrows. He was leaving without rations. The Fourth Zone was more than a rise away, almost two, when traveling at a heavy pace. He would need to hunt for food.

* * * *

Sera did not understand how she knew which way to go, she just did. The strange buzzing in her head seemed to guide her. She crossed the setway bridge, and followed a trail along a lake. It led to the Eighth Zone, confirmed by the Coat of Arms posted there. Here, she glimpsed her first sight of the glide flyers. Sera slowed her pace and watched in fascination as the two harnessed riders descended, landing their kites with impeccable skill. She was sure they would insist she turn back, but soon found out that they would not interfere with the pursuits of the legendary Ptino asteri. They merely hailed her and offered escort.

Sera was amazed at the distance the glide flyers were capable of achieving without losing height, flying high above her as she hastened toward her destination. They looked like enormous birds elegantly sweeping the skies, ascending, diving and crossing each other's paths with amazing precision.

The sound of a fast approaching steed caught her attention, but before she could react, the horse appeared at her side. With relative ease, its rider snatched Dex's reins and forced both horses to stop.

It was Aryan.

"Damn woman if you are not the faster rider I have ever been set to chase!" he growled. "Two quarters it took me to reach you! You are going to burst Dex's heart if you continue to force her at such a pace."

"Do not send me back, Aryan. I feel like I am about to shatter. I must go to Jerad."

Aryan regarded her silently for a long moment. He splayed his hands through his hair and breathed a heavy sigh. "I think my opinion may not be what the Edict intended, but we will go together."

Four more quarters they traveled, eventually crossing a shallow river, where they paused only briefly to refresh themselves and fill the canteen. From there, they passed through a bevy of trees and crested a ridge that brought them to the base of the Mountains of Eksaf 'anise.

From high in the sky, the glide flyers waved goodbye and turned back. They would not risk flying through the infamous mountains reputed as being the place where citizens have been know to vanish. Additionally, they were losing light, making it impossible for them to see.

"We will make camp here for the luna." Aryan dismounted from his horse.

Sera studied the grass-covered mountains, which looked more like very large hills. There were three peaks nearly pointed, one large, one medium and a smaller one. She felt a strong pull toward them, but was it because this was near where she landed, where she had met Jerad, or was it something else? Sera recognized

Eksaf's resemblance to the spectrocorde, but another memory wailed through her brain. Three stone structures came to mind, pyramids, the Egyptian ruins at Giza.

"There is a rough trail around the center peak. It is avoided by travelers, mostly out of fear, but it will shorten our journey by several quarters and take us directly into the Fourth kingdom."

"Are you not afraid to travel through them, Aryan?"

"Ochi, I am not afraid."

"What will we do when we get there?" Sera suddenly realized they had no plan. They certainly couldn't storm the kingdom, expecting to take command.

"I am without a notion, Sera. I had hoped our warriors would have arrived by now. Perhaps we should wait…"

"No!" Sera interrupted. "I can't. I feel like I am being ripped apart."

Aryan rubbed his forehead and implored the Origins to give him guidance. It was pure lunacy to enter the Zone as they were, but convinced Sera would refuse to tarry, he decided they would break camp at first light.

He did not sleep that luna, and Sera did not fare any better. He watched her toss and turn in her restless slumber, mumbling words he could not discern.

Sera was hearing voices. She was fighting against a tugging that threatened to snatch her away.

Inhibit Serotonin…forcing alpha waves…slowly now…

"Not yet," Sera cried. "Let me go…"

* * * *

It was by horrendous ill fortune the following *rise* that Aryan and Sera happened upon Ezra's tattered and bloodstained cloak. A bloodied misericorde was discarded nearby. Sera looked at the pick-like dagger and nearly retched. There was only one reason to use such weapon--to drive a death blow through the throat or chest of the intended victim.

Aryan clenched the cloak in fisted hands, his grip so tight his knuckles turned white. He turned to Sera with anguished eyes--the jade-colored eyes of Sondra whose glimmer dulled as death came to claim her.

Aryan's entire body began to quiver, and then, he lost all control.

He dropped the cloak and fell to his knees, while pulling his dagger from his belt. He lifted it over his head, held it with two hands and began stabbing the dirt over and over and over, roaring a tormented outcry, while Sera numbly stood by.

Suddenly realizing they were in dangerous territory, Aryan gritted his teeth to suppress the outrage that threatened to expose them to their enemies.

It was all for naught however. They were discovered and captured.

Chapter Twenty-four

"I did not waste twenty years of my life mastering the language, searching for answers, learning to manipulate their society to my benefit, only to come home and find my kingdom in anarchy!"

Moros crushed the red star on the warrior's jerkin with his fist and pulled him so close their faces nearly touched. His breath was hot with fury.

"Do you hear my words, Gorgar?"

"My lord, those who support the Noble Jerad's triumph for the throne might be swayed by your return."

"Yet my advisors tell me that it has not happened thus far, and likely will not unless the Noble Chancellor is executed."

With a glower, Moros released Gorgar, pushing him with such force he stumbled and fell into the throne chair behind him.

"What the hell made Zoren think he could rule my kingdom anyway!"

"My lord, he is...was your little brother. It was only fitting."

Moros slashed his hand through the air and sniffed with indignation. He cursed Zoren for the wager he had made. His sibling was never a wise thinker. The fact that Zoren had bargained the kingdom away had only served to complicate Moros' purpose. It was best his idiot brother went to Elysium without is head.

"What was that blasted fool thinking?"

"Zoren could not resist such a Challenge my lord. I was hidden in his private chamber that rise and I heard the terms. The Antheian descendant promised the Key if Zoren was the victor."

"Well, he certainly leapt for that dangling carrot, did he not?" Moros walked to the throne chair and grasped Gorgar by the upper arms. "Get out of my chair!"

Moros threw the large warrior from his seat. Gorgar stumbled and landed solidly against a column. Unscathed, he brushed himself off.

Moros shifted in his chair and leaned against the arm rail.

"What if the Noble Jerad had lost? Do you really think his people would give up the Key?"

"Perhaps we can barter the Noble's life for the Key to Orion's belt. If you execute him we surely will not acquire it."

"Not true my friend. The Key will be mine, if I have to steal it myself!"

"But Moros, we do not even know what it is."

"You have heard the rumors, idiot! The Ptino asteri is with them. If they are aware of who she is, then I am sure they have revealed the Key to her."

"But what makes you think she will reveal it to you."

"You are an ass, Gorgar. You forget the lady is mine. Her loyalty is preserved for me. After all, I did foster her."

"But what if she has learned nothing, lord?"

"It is fated, my most loyal warrior. She is the chosen one. Through her the Edict will be fulfilled and Protogio will be mine."

They turned their heads to the treading of heavy boots. Three men knelt before Moros.

"On your feet, I don't have all day."

"We have them, my lord. One appears to be the woman you described."

"Them?"

"*Nai*, she was with the Noble Chancellor, Aryan."

"Escort them here, and then bring in the other prisoner."

Sera and Aryan were led into the throne room. Their heads were hooded and iron shackles that cuffed their wrists and ankles restrained them. The weighty chains made moving about a laborious feat, but worse than the bonds that ensnared them, they were yoked by chain linked collars that tightened like a noose around their necks when pulled on. Sera struggled against her vanquishers several times and was rewarded with a sharp yank on her unwanted necklace, the tightening bond nearly choking her. From the gurgled sounds of Aryan's voice next to her, she assumed he suffered the same consequence.

Moros moved in front of Sera and pulled the covering from her head. He grasped her under the chin and lifted her face to look at her. "Finally, Sera."

Sera blinked several times to adjust her eyes to the light, then wrenched her chin from his clutches. Moros crooked an eyebrow at her and then turned to one of his men.

"Take the damn leashes off of her!"

"But my lord…"

"She will not try to harm me, will you, Sera?"

Sera was released from her bonds. She rubbed her wrists where the cuffs bit through her flesh and stared at her captor. He did not look like the rest of the men she had met on Protogio. Where most wore their hair at shoulder length, this one barely had any at all, it was cropped so closely to his skull. He had steely gray eyes and an angular jaw. He had handsome, but harsh features. Aside from being the enemy, something about him disturbed her. Sera knew that face, but from where?

"Who are you?"

Moros wrinkled his brows as he returned her gaze, searching Sera's confused looking eyes until understanding struck. "Oh isn't this rich! You've lost your memory!"

He strolled in front of Aryan and looked him up and down before returning his attention back to Sera. "I suppose it makes sense. You did suffer quite a blow to your head."

"How do you know that?"

Moros ignored her question and turned back to Aryan. He yanked the hood off his prisoner's head.

"Moros!"

"Very good, very good, Noble. You know who I am, at least."

"How could I forget the vile blackguard I beat to a pulp when I was sprig of a child!"

"Tsk, tsk, Noble. Insults will get you nowhere. In case you have not noticed, you are at a bit of a disadvantage at the moment."

"What have you done with the Noble Jerad, and where is the woman brought here with him?"

"*Nai*, a wild one she was. Bloodied one of my warriors before he knocked her senseless."

"Where is she?" Aryan demanded through gritted teeth.

"When I realized she was not this one," he paused to stroke Sera's hair. Sera shuddered, but not because of his touch. It was his name--*Moros*.

Recognition seized her brain.

"I threw her to my men. I am sure they used her well before they killed her." He turned to Aryan and grinned, "As for the other one…"

Aryan lunged at him, snarling his rage, but the guard behind him jerked the restraining chain and it tightened, seizing his neck in a choking grip. Aryan sputtered, grabbed at the chain with his fingers and dropped to his knees.

Moros' lip curled up menacingly. "Careful Noble, or you might crush your windpipe."

Sera was trembling. Her brain was in a tailspin. Though she was no longer restrained, she could not move. She could not speak.

Moros…Moros…Moros… she rolled the name through her thoughts.

Sera Moros…I'm Sera Moros.

The clinking of dragging metal drew her attention to a side entry.

Jerad was led into the throne room. It took four guardsmen to keep him restrained. He was shackled with wrist and ankle chains and a choker collar around his neck, bound in the same manner as Aryan.

"Jerad!" Sera shrieked. A tremendous amount of relief filled her at seeing him alive. She attempted to run toward him, but Moros caught her about the waist and pulled her back.

Sera thrashed and kicked to free herself, but with Moros' greater might, Sera's strength quickly withered. Moros laughed with smug satisfaction and handed her off to one of his guards.

Sera stared at Jerad with helpless desperation.

Jerad released a feral growl at seeing his wife in the grips of the Nyx monarch and struggled against his chains. He was immediately brought to heel. Moros signaled his guards with a hand gesture, and Jerad was dragged to a chair. His arms were forced to the table top in front of him and a spike was hammered through the chain connecting the irons clamped around his wrists. He was pinioned to the table. The same was done to the manacles at his feet, riveting his feet to the floor.

"I will kill you, Moros." Jerad stirred wildly, pulling at the chains that bound him.

"Be wise whom you threaten, Noble." Moros held out his hand. "Come to me, Sera."

Sera shook her head, but the warrior behind her shoved her forward.

Moros caressed her shoulders. Sera looked at him with dread. Her thoughts were racing. A myriad of disjointed pictures flashed through her brain.

"Lovely Sera. I was worried about you. He lifted her hand to kiss it, but halted upon seeing the Marks of Permanence.

"Married," he mumbled as he ran his thumb along the indelible engraving.

He darted a baneful sneer toward Jerad's fettered hands,

recognizing that he bore a similar mark. "So, Jerad, not only do you think to take possession of my kingdom, but it looks as though you wish to claim my woman as well." He turned back to Sera. "Don't fret my dear, you will be free of him when he is executed."

Sera tried to pull away from him but his grip on her arms tightened. "Yes, Sera. The best is yet to come."

The best is yet to come…

She grew up hearing that expression constantly. It was the last thing he said to her before…before their ship crashed.

There was no ship, no dead crew.

"Garret?"

"Ah, you recognize me, love."

"Sera!" Jerad furiously struggled against the chains that bound him. It was a futile effort.

Aryan attempted to move toward Sera and Moros, but was thrown forcefully to the stone floor by the guards.

The buzzing in Sera's head grew louder. The room started to fade then snapped back sharply. A memory jolted her to awareness.

"The POSSUM!" She looked to Garret for confirmation but it was not necessary, for she suddenly understood.

Then she heard voices.

…ease the beta waves… injecting epinephrine…not too fast…

"Shit! Not yet!" Garret yelled and pressed his fingers to the bridge of his nose.

Sera's eyes widened and she froze. Her breathing increased to a painfully abnormal rate. "You hear it too! Don't you?" She knew he did. They were sharing the same experience.

A barrier collapsed, and thousands of memories began pouring in. Sera threw a hand to her forehead. Her chest tightened as she gasped.

Sera was remembering.

"Jerad!" Sera cried and she started toward her husband. She needed to touch Jerad, to tell him…

Moros clasped his hands around Sera's upper arms. His fingers bit into her flesh. He pushed her closer to Jerad and shook her from behind.

"Behold Jerad of the Tenth Zone…" Garret Moros laughed banefully, "…I present my queen!"

"No!" Sera screamed.

Jerad bucked against his restraints and roared.

"My god! No…Jerad!" Sera reached for him, but Garret would not release her.

A tortured cry flew from Sera's throat. "You have to be real, Jerad. I love you!"

The colors in the chamber suddenly drained, leaving only shades of gray. The straight lines of the walls, crispness of the wooden furniture and hardness of the floor beneath her began to waver and implode.

"Sera!" Jerad watched as her image began to dissolve before his eyes.

Sera held out her vacant arms, reaching for Jerad's echoing voice. Suddenly it felt like she was being drawn backwards through a speeding tunnel. Jerad and the room surrounding him began shrinking rapidly until the scene before her became a tiny, black pinhole.

And then, it all vanished.

* * * *

…The Ptino Asteri…in truth will be of spirit but flesh to the touch…

Sera's eyes fluttered open to view a white ceiling with recessed lighting. She was surrounded by medics intent on beginning their routine exam. Sera bolted upright, tore the reciprocator from her head and opened her mouth to speak. She was choked with a throat culture swab.

"Damn it!" Garret was angry. He rose quickly from his girth and threw off his headpiece. He yanked out his intravenous line. A medic attempted to approach him, but Garret pushed him aside.

"Times up! How was your trip Major?" Melissa asked cheerfully.

Garret paused to stare at his medical research officer before responding. He drew a deep breath and composed himself. "It's been eight hours?"

In a lower voice, he mumbled, "Two months on Protogio."

"On What?" Melissa asked.

"Nothing, never mind."

Sera's chest was heaving with her fury. A medic was attempting to put an oxygen mask on her but she grabbed it and threw it to the ground.

Her eyes riveted onto Garret.

"You liar!" Enraged, Sera lunged at him. Garret was caught off guard and Sera knocked him to the floor. She landed on top of him

"You son-of-a-bitch!" Sera grabbed him around the throat and started slamming his head against the floor.

Two medics pulled her off of Garret as the physician prepared to inject her with a tranquilizer. She threw a fist to the doctor's jaw but missed, hitting his arm instead. The syringe flew from his hand and slid across the floor. Melissa ran to retrieve it.

At that moment their Commander and another officer entered the lab. They watched the melee with astonishment.

Sera was struggling against the two medics who had just pulled her off of Garret. She managed to bite one of them in the arm while kicking the other in the shin, causing them both to release their grasp on her. Sera took advantage of her temporary freedom and pounced on Garret again.

"Why did you tell him that!"

She was grabbed again and thrown to the floor. The lab team firmly restrained her.

"Calm down, Sera!" Garret rose to his feet and straightened his uniform. "You are out of your mind!"

"What is this behavior all about?" The Commander questioned, looking disappointedly at Sera.

"I'm going to kill you!" She spit angrily at Garret.

"She was a bit disoriented when we were awakened," Garret answered, grimacing as he looked down at Sera. She was prone on the floor. One of the medics placed a knee across the back of her neck, the other held her fisted hands behind her back. The staff physician sank the syringe needle into her arm and pushed the plunger.

"Well she is acting more like a lunatic, Major." The Commander barked. "I expect a full report on your success with this research within forty-eight hours."

He turned to leave. "And for god's sakes get the Lieutenant under control."

"Yes sir, I am sure she will regain her composure quickly," Garret assured him.

Chapter Twenty-five

Gaia:2063 AD

Sera awoke with a start. The infirmary room was dimmed by thick drapes covering the window, but she could tell it was daylight.

Where was she?

Gaia... Earth.

Sera was twenty years old.

Twenty!

Almost twenty-one. She wouldn't even be of legal drinking age for at least four more years.

She thought she was older, much older. Twenty-eight at least.

And she was *not* the Captain of a starship.

She was a Lieutenant, in the Air Force.

A Second Lieutenant!

Peon.

Low man on the totem pole.

A lackey.

The Captain of a starship, imagine that!

The space program had progressed as far as travel to Mars, but no farther. The IASA--*International Aeronautics and Space Administration,* landed a manned flight on the planet a little more than ten years ago, but it was only in the last two years that they had begun to colonize it. Their technology had only advanced that far, and Sera was not even a part of that project. Sera was a part of the POSSUM--*Project on Sub-sensory Understanding and Manipulation.* It was a military research endeavor, supported by the C.O.R.E.--*the Committee on Research Expansion.* Garret revived the study just one year ago after convincing the committee it had merit. Their assignment was to explore the possibilities of dream linking as an alternate and painless method of eliciting critical information from a reluctant individual.

Painless? Sera thought. *So much for that assumption.*

The theory behind the POSSUM held that the mind was most vulnerable to submission during REM sleep, or deep dream sleep. Scientists had proven that it was entirely possible to link two unconscious minds. While in a state of carefully controlled induced sleep, two technologically advanced headpieces, called reciprocators, transmitted precisely coordinated, digitally enhanced brain wave sequences between two people. Their sleeping thoughts could be connected. The military hoped that the project would lead to their ability to interrogate their enemies by entering their dreams, to coerce them into revealing their secrets.

Initially begun twelve years ago, the research had shown promise. Benign and specifically rehearsed information was actually passed between the study subjects. It was a six hour experiment and the tandem team was awakened every hour to record their findings. The project was scrapped as being too dangerous and unpredictable. Apparently the scientists created a mutual dream during which one was critically injured. The incident manifested physically while the scientist slept. His chest suddenly burst open and he bled to death before the medical team could save him. An immediate shut down of the project was ordered until further investigation could be conducted.

Some of the dream images were cited by the surviving scientist and the documentation included proof that he was able to obtain previously unknown information from his partner. The Captain involved in the study left the project shortly after and it was never resumed. An explanation of the phenomenon causing his partner's death was never found.

Argilos and Tomas.

Jerad told her they would often vanish from Protogio and then reappear…

Sera sucked in her breath when she realized what she was doing. She was confusing her dream thoughts with reality. Had she recreated Protogio in her mind based on what she had read about the previous project?

Jerad.

How could he not be real?

"N-o-o-o-o! Jerad!" Sera cried out his name, and squeezed her eyes shut. She sickened at the revelation washing through her. Her stomach clenched with unbelievable agony.

He had to be real.

She loved him.

Her chest constricted.

"Jerad," she whispered.

A wave of dizziness spun through her and the room felt like it was teetering.

She heard the clinking of chains and strong arms came protectively around her body. She was being cradled. Sera turned her face into the warmth of a muscular chest. His familiar scent soothed her. Sera sighed. A hand stroked her cheek, and lips brushed against her mouth.

"You're sitting in my supper, Starbird."

Sera's eyes fluttered open. "What?"

She brought a hand up to touch Jerad's face as he gazed down at her. Something wet was soaking through her clothing. When she turned to look, she saw that indeed, her rump was partly on top of a platter of food.

"Such nice garments you have on Gaia, Sera." Jerad smirked as he fingered the hem of her clothes and then grimaced.

Sera glanced down at herself. She was wearing an ugly hospital gown. Sera chuckled softly. "At least I didn't land on my head this time."

Sera looked around. The room was damp and dingy. The walls and floor were icy stone. There was a tiny window near the ceiling. An iron grating covered it. The entrance to the cell was also covered with iron bars. Sera returned her attention to Jerad. His wrists were shackled but the chains attached to them were slackened to allow him to eat. The other ends of the chains were spiked to the wall. His ankles were bound in cuffs attached to the floor, immobilizing his legs.

"Where are we?"

"The dungeon, in the castle of the First Kingdom."

"I must be sleeping…dreaming."

"You have returned to me, wife."

Jerad drew her closer and tightened his embrace around her. "I heard your words, woman, before you left me. I beg that they are the truth. Do you love only me?"

Sera pressed against him. His heartbeat thudded in her ear. It sounded…he felt…so real.

"I love you." Sera slipped her arms around Jerad and she clung to him. Her chest drew tight as her mind keeled with the unbearable truth that she was not really with him.

"Tell me you are not promised to Moros, woman." Jerad stiffened at the thought.

"No. I don't know why he lied. He is my brother."

Sera shifted from his lap and kneeled in front of him. She cupped his face between her hands and looked deeply into his eyes. "Tell me that you exist. Tell me that this is not a preoccupation in my head."

His dark gaze was penetrating…tangible…*real*. Her eyes welled with moisture. She closed them as Jerad brought his lips to her lids to kiss her tears away. His shackled arms came around her and he drew her close. "Sera, if I were an illusion, how could you believe my words if I told you I was not."

He could feel her fading from his presence, and knew no way to keep her there. Sera felt it too and slid her arms around him, begging him not to let go of her.

"I'm drifting away, Jerad." She looked up helplessly. The aggrieved expression on his face tore through her. "Help me."

Jerad inhaled sharply, clueless as to what he could do to help her, to help them both. He looked down at his platter of food, plucked a *kupa* from the plate, and placed it in her mouth. Then he bent for one last kiss.

"Remember me, Sera,"

She disintegrated from his arms.

Jerad threw his head back against the wall and growled with agony at the empty space where Sera was just moments before.

"Tell me you saw her, Aryan, and speak the truth. Did you witness her or am I going mad?"

Aryan, who had been silently watching from the cell across the hall, locked eyes with Jerad. His glare was both amazed and stupefied.

"She was there."

* * * *

… the bonded will be torn apart by flesh …but not of spirit…

Sera was staring at the sterile white ceiling of her hospital room. She never opened her eyes to view it. They were already opened. She was fully awake, fully aware--not sleeping. She could taste Jerad and *kupas* on her tongue. She sucked in a hard breath and held it, then cried out a moan, drew up her knees and hugged herself. She felt wet on her bottom, and got out of bed to investigate. She twisted her hospital gown around. It was stained the color of the deep orange *kupas*. Sera dropped her eyes to the untouched breakfast tray of grape juice and cereal--no *kupas* and no orange jam. She patted the dry sheets on the bed. Nothing had been spilled.

Sera wrenched her mouth with dismay. She was losing her mind. The team in the POSSUM lab had said so. Post-traumatic something-or-other. That's what she heard one of them say as they dumped her drugged filled body onto a gurney to transport her to the base infirmary. Though she was in a groggy state, Sera was able to put reason to their words. It was the thing that happened to soldiers after a horrible war. And now she had it.

Sera sat on the edge of the bed and combed her fingers through her hair. She released a grievous sob. Her heart was splitting with every beat. Death would be preferable to the torment she felt.

He wasn't real. None of it was real.

Except for Garret's sudden appearance at the end, that is. Where had his dream thoughts taken him? Apparently he was experiencing a similar illusion. Sera had the impression that he spent the entire time in the First Kingdom, certainly a part of Protogio. One of them conjured the images and the reciprocator must have transmitted at least some of those affects to the other sleeper. Without her memory intact, Sera did not think to search for Garret, but he was apparently searching for her.

*Garret….*Sera was so angry with her brother at the moment, though his behavior certainly was not out of character. It made perfect sense that he would attain a position of power even if it was within the realms of a fabricated dream. Garret was a military man, rigid in his manner, and touted as a natural born leader. Sera spent most of her life being dragged by him from base to base, as he embarked on new endeavors and climbed the military ladder. From his beginnings in the MP--military police, and then as an arms expert, Garret always pursued interests related to combat and with destroying the enemy. His specialty was in warfare maneuvers and terrorist interrogation. The latter earned Garret his present post with the C.O.R.E.

Garret was the reason Sera joined the military and trained at the officer's academy. He urged her to become a medical research technician and procured her assignment to the POSSUM. She never had a say in the course their lives would take. The one time Sera did protest, Garret became so upset over it that she never breached the subject again.

Garret dictated her life.

She couldn't even date without his approval, which he never gave. He threatened any man who got too close to her, managing to effectively gain her the reputation as being untouchable among their peers.

The *forbidden fruit* she was nicknamed. To her humiliation some took bets on who could get her into bed--until Garret found out about it and pummeled a few heads into the ground.

Sera should have hated him for that, but she didn't.

He loved her and she loved him. He was only trying to protect her. She was his only family. It had always been just the two of them, ever since their parents were killed in a terrorist attack while vacationing in Africa, leaving Sera and Garret orphaned. She was a baby at the time. He was a teenager. There was no other family. They were left with only each other to depend on.

Her only grudge against Garret was the lack of mementos from her parents and the life they shared. No pictures. No keepsakes. Garret told her he was so distraught after their deaths that he destroyed all reminders of them.

Sera scratched her head and then clenched her hands together. She was weary. She felt so empty and alone.

She missed Jerad.

She had to overcome this. He did not exist.

Sera took a deep breath and apprehensively opened her left palm. Her eyes widened. There were three small scars in her flesh, not old, but not new either. She rubbed her thumb along the purple and green bruises surrounding them. It didn't hurt.

An autonomic reaction to her subconscious machinations.

It seemed like a good explanation. She lifted her hospital gown and ran her fingers along the scar below the left side of her rib cage and shuddered.

If Sondra succeeded in killing her, she might have really died.

Sera lowered her gown.

She swallowed a hard, painful lump and stared at her hand again, tracing the bruises with her fingertips from her palm to her wrist, and twice around to the dorsum of her forearm.

Forever, Jerad. My memory of you will be with me forever.

She wrinkled her brow as she studied the faded marks. They looked so much like…

Don't do this to yourself, Sera.

She had to know.

Sera pulled open the drawer in the bedside stand. It was empty. She walked to the closet and opened it. Her clothes were hanging inside. She reached inside the pocket of her jacket, but the only item in there was her computer palm pad.

Sera got dressed and walked to the nurse's station.

"Oh, you're awake, lieutenant." The nurse behind the desk greeted her and then frowned as she noted Sera's attire. "And you're dressed."

"Yes, yes I am. I need a pen."

"A pen?"

Sera huffed. She leaned in to read the woman's name tag. "Yes, a pen, Lieutenant Thacker. Ya know, the tube thing that has ink in it."

Unperturbed by Sera's obviously annoyed attitude, the lieutenant smiled. "Well, we don't use them much anymore, with everything being recorded digitally, but the staff is still fond of post-its. There must be one around here somewhere."

She pulled out a drawer and began rifling through it.

Sera tapped her fingers impatiently on the desk-top.

"Ah hah! Found it." The nurse handed the pen to Sera and watched with confused dismay as Sera began sketching on the skin of her hand and arm. When she was finished, Sera studied the finished product. She had outlined a perfect leafy vine adorned with rosebuds.

"Check this out, Thacker?" Sera held up her palm to the nurse. "Nice body art, don't you think?" Sera turned and started to walk away. "I think I'll have it tattooed."

"Lieutenant Moros, where are you going?" the nurse asked her.

"I'm outta here." Sera continued walking toward the door.

"But the doctor hasn't discharged you."

Sera stopped and looked over her shoulder, not caring that she was being unjustly rude, fueled by her irritation and frazzled emotions.

"Yah? So court martial me. I'm leaving."

Sera hit the button on the wall and the door slid open. She left the base hospital dragging her melancholy spirit like a ball and chain.

Sera's heart was wilting, enhanced when she remembered that the POSSUM lab was located in the third corridor of C.O.R.E. building. Bewildered, Sera wondered how much more of her life she would discover had been interjected into her dream.

The door to the lab was open. Sera heard voices inside, but stopped abruptly when she realized they were arguing.

It was Garret and Melissa.

"I'm telling you I never touched her, Melissa!"

"Then how do you explain it?"

It was another lover's spat.

Sera pressed her body against the wall. She really shouldn't be listening, but their arguments were always so amusing. Garret never could tolerate Melissa's jealousy, and Melissa had so much trouble tolerating Garret's infidelity.

Imagine that.

Who was it this time? The nurse in the infirmary or the cute little blond in Sheet Metal Shop? Garret was a free spirit or a louse, depending on whose side you were on.

"I should have never told you that I wasn't her brother!"

A numbing rush assaulted Sera's nerves. She listened with disbelief.

Not my brother?

Like she needed to hear this right now.

Before she could dwell on it further, a sharp pain stabbed like a knife, low in her belly

If there was anyone who knew what that felt like, Sera surely did.

Sera's knees buckled as she grabbed her abdomen. She leaned against the wall for support. The hallway felt like it was tipping.

Music threaded through her eardrums, an enchanting melody that captivated her senses, seized her soul.

She lifted her head to locate the sound.

Shegarth and the Magistrate Council stood around the table of his private chamber, staring at the spectrocorde that was placed in the center. Colorful beams of light danced from the prisms in rhythmic accord with the music it played.

In near unison, their heads turned toward Sera. Shegarth approached and crouched down in front of her. "Daughter of the Mark, from where did you come?"

"I was there, on Gaia. Now I am here," she answered shakily.

"We are at war, Sera. The Nyx warriors believe that you abducted their Monarch and have brought him here. They bargain Jerad's life for his and they seek the Key to Orion's belt, but we will not succumb."

"You will let Jerad die?"

"We will do everything that we are able to free him."

Sera looked beyond him to the worried expressions of the Magistrate members and then to the spectrocorde.

"It has played incessantly since you were taken."

"I'm afraid, Shegarth. What can I do?"

Shegarth's face suddenly faded and Garret's grew solid before her.

"Sera, are you okay?" Garret was stooped down in front of her. Melissa was watching from over his shoulder.

"What language was that?" Melissa asked.

Apparently Sera had been speaking out loud. Garret would know what she said. Would he think she was crazy?

Sera stared at her brother--who was not her brother. His eyes were nearly silver. His hair so blonde it was almost white. They looked nothing alike.

"Uh, it's Greek. I taught it to her."

Taught it to her?

Forced it on her was more like it. From the time she was very young, Garret insisted she speak only in Greek when they were alone. He even insisted that her schoolwork be written with Greek lettering as well, before he would allow her to translate it into its Latin syllables. Thank goodness for modern technology. With a touch of a button on her palm pad, that task was easily performed.

"Well, why is she speaking it now?"

Sera's eyes drifted from Garret to Melissa. "Temporary delusional psychosis, post trauma. Haven't you heard, Melissa?"

Melissa raised a brow and went back inside the lab. She returned moments later holding a small container and handed it to Sera.

"What is it?"

"Sedatives. Take one and get some sleep. You look like hell."

Sera took the container and slipped it into her jacket pocket.

"Come on, Sera. I'll take you home." Garret helped her stand.

Sera pursed her lips and jerked her arm free. She started to walk away. Garret grabbed her arm and turned her around.

"You are still angry with me."

"You messed with my head while we were linked, Garret, and you're still doing it," Sera responded bitterly.

Garret eyed her suspiciously, wondering how much of his and Melissa's argument she had heard. He would have to watch her closely. He followed her down the hall.

The C.O.R.E building was on Jupiter Air Force Base located on the Atlantic coastline of Florida. The installation housed several medical research facilities, including a major research hospital. It was a self-contained site containing a shopping center, theaters, schools, a park and several swimming pools, among other conveniences. Over four thousand military members and their families lived within the confines of the Jupiter facility. Sera and Garret's quarters was located within it and only a five minute ride away.

Jupiter… How fitting, Sera stared out the window of the monorail transport. Right now her head felt as though it were a big ball of gas. Her gut felt like a feather swirling in an empty void. The world seemed to be moving in slow motion, but Sera didn't care. She had gone numb.

Garret tried to speak to her several times during both the ride home and short walk to their apartment, but Sera offered him nothing more than a frigid facade. He made another attempt to speak to her when they entered their apartment, but she merely stared at him, then plopped down on the couch and turned on the TV viewer with the remote.

...a man was arrested today after he held his girlfriend hostage for nearly four hours and then shot and killed her. Another man, who bystanders said, was having an affair with the woman, attempted to rescue her but was shot twice in the head as he tried to enter the house. He died at the scene. The gunman, identified as...

Sera stared blankly at the screen...for hours.

Life was so much more civilized on Protogio...

She was only half aware that Garret brought her food, stroked her hair to give her comfort, and covered her with a blanket. She supposed he wasn't so bad for someone who suddenly felt like a stranger to her.

Sera threw off the covering and went to the bathroom. She bent over the toilet and vomited. When she was through, she pulled herself up to the sink and leaned heavily on it. She turned on the cold water, rinsed her mouth and wiped the sweat from her brow with a washcloth. She studied her face in the mirror. Gold eyes reflected against gold eyes. They weren't always that color. Sera woke up one morning when she was about eight years old and started screaming when she saw herself. Her dark brown eyes had turned to a honey shade of gold.

Was it a coincidence that it happened twelve years ago...the last time the POSSUM...

Garret had teased her relentless...

The thought faded as Sera blinked at her image and bent forward for a closer look.

It couldn't be.

Sera stormed from the bathroom and stalked across the living room to a desk on the other side. She opened a cabinet door and began thumbing through her collection of bittie discs, *BDs*, as they were called because of their small one-inch by one-inch size. When Sera located the one she wanted, she slipped it into the slot on the note pad computer that was sitting on top of the desk.

"Scan BD."

The computer began booting a series of photographs, Sera's personal photo album, until the snapshot she was searching for appeared.

"Stop...enlarge...edit mode."

It was her academy graduation picture.

"What are you doing, Sera?" Garret strode up beside her and

crossed his arms.

Sera ignored him and kept working, touching the stylus to the areas she wanted to alter. She angled her jaw line and nose, but just a touch, not enough to change her characteristic features. She erased her military hat and added light brown, wavy hair. When Sera darkened the honey golden eyes in the portrait to a dark brown, she sat back and shuddered. Then, she snickered a few times before giving way to a tremulous, bemused chuckle.

Sera had projected her own likeness into her illusion of Mekal. In fact, her feminine face, only slightly modified, was nearly identical to his masculine form.

Garret examined the image Sera had composed on the screen. "Who is that?"

"Don't you see?" she tittered, pointing at the screen. "It's my phantom brother!"

Her expression grew angry as she narrowed her eyes at Garret. "But then again, isn't that who you are?"

She stared at him for several seconds before she burst into disconcerted, hysterical laughter.

"You need to get a hold of yourself, Sera!" He grabbed Sera and shook her.

"I'm freakin' cracking up, Garret! You gotta problem with that?" She swiped a tear from the corner of her eye.

…In other news from around the world, an earthquake registering at one point zero, touched the area of Giza last night. No one was hurt and there was no damage to the ancient pyramids …

Sera's head snapped back at the mention of the pyramids. Her hysteria was immediately sobered. She and Garret looked at the TV viewer and listened intently to the commentary.

…witnesses claim the ground shook for nearly thirty seconds before it was over. A bizarre buzzing sound was recorded by tourists in the area and visitors claim that the sound could be heard for nearly eight hours prior to the earthquake. It disappeared following the quake. Seismologists could not explain…

Sera's astonished expression fixed on Garret. Incredibly, he smiled at her. There was a wicked glimmer in his eyes. Her respiration suddenly increased to unbreathable proportions and Sera began choking on her own air.

Garret helped Sera to sit on the couch and cupped her hands over her mouth.

"Easy, Sera. Breath slow," he soothed until her panicked gulps eased. "We need to discuss what happened, Sera."

Sera nodded and relaxed a bit. She really did need to talk about it, and so, she opened her mouth and started to speak. She told Garret about the Magistrate Council and the Challenges. She described the beauty of the castle, and of the *crukis* bulbs. She talked about the culture, their herbal medicines and the monetary value of the gemstones. She even detailed the shatter arrows used by the Nyx warriors, and how she first thought their blasts were from her exploding spaceship.

When Sera expressed her love for Jerad with poignant emotion, she noticed that Garret clenched the arms of his chair forcefully and his face reddened with anger.

She purposefully omitted the spectrocorde and who the citizens thought she was. She was therefore caught unaware when Garret asked her what she knew about the Edict and pressured her for information about the Key to Orion's belt. She regained her composure quickly, however.

"I know nothing about that." Sera watched his lips thin and nostrils flare in irritation to her statement.

Garret was a bit too interested and a tad overanxious about their conjoined dream. It would have been more relevant for him to ask her about the data they were given to communicate to each other while they were linked. It pained her to distrust the only person she ever knew as family, but an inner warning told her it would be best to reveal nothing more to him. Sera might be young, but she was not stupid.

"Why did you capture Jerad?"

"He is my enemy."

"He isn't my enemy."

"How was I to know that?"

"Would it have made a difference?"

"Probably not."

Something in the way Garret responded sent an eerie chill up Sera's spine. She had the foreboding sense to be weary of him. He lied to her about their kinship, but for what reason, she could not even guess.

If he wasn't her brother, than who the hell was he?

Why was she with him?

Sera shook her head. Garret emerged from the POSSUM unscathed, while she was coming apart at the seams.

"I'm going to bed. Goodnight Garret."

Chapter Twenty-six

...there within this melding, the mystery of the Key will be revealed...

Sera slumped against the ceramic tile wall as the steaming water doused her head and body. It was three-thirty in the morning. She spent much of the night rolling from one side of her bed to the other. Each time she was about to fall asleep, she would see Jerad's face, his image would jolt against her shaky slumber and she would awaken. Surrendering to a certainty that she was not going to get any rest, Sera slid out of bed and decided to take a shower.

Sera pressed her hands against the shower stall and dropped her head, allowing the steaming water to drench her hair and slide along her back. But nothing, it seemed was going to sooth her tension. She felt like she was being pulled apart by two worlds. It was like being trapped in a bipolar field with invisible tentacles seeking her from every direction, a force so compelling and so disturbing she would have preferred to have her eyelashes plucked out.

A very old cliché--*Stop the world I want to get off*--came to her mind, but Sera just wished she could jump onto one world and stay there.

In whatever level of consciousness she presently existed, her wits were definitely on overload. In the last forty-eight hours her life had turned a full circle. She entered a reality called Protogio dazed and nearly vomiting, she knew nothing about her life or where she belonged. Now she was back in another reality losing her mind and retching her guts out. She had a brother she couldn't recall, who she then remembered, who was now not her brother.

And when she considered all she had gained and lost with Jerad...

Sera released a sob. It was unbearable to think about.

Her life was so much simpler when Garret was running it.

The news report rattled her, contributing to her already disheveled nerves. It was too much of coincidence for her to think there was no connection. It was crazy to think…

She had to believe.

But Sera needed answers. She got dressed and headed for the lab, hoping to find something, anything that would put the pieces of the puzzle together.

It was a tepid evening, so Sera opted for the half-hour walk it would take to reach the C.O.R.E building. It might help to clear her thoughts. She inhaled deeply taking comfort in the peacefulness of the dark early morning. Orion's constellation was clearly visible in the cloudless sky. Sera stopped briefly to watch it move in its clockwise path through heavens.

The lab was deserted, not surprising at four-thirty in the morning. In a few hours the team would begin anew, analyzing the information gathered and recalibrating the equipment for Sera and Garret's planned, second trip into dreamland. The thought of submitting to another dream linking made Sera ill, but if that was where her answers could be found she would do it. This time however, she would go armed with information that might be useful on the other side. Sera flicked on the lights and sat down in front of the data processor.

"Voice mode."

The mainframe hummed to life.

"Scan, POSSUM research, year two-thousand and fifty-one." She would start in the beginning, with the earlier project conducted twelve years ago. She read the documentation and the commentary on the dream sequencing that emerged during their linking. First Lieutenant Thomas Ormond and Captain Clay Jackson successfully passed the information they were given, but it was their experience on Protogio that interested Sera. There was very little detail provided, however. Other than the bizarre incident that left the lieutenant dead, the contrived dream was considered irrelevant to the mission of the project.

The data briefly mentioned the Edict and there was even a minor reference to the spectrocorde, grouped in their descriptions of the artwork they found there. A vague description of the Tenth Zone was given, and the citizens who dwelled there were also mentioned, referring to some of them by name. She read about the couple, Shegarth and his wife Corinne, and of the boy called Jerad, who followed them relentlessly, attempting to learn their language. It was Jerad who called Captain Jackson, *Argilos*. Interpreted from Greek to English, it translated as the modeling dough used for sculpting, not a person's name. Sera smiled as she pictured her husband as a curious young boy.

My husband. Sera flinched. She still thought of him that way.

Sera leaned back in her chair and sighed. She read this documentation before and she could accept that they were embedded somewhere in her subconscious. They could have contributed to their mental processings while linked. The only difference was that Sera had moved the dream forward in time. She found that piece of information quite puzzling. On Sera's Protogio, there were no images confusing its past with its present. It was as if life had continued in an organized, purposeful manner. She didn't think that even the most stalwart and imaginative mind could have pulled that one off.

Sera turned her attention to the *KNOE*. She was curious to view the data on the numerous physical transformations that occurred to her body while she was sleep induced. There was no doubt that things had happened to her. She had the scars to prove it.

"Play, biological information, Second Lieutenant Sera Moros."

The three-dimensional scan of Sera's body appeared on the *KNOE*. Various readouts began flashing around the perimeter.

"Voice presentation."

Respirations, twelve per minute… pulse, sixty-two… a drone female voice reverberated.

Inducing R.E.M. sleep.

The figure on the screen began to rotate, pausing to outline the various areas of her skin, skeleton and internal organs. The *KNOE* reviewed her injuries, including the concussion to her head.

She watched as the infliction healed within minutes. The same thing occurred to the slash under her ribs and the piercings in her hand. They all healed with miraculous swiftness, leaving only remnants as proof that they occurred.

Sera leaned back in her chair and yawned. She wasn't finding any useful information from what she was seeing

New human life form…

Sera bolted upright. "Stop!"

The *KNOE* halted.

Sera leaned toward the screen. "Enhance."

The screen zoomed in to focus on her lower belly

"Microscopic level and replay."

Sera intently watched the screen as a minuscule cell appeared in the wall of her womb. It divided into two cells and those cells divided. The process continued until a curved form took shape. A tiny dot appeared within it and began pulsating--a heart.

A primitive brain and skeleton formed, and little arm buds burst from the body.

End of data…

Sera stared at the image for several seconds, stunned by what she was seeing.

Sera was…*pregnant?*

"Age of fetus," she choked out.

Data is conflicting…

"Maturation age of fetus," Sera re-worded.

Physical maturation is at six point five weeks, fifteen hours, thirty-six minutes…

"Stop. Time of conception."

Her child was conceived forty-five minutes into the experiment.

A phantom child created in the depths of her own mind, by a phantom lover?

I don't think so.

"Did someone..." Sera gasped and frantically checked the logs. No.

There were at least three people on duty at all times, plus the lab had visual monitors. No one would have dared touch her. Besides that, the fetus was well over a month old.

"There is no way in hell I impregnated myself." Sera did some quick calculations to correlate her sleep time to her time on Protogio, and found that her child was conceived near the first time she and Jerad were together.

I'm having your baby, Jerad. Can you hear me? Sera spoke in Greek. She placed a hand on her lower belly and smiled. Her stomach cramped painfully, but her heart was flying.

Sera pulled her palm pad from her pocket and plugged it into a slot in the *KNOE*. She hit download and recorded the entire course of her baby's short little life.

...This bond will be a joining so seamless it will cross the boundaries of the heavens…

It was eight a.m. Sera was running on little sleep but she was driven by a determination so fierce nothing was going to stop her from figuring it out. She removed her palm pad from the computer, hit the phone button on it and entered a number.

"Jupiter Air Force Base, Personnel Services, Sergeant Roberts speaking, how may I help you?" A voice on the other end spoke.

"Jen?"

"Sera? Hey! How's it going?"

"Oh just dandy. This project is keeping me busy."

"You mean that top secret, nobody can know about it, not even your best friend it's so highly classified, project?"

Sera chuckled. Jennifer was her best friend, and one of the few that Garret allowed her to have. They met at a base picnic when Sera first arrived in Jupiter, and they immediately liked each other.

"Listen Jen, I need a favor."

"Anything for you, hon."

"I need information on a Captain Clay Jackson. He worked at the C.O.R.E twelve years ago."

While Sera waited for the information, she stared at her child's image, watched its gentle floating motions within the safety of her womb. Sera couldn't believe it. She was going to have a baby. Did Garret know? Was that what he and Melissa were arguing about yesterday? Sera decided immediately that it had to be about something else. If Garret knew that she was pregnant, he would have told her.

Wouldn't he?

"Okay, what do you want to know."

"Tell me what you've got."

"Well, let's see. He left the C.O.R.E in two thousand fifty-one. He's a Major now...stationed with the IASA...flying Mars transport shuttles...."

"Do you have and address or phone number?"

"Yep, sure do."

Sera entered the information into her palm pad.

"Gotta go, Sera. The big boss just walked in. Let's do lunch."

"Sure, Jen. I'll call you soon."

The line disconnected and Sera entered the number to Clay Jackson's home. He answered on the second ring.

"Major Jackson, my name is Sera Moros, uh, Lieutenant Sera Moros. I am a Research Technician working on a project called the POSSUM. I was wondering if we could meet."

"I left that project twelve years ago."

"Please, it is important. I just...something has happened to me. I thought that you might be able to help me."

"No... No I don't think so. I'm really not interested in the POSSUM anymore. Good day, Lieutenant."

"Please, no....Don't hang up! Please, Argilos!"

"What did you call me?"

"Argilos."

"There was only one place that I was ever referred to as a lump of modeling material." He paused for a moment and Sera waited for him to continue, but he did not respond further.

"I...I...," Sera stammered over her words. What if he didn't believe her? "I have been to the Third Corridor."

There was an endless silence on the other end of the phone. Sera steeled against the anxiety wracking her.

"They called me the Ptino asteri, sir."

More silence. Sera knew they were still connected. She could hear him breathing.

"Major, sir?"

"I have some time this afternoon," he finally responded.

If relief was an audible thing, Sera's would have been heard across the compound. She left the POSSUM lab filled with hope.

Garret watched Sera disappear around the corner of the hallway. He stepped from the utility closet he hid in to avoid be being seen by her. He overheard her telling someone she would leave within the hour and now his aim was to find out *who* that somebody was. He entered the lab and checked the computer's history to see what Sera had been reviewing. Garret then noticed her palm pad sitting forgotten next to the KNOE. He grinned with satisfaction. The device would give him the information he needed. Sera never kept a lock on her portable computer, let alone its phone.

* * * *

Sera and Clay Jackson agreed to meet in the carrels at the IASA's library at twelve o'clock that day. She hopped the monorail heading north. The IASA was in Cape Canaveral, two hundred miles away, a forty-five minute ride by direct transit. Canaveral was the launching site for the Mars shuttles. The library was located at the large military complex nearby.

Major Jackson was twenty minutes late, but at least he showed up. He was mature, but not old, a man of about forty-five years. Though Sera had read his profile and viewed his picture she was taken back by his rugged good looks and lean, strong appearance. He wasn't tall, about five feet, eleven inches, but carried himself with the proud gait of a seasoned military officer. His dark blond hair, graying slightly at the temples, was cut short in regulation style, and he had a mustache with traces of silver intermittent among the blond. His expression was stern and focused directly on her as he approached.

"Lieutenant Moros?"

"Yes Sir." Sera stood rigid in front of her superior.

He glanced at her wrenching hands and then opened the door to an empty carrel. They stepped inside of the private reading room. He pulled out a chair at the table, seated her and then took a chair on the opposite side. He inhaled and exhaled sharply as he stared at Sera from across the table.

"State your piece, Lieutenant."

Sera tensed at the irritation in his voice, suddenly worried that it might have been a mistake to seek him out.

"I wanted to know more about the dream you had while you were linked."

"You have read my report?"

"Yes."

"Then why are you here? There is little else I can offer you about the POSSUM."

Sera took a deep breath. She was truly taking a risk. Even if Major Jackson did believe her, what could he possibly do to help? And if he didn't, he could report her irrational thinking to her superiors. They might have her declared as being mentally incompetent and she could be discharged from military service.

Garret would be furious.

Sera bit her lip. She didn't care what Garret thought, and her emotions were in such a turmoil at the moment that only two things mattered--Jerad and their unborn child.

"I don't believe it was just a dream. I...I think we were really there."

Okay, she said it. Now what?

The Captain smoothed a hand over the top of his head. He waited for several tension filled moments before answering her.

"Lieutenant Moros, I agreed to meet with you because you sounded distraught. I was quite unsettled myself after working on the POSSUM. I am sure you are aware of the details. I would have to say that your imagination is much more creative than mine and perhaps augmented by a seed already planted."

He rose from his chair and headed toward the door. "Good day, Lieutenant. I have work to do."

"I'm pregnant!" Sera blurted.

The major turned to her and crooked his eyebrows. "Congratulations Lieutenant Moros, but I don't see how that has anything to do with me. Now, if you'll excuse me."

"No," Sera briskly crossed the room and grabbed his arm.

"You don't understand. It's…" Sera paused. She knew how insane it sounded. "… it's Jerad's baby."

The major rubbed his hand across his forehead and shook his head. He removed her hand from his arm and gently patted it. "I urge you contact a psychiatrist."

He pressed the wall button and stepped through the open doorway.

"Please, Argilos," Sera pleaded. "You have to listen to me,"

"I believe we are done with this conversation, Ms. Moros."

"No Major, please don't go!"

Major Jackson blew out an exasperated gust of air. "Young lady, I suggest you return to your life and disregard your obsession with this castle in the air."

He turned to walk away.

Sera closed her eyes. "I will never forget you, my castle in the air."

Sera spoke to his back, quoting the last entry to Argilos' diary. Her voice was low and barely audible, but he heard what she said.

Clay Jackson froze and then slowly turned toward her.

Sera continued, "In the quiet of the night when cool, gentle whispers of breezes caress my face…"

She recited the verse, nearly unerringly, keeping her eyes closed, as the words flowed through her mind. When she finished, she lifted her lids to look at Clay. His eyes were alive with shock. His gazed darted back and forth across her face as if searching for some unknown truth.

"I wrote that, in one place, in one time. It was never mentioned again."

"Jerad saved your journal." Sera gulped. Her eyes began to well with tears. The journal was mentioned nowhere in his documentation.

"It was true," Jackson grimaced and pressed his fingers against his temple. "All true?"

He moved back to the table and unsteadily lowered into a chair. His hands were trembling.

Sera nodded. "We were really there."

An array of emotions crossed Clay's face. He rubbed his jaw, searched the floor, propped his elbows on the table and dropped his face to his hands. Finally he leaned back in his chair, threw his head back and stared at the ceiling. During it all Sera told him everything--every detail of her saga from beginning to end.

When she was finished he stood abruptly and stomped toward the door. Sera's shoulders slumped in defeat. It was over. There was nothing more she could do other than re-link and hope it took her back to Jerad. Perhaps she could find a way to stay this time.

"Come with me."

Sera looked up. Major Jackson was holding his hand out toward her. She hesitated with uncertainty. Was he going to commit her himself?

"Don't look so worried. You have found an ally, Lieutenant." He took her hand into his and guided her from the building.

"Where are we going?"

"To the observatory."

Garret was crossing the quad and caught a glimpse of Sera passing through on the other side. She was with Clay Jackson. He recognized the Major from the profiles of the previous POSSUM team, stored in the lab. Garret started to follow them but ducked behind a tree when Sera suddenly doubled over and fell to the ground.

The ground dropped out from beneath Sera's feet. She looked down and started to scream. Her body was dangling at least two hundred feet in the air. Sera sucked in a raspy gasp as the ground below her sped by.

"Hades breath, woman, where did you come from?"

Sera looked up to see Mekal's stunned face peering down at her. He was holding her by the upper arms.

"Wrap your legs around me before you fall."

Through her panic, Sera managed to throw her legs upward and hooked them around his body. He released one of her arms and then the other. She wrapped them around his back, then hid her face against his shoulder. Mekal guided his glide flyer and they drifted downward. He landed on his feet with complete control, but Sera clung to him for dear life refusing to let go.

"Although I am glad to see you Sera, it is good that Jerad is not here to witness how glad you are to see me, less we have more explaining to do."

Sera was too frightened to be embarrassed, but she released her hold on him and sank to the ground. Mekal undid the harness, freeing himself from the kite and squatted in front of her.

"Your sudden appearance nearly drove my flyer to the ground. It is good that you are as light as a feather, otherwise..."

Sera threw her head back and began to scream again. She was shaking uncontrollably. Mekal wrapped his arms around her and tried to comfort her.

"Gain a hold, Sera. You are safe now."

"I can't take this anymore, Mekal! I'm not really here!"

"You are as clear to me as the sky above, but I know you are an apparition."

His image began to dim and then it faded to black. Through the darkness, tiny bursts of light grew brighter. Sera was staring at the sky. Clay kneeled over her. She sat up and looked around at the crowd that gathered.

"Are you okay, Sera?"

"I'm fine. Just help me get out of here."

Clay assisted Sera to her feet and pulled her through the crowd. As they continued their walk to the observatory, Sera explained the incident to Clay and also told him about the others. He denied ever moving between Earth to Protogio after his dream link, and as far as Sera knew, it hadn't occurred with Garret either. Why then was it happening to her?

"This place is an astronomer's dream," Major Jackson told Sera as they entered one of the several planetariums available. "The observatory has the most technologically advanced equipment and current database available to study the stars. I used to come here looking for answers."

"To what, Argilos?"

The Major moved to the computer panel in the center of the room and activated it. The room darkened and the dome above them began to sparkle. They were surrounded by billions of photo-simulated stars, a visual record of the universe.

"Thomas and I had our suspicions and discussed it each time we were awakened. We wondered if we weren't half-mad, but what we experienced was much too existent to ignore. Unfortunately, as you know, we never got the opportunity to explore the possibility."

"His death?"

Clay nodded. "I took a one year medical leave after my stint with the POSSUM, citing extreme duress because of Thomas' death and anxiety caused by having my sleep induced mind tampered with. During that year I did some research."

Sera sat beside him and listened.

"I gathered quite a bit of information on the Greek gods, which I knew little about before the POSSUM, but had a head full of afterwards. One thing I discovered was that Hypnos, god of rest or sleep, sired the four deities, collectively called the Oneroi. They controlled every type of dream from nightmares to ghostly visions."

He pressed a button on the panel and the images in the dome rotated until Orion's Constellation came into view.

"The observatory maintains an ongoing record of the universe. Every change that occurs is recorded here. Do you know who the Protogenoi are, Sera?"

Sera shook her head.

"In Greek mythology they are the first-born gods, the beginning of life. Proto, when translated means first or original. Gen, refers to being produced or born, and geo means, of the earth."

"Protogio...*Proto-geo*. First Earth?"

"Interesting, isn't it? And I believe the Origins traveled between the planets. For what reason, I can only surmise. But I don't think it ended there."

"I learned on Protogio that there is connection between Eksaf 'anise and the great Egyptian pyramids, and astronomers have known for years that the three great pyramids align themselves with Orion's belt. Watch the stars on the belt. I discovered this several years ago."

Clay entered some calculations on the keyboard and froze the image that appeared. He highlighted an area on the viewer in front of him and it appeared on the dome above. "It is barely noticeable to the naked eye, but I found it."

"What is that?" Sera gazed up at the dome. There was linear shadow extending from Alnilam, the center star on Orion's belt. It looked as thought the universe was folding in on itself.

"It's an anomaly. I call it a temporal fold. Now, I am going to trace the line. Watch where it leads to."

Sera's mouth dropped open as Clay revealed the path that the temporal fold was taking. It seemed to pierce the Earth's atmosphere and come to stop directly at the center pyramid in Giza.

"This particular fold occurred on July fifteenth, two thousand and fifty-one, the exact same day we conducted the POSSUM experiment. Well, my curiosity got the best of me and I checked further back in time. A temporal fold also occurred a little over twenty years ago, but that was the last one I could find in this millennium and there were none during the nineteen hundreds. Because no method of recording images of the universe existed before the twentieth century, I couldn't determine if there were any folds before then, but I suspect there was."

"Do you think it's a porthole, Clay?"

"Yes, I do, and if my assumption is correct, there should have been another one during your POSSUM induced sleep." Clay punched the date into the computer and a new picture appeared. It was there, another temporal fold and the computer indicated that it lasted for approximately eight hours.

Sera furled her brow. "The descendants on Protogio are from Greek origins. Why would an Egyptian monument be used for their runes?"

"I thought about that myself and did some further investigating. In ancient mythology there was a Greek woman by the name of Io."

"Jerad called the Key, Io's curse of the tombs."

Clay nodded. "I read the *Protogian Principles*. Demeter, according to the historical documentation is responsible for creating the Key. According to Greek mythology here on Earth, Io worshipped Demeter and Demeter adored her. Io was banished from Greece and eventually came to settle in the area known as Egypt. She is associated with the Egyptian goddess Isis, but more importantly Io is also the progenitor of Aegyptus, father of the Egypt. It is believed that from him, the great pharaohs descended. So you see, there is a connection, though we may never know the particulars of how it all came to be."

"This is incredible."

"And an ingenious idea you have to admit. After all, would you hide the key to your home in your own backyard, or would it be safer in your neighbor's lot?

"But how could the POSSUM have produced that?"

"My theory is that the calibrated brain waves we used opened the porthole and transported us mentally to the planet."

"The Edict said that the Ptino asteri will in truth be a spirit, but flesh to the touch."

"Yes, Sera, and we know so little about where the mind ends and the spirit begins."

Sera was speechless. Never could she imagine that she would find herself on the cusp of something so remarkable.

"A shuttle passed through the temporal fold twelve years ago," Clay continued. "There was no damage, but the crew reported a major disturbance in their flight pattern, similar to a jet's wake. It threw them off course, but not significantly. I believe that the *KNOE's* calibrations opened the porthole, but the signal was too weak to allow an actual object to move through it. However, with a stronger signal aimed directly into the pyramid…"

Sera shot out of her chair. She was completely overwhelmed with the possibility.

"We could physically go to Protogio! We have to tell the IASA. They could research this, they could…"

"No, Sera!" he yelled at her. Sera clamped her mouth shut and gave him a perplexed look.

"Even if we could convince them that this actually did happen, how long do you think it would take for them to get approval, conduct their own research and then execute the necessary experiments to prove it were true, months, maybe years? I don't believe you have that much time."

"What do you mean?"

"If you remain here, I don't think your child is going to survive, and you may not as well."

Sera hugged her belly protectively. "Why would you say such a horrible thing?"

Clay's eyes darted to Sera's abdomen and then back to her face. "The baby you carry was conceived somewhere in the cosmos, between two worlds. I believe it is the reason you drift between here and Protogio. You told me that each time you link the pains worsen. It is not you that is being drawn there, Sera. Your child is being torn apart."

"Oh my god!" Sera placed a trembling hand over her mouth. "My baby, how can I save my baby?"

"I can think of no other solution other than your returning to Protogio."

"But how?"

"Simple. We are going to steal a shuttle."

Sera looked at him wide-eyed. "You would do this for me?"

"I would do it for both of us, Sera. The POSSUM ruined my life. I lost a very good friend that day, and my obsession following the experiment destroyed my marriage. My wife left me. My kids don't even speak to me. I tried to put it out of my mind, and when you showed up on my doorstep I was determined to deny it, but I really never could let go of the POSSUM completely. You were all the proof I needed to tell me I wasn't insane."

Sera inhaled deeply and sat down in her chair. They sat in amiable silence for a long time. Neither of them noticed the shadowy figure that leaned against the wall at the far end of the room, or when it disappeared through the exit door.

* * * *

…The Ptino Asteri will deliver unto you the prior one…

Chapter Twenty-Seven

...Be not caught unaware, for a baneful warrior through the line of Nyx will seek to annihilate your people and claim that which is not his to hold…

The elevator doors opened and Garret, dressed in civilian clothing, stepped out. He crossed the base, and headed for his pick-up truck in the parking lot. He took a leisurely drive to the front gates. A soldier stationed in the guardhouse saluted. Garret returned a quick nod. The guard pressed a button and opened the security gate.

The drive to the privately owned storage buildings was ten miles away. It was dark when Garret pulled up. This was a good thing. As always, the less he was observed the better. Renting a storage cubicle with this company was a brilliant idea. The manager, who provided him with the key, allowed him access to his possessions day or night. The employees, indifferent in their attitudes, never paid much heed to his comings and goings. It had been an easy ploy bringing the documents, weapons and explosives to this place for safe keeping. He even managed to secure a dirty bomb. Being a terrorist interrogator had its advantages.

Garret drove his truck along the rows of garages until he reach the one he had rented. He reached into his pocket, removed an oval key and depressed the button on it. The security panel on the cubicle caught the identifying signal and the garage door rose. Garret exited his truck and stepped through the opening. He flicked the light switch, pressed another button to close the entrance and concealed himself inside.

He smiled with satisfaction as he surveyed his accumulated bounty.

Within a short time he heard the sound of a vehicle arriving and peered out a small window. A military truck idled outside.

Right on time.

Garret opened the garage door.

"Major Moros?" one of the enlisted men asked as he examined

Garret's civilian attire.

Another soldier lowered the ramp on the back of the vehicle, hopped in and steered a motorized, hand tow from it. Garret indicated the crates inside of the storage compartment

"Where to, Major?"

"IASA, dock four. Do not load them. One of the passengers will be expecting them and will take care of that. Here are the authorization papers to transport this cargo."

Garret handed the illicitly obtained documents to the soldier. He leaned against the wall, folded his arms across his chest and watched the two enlisted men load the four crates onto the military truck.

Bribery was such child's play.

* * * *

Mars settlement shuttles departed two at a time, twenty-four hours apart, once per month. Their mission was to transport supplies, equipment and any passengers that might be going to the planet. The first shuttle for the month was scheduled to leave in twelve hours. Major Clay Jackson's shuttle would be the second one after that.

The biospheres on Mars proved to be relatively safe and at present over two thousand people, mostly military personnel, lived within their walls. The wage and benefits for working and living on the planet was extremely generous. Despite this, many people were still apprehensive about a project that was relatively in its early stages, and the government was reluctant to implement enforced commitments off planet. To that end, the Mars settlements were in desperate need of well-trained employees to work within its atmosphere. Research specialists were among the neediest, and Clay assured Sera that he could pull some strings and have a transfer for her approved before his flight departed. He would then schedule her as a passenger on his shuttle.

There were a few minor details to consider. First, the Major did not want to involve his co-pilot and friend in a scandal, or risk his life should something go wrong. That problem was easily remedied when Sera produced her bottle of sedatives. Clay took them from her saying he would take care of it. Second, they needed the brain wave coordinates used during the POSSUM. The information was classified and if Sera was caught trying to remove the data from the lab she could be detained, discharged, or worse yet, be convicted for tampering with government property. In fact, she might already be locked out of the lab if anyone found out she had copied some of the information, even though it was only the record of her pregnancy.

Sera stood in front of her apartment door and punched the security number into the panel on the wall. Her heart was racing and she was shaking with both trepidation and elation.

She was stealing a shuttle!

If she and Clay were caught it could mean a court martial and life in a military prison, but if it would take her back to Jerad, Sera was more than willing to risk it. The Edict was true. She *was* the Ptino asteri. The only mystery that remained was how she was going to save his world, and from what?

The door slid open. Sera was so consumed with her thoughts, she did not see Garret standing in the doorway. Startled, Sera let out a shriek and jumped back.

"*Geez* Garret, you scared the hell out of me."

"I knew you could do it, Sera." He grabbed her and hugged her.

"Do what?" Sera pulled away from him.

He laughed heartily, then turned and walked into his bedroom. Sera curiously followed him.

Garret opened the lid to a wooden box that sat on top of his dresser. He removed an old-fashioned key. "Do you know who Moros is, Sera?"

Sera blankly stared at him.

Garret continued. "Moros aligns with Doom. He is the begat of Nyx, who is one of the most feared Origins in the universe. Nyx was the sovereign who ruled the First Kingdom. Moros is the name given to all first-born males in her lineage. I am Moros, fifteenth generation in the bloodline of Nyx. I am the true ruler of the Fourth Zone and soon all of the Zones will be mine."

Sera forced a cool demeanor, but she was far from feeling at ease. Garret was truly frightening her with his declaration.

She started backing up toward the door. "I know you have a library full of mythological literature, Garret, but don't you think you're taking it a little too far."

"Am I?" Garret moved forward and grabbed her wrist. He turned her palm up and place the key in her hand. He indicated a trunk at the foot of his bed. "Open it."

Sera's instincts told her to run, but her questioning mind was overriding any rational thought. She inserted the key into the trunk and popped open the lid. Inside, she found a sword with a star-etched bezel, gauntlet styled gloves and an old pair of boots. Her mouth fell open as she lifted out a worn, brown tunic. A red star pierced with a silver dagger was embroidered in the upper left corner.

Sera angled her head up to look at Garret.

His lips thinned into a smile. "I received my badge at an early age."

"Where did you get this?" Sera asked with dismay. It was impossible for him to have had it made in such a short time.

"I was wearing it when we arrived. There's more, Sera. Take a look."

Sera examined the other items in the trunk, listening as Garret delivered his tale.

"I went to Eskaf that rise, some twenty term cycles ago." He spoke to Sera in Greek. "I was ordered to go there through a vision I received in a dream. A woman waited for me there. She was carrying a babe. She hugged her child gently and handed it to me. I opened my mouth to speak, but before I could form any words, an odd vibration surged through my body and the land around me vanished. The mountains turned to stone. I didn't know it then, but I was suddenly sitting, with you in my arms, at the base of the Great Pyramids in Egypt."

Sera rose to her feet and faced Garret. "With…me?"

Garret smirked and moved to stand in front of her. He looked down at the cloth she was holding. "You were wrapped in that. Of course I did not know your name and had to give you a new one."

Sera studied the thin coverlet she held in her hands, small enough to wrap only a tiny baby in. It was made of a soft woven material. A blue feather patch was sewn in its center. There were hundreds of markings dyed into the material, covering it on both the front and the back. They looked like symbols, letters perhaps, but it was nothing she recognized.

"There's something else." Garret bent toward the trunk and removed a scroll. He handed it to Sera. She set the baby blanket-- *her baby blanket* aside and slowly unrolled the piece of paper. It was the Edict of Oneroi. Sera read it aloud.

"By these teachings we unveil the prophecy which will come to pass…Be not caught unaware for a *great* warrior through the line of Nyx will come to claim the kingdom that was *stolen*…One will be called the Ptino Asteri…and will forge a bond with the *ruler of the great kingdom*. This will be a joining so inherently seamless it will cross the boundaries…"

Sera lifted her chin and narrowed her eyes at Garret. "This is wrong. It's not what the Edict says."

Garret smiled gleefully and planted a very *unbrotherly* kiss on her lips. Sera stepped back from him and wiped her mouth with the back of her hand.

"It is the correct version, love. And as you can see, you, the Ptino asteri was delivered to me. You are mine, you will be my wife, and together we will rule Protogio."

Be his wife? Yuck. It didn't matter that he wasn't really her brother. She still thought of him that way.

"You're forgetting something, Garret. I am already married."

Garret's expression turned angry. "You won't be, once I execute him!"

He spun on his heels, and stalked away from her. Sera jumped when he slammed his fist down on the dresser. "It sickens me that he touched you, when all of these years I kept you pure for my touch only!"

Garret circled around until he was behind Sera. He wrapped his arms around her and pressed her against him. He kissed the side of her neck. Sera grimaced with disgust.

"Don't worry, my Starbird. I forgive you."

"Don't call me that." Sera tensed. *Starbird* had become Jerad's endearment for her. She did not like the sound of it coming from Garret's mouth one bit.

Garret pushed her and roughly twisted her around. "I will call you what I wish. I am your king and you will obey me!"

Sera stared at him defiantly. "Why did you keep all of this from me?"

"Would you have believed me? And suppose you told someone. I was already having enough trouble keeping you in my care with the social department constantly breathing down my neck. It was good that I learned early on the importance of aligning myself with powerful people."

He lifted his hand and stroked his knuckles against her cheek. "Now we will return home and I will make you my queen."

"And how do you suppose we will do that? We can't stay linked to the POSSUM for the rest of our lives." Sera folded her arms across her chest and flashed him a scathing look.

Garret smirked. "You are going to take me with you when you leave."

"What do you mean?" she asked apprehensively. He couldn't possibly know of her plan.

Garret reached into his pocket and removed an object. "You wouldn't make a very good spy, Sera. You really should secure your private affairs. I had little difficulty ascertaining the number you called, and from that was able to surmise where you were heading."

Sera's face fell when she saw her palm device in Garret's hand. She patted her jacket pocket realizing at the same time that she had left her palm pad in the POSSUM lab. He gave the notepad to Sera and she opened it. Her email activated. It was a message from the IASA and instructions for her departure. Sera's transfer was approved.

"I followed you. I heard it all, every last word of exchange between you and Major Jackson as you devised your plot."

"How do you expect me to get you onto a Mars shuttle?"

Garret snorted. "You're going to smuggle me on board."

"You're crazy." Sera rubbed her forehead and stalked out to the living room. Garret followed her.

"*Nai*. It is a brilliant plan. Even now, four crates with your name on them are being delivered to the shuttle launch. One of them is nearly empty. I will come to wish my dear sister goodbye and you will smuggle me into the crate before it is loaded. I would request a transfer to the Mars settlement myself if it would get me aboard the shuttle. Unfortunately, there is little need for a combat specialist on Mars, at least at this time."

"And what if I refuse?" Sera bit the tip of her thumbnail and nervously paced across the room. Defying Garret was something she was not used to doing.

"You won't. One phone call from me, and you, and your accomplice will be arrested."

"For what reason?" Sera looked at him crossly.

"Treason, tampering with government property, any number of things."

"Why would they believe you?"

Garret inhaled deeply and blew out a gust of air. "They only need to open those crates, although I much prefer to use what is inside to reclaim my land."

Sera's blood ran cold. What had he done? "What—is—inside—of those crates?"

"Contraband..." Garret snickered. "... of the terrorist kind."

"But how did you..."

"Corruption, blackmail, bribery you name it! I have many connections, Sera, legal and illegal. Such weak governments this planet has. There are many who will turn a coat for a quick buck, or to save their mighty reputations."

"You're lying!" Sera cried out. Would he actually ruin her life on purpose? How could he be so malicious?

Garret plopped down in the center of the couch and spread his arms along the length of the back. He casually stretched out his leg and crossed them at the ankle.

"Test me." A slanted smile tugged one corner of his lips.

Sera straightened against the cramping in her belly that was growing worse by the hour. She considered Garret for a long moment. Finally she relented.

What choice did she have? She would worry about the weapons he was planning to use against the Zones, later.

"Fine, Garret. I will try to get you on board."

Garret smiled smugly. "Go do what you need to do, Sera. I have a few details to attend to myself. I will see you at the launch."

Less than a half-hour later, Sera entered the POSSUM lab. She had stopped on her way to grab a bite to eat at the base mess hall, not that she felt much like eating, but she had her child's health to think of.

A child she might lose if this didn't work, Sera thought sadly.

Melissa was sitting at the *KNOE*.

Damn, Sera would have to wait for Melissa to leave.

"Hi, Sera. How are you feeling?"

"Wonderful," Sera said dully. "You're working late."

Melissa blew out a gust of air. "Yah, I have to make sure everything is correctly calibrated. You and Garret are scheduled to link again soon. We have to keep you two safe, right?"

"Whatever," Sera shrugged. She walked over to a cot, sat down and yawned. She was so tired.

I'll just close my eyes and rest them. Sera reclined on the cot. The last thing she saw was the white recessed lights in the ceiling. She remembered waking up during the POSSUM experiment. Right after Sondra had slashed her. Had the medics really been the ones to save her life?

Sera's eyes fluttered opened. She had been dreaming, or linking. She really wasn't sure. This time she stood at the top of Eksaf, watching a horrid battle taking place across the plain. Sera searched frantically for Jerad amid the warriors below. She knew he was down there, she could feel his presence, but she could not locate him.

Sera sat up and stretched. Her eyes darted to the empty chair in front of the computer panel. Melissa was gone at least. Her gaze wandered to the clock on the wall. It was seven o'clock--*in the morning!*

Oh god! Sera flew from the cot. She had slept through the night. Sera moved quickly to the *KNOE* and sat down. It would only take a few minutes to retrieve the data she needed. She slid her palm pad into the slot, but was startled by the hand that reached over her shoulder and pulled it out. Sera swiveled around in her chair and stiffened when she discovered her commander peering down at her.

"What are you doing lieutenant?"

Damn! Busted! She never heard him enter the room.

"I... uh... Well, sir, I've been so exhausted lately. I was just going to download some of the information and work on my report from home."

Her commander handed her palm computer back to her and frowned. "You know this information is classified lieutenant. It can't be removed from the lab."

"Uh, yes sir. I don't know what I was thinking."

Her phone rang.

"Don't let it happen again." The commander sat down next to her and started sifting through the data. "And have your report on my desk this afternoon."

"Yes sir."

She hit the receive button on her phone. "Hello, Lieutenant Moros speaking."

"Yes, Lieutenant Moros," the voice on the other end spoke. "This is Sergeant Lewis at the IASA. Major Jackson had me put a call in to you. The first shuttle launch was grounded due to mechanical problems. The Major's departure time has been moved up. You need to be here within three hours or you'll have to wait until next month."

Shit!

Sera did not have that much time. "I'll be there."

Panic bubbled up inside of Sera as she shut off the phone. What was she going to do? Maybe Clay could hack into the POSSUM and retrieve the information. It was hoping beyond hope. Security protecting government computers was nearly impenetrable, but they could try. One thing was certain, she could not wait another month. It would be certain death for her unborn child and perhaps for herself, as well.

Sera went back to her apartment and was grateful to discover that Garret wasn't home. Another thought occurred to her. There was a good chance that Garret did not know the shuttle departure time had been changed. She could leave without him. A twinge of guilt poked at her, but she brushed it away.

Sera packed a small bag and hurried toward the monorail. She racked her brain throughout the ride to Cape Canaveral. There had to be something they could do about the coordinates they needed. After all, she was the Starbird of the Edict, sent to unlock the mystery of the Key to Orion's belt. Somewhere, locked inside her head was the answer.

Then, it came to her.

* * * *

"I got caught, but I think I know what to do."

Sera explained her thoughts as she and Clay headed toward the launching dock. She paused to watch Garret's crates being loaded into the cargo bay. As Garret assured her, Sera's name was on them. To her relief, Garret was nowhere in sight.

"I hope you are right with your assumption, Sera. This may be our only chance to open the temporal fold. But I guess we don't have much of a choice do we?"

"Not unless we wait another month. I might have another opportunity to retrieve the coordinates."

"It may be too late by then. We have to do this now."

Clay looked as nervous as Sera felt.

She had to be right--for the sake of their baby, for *Jerad,* and for whatever purpose the Edict intended for her.

Sera's heart wrenched. She was going home.

"Your personal effects are on the shuttle, ma'am."

Sera turned to face the airman who spoke. He was referring to the crates. "Uh… yes. Thanks."

A wave of great destruction the likes of which have never witnessed before.

The weapons--Garret's sole intent all of these years had been to gather an arsenal large enough to destroy and control Protogio. But he would not be delivering those weapons. She would be, and she would have to figure out how to keep them out of enemy hands. Sera shuddered and the enormity of her task.

Clay took Sera by the upper arm and steered her toward the shuttle's entrance. She froze when she saw the name painted on the side.

Starbird.

The lettering was written in English, and just below it, the Greek symbols and translation--*Ptino asteri.*

Clay smiled at the surprised look on her face.

"Prophetic, isn't it?" Clay placed a hand on Sera's shoulder blade and guided her inside.

Clay spent thirty minutes engaged in safety checks and status reports, while Sera sat buckled in the co-pilot's seat. She concentrated on humming the music from the spectrocorde, hoping she wasn't tone deaf. The spectrocorde was the Key to Orion's belt. It had to be the answer.

Launch sequencing complete. A voice came over the intercom. *Assume launch position.*

Clay rolled the shuttle to the runway and maneuvered it into position.

Clear to launch.

With inherent expertise, Clay controlled the shuttle and they lifted off. Within ten minutes they broke through the earth's atmosphere and were in orbit. They experienced a brief moment of weightlessness until Clay flipped on the gravity simulator. Under normal circumstances Sera would have been thrilled, this being her first time in space, but this was most certainly not a normal situation. Her anxiety was causing her stomach to flip all over the place.

Clay switched off the video recorder.

…There appears to a problem with your video feed, Major…

"I'll check into it," he responded, but remained in his seat.

…Your shuttle is off course, Major…

"I'm taking care of it."

Sera nibbled her lip. She could hear the buzzing of voices in the background as the controller spoke to them. They were concerned, but not yet suspicious.

"There it is Sera." Clay gaze was fixed forward, concentrating on his target.

Sera peered through the shuttle's window to view the object spinning within the Earth's orbit. "What is it?"

"The Egyptian satellite." Clay manipulated the controls in front of him.

Sera watched as the satellite tipped and turned.

"I just aimed it directly toward the pyramids."

…Major, why are you tampering with the Egyptian satellite?

"Sing, Sera. I am going to convert the musical sounds to transmittable waves and direct it toward the satellite. The signal will be sent to Giza. Keep your fingers crossed."

Sera opened her mouth and crooned the tune she knew so well. Clay converted the signal and transmitted it.

...Major, is someone singing up there?

Clay turned off the radio transmitter, but left the receiver on. A number of frantic sounding voices were exchanging conversation in the background.

...We lost transmission with the shuttle, sir.

"Nothing's happening, Sera. The signal is not working."

Sera's anxiety rose to monstrous proportions. She felt like she was going to faint. She unbuckled herself from her seat and started to pace. She was missing something. The spectrocorde had to be the answer.

It just had to be.

"The lights, the colors." She abruptly stopped her pacing. "The sculpture emitted a spectrum of colored lights when it played."

...Major, we seemed to have lost contact...Do you copy? ...I'm getting no response...

"Do you know the sequence?"

"I think so."

...Major, let us speak to your co-pilot...

"You better know so. This is our only chance." He ignored command control's request.

Sera gave him the color sequences. He converted them into wavelengths and transmitted them in combination with the musical sounds.

...Major, would you mind telling us why we just found your co-pilot drugged and tied up in a broom closet?

"Damn! They're onto us. Think Sera! The combination is not working either!"

...Major Jackson, you are ordered to turn your craft around. Return to home base...

"Oh god! Clay!" Sera searched the deepest corners of her mind, reviewing her memories for every little detail.

...Why are there weapons on your shuttle Major?

"Oh shit, Sera! They've scanned the ship. Damn your brother!"

Sera's heart was frantically thumping against her chest. She was terrified.

We are activating the destruct mechanism, Major. Turn your ship around or you will be destroyed...I'm getting no response from the shuttle, sir...

"What's going on, Clay?" Sera shuddered.

"They think we're terrorists. They are going to destroy the shuttle."

"Can they do that?"

"Without a doubt. There is a destruct mechanism on every shuttle. It can be engaged by the crew or by command control."

Clay, this is Commander Militello. Are you being held hostage? ...I'm not getting anything.

"Can't you turn it off?"

Clay shook his head. "Not when Command Control has activated it. Only they can abort."

Sera squeezed her palms against her temples. *If only she had gotten those damn coordinates!* They were running out of time.

...Three minutes to destruct...Major Jackson, surrender your ship...

Sera started pacing again. "Think, Sera," she commanded herself out loud, once again searching the crevices in her mind. The spectrocorde, the lights and the music, she was sure she had gotten them right. This was supposed to work. She and Garret traveled from Protogio to Earth. There had to be a way back. Was there a clue in the castle's mural? She had studied that piece of art time and time again. Orion's Belt, the stars, the rising moving counterclockwise through the sky--something about them was perturbing.

One minute to destruct...

A light dawned on Sera, brighter than any star in the universe.

"Clay!" Sera flew to his side. "Bring up a view of Orion's belt."

He did as she instructed. Sera studied the image.

This is your final warning...

"Hurry, Sera. We are about to be turned into space junk." Clay gritted anxiously, through clenched teeth.

Thirty seconds...

"Oh my god! That's it! Reverse the signals!" Sera moved quickly to the co-pilot's chair and buckled in.

"You better be right about this." Clay reversed the transmission and sent it to the Egyptian satellite.

Ten seconds...

The shuttle violently tipped from side to side until the vessel inverted, righted, and then flew into a roll. The entire ship rattled, alarms shrieked out their warning as the shell of the shuttle came dangerously close to fracturing. Sera squeezed her eyes shut, terror gripping every nerve in her body. Then a dreamy wave encompassed her and when she opened her eyes again. The stars were sliding past them.

"What happened?" Sera's entire body was fitfully trembling.

Clay leaned back in his chair, breathing heavily. He wiped the sweat from his brow with his jacket sleeve. "It worked. We are in the temporal fold."

Clay switched off the engines allowing the porthole to guide them. He would ignite them when they came out on the other side.

"Would you mind telling me what that was all about?"

Relief gushed through Sera and she started bawling like a baby. Clay frowned, unbuckled his belt and went to her. He knelt by the side of her chair and drew her head to his chest to comfort her. Sera pulled back from his embrace.

"When the spectrocorde was played, it must have opened the temporal fold and directed a signal *from* Protogio toward Orion's belt, and from there to Earth." She took a deep breath and swiped at her tears.

"A one way transmission? How did you come up with that?"

"Orion's constellation, the rising and setting of the sun…everything on Protogio was moving counterclockwise through the skies. That means the planet was rotating clockwise, doesn't it?"

Clay nodded. "The opposite of Earth. I noticed that when I was on Protogio, but it never occurred to me that it would later prove significant. I didn't even include that fact in my documentation."

"It suddenly hit me. If the music from the spectrocorde opened a pathway from Protogio to Earth, it only made sense that reversing the signal would open the porthole in the other direction."

Clay blew out a gust of air. "Well thank god or the cosmos for that. We nearly bit the stardust back there."

Sera closed her eyes. The pain in her womb was gone.

Chapter Twenty-eight

Garret almost spit out his coffee when he overheard the conversation in the booth behind him.

"I just got off the phone with the IASA. Seems the shuttle they launched today was hijacked."

"No kidding."

"Yah, they messed with the Egyptian satellite. Command control was alerted that something was wrong, so they scanned the ship. Apparently there were weapons aboard."

"Good lord, a terrorist attempt?"

"That's what they suspected. The co-pilot was drugged and tied up. They found him in a closet. Command control tried to destroy the bird but, and you're not going to believe this one, the damn shuttle suddenly disappeared."

"No shit. Did it blow up?"

"Nope. Satellite picked up a clear image. The thing just vanished into thin air, or should I say thin space."

Son of a bitch! Garret rose from his seat and hurried from the mess hall.

* * * *

…There will be two in number, separated by past and present…They will face and exterminate thine enemy…

Sera stared in awe as the small planet of Protogio came into view. It was a beautiful and welcoming sight. The temporal fold seemed to be purposefully directing the shuttle, guiding them to the circular pattern of the planet's orbit. Protogio was half the size of Earth and was covered mostly in water. There were a number of tiny islands dotting the globe and one large land mass in its upper hemisphere.

The Zones.

Clay re-ignited the shuttle's engines and assumed control of the craft. The land slowly drew closer as they descended. Details of terrain below became clearer. They crossed a ravine so deep Sera could not see its bottom. Eksaf 'anise came into view. Through the shuttle's windows they could clearly see the war raging below. Hundreds of warriors clashed in battle as the *Starbird* cut through the skies. Sera strained for recognition of the combatants, searching for Jerad, but they were moving too fast. She wondered how the warriors might be reacting to the mighty flying craft passing over them. The shuttle had to be creating an ear-shattering sound.

"I'm circling around. We can land there." Clay pointed to a large flatland beyond Eksaf. "It's awfully close to the battleground, but we should be safe inside of the shuttle."

Sera braced herself as the ground drew up beneath them. They landed with a harsh thump, bounced mercilessly along the uneven ground and then came to a jerking halt.

Clay reached forward and shut down the engines. His shoulders slumped as he sank into the back of his chair. They both sat immobile for long moments, rapt in the acumen of an alternate reality, stunned that they defied an entire nation, crossed a universe in a matter of minutes to chase the thread of a dream they shared.

They could scarcely believe that they made it.

Sera moved first. She picked up a pair of binoculars from a supply bin and studied the terrain. Glide flyers soared in the distance and there were explosions from what Sera assumed to be shatter arrows. Then, she caught a glimpse of Aryan running across one of the hills. In her excitement, Sera could not contain herself. She bounded from where she stood and released the mechanism sealing the shuttle's hatch. A retracted ladder unfolded from a compartment on the outside of the shuttle.

"Wait Sera! You can't go out there. It's too dangerous!"

Sera did not wait for him, she needed to find Jerad. She scurried down the ladder and dashed across the field, heading toward the hill. She was met head on by a Nyx warrior, who jumped from behind the brush. He was coming at her with his sword held out at his side. Sera dug in her heals to stop her forward progress, realizing belatedly that she should have broken into the crates to retrieve one of Garret's weapons before she left the shuttle.

She started backing away from him and he followed her step for step. Sera looked around for something--anything that could be used to defend herself, but the nearest thing Sera could find was a three-foot high plant stalk topped with a lily shaped flower. She grabbed the long stem and yanked it from the ground. The warriors eyes darted to her inefficient weapon and a feral snicker escaped his lips. Sera did not hesitate. She whipped the rooted end of the plant toward his face, hoping against odds that the dirt that clung to the roots would at least blind him temporarily--but there was no root. There was only a large white bulb--a *crukis* bulb. It burst against his cheek. Within seconds, he was yowling as the splattered *crukis* gel peeled the flesh from his face. The angry, injured warrior rushed toward her.

Sera screamed.

He reached for her but suddenly halted. Both their gazes flicked to his belly. The point of a sword protruded through it and then retracted. He had been skewered from behind. Sera jumped out of the way as the warrior took one faltered step and fell forward. Aryan stood behind him, bloody sword in hand.

"Welcome home, Ptino asteri,"

"Thanks, Aryan." She grimaced at the dead warrior on the ground. "I think."

She walked to Aryan's side and shook her head. "I didn't care much for the idea of becoming an acid wipe."

Aryan scanned the hillside, stiffening as he watched his men attempting to stave off the advancing Nyx warriors.

"Where's Jerad?" Sera looked at him hopefully.

Aryan waved his hand in the air. "He is about somewhere."

Jerad was still alive.

Relief filled Sera but immediately evaporated when she spied a Nyx warrior raise a shatter arrow in their direction and release it. She leapt sideways, and with lightening speed her hand flew out and closed around the shaft of the shatter arrow. It skidded along the flesh of her palm, ripping it open, stopping just inches from Aryan's chest.

"Ouch!" She yelped and opened her hand to release it. Aryan snatched it out of the air before it hit the ground. He threw it like a spear and it exploded a safe distance away, taking two Nyx warriors with it.

Sera clenched her teeth, vigorously shaking her hand against the burning tear in her skin.

"*Nai*, such talent my wife possesses."

Sera stilled at the sound of the familiar voice. Her heart thumped with joy.

Pain forgotten, she spun around. "Jerad!"

Sera ran and jumped into his arms. She wrapped her legs around his waist and buried her face in the crook of his neck.

Jerad held her tightly. "I have sorely missed you, woman."

Sera tipped her head back to look at him and he tenderly kissed her mouth.

"Do I get welcome kiss too?"

"Argilos!" Jerad released Sera as Clay approached.

"Look at you." Clay patted Jerad's shoulders. "All grown up."

"And married too." Jerad looked at Sera endearingly and slipped his arm around her.

At the mention of her marriage, Sera opened her left hand and beamed happily when she discovered the Marks of Permanence brilliantly displayed on her palm.

"Ah Argilos, you are speaking my language well."

"I had twelve term cycles to learn it my friend."

The two men embraced and laughed.

"It dismays me to break up this festive reunion," Aryan interrupted, "but it would befit us much to find safer ground."

The clashing of swords drew their attention to the plain. The battle was moving dangerously close to where they stood.

"I would ask you to fight at my side, Argilos, but my wife's safety is of first importance."

"I will get her back to the shuttle."

"*Ochi!* We all saw the great bird fly over. The Nyx warriors will seek to capture it."

"We can't let them, Jerad." Sera placed her hands on his chest. "There are terrible weapons inside."

"Worse than shatter arrows?"

"Much, much worse--powerful enough to destroy the Corridors."

"I have a band of warriors just over the ridge. I will gather them and signal the glide flyers. We will protect the bird," Aryan suggested.

Jerad nodded. He, Sera and Clay hurried toward the shuttle. Once safely inside, Clay sealed the hatch. Jerad examined the interior of the craft, amazed by the complexities of the equipment it contained, momentarily forgetting the war outside.

A shatter arrow hit the outside of the shuttle and exploded.

"We have to stop them," Clay asserted. "They can't do much damage to the shuttle's shell, but if they hit the fuel chamber we'll be blown to kingdom come."

"Can we stop them with the weapons you brought?"

"Not unless you want to risk losing some of your own men." Clay turned to Sera and handed her a wireless transmitter. "I have a better idea."

"What's this for?"

"I'll amplify your voice and you can order them to stop."

"Why would they listen to me?"

Jerad flashed Clay a wry smile. "You are the Ptino asteri, Sera. Why would they not?"

A resolute look crossed her face.

"I'm going on top," Sera opened the shuttle hatch and reached for the ladder.

Jerad caught her by the arm. "Not without me, wife."

They climbed the ladder and came to stand on top of the shuttle. Sera forced out as loud a voice as she could muster, but with the clatter and yelling among the combatants, her voice was ignored.

Clay realized what was happening and hit a switch. A shrilling alarm boomed out over the battlefield. He laughed at the wincing faces, as warrior after warrior pressed their hands to their ears. Many dropped to their knees, as well. The battle came to an abrupt halt.

"For the love of the Origins, my ears are splitting!" Jerad yelled, but Sera could not hear what he said. She was protecting her own ears.

Clay switched off the alarm and the blood curdling siren ceased. All eyes were fixed on Sera.

Sera raised the transmitter to her lips. "This is the Ptino asteri! I command the Nyx warriors to retreat or you will be destroyed!" Sera scanned the faces below.

"NOW!" she screamed. At that moment, Clay hit the alarm again. Hundreds of Nyx warriors dropped their swords and began backing away. Clay turned off the alarm and joined them on top of the shuttle.

"The Oneroi!" someone yelled.

The Nyx warriors turned and ran.

A heady feeling came over Sera. She knew what was occurring. In like with the mural in the Third Corridor, they were seeing a great silver bird with the Oneroi on top, giving it powerful command. The name was even labeled on the side of the shuttle. It would have been a humorous thing under lighter circumstances.

Wait.

There were *four* Oneroi, but only three people stood atop the shuttle.

Sera whirled around and gasped. Garret stood behind Clay holding a gun to his head. Jerad did not move. Though he had never seen such a device afore, he knew deep in his gut it was a very dangerous weapon.

"Blasted cowards," Garret remarked as he watched his warriors retreat. "Those disgusting weaklings will pay."

"Where did you…" Sera's mouth dropped open. "You're in the POSSUM lab, aren't you? You're linking!"

Her eyes flicked to the gun. He must have retrieved it from one of the crates before he climbed to the top of the shuttle.

Garret brushed past Jerad, still aiming his gun at Clay, until he was within Sera's reach. With a quick exchange he pushed Clay away and pressed the barrel of his weapon to Sera's temple.

"You might risk that one's life, Noble, but I doubt you will risk hers."

Jerad flinched and snarled at Moros.

"Inside the shuttle now," Garret ordered. "Oh, and Chancellor, wave off that glide flyer above me. If he pierces my flesh with that arrow he is raising, I just might slip and pull the trigger."

He puckered Sera's mouth between his fingers and thumb. "It

would be such a shame to split open this beautiful face."

Jerad had been watching his men on the ground. They were ready with their arrows, waiting for his signal. He was also aware that the glide flyers overhead did the same. He turned to Clay to confirm if what Moros warned him about were true. Clay nodded and Jerad signaled his warriors to lower their weapons. There was nothing he could do.

For now.

He and Clay climbed down the ladder and went inside of the shuttle.

"If you kill me Garret, not one warrior will spare you, and I don't need to tell you what Jerad would do to you."

Garret pushed her towards the ladder. "Ah *Nai,* Sera. And you would risk your life to save the Noble wouldn't you?"

"Yes," Sera stated firmly.

"Thanks for the warning." He moved the gun to her lower belly. "You might live, but I could do grave harm to the brat you carry. Will you risk its life, Sera?"

Sera froze and a chilling terror swept through her.

"Yes Sera, I know about it."

Sera's stomach churned with repugnance. All those years he raised her as family, claimed he loved her. Even if it was other than a brotherly love, still, he claimed it. Would he actually destroy her unborn child? Sera bit her lip and tried to tamp down the emotional hurt. Her loathing of him could not be greater.

As if Garret could read her mind, he responded. "I could care less for the life of that imp. I will do anything to rule Protogio. The planet belongs to me. Once the Noble realizes you carry his child, he will not risk both of your lives. He will bring me the Key to Orion's belt and I will have access to both planets. Think of the power I could gain."

"Oh god, you're insane," Sera gulped.

"Get moving, Sera." Garret pushed her and Sera climbed down the ladder. He then shoved her through the shuttle's door.

Garret kept Sera close to him while they moved to the cockpit. Jerad stood rigid, eyeing Garret with vicious anger. One wrong move and Jerad would personally snap his neck.

"Now what?" Clay asked Garret.

"You're going to fly this bird to the Fourth Zone."

Clay ignited the engines and worked the controls. The shuttle rolled forward--at a turtle's pace.

"What the hell are trying to pull?"

"Something wrong, Major Moros?"

"Do you take me for a fool? I know you can't get lift at this speed."

"Hmn, I suppose you're right," Clay responded with sarcasm.

He flashed Jerad an unblinking glare. "You might want to hold on to that safety bar as tight as you can, Jerad."

Jerad nodded as he reached back and closed his hands around the bar. He might not fully understand all the silver bird was capable of, but he comprehended by the look from Argilos, to be alert.

Garret shoved Sera towards the co-pilot's seat.

As Garret moved across the bay, Clay slammed the brake lever. Simultaneously, he reached under the control deck to activate the shuttle's self-destruct mechanism. The shuttle lurched and threw Garret off balance. Jerad lunged forward and yanked Moros' gun hand away from Sera's body.

Sera scrambled away.

The gun went off and the bullet lodged into the control deck. It sizzled and a fire erupted. Alarms began to screech. Clay flew from his seat and both he Jerad struggled to subdue Garret. The shuttle started rolling forward again.

"Get Sera out of here!" Clay yelled over the noise of the sirens. "The damn ship is going to blow!"

Jerad grabbed Sera's wrist and dragged her to the shuttle's open hatch.

"Out, now!" he ordered Sera and turned to assist Argilos. The two men dragged Garret toward the hatch.

Sera climbed down the ladder with the three men just behind her.

Well, this escape is a bit less than impressive, Sera thought as she looked at the ground.

The shuttle was moving so slowly it was like jumping from a tricycle being pedaled by a three year old, but then she looked beyond the shuttle's nose. The craft was rolling straight towards the ravine.

"Jump, Sera!" Clay urged from behind her.

"Yep, time to go!" She leapt to the ground, landing on her feet. Clay was right behind her. They turned in time to see Garret break free from Jerad.

"My weapons! I have to save my weapons!" Garret climbed back through the hatch.

Jerad shook his head at the monarch's foolishness and jumped from the ladder just before the shuttle reached the brim of the ravine. The nose tipped over the edge. The shuttle teetered a few times and then plummeted.

Sera, Jerad and Clay ran like the wind just as the shuttle burst into several ear-piercing explosions. They dove for cover beside a large bolder. A small amount of debris rained down. Most of it was contained between the walls of the ravine when the craft tumbled into it.

Sera experienced a grievous moment when she realized that Garret was probably dead. Even though he held hateful intentions toward Sera and the people she loved, it did not erase all of the years of caring she felt for him. Also, in truth, he was the cause of her meeting Jerad, bless his angry, black soul.

Garret reached Protogio through the POSSUM. Sera wondered what was happening in the lab. Was he disengaged in time, or was it too late?

* * * *

Melissa was in the hall, on her way to the POSSUM lab when the sounds of alarms reached her ears. She quickened her pace, but found the door locked. She reached into her pocket and fumbled for her access card. She then swiped it through the key slot, shifting on her feet until she was permitted access.

Garret was lying on the cot, convulsing violently. The computer panel was nearly overheating in a frenzy of flashing emergency warnings. Melissa noticed that Garret was connected to one of the reciprocator headpieces, and darted toward the *KNOE* to disengage him, but before she reached it, his body burst into shards of exploding flesh, leaving only the remains of torn, bloody tissue scattered about the room.

Melissa's screams echoed throughout the third corridor of the C.O.R.E.

Chapter Twenty-nine

Sera, Jerad and Clay stood and brushed themselves off. Several glide flyers, including Mekal, landed nearby. The allied warriors on the ground began moving closer to them, but all movement stopped when a low vibration rumbled along the ground beneath their feet. It increased in intensity as it reached Eksaf 'anise--

riseward across the plain. Orion's constellation brightened in the dusky sky above.

All eyes turned to watch.

The air above the middle peak became dense and started to spiral. Alnilam, the center star on Orion's belt illuminated brighter than all the stars in the sky. A beam of light fanned around Eksaf's center peak and began to glow in a sequencing of colors as a euphony echoed from it--the melody of the spectrocorde.

Earth appeared inside and then the globe shrank as the image soared along Mars, Jupiter, Saturn, the rest of the planets and beyond. Orion's constellation grew large, then small, and Protogio appeared.

Two more beams of light encased the other two peaks of Eksaf. A vast number of stars twinkled inside, encased in a gray, misty looking universe, but no other images emerged.

An ethereal voice that seemed to come directly from the mountains reverberated across the land.

Time brings all to light. Light of the dawn, dawn of new light will glorify. Here in lies your future my children...the beginning of the Starbird's rising...be at peace.

The beams of light faded and vanished.

"What must this all mean?" Mekal scratched his head as he stared at the now silent mountains

Sera unzipped her flight suit and pulled out the blanket she had wrapped around her body. "Do you think this has anything to do with it?"

Clay peered over Sera's shoulder to look at the cloth. "It looks like a bunch of symbols."

He scanned the cloth and then he lifted his head toward Eksaf 'anise. "Perhaps it unlocks the temporal folds to the rest of the universe."

Sera threw back her head. "*Pfft*. Well you can count me out. I'm done planet hopping."

"This is the shroud of Daedalus." Mekal took the cloth from Sera and studied it. He looked at the blue feather embroidered in its center. "It bears the crest of my clan and has been bequeathed through our lineage for centenaries. Where did you get this, Sera?"

"I was wrapped in it when Moros took me from my mother."

"My sister was wrapped in this when my mother left with her."

He grabbed Sera by the shoulders and studied her face with

dismayed awe. "But your eyes."

Sera smiled up at him. "They were not always this color. They used to be a very deep brown. I didn't remember that before."

The confused expression on Mekal's face melted to a heart-filled joy. He drew Sera into his arms and hugged her close. "Ekaterina, you have come home. Our clan will be elated. We will leave immediately for the Eighth Zone…"

Jerad grabbed Sera's arm and pulled her from Mekal's embrace. "What is your meaning by this? Sera will return to the Tenth Zone with me."

"She is my sister and I am bound to her honor. This marriage will be dissolved."

Oh god! Not again. Sera cupped her forehead.

"By what reason!" Jerad demanded.

"You, my confidante, are not fit to husband with her. You attempted to force your way with her…twice! You took her hand in marriage against her will…"

Mekal's stance stiffened and he drew his sword. "Consider yourself challenged!"

Jerad rolled his eyes. The warrior could not possibly be serious. "This is much like closing the stable door after the horse has run off. Is it not my friend?"

Nevertheless he drew his sword to meet Mekal's challenge.

Sera groaned, but she knew deep down her brother and husband would never hurt each other. A wave of dizziness and nausea grabbed hold of her and she dropped to her knees.

"Sera!"

"Kati!"

Both men dropped their swords and were immediately at her side. She promptly threw up on Mekal's boots.

Mekal jumped back and glared at Jerad.

"Look what you have done. You have made her sick. And now my boots need polishing!"

"*Ochi!* I did not make her ill, she is carrying my child." Jerad knelt before Sera and held back her hair for her until she was through emptying her stomach.

"How did you know?" Sera croaked out.

Jerad handed her a canteen of water. "We were never truly separated, Starbird. I heard all of your words while you were gone from me. Though I knew some of the words you were saying, only clearly could I understand those you spoke in my language."

Sera nodded as she recalled that she had spoken in Greek about their baby while reading the *KNOE* in the lab.

"You have impregnated my sister!"

Jerad stood and faced Sera's true brother. "I am her husband fool! Aside, you are the one who gave advice to me on how to seduce her!"

Mekal blushed.

Sera looked at them, mortified.

"Enough!" Aryan bellowed at the two men. "I have neither a sister nor a wife to banter over."

"Do not be so quick to bury your wife, husband."

Aryan turned on his heels. Ezra stood with Dex and a Nyx warrior.

"It seems we have friends in the Fourth Kingdom." Ezra held out her arms and Aryan moved quickly to embrace her.

"I thought I lost you, woman." He drew her into his arms and spread kisses over her face and neck.

He nodded his thanks to the warrior who returned her safely.

"Let me in there." Sera pushed between them and hugged Ezra. "I was so devastated when I thought you were dead. You have been such a good friend to me."

"As you have also been, Sera." Ezra hugged her back. "Despite my husband."

Ezra winked at her husband, and Aryan, who usually wore a grim facade, winked back and smiled.

Sera walked up to Jerad and placed her hands on his chest. "You will take me to meet my mother?"

"*Nai,* of course, my heart."

Mekal flashed a devilish grin in Jerad's direction.

Jerad narrowed his eyes at him. "What are you about my brother of the Mark? You look like the *gatos* that swallowed the *kanarini.*"

"I was thinking about your raging jealousy over the caring that Kati and I share."

"Do not remind me of my foolish behavior." Jerad looked away with chagrin.

Mekal tramped over to Sera. A mischievous grin graced his face.

"Well then, since she is my sister, it really would not be compromising if I say, oh…" He grabbed Sera and wrapped his arms around her. "…decide to give her a great hug."

Mekal tightened his hold and swung her from side to side. Jerad crooked an eyebrow.

"Let me go, Mekal." Sera laughed and tried to pull away from him.

Mekal tightened his embrace. "And I suppose, since I *am* her brother, it should matter not if I took her in my arms and bent her back and gave her a big, wet kiss on the mouth."

He bent Sera back, leaned over her and looked at Jerad. "In a brotherly way of course." Mekal smacked Sera's lips with his own.

"Mekal!" Sera sputtered and wiped her lips with the back of her hand, just the way a sister might if being teased by a brother. She mused at the thought. She really had a brother.

Jerad stalked over to them. He was not amused. "You will forever torment me about it, *Nai?*"

"Hmn. Of course. What else are confidantes for?" Mekal released Sera and gave her a hardy whack on her bottom. Sera jumped, her jaw dropped and her eyes went wide.

Mekal released a boisterous laugh. "After all, she is my sister." He then wrapped an arm around Jerad's neck and one around Sera's. He gave Jerad a smacking kiss on his cheek. "*Ack.* I suppose you are suitable to husband her."

With a chortle Mekal released them both. Jerad grinned at him and held his hand up. The two warriors grasped palms, then knocked knuckles.

Sera gasped, suddenly remembering that she brought something else with her from Earth. She patted her jacket pocket, reached inside and withdrew her palm pad. Sera motion Jerad to sit. She snuggled between his thighs and leaned against his chest.

"I want to show you something." Sera activated the record of their child's conception and birth, explaining to Jerad all that was happening on the screen.

"This is a remarkable thing, Starbird."

Mekal approached and sat down beside them.

"Look at this, Mekal." Jerad pointed to the viewer.

"It is my seed," he announced arrogantly--proudly.

Sera's face lit to a deep red at the thought of what she and Jerad were doing at that moment.

"They look lost," Mekal observed.

"*Nai,* but watch. It will take just one to make our child."

The three of them silently watched the viewer of Sera's palm pad as the miracle of creating human life took place and the tiny embryo reshaped into an odd looking human form.

"Oh, I am so sorry."

"*Why?*" Jerad and Sera asked simultaneously and turned to look at Mekal.

"Your poor child resembles its father."

Sera snorted.

Jerad snarled.

Mekal stood and harnessed his glide flyer. With a wave he was off to the skies.

"I will see you soon in the Corridor. I expect a grand celebration," he called as he drifted upward.

"Just as long as its not a Challenge." Sera furled her brow.

"No more Challenges," Jerad assured her. Then he smirked. "But I might let you tie me up."

Jerad wagged his eyebrows at her and kissed her cheek. He wrapped his arms tightly around her, caging her within his embrace. This was one starbird he would never again, let fly away.

A Possum Rescue

The first thing you must do to save a baby possum is to get it warm. Being away from the protective heat that a mother's body provides could be fatal. If you decide to pick up a baby possum, get it warm as soon as possible by wrapping it in a warm cloth. If this doesn't work, place it against the skin of your chest beneath your clothing. Be careful it might scratch. Transport it for medical help.

Note: Adult possums require special handling. Proceed with caution. You may get bitten…
… or you may fall in love.

Epilogue

"Well, that was amusing." Demeter gazed at the tiny, crystal pyramid floating above her palm. She strummed her fingers through the variegated color beams emanating as it rotated. A melody sprang forth and then abruptly stopped before the prism descended and disappeared into the flesh of her palm.

"Amusing for whom," a voice, sounding a bit disgruntled, griped from behind her.

"Oh stop your grumbling, Moros. Did you really think I was going to let you have her? She carries my legacy, be aware," Daedalus warned as he flashed Moros a smug look.

Moros sneered.

"And there was no way in the universe I would allow you to recapture my darling little Protogio. I have better plans for it than to watch it crumble at the feet of those barbarians your mother, Nyx, sired." Demeter added.

"You forget that I am also from her loins, Demeter."

"Ah yes, and be glad I took pity on you for it."

"Is it why you have condemned me to live only in mortal flesh, Demeter?"

"It is to keep your devious nature in check. After all, I can't have you running about the universe casting doom wherever you wish."

"So what do you plan to do with them now, Demeter?" Daedalus asked. His mighty wings spread from his shoulder blades and shimmered a bright cyan blue. He flapped them gracefully a few times, as he stretched his muscular form, and then folded them back into his body.

"My little progenies deserve a time of peace. I think I will let them rest for awhile and enjoy some progression."

"Oh please let me stay with them. I so love the Protogians!" Eros exclaimed, clasping his hands and bouncing up and down.

Demeter looked at the sprite and shook her head. "Ah yes, Eros. You did make a pretty little sum on that silly little poem of yours did you not?"

Eros' face alighted. "Our little Kati was quite generous."

Moros flapped his hand near his ear. "Damn annoying buzz."

"Another mortal womb calls you Moros?" Demeter sighed. "I suppose doom will always be part of the universe. I had so hoped we would enjoy a bit of reprieve before you were called to disrupt harmony again."

"Why, Demeter? Why must I suffer so? Do I not deserve the immortality that the rest of you enjoy?" Moros slashed a hand through the air. "I grow weary of living in the flesh and dying again and again. It is not very pleasant I'll have you know."

"Had you turned from your mother's deeds, Moros, you would have been spared, but instead you followed her." She paused and drew her cape in a sweeping motion as she twirled. A powder of glittering, silvery, cosmic dust swirled around her. "Did you think I would let you bring second Earth's devastating technology to my first Earth. Protogio is my purest of planets and I wish for her to remain so."

"But the Edict…"

"You are a fool, Moros. Have you not realized that Nyx altered the Edict? Protogio was never yours to take."

Moros frowned at her.

"Now off with you, and be born flesh again. Perhaps this time you will redeem yourself. But be warned, we will be watching."

Demeter opened her palm again to release the pyramid spectrum. She directed it to the ground and waved her hand over it. Musical sounds rang forth and blazing colors appeared to form a large cone-shaped configuration.

"Remember, the best is yet to come." Moros begrudgingly stepped into the beam of light and was gone.

"Don't you just love happy endings?" Eratos crooned and batted his lashes.

"Indeed I do. Indeed I do my lovesick little friend." Demeter caressed Eratos' cheek. "Come now, the dream shifters are bending the stars again. We have much work to do."

Demeter waved her hand through the spectrum, the Origins stepped through the temporal fold and vanished.

Printed in the United States
31686LVS00001B/28-30